ALSO BY LEIF GW PERSSON

Between Summer's Longing and Winter's End

Another Time, Another Life

Free Falling,
As If in a Dream

Free Falling,
As If in a Dream

THE STORY OF A CRIME

Leif GW Persson

Translated from the Swedish by Paul Norlen

Pantheon Books

NEW YORK

Translation copyright © 2014 by Pantheon Books, a division of Random House, Inc.

All rights reserved. Published in the United States by Pantheon Books,
a division of Random House, LLC, New York, a Penguin Random House Company,
and in Canada by Random House of Canada Limited, Toronto.
Originally published in Sweden as *Faller fritt som I en dröm*
by Albert Bonniers Förlag, Stockholm, in 2007.
Copyright © 2007 by Leif GW Persson.

Library of Congress Cataloging-in-Publication Data
Persson, Leif GW
[Faller fritt som i en dröm. English]
Free falling, as if in a dream : the story of a crime / Leif GW Persson ;
translated from the Swedish by Paul Norlen.
pages cm
ISBN 978-0-307-37747-0
1. Palme, Olof, 1927-1986—Assassination—Fiction. 2. Prime ministers—
Sweden—Death—Fiction. 3. Assassination—Investigation—Sweden—Fiction.
4. Cold cases (Criminal investigation)—Sweden—Fiction.
I. Norlen, Paul R. II. Title.
PT9876.26.E7225F3513   2013   839.73'74—dc23 2012050987

www.pantheonbooks.com

Jacket photograph by Jessica Hines
Jacket design by Brian Barth

Printed in the United States of America
First American Edition
2 4 6 8 9 7 5 3 1

To Mikael and the Bear

Regardless of whether truth is absolute or relative, and quite apart from the fact that many of us constantly seek it, in the end it is still hidden from almost all of us. As a rule out of necessity, and if for no other reason out of concern for those who wouldn't understand anyway. There is no law of public access with regard to the truth. We have a practical problem that we have to solve, and it's no more difficult than that.

—*The Professor*

Witness One (W1) is on Tunnelgatan when he catches sight of the murderer, who he runs after, up the steps to Malmskillnadsgatan where he meets Witness Two (W2), who has seen a man running down David Bagares gata. Witnesses Three and Four (W3, W4) have seen a man turn to the left onto Regeringsgatan. A fifth witness, the "Cartoonist" (C) saw a man running through Smala gränd and out onto Birger Jarlsgatan.

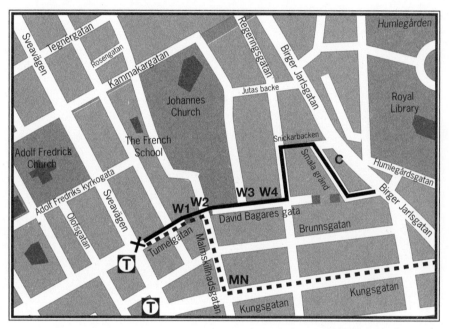

Image source © Kartena AB

Witness Madeleine Nilsson (MN) claims on the other hand to have met a suspicious man on the stairs between Malmskillnadsgatan and Kungsgatan, which suggests a completely different escape route.

X Crime scene   ━━━━━ Old theory of escape route

━ ━ ━ ━ New theory of escape route

Wednesday, October 10.
The harbor in Puerto Pollensa on north Mallorca

Just before seven o'clock in the morning Esperanza left her usual place at the charter pier in the harbor. A beautiful little boat with a beautiful name.

1

Eight weeks earlier, Wednesday, August 15.
Headquarters of the National Bureau of Criminal
Investigation on Kungsholmen in Stockholm

"Olof Palme," said the chief of the National Bureau of Criminal Investigation, Lars Martin Johansson. "Are you familiar with that name, ladies and gentlemen?"

For some reason he seemed almost joyful as he said it. Just back from vacation with a becoming suntan, red suspenders, and linen shirt with no tie as a lighthearted signal of the transition from relaxation to responsibility. He leaned forward in his seat at the short end of the conference table, letting his gaze wander across the four others gathered around the same table.

The joy seemed to be his alone. Doubtful looks were exchanged among three of the four—Police Superintendent Anna Holt, Detective Chief Inspector Jan Lewin, and Detective Chief Inspector Lisa Mattei—while the fourth in the group, Chief Inspector Yngve Flykt, who was head of the Palme group, seemed if anything embarrassed by the question and tried to compensate by looking politely preoccupied.

"Olof Palme," Johansson repeated, his voice now sounding more urgent. "Does that ring any bells?"

The one who finally answered was Lisa Mattei, the youngest of the group, but long accustomed to the role of best in class. First she glanced

3

at the head of the Palme investigation, who only nodded and looked tired, then she looked down at her notepad, which incidentally was free of any notes or the doodling with which she usually filled it, whatever was being discussed. Then in two sentences she summarized Olof Palme's political career, and in four sentences his end.

"Olof Palme," said Mattei. "Social Democrat and Sweden's most well-known politician during the postwar period. Prime minister for two terms, from 1969 to 1976 and from 1982 to 1986. Was murdered at the intersection of Sveavägen and Tunnelgatan in central Stockholm twenty-one years, five months, and fourteen days ago. It was Friday the twenty-eighth of February 1986, twenty minutes past eleven. He was shot from behind with one shot and appears to have died almost immediately. I was eleven years old when it happened, so I'm afraid I don't have much more to contribute," Mattei concluded.

"Don't say that," said Johansson with a Norrland drawl. "Our victim was the prime minister and a fine fellow, and how common is this kind of crime victim at this sort of place? True, I'm only the head of the National Bureau of Criminal Investigation, but I'm also an orderly person and extremely allergic to unsolved cases," he continued. "I take them personally, if you're wondering why you're here."

No one had wondered about that. No one seemed particularly enthusiastic either. Regardless, the whole thing started as it almost always does, with a few police officers sitting around a table, talking about a case. No flashing lights, no sirens, and definitely no drawn service revolvers. Although when the crime happened, over twenty years ago, it had started with flashing lights, sirens, and drawn service revolvers. Nothing had helped. The case had ended badly.

Johansson elaborated on his ideas about what ought to be done, the motive for doing it, and how it should all be arranged in practical terms. As so often before, he also relied on his personal experience without the slightest trace of either genuine or false modesty.

"In my personal experience, when a case has come to a standstill so to speak, it's often worth calling in some new folks who can look at the case with fresh eyes. It's easy to overlook things," said Johansson.

"I hear you," Anna Holt answered, sounding more sarcastic than she intended. "But if you'll excuse—"

"Sure," Johansson interrupted. "Just let me finish my sentence first."

"I'm listening," said Holt. I never learn, she thought.

"When you're starting to get up in years like me, unfortunately the risk increases that you don't remember what you meant to say, if you get interrupted, that is," Johansson explained. "Where was I now?" he continued.

"How you intended to organize the whole thing, boss," Mattei interjected. "Our investigation, that is," she clarified.

"Thanks, Lisa," said Johansson. "Thanks for helping an old man."

How does he do it? thought Holt. Even with Lisa of all people?

According to Johansson it was not a question of forming a new Palme investigation, and the investigators who were already in the Palme group—several of whom had spent almost their entire active time as detectives there—would of course retain sole responsibility.

"So I want to make that clear from the start, Yngve," said Johansson, nodding at the head of the Palme group, who still seemed more worried than relieved.

"No way," said Johansson. "You can forget any such ideas. I've imagined something a lot simpler and more informal. What I want simply is a second opinion. Not a new investigation. Just a second opinion from a few wise officers who can look at the case with fresh eyes.

"I want you to go through the investigation," he continued. "Is there anything we haven't done that we should have done? Is there anything in the material itself that we've missed and that's worth looking into? That can still be looked into? If so, I want to know about it, and it's no more difficult than that."

Regardless of his hopes on the last point, the following hour was devoted to discussing objections from three of the four others in the room. The only one who didn't say anything was Lisa Mattei, but when their meeting was over, her notepad was as full of scribbling as always. Partly with what her colleagues had said. Partly with her usual doodling regardless of what was being said.

First up was Chief Inspector Jan Lewin, who after some introductory, cautious throat clearing quickly zeroed in on Johansson's fundamental motive, namely the need for fresh eyes. The idea as such was excellent. He himself had advocated it often enough. Not least during his time as head of the group that dealt with so-called cold cases. But for that very reason he thought he was particularly poorly suited for this case.

During the initial year of the investigation—while Lewin was working at the homicide squad in Stockholm—he had primary responsibility for the collection of significant portions of the material evidence. Not until the investigation was taken over by the national bureau did he return to his old assignment at the homicide squad in Stockholm. Several years later he moved over to the national bureau, and once there he had also helped on the Palme investigation for a few brief periods with the registration and review of new leads that had come in.

"I don't know if you remember, boss, but the investigation leader, Hans Holmér, the police chief in Stockholm at that time, collected large quantities of information that perhaps didn't have anything directly to do with the murder itself but might prove to be of value." Lewin nodded at Lisa Mattei, who had been only a little girl in those days.

"I remember the police chief at that time," said Johansson. Of unblessed memory, he thought. "Though most of what he found I've managed to repress. What was it that landed on your desk, Lewin?"

At best, quite a bit of questionable value, according to Lewin.

"All hotel registrations in the Stockholm area around the time of the murder. All arrivals into and departures from the country that could be substantiated with the usual passport and border checks, all parking violations in greater Stockholm around the time of the crime, all speeding violations and other traffic offenses in the whole country the day of the murder, the day before and the day after, all other crimes and arrests in the Stockholm area at the time of the crime. We took in everything from drunkenness and domestic disturbances to all ordinary crimes reported during the twenty-four-hour period in question. We also collected accident reports. Plus all suicides and strange causes of death that happened both before and after the murder. I know when I left the investigation they were still working on that part. As you know, it added up to quite a bit. Hundreds of pounds of paper, thousands of pages actually, and I'm only talking about what came in during my time."

"The broad, unbiased effort," Johansson observed.

"Yes, that's what it's called," said Lewin. "Sometimes it works, but this time almost all of it remained unprocessed. There simply wasn't time to do anything. I sat and skimmed through what came in, and I had my hands full just with what first jumped out at me. Ninety percent of the paperwork was basically put right back in the boxes where it had been from the start."

"Give me some examples," said Johansson. "What things jumped out at you, Lewin?"

"I remember four different suicides," said Lewin. "The first took place only a few hours after the murder of the prime minister. I remember it in detail, because when I got the papers on my desk I actually felt some of those old vibrations you feel when things are starting to heat up." Lewin shook his head thoughtfully.

"The man who committed suicide had hung himself in the rec room of his house. A guard who took early retirement who lived on Ekerö a few miles outside Stockholm. He was the neighbor of a police officer, so I got the tip through him. He also had a license for a handgun, to top it off a revolver that might very well have matched what we knew about the murder weapon at that time. He was generally considered strange by those who knew him. Antisocial, divorced for several years, problems with alcohol, the usual stuff. In brief, he seemed pretty good, but he had an alibi for the evening of the murder. For one thing, he'd quarreled with some neighbors who were out with their dog at about ten o'clock. Then he called his ex-wife from his home phone, a total of three times if I remember correctly, and carried on with her about the same time as Palme was shot. I had no problem ruling him out. We found his revolver in the house search. It was test fired, even though we already knew it was the wrong caliber."

"And the others?" Johansson was looking almost greedily at his colleague.

"No," said Lewin, "at the risk of disappointing you, and I was pretty careful about these cases. I remember when the media started making a row about the so-called police track, that it was some of our fellow officers who murdered Palme, I went into the material on my own and checked for that specifically—all the parking violations and other traffic offenses where the vehicle or the perpetrator could be connected to our colleagues, whether or not they were on duty."

"But that didn't produce anything either," said Johansson.

"No," said Lewin. "Other than some pretty imaginative explanations of why a particular officer shouldn't have to pay his parking tickets or why his car ended up in such a strange place."

"Exactly," said Johansson. "The same old women problems if you ask me. Nevertheless, wouldn't it be interesting for you to take another look at your old boxes? Now when you've got some perspective, I mean. I can't help sensing that you don't seem completely uncomfortable with the job. And you could take a look at all the rest, once you're at it any-way, I mean."

"With some reservations about fresh eyes," said Lewin, sounding more positive than he intended. "Well, maybe so. The basic idea is good enough."

Coward, thought Anna Holt, who didn't intend to let Johansson get off that easily.

"With all due respect, boss, even though I also believe the part about fresh eyes, and even though I've never been anywhere near this inves-tigation, I really don't believe in the idea," said Holt. Now it's said, she thought.

"I'm listening, Anna," said Johansson, with the same expression in his eyes he'd learned from his first elkhound. The gaze that naturally ensues from undivided positive attention. As when he and the dog took a break in the hunt, when he told him to sit nicely, just before he gave him a slice of sausage from the lunch sack. "What do you mean?"

"What I mean is that I can't imagine a more thrashed-out case in Swedish police history. Investigated over and over again in every con-ceivable and inconceivable respect. Without technical evidence worth the name. With witnesses who were pumped dry twenty years ago, most of whom are now probably either dead or in no shape to be talked with. Where the only suspect worth the name, I'm thinking of Christer Pettersson, obviously, was convicted in Stockholm District Court almost twenty years ago, only to be released by Svea Court of Appeal six months later. The same Pettersson they tried to indict again ten years ago, but the prosecutor couldn't even get a new trial. The same Pettersson who died a few years ago. As if everything that happened before wasn't more than enough to close the investigation against him."

"You're making me think of that classic skit, Anna. I think it won a prize as the world's best TV sketch. That Monty Python thing about the dead parrot," said Johansson. "Wasn't it a Norwegian blue? Wasn't that what it was called? The parrot that is.

"'This parrot is dead.' You know that scene where the upset customer is in the pet shop and slams the dead parrot on the counter," Johansson explained as he slammed his desktop to illustrate.

"Sure," said Holt. "If you like. This investigation is dead. Just as dead as Monty Python's parrot."

"Maybe it's just a little tired," said Johansson. "Isn't that what the shop owner says—the one who sold the customer the parrot, when the customer comes in to complain? 'He's not dead, just a little tired.'"

Don't try that with me, thought Holt. Giving in was the last thing she intended to do, regardless of all the smoke screens and easy-to-see-through jokes from her boss.

"The Palme investigation has not come to a standstill," Holt repeated. "The Palme investigation has been thrashed to death. It's not a cold case; it's not even an ice-cold case. The Palme investigation is dead."

"You don't need to get upset, Holt. I hear what you're saying," said Johansson, who suddenly didn't sound the least bit nice and friendly anymore. "Personally I think it's maybe just a little tired. And maybe it should be looked at with fresh eyes. That you proceed from the basic police ground rule that always applies when you're involved in such things."

"Like the situation," said Holt, who knew Johansson after a number of years and cases.

"Exactly," said Johansson, smiling again. "Nice to know we're in agreement, Anna."

. . .

Last up was Chief Inspector Yngve Flykt, head of the Palme group. If he'd had anything to say about it, this meeting never would have happened. Personally he was a man of peace, and what he'd heard about his top boss, not least that he was capable of thinking up all kinds of things to happen to co-workers who didn't do what he said, made him irretrievably lost from the start.

With all due respect for his boss, and being both happy and grateful for the boss's clear and definite opinion that any changes in a well-established, functioning organization were not even an issue, with respect for all this and everything else that in haste he might have forgotten, he would still, however, and obviously with all good intentions, like to point out a few practical problems, which his colleague Lewin had already touched on.

"What are you talking about?" interrupted Johansson.

"Our case files," said the head of the Palme investigation, looking almost imploringly at Johansson. "It's no ordinary body of material even for a very big case. I don't know if you've been down and looked at it, but it's a colossal amount of material. Gigantic. As perhaps you know, it takes up six whole cubicles in the corridor where we're located. We've already taken down five partitions, and soon it'll be time for the next one. There are binders and boxes from floor to ceiling."

"I'm listening," said Johansson, forming his long fingers into an arch and leaning back in his chair. Flykt, thought Johansson. It must be congenital.

"From what my colleagues and I have understood, it's actually the largest amount of investigative material in world police history. It's supposed to be even larger than the pre-investigation material on the Kennedy assassination and the investigation of the attack on the jumbo jet over Lockerbie in Scotland."

"I hear what you're saying," Johansson interrupted. "What's the problem? A lot of it must be entered on computers by now."

"Obviously, and there's more and more every day, but it's not something you just sit down and browse through. We're talking about roughly a million pages. Most are transcripts of interviews, and there are thousands of those that are tens of pages and sometimes longer. In round numbers, a hundred thousand different documents stored in almost a thousand binders. Not to mention all the boxes where we've stored the things you can't keep in binders. There was an expert in the latest government commission who calculated that even then, and this must have been two years ago, it would have required ten years of full-time work for a qualified investigator simply to scan through the material. If you ask me, I think it would take even longer, and new information is coming in all the time."

"I hear what you're saying," said Johansson, making a slightly dismissive gesture with his right hand. "But some type of sorting out must still be possible, no? If I'm not mistaken, there are tens of thousands of pages of the usual crazy tips. Couldn't those be set aside?"

"I'm afraid that's not enough," Flykt objected. "There are a lot more crazy tips than that. The problem with them too, and you know this as well as I do, boss, is that some may appear convincing to start with. I saw a newspaper interview a while ago with our own professor here at the National Police Board where he maintained that if we suddenly solved the Palme assassination and knew what had happened, it would prove that ninety-nine percent of the whole case file was irrelevant, and that almost everything we'd collected had been directly misleading. For once we were in complete agreement, he and I."

"That's a pity," said Johansson. "To hear that you're in agreement with such a person, I mean. What I'm trying to say is simply that of course there must be a way to sort the material. For some clever colleagues with fresh eyes. Personally I've gotten by well enough over the years with the event description, the most important eyewitnesses, that is, the technical investigation and the forensic report," Johansson said, counting on his fingers as he spoke, smiling as he held up three of them.

"Besides," he continued, "there must be a nice summary or two in this case that explains the usual where, when, and how. Even the officers in the uniformed police seem to have understood who the victim was a few minutes after the crime."

"That's correct." Flykt nodded and seemed almost relieved, as if suddenly he was on firmer ground. "Our own perpetrator profile group produced both an analysis of the crime and a profile of the perpetrator in collaboration with the FBI. Besides that there were several other analyses made by external experts that we turned to. Both of the crime itself in its main features and of various details. For example, the murder weapon and the two bullets that were secured at the crime scene. We got quite a bit actually."

"Of course," said Johansson, throwing out his hands with the secure conviction of a Bible-thumper from his provincial childhood. "So what are we waiting for?"

As soon as Johansson released his hold on the head of the Palme group, everyone in the room started carefully inching their chairs back, but Johansson ignored their hopes.

"I realize you're eager to get going, ladies and gentlemen," said Johansson with a crooked smile, "but before we part company there's one thing I want to emphasize. A word of warning on the way." He nodded emphatically and looked at them in turn with a stern expression.

"You must not say a word about this. You may talk with each other as needed in order to do what you should. If for the same reason you need to talk with anyone else, you must first obtain my permission to do so."

"What do I say to my co-workers?" The head of the Palme group did not look happy. "I mean—"

"Nothing," Johansson interrupted. "If anyone wonders about anything, you can send him or her to me. You should understand that better than anyone," he added. "What a hell the media has created for the Palme investigation all these years. I don't want a lot of other officers running around talking nonsense. How do you think the media gets hold of all the shit they write about? The last thing I want to read in the newspaper when I open my eyes in the morning is that I've appointed a new investigation of the assassination of Olof Palme."

"Which is precisely why I think providing a little information to the people in my group would be good. To avoid a lot of unnecessary talk, I mean." Flykt looked almost imploring as he said this. "One solution would be to say that we've asked Holt, Lewin, and Mattei to look over the case indexing. I mean that sort of work goes on all the time and is often done by colleagues outside the group. Or perhaps it's a purely administrative overview."

"Like I said," said Johansson, "not a word. Send all the curiosity seekers to me so I can slake their thirst for knowledge, and if they're not satisfied I'm sure I can arrange other duties for them. All of us in this room will meet in a week. Same time, same place. Any questions?"

No one had any questions, and as they were leaving Johansson first nodded curtly at Flykt. Then he smiled broadly at Lisa Mattei, asked for a copy of her typed-up meeting notes, and told her to take care of herself. Holt he completely ignored, and as they left he took Lewin aside.

"There's one thing that disturbs me about this case," said Johansson.

"That it may have been wrongly conceived from the start," Lewin replied, who had been around before and heard Johansson expound on the same text on more than one occasion.

"Exactly," Johansson agreed. "A lone madman who by pure chance runs into a completely unprotected prime minister and just happens to have a revolver the size of a suckling pig in his pocket. That's what most people seem to believe, including the majority of our dear colleagues. So—a quiet question from a man in mature middle age: Just how common is that?"

"I understand what you mean," said Lewin.

"Good," said Johansson. "Then I'll see you in a week, and if you happen to get hold of the bastard before that please let me know."

2

After the meeting with Johansson, Anna Holt returned to her office at the national liaison office where she'd been working as a superintendent for over a year. She was careful to close the door before sitting down at her desk and exhaling deeply three times. Then she swore loudly and fervently on the theme of adult boys forty pounds overweight with red suspenders and the dual role of country boy comedian and head of the country's National Bureau of Criminal Investigation. That gave her some relief, but not as much as she'd hoped, so when Lisa Mattei knocked on her door half an hour later she was still in a bad mood.

"How's it going, Anna?" said Mattei. "You seem a little down."

"What do you think?" interrupted Anna.

"Don't get hung up on Johansson," Mattei said for some reason. "Johansson is who he is, but he's also actually Johansson. I've talked with Flykt, so we can jump right in. He'll arrange it so we have our own access cards."

"It's time to embrace the situation," said Holt. "High time to resurrect a dead parrot."

"Exactly," said Mattei. "You know yourself there's more than one way to skin a cat, as Lars Martin would say."

"Okay, okay, okay," said Holt, sighing and getting up. So now we're suddenly on a first-name basis with the world's best Johansson, she thought. Lisa of all people.

Lewin had also returned to his desk. There he sat for a good quarter of an hour, criticizing himself for once again ending up in a situation that he could have avoided. Together with his top boss, Lars Martin Johansson, besides, with whom he tried not to have any contact otherwise.

The man who can see around corners, thought Lewin mournfully. That was how many officers always described him, especially when they had a few shots under their belt. The legend Lars Martin Johansson from north Ådalen in the province of Ångermanland. Policeman and hunter, with the same view of both justice and hunting, regardless of whether he took it out on people or on innocent animals. Johansson with his large nose and uncanny ability to sniff out the faintest scent of human weakness. With his jovial image and human warmth that he could switch on and off as he pleased. Shrewd, hard, and merciless as soon as it mattered, as soon as his prey came within reach and was worth the trouble.

Then he had a twinge of conscience. Johansson was in spite of it all a fellow officer, his boss besides, and who was he to judge a fellow human being he'd never had close contact with and really didn't know that well?

High time to embrace the situation, Lewin thought. He picked up his desk phone and entered Flykt's direct number.

"Welcome to the holy of holies," said Flykt, nodding at the mountain of papers that surrounded Lewin, Holt, and Mattei. Binders and boxes lined the walls from floor to ceiling. Stacks of boxes arranged in neat rows out on the floor. A room of over two hundred square feet that already seemed too small.

"Well, Jan, I know you've been here before," Flykt continued, turning to Lewin, "but for you, Anna and Lisa, this may be the first time?"

"I've been here on a guided tour," said Holt. "True, it was a few years ago, but the piles don't look any smaller." If Johansson has been here he's either blind or crazy, she thought.

"A question," said Holt to Flykt. "Has Johansson seen this material? At our meeting this morning I got the feeling he hadn't."

"I thought so too," said Flykt, "but a little while ago one of my colleagues here at the group said that evidently the boss stopped by before his vacation. Although I was out so I missed that visit. I also suspect he's gone through the parts of the material that are with SePo. I remember we got a request for additional information while he was head of operations there. Though perhaps you know better than I do, because you've worked there. And we shouldn't forget that he's been called in as an adviser to all the government commissions that reviewed how we more humble police officers have conducted ourselves over the years. If you ask me Johansson probably knows more than most of us."

"God moves in mysterious ways," Holt answered.

"So true, so true," Flykt agreed with a smile. "Any questions, anyone?" For some reason he looked at Mattei.

Oy, thought Lisa Mattei, who had a hard time taking her eyes off all the papers. Working with this stuff must be like climbing a mountain. And I'm afraid of heights.

"It's my first time here," she said. "It will be interesting to see what you've collected." Like climbing a mountain, she thought again as she let her gaze wander over the rows of binders.

"Yes, it has turned into quite a lot over the years, and there's still a new binder every week. Mostly so-called crazy tips if you ask me," said Flykt. "So I guess the least I can do is wish you luck," he continued. "If you do happen to find something that my colleagues and I have missed, no one will be happier than we will be."

Sounds like a pretty risk-free promise, thought Holt, who just smiled and nodded.

Unfortunately the age of miracles is probably past, thought Lewin, which of course he didn't say.

And I'm scared of heights, thought Mattei, but that was not something she intended to tell her colleagues, not even Anna.

Lars Martin Johansson was in a great mood. He was satisfied in general terms and even more so with himself. He was most satisfied that he'd finally decided to do something about the police misfortune that went by the name of the Palme investigation. For more than twenty years the case had been the responsibility of the National Bureau of Criminal Investigation, for a few years ultimately his own, and it was about time for something to happen. During the last decade, after the last failure with the now deceased "Palme assassin" Christer Pettersson, the group that worked on the case had mostly been engaged in other things.

Identifying the Swedish victims of the tsunami catastrophe in Thailand demanded all their resources for more than a year. After that similar assignments had literally poured in to the Palme investigators. Swedish citizens who were abroad and subjected to political attacks, natural disasters and accidents. The little now being done about the Palme assassination mainly consisted of tending the circle of private investigators, conspiracy theorists, and those whom the police called, regardless of gender, bag ladies. All those who wanted to help and have complete knowledge of what he and his officers might contribute besides. We can't have it that way, naturally, because then we might as well shut down the whole damn thing, thought Johansson. Then he'd made his decision.

As soon as Flykt left, Holt proposed that they withdraw for some private deliberations. But not in the Palme room—the mountain of papers all around them filled her with physical displeasure, although she didn't say so of course. Instead perhaps they could go someplace where they could sit more comfortably. No one had any objections. First they got coffee, then they went into an empty conference room and closed the door.

"All right," said Holt. "So here we are. And it's time we start embracing the situation, considering what's waiting. The good news is that if we divide up the material, at least there'll be less to read."

"In that case I suggest I take care of the incident itself," said Lewin. "What Johansson mentioned, with the witness statements from the crime scene, the technical investigation, and the forensic report. At least I thought I could start there."

"I have no objections whatsoever," said Holt. "Here's your chance, Lisa," she continued. "Is there any particular piece you're longing for? Now that you've got the chance."

"I don't know enough about the case," said Mattei. "I need to get a better overview. All those tracks, or working hypotheses to be correct, that I've heard about since I became a police officer. You know— Kurdish terrorists and lone madmen and mysterious arms deals and our colleagues, the so-called police track."

"Excellent," said Holt. "I don't think you'll have a shortage of reading material." One of us at least likes the situation, she thought.

"What about you, Anna?" asked Lewin, cautiously clearing his throat.

"I thought I'd supervise and divide the work between you and Lisa," said Holt.

"Kidding aside," she continued, "I think I'll focus on Christer Pettersson. Regardless of what Johansson thinks about my fresh eyes, and even though I don't know any more about the case than what I've read in the newspapers and heard ad nauseam at work, I've always thought it was Christer Pettersson who shot Olof Palme. I still think so if anyone's wondering, but because it has happened before that I've been wrong, I'm willing to make a fresh attempt."

"I see," said Lewin, nodding. "Then that's how we'll do it. To start with at least."

"Sounds good," Mattei confirmed, getting up.

"Yes," said Holt. "Do we have any choice?" Then she sighed audibly and shook her head, despite the promise that Johansson had forced out of her.

3

Satisfied with himself and the decision he'd made, even though it was the first day after vacation, Johansson decided to leave early and work at home. His secretary thought this sounded excellent, not least considering the beautiful summer weather. She would gladly have done the same if she'd had the opportunity to choose or even express a wish in that direction.

"Sounds wise, boss," she agreed. "Considering the weather, I mean. Is there anything else I need to know?"

"I'm to be reached only in an emergency. Plus the usual, you know," said Johansson.

"That I should take care of myself," said his secretary.

"Exactly. You have to promise to take care of yourself."

"I promise," she answered. "Although this evening I hadn't planned any major adventures. Thought about watering the flower boxes on the balcony when I get home, if that's all right?"

"Sounds like an excellent idea," said her boss, whose thoughts already seemed to be elsewhere. "Just so you don't fall over the railing."

"I promise," she said. What could happen to me? she thought as he vanished out the door. I'm fifty years old, single with no children, my only girlfriend on vacation with her new boyfriend, and I don't even have a cat I can pet.

Johansson walked the whole way home along the city's wharfs in the pleasant summer breeze that passed over the waters of Mälaren and cooled his Norrland body. An American in Paris, Johansson thought for some reason, and then he started wondering about himself along the same lines. A simple boy from the country, from Näsåker and red Ådalen in north Ångermanland, who had traveled to the royal capital forty years ago to start at the police academy in Solna. Who'd taken his fate in his own hands and borne it on strong arms, who'd done it well and patrolled his way to the top of the police pyramid. A simple boy from the country who was now approaching the end of the journey and would retire about the same time as the murder of the country's prime minister would pass the statute of limitations. What would be a better finale than clearing up this case before he said goodbye?

In these and equally pleasant musings he walked the whole way along Norr Mälarstrand, Riddarholmen, and up on the heights of Söder. There he made a detour by way of the indoor market to shop for various delicacies for the summer dinner with which he intended to surprise his wife when she came home from her job at the bank. A few goodies, mostly fish, seafood, and vegetables, but still two well-filled bags that he carried home to the apartment on Wollmar Yxkullsgatan.

The rest of the afternoon he was diligently busy as a cook. Because the weather was right, he set the table on their new balcony facing the courtyard; it had been finished just before they went on vacation and could not be inaugurated until now. He made a salad of fresh salmon, avocado, and mild arugula, cut fresh tuna in nice thick slices, placed chopped herbs on top, and put everything back in the fridge until it was time.

Then he scrubbed carrots and potatoes, put them in separate saucepans, and poured in water. He checked the temperature of the dry German Riesling he planned to serve as the main wine. After a brief inner deliberation he also put a bottle of champagne on ice in a table-cooler. Both he and his wife preferred it really cold.

Then he did everything else from the fresh asparagus with whipped butter, to the cheese tray, to the concluding raspberries. Everything in the right order, of course, and while he was still at it he rewarded himself with a cold Czech pilsner. When his wife called and said she'd just left work and would be home in fifteen minutes, he put the saucepans on the stove and made a toast to himself.

Cheers, Lars, thought the head of the National Bureau of Criminal Investigation, Lars Martin Johansson, raising his glass. In all likelihood there's not a soul on the planet who can say anything other than that you are one outstanding, well-stocked SOB.

"God," Pia Johansson exclaimed as soon as she stepped into the hall and set her handbag down on the hall table. "I'm so hungry I could devour a boiled puppy. With the fur on."

"That probably won't be necessary," Johansson answered. He bent forward, placed his right hand around her slender throat, his thumb against the hollow in her neck, letting his left hand rest lightly against her right cheek, breathing in her scent while he let his lips brush her hairline.

"What do you say we eat first?" asked Pia.

"Of course," said Johansson. "Otherwise I would've wrestled you to the floor right away."

"God, this is good." Pia sighed two hours later when they had arrived at the raspberries and a more frostbitten Riesling that Johansson had up his sleeve for just this purpose. "If I were forty years younger I would have belched."

"Impossible," said Johansson. "Only small children belch. And Chinese," he added. "It's supposed to be a tradition they have in China to say thanks for the food."

"You're lucky I'm the only one listening. Okay then, if I were forty-five years younger, then I would have belched."

"Children belch; men snore, fart in secret, even let out real juicy ones if they're alone or feel comfortable with who they're with. Women do nothing of the sort."

"Why do you suppose that is?"

"I don't have the faintest idea." Johansson shook his head. "What do you think about a cup of coffee, by the way?"

"Of course," Pia agreed. "Though first I meant to say thanks for this princely meal."

"Just a simple banquet," said Johansson modestly. "Necessary nourishment for our solitary earthly wandering."

"I'm almost getting a little nervous," she continued. "You're not up to something, are you?"

"Not really," said Johansson. "I simply wanted to ingratiate myself in general terms with the woman in my life."

"You don't need to borrow money?"

"Borrow money," Johansson snorted. "A free man doesn't borrow money."

"Okay then," said Pia. "Then I'll take a double espresso with hot milk."

"Good choice," Johansson agreed. "Personally I was thinking about having a small cognac to help my digestion."

"Not for me," said Pia. "Considering tomorrow. There's a lot to do after vacation." But mostly because I'm a woman, she thought.

"Personally I was thinking about taking it very easy tomorrow," said Johansson. I am the boss after all, he thought.

Tomorrow can wait, thought Johansson as he loaded up the espresso machine and poured a short one to help his digestion. I'm a fortunate man, and some days are better than others.

After dinner was over they sat on the couch in Johansson's study. Johansson turned on the TV and looked at the late news. But everything was quiet, and given that his red cell phone had been silent the whole evening, his concluding message at the meeting had evidently done the trick. Not a peep about a prime minister assassinated long ago. In the midst of all this Pia fell asleep on the couch with her head on his lap. Without making a sound and while he stroked her forehead. You sleep like a child in any event, he thought. Motionless, soundless, now and then just a light trembling of the eyelids. Change of plans, and just as well considering all the food and wine, and what do I do now?

His wife solved the problem for him. Suddenly she sat up with a jerk, looked at the clock, and shook her head.

"Good Lord," said Pia. "Already eleven. Now I'm going to bed. Don't stay up too late. Tomorrow's a work day."

"I promise," said Johansson. Tomorrow can wait, he thought, reaching for the TV guide.

First he sat surfing between the twelve or more movie channels to which he now had access. Most of the films he'd seen before, and the ones he hadn't didn't seem worth the trouble. Mostly a lot of nonsense about serial killers who had the good taste to stay away from his desk anyway, and in the midst of this he suddenly had an idea.

In the Palme room were binders, folders, and boxes that covered all the existing wall space and a good share of the floor. In Johansson's large study there were books from floor to ceiling. Books about everything under the sun, assuming it was something that interested him. What didn't interest him he would take up to the attic or give away. True, the Palme room was twice the size of Johansson's study, but the difference in letters and words was less than that. Books, books, books . . . videocassettes, DVDs and CDs plus numerous good old-fashioned LPs. But mostly books, almost all books. Books he'd read and appreciated and could imagine reading again. Books he needed to learn about things and to be able to think better. Books he loved literally because their physical existence showed that for a long time he had become the master of his own life and that he had made the most of himself. All these books he'd missed so deeply while growing up on the farm outside Näsåker that the absence sometimes gnawed at his chest. But never a mountain he was forced to climb.

In Johansson's childhood home there had been few books. The life they lived left little room for reading. In the parlor there was a bookcase with old Bibles, hymnbooks, farming guides, and the devotional tracts that were a natural part of the region's cultural heritage and considered remarkable enough to have bound. But not much else.

In his father's study—the farm office—there were thick catalogs for everything under the sun having to do with work. From manufacturers of tractors, farm and forest machinery, to sellers of guns and ammunition, fishing tackle, screws, nails, tar, paint and varnish, bolts and lumber, motor saws, tools, seed, breeding animals and other lighter goods that were part of life on the farm, and could be shipped through the postal service, paid for COD with the deal concluded by a handshake with the mail carrier.

In his older brothers' room were numerous worn-out volumes of *Rekord* magazine, *Se* and *Lektyr*, carelessly stacked on their one rickety bookshelf. Besides very different publications in which a picture said more than a thousand words, and which they preferred to hide under their mattresses.

The latter publications were obviously lacking in his sister's room. Instead there were *Anne of Green Gables*, *Pollyanna*, *The Children from Frostmo Mountain*, and everything else on the same theme that shaped little girls into conscientious young women and good mothers.

Not so for Johansson, who even as a little boy read as if he were possessed. Who somehow learned to read the year before he started grade school. Little Lars Martin, whose love of reading deeply worried his kindly father and was the reason that his older brothers teased him and gave him a licking whenever they caught him with a thick book without any pictures.

It started with crime. Ture Sventon, Agaton Sax, Master Detective Blomkvist, and Sherlock Holmes, the greatest of them all. He was forced to hide in toolsheds, carriage houses, and outhouses so he could harvest the fruits of such reading in peace. Not until he was big enough to defend himself could he visit his own room, his own reading lamp, and the relative lack of disturbance this calling required.

He continued with adventure in the most general terms, from another time and reality than his own, and for just that reason he could give his imagination free rein. All the adventures of Biggles, the solidarity of the three musketeers, and the solitude of Robinson Crusoe. *Around the World in 80 Days* and *Gulliver's Travels*. He traveled in time and space, in free flight between reality and imagination, and as far away as the public library in Näsåker could issue the ticket. The happiest of all the journeys a person could undertake if anyone had thought to ask little Lars Martin.

When he was nine, his father put him in the car and took him on another journey, an eighteen-mile trip to the district doctor. High time, imminent danger, and his youngest son was wearing his eyes out reading books like a veritable madman. Because little Lars seemed completely normal in all other respects, his father couldn't rule out that something in his head had gotten stuck. Like a gramophone record with a skip in it, if you were to ask a layman.

"So it's not that he's strange or anything," his father, Evert, told the doctor, when he'd shut the door, leaving the little patient in the waiting room outside.

"No, it's nothing like that if you ask me. He's easy enough to deal with, likes fishing, and he's a real crackerjack with the air rifle I gave him for Christmas. It's this reading stuff. He's in a conspiracy with the library lady down in the village and his teacher, and as soon as I take my eye off the kid he's dragging home sacks of books that they pile on him. I'm worried his eyes are going straight to hell."

The doctor investigated the matter. Shone a light in the eyes, ears, and nose of Lars Martin Johansson, nine years old. Squeezed him on the head and hit him on the knee with a little hammer, and so far all seemed well and good. Then the boy had to read the bottom line of letters on the chart on the wall. First with both eyes and then with his hand in front of first the left, then the right eye, and no big deal there.

"The kid's as healthy as a jay," the doctor summarized after his patient returned to the waiting room.

"But you don't think he needs glasses? There must be some help," Evert persisted.

"About as much as a hawk, if you ask me," said the doctor.

"But what about all the reading? The boy seems possessed. You didn't find anything wrong in his head?"

"I guess he likes to read. Some people do," said the district medical officer, sighing for some reason. "The worst thing that can happen is that he'll become a country doctor," he observed and sighed again.

Then Evert and his youngest son drove home to the farm and never talked about the matter again. Ten years later Lars Martin went to Stockholm to become a cop and so that he would be able to read in peace. Mostly about crime as it turned out, mostly gathered from reality, less often from the world of imagination. A considerable detour it might seem, but not all journeys are simple, and there are often more routes than one that lead to the journey's end.

After some rooting in his shelves, Johansson at last found the book he was looking for. Volume seven, on the Gustavian period, of Carl Grimberg's classic work on Swedish history: *The Marvelous Destiny of the Swedish People*. A beautiful little book that could be sensuously weighed in the hands, first edition, leather bound, gold tooling on the spine.

This is what the computer wizards have missed, despite all the networks and search engines, thought Johansson contentedly as he poured the last drops of wine from dinner into his glass, made himself comfortable on the couch, and started reading about the assassination of Gustav III and the times in which he lived. It was as close as he could get to his own murder victim and a comparable Swedish crime case, he thought.

The reading had taken an hour, most of it he already knew, and then he took out paper and pen to make notes while he thought.

The masked ball at the Royal Opera House in Stockholm on March 16, 1792. A circle of perpetrators in the victim's vicinity who hated him and what he stood for. Aristocrats, courtiers, members of the king's own guard. A circle of perpetrators whose opportunity was served up on a silver platter. With a personal invitation and far enough in advance to make the most of it. A circle of perpetrators who were expected to wear masks even before they set to work.

A circle of perpetrators who had access to firearms. Johansson smiled wryly as he made a note of this. One of them was motivated enough to approach the victim, draw his weapon, aim, and fire. Motive, opportunity, and means, Johansson summarized the same way his colleagues at that earlier time must have done.

A victim who was hated by many—aristocrats, military officers, rich citizens. Fine people, in brief, who held power in their swords, their moneybags, their history, and feared that an absolute monarch would take it away from them for good. A victim who was loved by many. By poets and artists, for the shimmer they maintained was a result of King Gustaf's reign, and for them in particular on good economic grounds, thought Johansson.

The fact that large segments of the peasantry also seemed to have liked their king was not as easy to understand. Plagued as they were by constant wars that drove the finances of the realm to the bottom, and suffering all the everyday misery of crop failure, starvation, epidemics, and common diseases. People must not have known any better, thought the farmer's son Johansson, sighing.

Hated by many, loved by many, but with no room for many feelings in between. What more can one ask of a so-called motive, Johansson summarized as he brushed his teeth in front of the bathroom mirror after a day of hard work, an excellent meal he'd made himself, and a little reading purely for the sake of enjoyment. At best I've learned something too, he thought.

Ten minutes later he was asleep. With a smile on his lips but otherwise exactly as usual. On his back with his hands clasped over his chest, with manly snoring, secure in his own body, free from dreams. Or in any case the kind of dreams he would remember, even vaguely, when he woke up the next morning.

Most often it was Lars Martin Johansson who fell asleep last and woke up first, but for once his wife had evidently gotten up before him. It was the faint aroma of coffee that alarmed his sensitive nose and woke him. Although it was only seven o'clock it was still a few hours late compared to his usual routine. His wife, Pia, had already had time to set out breakfast—"I've labored like a beast to start paying you back for dinner last night"—and in passing she alerted him to the morning paper with an innocent smile.

"You're in the newspaper, by the way," said Pia as she poured coffee for him. "Why didn't you say anything?"

"About what?" asked Johansson as he splashed warm milk in his coffee cup.

"That you've appointed a new Palme investigation."

What the hell are you saying, woman? thought Johansson, who would never dream of saying that out loud. Not to his beloved wife and after almost twenty years of marriage. The fact that all days hadn't been good weighed easily against the fact that many had been good enough and several far better than anyone had the right to ask for, even from his wife.

"What is that you're saying, dear?" said Johansson. What the hell is it she's saying? he thought.

"Read it yourself," said Pia, handing over the copy of *Dagens Nyheter* that for some reason she had chosen to set on the floor next to her own chair.

"Sweet Jesus," Johansson moaned, glaring at the unflattering picture of himself on the front page of the country's largest morning paper.

"High time if you ask me," said his wife. "A new Palme investigation, I mean," she clarified. "Though maybe you should make sure they get a better picture of you. You've actually lost quite a bit of weight since they took that one."

4

When Johansson had finished his breakfast, he showered then dressed with care. No linen shirt open at the collar, no red suspenders. Instead a gray suit, white shirt with discreet tie, black polished shoes: the necessary armor for someone like him when it was time to take the field. Then he went to the kitchen, folded up the newspaper, stuck it in his jacket pocket, and went to work. He hadn't read the article. Didn't need to, because a quick glance was enough for him to know what was in it.

Once at work he greeted his secretary amiably, waved the newspaper deprecatingly, went into his office and closed the door. Only then did he read through, carefully and with pen in hand, what was the day's major media event. That the head of the National Bureau of Criminal Investigation had appointed a "new, secret investigation of the assassination of Olof Palme." Was I right or was I right? thought Johansson, sighing because everything in it confirmed his misgivings.

Even the picture. A few years old with a Lars Martin Johansson forty pounds heavier glaring at the camera. Obviously such a character could not be reached for comment; instead the newspaper's two anonymous sources had been allowed to carry on freely and tell about all their sufferings. Inadequate resources, unsympathetic bosses, and now their jobs had been taken from them.

The fat, mean boss who takes out his own shortcomings on his poor, innocent employees, thought Lars Martin Johansson.

"Seems like we have a lot to get to work on," said Johansson to his secretary as soon as she sat down on the opposite side of his big desk.

"There are a number of persons who have called wanting to talk with you," she replied with an expression as innocent as his wife's.

"So what was on their minds?"

"Something they read in the newspaper," answered his secretary. "About a new secret investigation of the assassination of Olof Palme you supposedly set up yesterday."

"So who are they? Who called, I mean."

"Basically everyone, it seems," answered his secretary as her eyes searched the paper she held in her hand.

"Give me a few names," said Johansson.

"Well, Flykt of course. He's already been here twice. He wanted to see you personally to work out any misunderstandings that might result from what's in the article."

"Imagine that," said Johansson. "I had no idea Flykt was working at *Dagens Nyheter*. Tell the SOB he can wait," said Johansson.

"Yes, perhaps not word for word," answered his secretary. "Because in that case it's best if you say it yourself. I'll let him know you'll call him during the day and that you want him to be in his office."

"Excellent," said Johansson, because he knew that Flykt preferred to end his workday early, especially on days like this when the weather promised to be excellent for playing golf. "Make sure he remains here in the building until I call him."

"I understand exactly what you mean," said his secretary, who knew her boss and right now did not envy Inspector Yngve Flykt with the Palme group.

"So who are the others?" Johansson repeated.

"Basically everyone, as I said. Everyone from the media at least, because they're calling like crazy, so I'm forwarding them to our own press department. But if we start here in the building, we have the chief of national police who contacted us through our communications director, you know, the new one. The police chief is on a visit to the police in Haparanda. Our director general also called and wondered if there's something she needs to know about or can help with. I promised to relay that. Then Anna Holt called and asked if there's anything new that she and her colleagues ought to know about. Your best friend called too, if you haven't had a falling out again, of course."

"Jarnebring," said Johansson. "Did Bo call? What did he want?"

"Yes," said his secretary. "What did he want? Well, he wanted to talk with you. Said he'd read the morning paper and he was worried about you."

"Word for word, please," said Johansson.

"Okay," she sighed. "He wondered if you'd had a stroke. If he could help you with anything, and that you should call him as soon as you had the time."

"So that's what he said," said Johansson.

"The chief prosecutor in Stockholm called. Twice already. She's very anxious to talk with you. If I remember correctly she's the head of the preliminary Palme investigation, so it may very well have something to do with that case."

"That's what you think," said Johansson. "Okay then. Let's do this. Call that skinny woman at the prosecutor's office and say that if she still wants to talk with me that's fine of course. Otherwise you can just inform her that she shouldn't believe all the shit she reads in the papers. I can meet with our own media gnomes in fifteen minutes, and that can be here in my office. The others can wait until I contact them. Was there anything else?"

"We can start with this," his secretary agreed.

First in and first out on Johansson's phone was the female chief prosecutor in Stockholm. The head of the preliminary investigation and in a formal sense the highest-ranking person responsible for the investigation of the assassination of the prime minister, if one were to be precise and look at the formalities more than the circumstances. Why would anyone do that? Johansson's role in this context was more modest and consisted of supplying her with the police resources she thought she needed to carry out her assignment. He was obviously well aware of all this, and before he made his decision to go forward he had thought many hours about how he would handle this issue. How he would see to it that something was done and that those who did it got peace and quiet around them while they were doing it. The high risk of leaks decided the matter. That's how he'd thought, and everything else could advantageously wait until later, but then it hadn't turned out the way he'd hoped and now it was high time to regroup.

"I see in *Dagens Nyheter* that you've appointed a new Palme investigation," the chief prosecutor began in a well-controlled, suspiciously courteous tone of voice. "What I'm wondering about is simply—"

"Yes, I saw that too," Johansson interrupted gently. "What fucking nutcases! Where do they get all this from?"

"Excuse me?"

"Slow news day," said Johansson. "Pure fantasies. Typical slow news day story. Although at that rag it's like they have slow news days all year long."

"So I should interpret this as meaning that you haven't appointed a new investigation or gone in and made any changes to the investigation that I'm actually leading?"

She was not as controlled now. Not as courteous. It is high time to put a stop to it, thought Johansson.

"How would that look?" said Johansson with a resentful face, even though he was alone in his office. "I think you know that even better than I do. You're the head of the Palme investigation. Besides, between the two of us you're the one who's the lawyer, if I'm not mistaken."

"Then I really don't understand a thing."

"Me neither," Johansson agreed with emphasis. "As I'm sure you know, all the case files have been packed up in boxes for years, and it was only a few months ago that we were able to make room for all of them and put them on the shelves again. You do know about that?"

"Of course," she said. "I was the one who made that decision, in consultation with Flykt and the others in the group."

"Exactly," Johansson agreed. "But then they've been on me about that. They said they need even more room, and if the rest of us who work here aren't going to end up on the street because we have no place to put our rear ends, then I thought it was high time to take a look at the case indexing. Find a better, more modern system, simply. Maybe transfer it onto those little diskettes, you know, and move all the papers to the basement. Or some of them, at least. It was Flykt, by the way, who pointed that out to me. I thought it was an excellent idea, and so I asked a few of my younger officers to see if they had any good ideas. Modern computer processing and data storage, and all that, you know, which old geezers like me have completely missed despite all the courses we have to take."

"Lewin then?" asked the chief prosecutor, who still did not sound completely convinced. "True, he's not ancient, but describing him as a younger colleague is still a stretch."

"He knows the material from before, and the people who work for you seem to be busy with other things," Johansson clarified. You must have talked with someone here in the building, thought Johansson. In the article there wasn't a word about Lewin. At the bureau there are more than seven hundred police officers, but only one with that surname, and it's lucky for you you're not sitting in an interrogation with me, he thought.

"Obviously it would be out of line for me to intervene in your administrative procedures," the prosecutor agreed.

"No, how would that look?" said Johansson, sounding as happy as someone who hadn't heard what he just said.

The rest went like a dance where Johansson was leading. For the sake of a good cause he set aside five whole minutes for the usual courtesies and concluded the conversation by expressing the hope that they would meet again soon for social activities. For a long time Johansson and his wife had talked about inviting the chief prosecutor and her husband to dinner. Eat and drink well, and as far as the media was concerned she wasn't the least bit worried. He would take care of the media himself because it was his table, and no one else's, they'd had the bad taste to shit on.

"You have to wonder where they get all this from," sighed Johansson, shaking his head to further his point, even though he was still all alone in his office.

Then he had a meeting with the national police chief's information director and his own information department to firm up the media strategy. According to Johansson it was very simple. He had not formed a new Palme investigation. He had not even made the slightest change in the investigation that had been ongoing for the last twenty years. In other words the Palme investigation wasn't his responsibility but rather the leader of the preliminary investigation's responsibility, and as they knew she was chief prosecutor in Stockholm.

"What this is about," said Johansson as he leaned forward, supporting his elbows on the table, "is that I've asked three investigators here at the bureau who have particular experience in how to handle large quantities of preliminary investigation material according to the latest methods—computer technology goes forward with giant leaps, to say the least, and you youngsters know that better than I do, by the way—how we could store the material so that the Palme group can work with it without our needing to build an extra floor here in the building. It was Flykt's idea by the way, if anyone's wondering."

"Yes, I realized that the case files have been packed up in boxes for years," said the information director with a sly expression.

"Exactly," Johansson agreed. "We can't have it that way. The stuff has to be easily accessible for the people in the group so they can work with it. Otherwise we might just as well carry it down to the basement and close the case." Clever boy, he thought.

"What do we do with the media?" asked his own information manager.

"Usual press release. I want to see it before it goes out. I'm sure the police chief wants to see it too," said Johansson, checking with a glance in the direction of the police chief's information director.

"What do we do about TV?" his colleague at the bureau wondered. "Should I set a time for interviews this afternoon here with you, boss?"

"So they can sit in their fucking studios and cut and paste the tape as they like? Definitely not," said Johansson, letting his own media manager taste the old police gaze he'd learned from his best friend Bo Jarnebring. "If they're still interested, I can be available for a live broadcast this evening, on channels one, two, and four. Just me, no one else, and above all no so-called experts." I'll have to keep an eye on you, he thought.

· · ·

Flykt can wait, thought Johansson two hours later after he'd cleared the papers off his desk, had lunch at a Japanese restaurant in the vicinity of police headquarters, and was starting to feel that he was regaining a firm grip on the rudder of his own boat. On the other hand perhaps I should have a conversation with little Anna, he thought. True, she can be annoyingly pigheaded, but you can count on her saying what she thinks.

Five minutes later "little Anna," that is, Police Superintendent Anna Holt, forty-seven, was sitting in the visitor's chair in his office.

"How's it going?" said Johansson with a friendly smile and interested blue eyes.

"You mean with our overview of the data processing of the Palme material," said Holt acidly. No "boss" this time, she thought. They were alone in the room, had known each other well for many years, and to be honest she wasn't in the mood for it.

"Exactly," said Johansson. "Have you found the bastard who did it?"

"I don't think you need to worry about me, Lisa, or Lewin," Holt replied. "True, the media have been chasing us like madmen, but none of us has talked with any of them. We won't either."

"So you know that?" said Johansson.

"Yes," said Holt.

Then it's probably that way, thought Johansson. Holt was not one to lie. It was probably so bad that she didn't even know how to. And Mattei was, well, Mattei. And Lewin? That coward didn't talk with a living soul unless he was forced to.

"On the other hand there are two other things that perhaps you ought to think about," said Holt.

"I'm listening," said Johansson, leaning back in his chair.

"First," said Holt, "I think the whole idea is crazy. How can three pairs of so-called fresh eyes find anything new of value when hundreds of our colleagues haven't, in more than twenty years? You can't really mean in complete seriousness that everyone who has worked with the Palme case for all these years is a nutcase, featherbrain, blind bat, nitwit, and glowworm, to use a few of your own favorite epithets."

"No, not all," Johansson agreed. Favorite epithet, he thought. Anna's starting to become an educated woman. Must be the association with little Mattei, the string bean who got her PhD a few years ago. True, she wrote an incomprehensible dissertation on what a shame it is about women being killed by their boyfriends, but in any case it was good for tossing into the jaws of hungry media vultures when needed, he thought.

"The material is gigantic," said Holt. "It's a mountain, not a regular haystack where there might be a needle. Regardless of whether it's there, we're not going to find it. Although I'm sure you already know that."

"Sure," said Johansson. "So that means we really have to like the situation. The other thing you were talking about? What's that?"

"Okay," said Holt. "Assume that we do it anyway. Assume that we find something decisive that could give us a breakthrough in the investigation. Then I would say that you're going to have major problems with a number of people in your vicinity. Considering that you've actually been lying to their faces. Not to mention the media. I went past our information department before lunch and happened to see a draft of your press release. I don't understand how you dare."

"I hear what you're saying," said Johansson, whose thoughts already seemed elsewhere.

"I learned something from my father," he continued.

"Yes?"

"When I was a little boy at home on the farm, Dad had a visit from an insurance agent who wanted to sell him a policy on a forest parcel he'd just bought. It was an iffy location if the wind was strong, and windfalls and trees with their tops lopped off aren't good business. The problem was that the insurance cost more than he'd paid for the parcel. So that wasn't a good deal either. Do you know what my old man said?"

Here we go again, she thought. One-way trip fifty years back in time. From the Palme investigation, a current, very concrete problem, to yet another of Johansson's childhood memories.

"No," said Holt. How could I know? I guess that's the point, she thought.

"We'll cross that bridge when we come to it," said Johansson. "That's what he said. 'We'll cross that bridge when we come to it.' So there was no insurance, but on the other hand when he cut down the forest after twenty years there was a tidy profit. You don't seriously believe I would be a social outcast if—granted, against all odds—we could put some order into this story? The only risk I run in that case is that they'd erect a monument to me outside the entryway down on Polhemsgatan."

"I'm not so sure about that," said Holt.

"Let's cross that bridge when we come to it," said Johansson, shrugging his shoulders.

5

Chief Inspector Flykt's wait was not over until a quarter past six. He'd already made three calls to soothe his increasingly sarcastic golf buddies, when suddenly his boss opened the door and just strode right in.

"Knock, knock," said Johansson, smiling and waving his big right hand. Wonder where the asshole put his golf bag? he thought after a quick inspection of Flykt's office.

"Well, I realize you've been very busy, Chief," said Flykt, trying to sound as unperturbed as Johansson. "This is a sorry story but I did try to warn—"

"Forget about that now, Flykt," said Johansson. "It would be inconceivable for me to try to find out which of your many associates let his tongue run ahead of his feeble intelligence. I've understood from the start it wasn't you personally."

"Yes, I really hope you don't think so, boss," said Flykt.

No, thought Johansson. I'm sure you just ran off at the mouth as usual.

"You've seen the press release?" asked Johansson. "No objections if I've understood things correctly?"

"No," said Flykt, shaking his head to make it seem more convincing.

"Good," said Johansson. "Then it's high time you and I took off to talk with the TV people," said Johansson. "We'll have to grab a bite to eat between channels."

"But I'm not prepared to be part of any TV interview," Flykt objected.

"You won't be either," said Johansson. "You're just coming along so the vultures can learn what a united front looks like." Even though you probably already put your golf bag in the car, he thought.

. . .

It was almost eleven o'clock before Johansson could step into his own abode on Wollmar Yxkullsgatan. First there were the two interviews for three different TV channels, and then his chauffeur let Flykt off outside the office because he needed to get his car in the police headquarters garage.

The lights were off and it was quiet in the apartment. His wife was at a kickoff meeting for the bank at a conference center hotel out in the archipelago and wouldn't be home until the next day. Johansson was looking forward to a few hours of peace and quiet after a hard day, which could have ended badly but he hoped had ended well. In the basket under the mail slot was a CD with his TV appearances that his secretary had recorded and one of his many associates had then delivered to him.

"Home at last," said Johansson, who was satisfied with himself and the evening.

First he arranged a tray with a suitable selection of yesterday's leftovers and a cold beer. After a quick deliberation he also poured an ample shot. It's Thursday after all and almost the weekend, thought Johansson.

Then he carried the tray to his study, poured the beer, and prepared an old-fashioned open-faced sandwich, put in the CD, and took a seat in his large armchair in front of the TV.

Let's see now, said blind Sarah, thought Johansson, taking a substantial bite. He swallowed half the shot chased with pilsner and switched on the TV.

Basically it was the same feature in the early and late news programs on the two public television stations. There hadn't been enough time to cut and paste very much. The essential difference was that the story was shorter in the later program. A good sign that the whole thing would soon blow over.

A correct male news anchor asked the expected questions, but toward the end he had trouble concealing his amusement at Johansson's categorical denial of the information that had appeared in the country's largest morning newspaper. Most of all at the way Johansson did it, which is probably also why he was content with the concluding routine attempts.

"But surely someone in your position must have wondered how such a rumor can arise?" the male news anchor asked.

"Of course I have," said Johansson. "Spreading rumors is just as big a problem at my place of employment as at yours, and the reasons are probably the same. But most of what the media reports is actually true, and most of what we talk about at my job is true too. Things that are only speculations or that someone's got turned around or just plain wrong are the price we pay for being able to carry on a dialogue with one another."

"And this time it was completely upside down," the interviewer suggested.

"Yes, it was," said Johansson. "But let's not forget that ultimately this is about the assassination of our country's prime minister, and personally I would be seriously worried if I were to discover one day that the media was completely uninterested in talking about that."

"Since you're here anyway . . . are you ever going to solve the murder of Olof Palme?"

This is it, thought Johansson. Time to move into silver-tongue mode.

"When you're a police officer working on a murder investigation, there's only one thing that matters. Liking the situation," said Johansson.

"But what do you think personally?"

"During all my years as a policeman, I've been involved in investigating far too many murders," said Johansson, whose thoughts suddenly seemed elsewhere. "But I've never been involved in this investigation." Time for heavy, brooding old cop, he thought. Plus that inward-gazing murder investigator look he had never really succeeded in teaching his best friend.

"But you must still—"

"You're asking the wrong person," Johansson interrupted. "That question should go to the chief prosecutor in Stockholm, who is the leader of the investigation, or to the investigators at the Palme group who manage the practical aspects of the case."

"But you have great confidence in them?"

"Obviously," said Johansson. "They're good people."

That was that, thought Johansson contentedly. He hit the pause button, finished his good sandwich and the last half of the shot, chased it with beer, and turned on the TV again. Time for somewhat harder moves, he thought. Female reporter, considerably younger than him, almost as good-looking as his wife, and he hoped she was a little too sly for her own good.

First he got to speak his piece. Summarize the message in his own press release. Then suddenly it got serious.

"What I don't really understand is that you appointed three of the country's most experienced murder investigators to do something that sounds to me like a routine task for computer experts," she said with a smile so friendly it certainly portended something else.

"To me it's pretty obvious," said Johansson. "If this sort of material is going to be sorted out, it's necessary for the work to be done, as you yourself say, by a very experienced murder investigator."

"But computers and data processing are not really their field, are they?"

"I'm afraid you underestimate my co-workers," said Johansson. "All have extensive academic backgrounds, alongside purely police-related training, and one of them is a PhD. If you ask me she may be the police officer in this country with the greatest combined experience in these issues. She has considerable experience as a murder investigator. As a police officer she has unique expertise in science and statistics and, when it comes to computer issues, she knows how large quantities of investigative material are best handled."

"But you yourself," she asked suddenly. "You're a legendary murder investigator. You've never felt tempted to solve the murder of the prime minister?"

"Where computers and a lot of data and that sort of thing are concerned, I'm an old geezer," said Johansson. "I'm overjoyed every day I manage to log on to my own computer."

"So you've never felt tempted?"

"Of course I have," said Johansson. "But fortunately I'm old now and wise enough to leave it to those who have better understanding about that than I do. I have good people working on the Palme case. My job is to see that they don't drown in all the paper they've collected."

"You make it sound like a simple work environment issue."

"Yes," said Johansson. "Those are exactly the sort of issues someone like me should be concerned with. Creating a good work environment so my people can function. I'm sure you remember how things went earlier in this case when a lot of old bosses got the notion they should run around playing murder investigator."

Anna Holt, Jan Lewin, and Lisa Mattei had also devoted a good portion of the evening to following Johansson's TV appearances.

The man defies all description, thought Anna Holt as she turned on the late news on TV4. Time after time he manages to get completely normal people to lose the thread and suddenly start talking about something completely different, just because he's decided to talk about it. It was time she went to bed if she was going to be able to crawl out from under the mountain of papers under which Johansson had buried her.

The man who can see around corners, thought Lisa Mattei solemnly, and suddenly she didn't feel the least bit afraid of heights any longer. Then she went to her computer because she'd just had an idea.

Extensive academic educations, that's one way to describe it, thought Jan Lewin in the absolute solitude of his small apartment up at Gärdet. In his case it was a matter of an intro course in law, forty credits in criminology, and a basic course in statistics that he dropped because he couldn't make any sense of all the formulas and numbers.

Still, worst of all was that the little he'd learned during his academic education was either obvious or the sort of thing he already knew. Apart from statistics, of course, because that mostly confused him. It's high time to hit the sack, he thought. Then he undressed, brushed his teeth, and went to bed. As usual he twisted and turned for a few hours before he finally fell asleep.

Like the situation, he thought. How do you do that when loneliness has robbed your life of both purpose and meaning?

Johansson himself was feeling splendid. He finished the evening by reading a few more chapters in Grimberg's book about the Gustavian period and the assassination of Gustav III. Then he sat down in front of his computer and searched the Internet to learn more about murders of people like Gustav III and his own murder victim. The way he went about it would surely have surprised at least one female reporter at TV4.

Interesting, thought Johansson. Although you've suspected as much all along, he thought as he stood in the shower two hours later, pondering his new insights as a completely separate idea began to take shape in his head.

Then for some reason he started thinking about the police work in the investigation of the murder of the great king Gustav more than two hundred years ago. An excellent investigation. Based on the conditions of the time, the police chief, Liljensparre, had done everything a real policeman could be expected to do. Everything that his successor in the position 194 years later had failed to do.

First Liljensparre closed the doors to the opera house before anyone had a chance to slip out. He wrote down the names of everyone in the place and did some initial questioning. Then he personally inspected the two pistols that the perpetrator had thrown aside at the scene of the crime. One loaded, one recently fired, both recently repaired. He'd been able to do that without having to worry about fingerprints or DNA traces, thought Johansson, letting the water cascade around him.

The following day Liljensparre summoned the city's gunsmiths, one of whom immediately recognized the weapons. He had repaired them himself a fortnight earlier for a captain by the name of Jacob Johan Anckarström. The same Anckarström who had attended the masquerade ball the evening before and had a reputation for hating the king.

Anckarström was picked up for interrogation, confessed more or less immediately, and Liljensparre trudged happily on. Quite certainly in the same red woolen stockings he was wearing in the full-length portrait that still hangs in the police chief's corridor in the old police headquarters in Stockholm. One by one ringleaders, accomplices, conspirators, and opposition elements in general ended up in jail, where a good percentage of them more or less immediately tried to talk their way out by informing on all the others who were already there.

We must have had good interrogators at that time, thought Johansson as he soaped in extra under his arms.

With the number arrested passing a hundred, and a police chief who was getting more zealous every day, apparently the powers that be thought enough was enough. Liljensparre was released from his duties, the investigation was ended, and the majority of those who had been arrested were let out. Only the ones most closely involved were convicted, and they received surprisingly mild sentences considering the time and the crime—with the exception of Anckarström, who was, to put it simply, hacked to pieces.

Ingratitude is the world's reward for a poor policeman, regardless of how it ends, thought Lars Martin Johansson. We'll cross that bridge when we come to it, he thought, turning off the water and reaching for a towel.

Five minutes after going to bed he was sleeping deeply, his snores disturbing nobody in the whole world.

6

Despite what he'd said to Holt and Mattei at their introductory meeting, Lewin started with his old boxes. The same boxes that held everything under the sun that was at best of doubtful police value. The results of the internal investigation he'd been responsible for over twenty years earlier.

Back then he hadn't found anything, and since then no one seemed to have even tried. Three ordinary cardboard moving boxes piled among hundreds of others. At the bottom of each pile, of course, that's how it always was. He found them with the help of his own handwritten lists of contents that he'd taped to the boxes twenty years earlier.

Apart from the fact that someone must have moved the boxes, surely a number of times, the papers in them were arranged exactly as he'd left them. The only thing missing was cobwebs, thought Lewin. First he took out the old suicide on the islands in Mälaren. Mostly out of piety and to check his own recollections. He had no factual reason whatsoever.

The initial report—"suspected cause of death"—was dated the day after the assassination of the prime minister, Saturday the first of March 1986, and prepared by the Norrmalm police after a tip from the same colleague who'd contacted him. It was unclear why the case had ended up with the Norrmalm police—the Mälaren islands belonged to a different police district—but it was probably due to the fact that the officer who submitted the tip worked there, as well as the general chaos that prevailed after the assassination.

The report was topmost in a binder that also included an autopsy report, a technical investigation of the house on Ekerö where the former watchman who'd hung himself in the rec room was found, a ballistics report on the revolver found in the house search but which had nothing to do with the suicide, a test firing of the same weapon and a ballistic comparison with the two bullets secured at the crime scene where the prime minister had been murdered. Even though it was already known that the suicide's weapon had a different, considerably smaller, caliber than the gun the perpetrator used to shoot the prime minister.

At the back of the binder were interviews with five different witnesses, the ex-wife, and four neighbors. At the very back was the memorandum that Lewin had prepared when he closed the case. Convinced as he then was, far beyond all the doubts that tormented him more than almost any of his colleagues, that the man who had taken his life had nothing whatsoever to do with the murder of Olof Palme.

How much simpler it all would have been if it had been the watchman after all, thought Lewin and sighed.

The copies of old parking tickets required a separate box. From the afternoon of Friday, February 28, 1986, until Saturday afternoon on March 1, the traffic wardens and police had ticketed almost two thousand illegally parked vehicles in the Stockholm region, at Arlanda airport; the central stations in Uppsala, Enköping, and Södertälje; plus the ferry terminals in Nynäshamn, Norrtälje, Kapellskär, and Hargshamn up in north Uppland. They were sorted into piles for the various police districts as well as the various traffic districts in Stockholm. Arranged in chronological order according to the time on the ticket. Neatly bundled with rubber bands, and he was probably the one who had organized most of them.

At the top of the piles was a blue binder. In it were copies of nineteen different parking tickets that Lewin had traced to his own agency or to individual police officers. Six of them involved civilian service vehicles, and all the tickets were canceled. The remaining thirteen applied to cars whose registered owners were fellow police officers.

. . .

Nine of them paid their fines within the stated time, and because their vehicles were parked near their home addresses there was certainly nothing remarkable about those tickets. Two of them paid after a reminder, and Lewin hadn't been able to find anything strange there either.

He talked with both of the vehicle owners, and one of them frankly admitted he'd been at home with a woman other than the one he was married to. A colleague of his moreover, and if the Palme investigators didn't have anything better to do then of course it would be fine to talk with her too. Better that than ending up on TV as part of the so-called police track. If Lewin would be so kind as to not talk with his wife about it, no one would be happier than he. Lewin let the matter rest with the female police officer/lover, and after that conversation crossed out yet another person as a conceivable perpetrator in the murder of the prime minister.

Remaining were two tickets dated the day of the murder for illegally parked vehicles owned by police officers who used their own cars on duty; both of the parking tickets had been canceled. One was a detective with the narcotics squad who'd met one of his informants and preferred his own Alfa Romeo because he felt that the police agency's Saabs and Volvos were a red flag for the people he was after.

The other was an officer with the secret police who had looked in on a person that SePo kept hidden at one of their secure addresses. Otherwise everything seemed in order. Both the addresses where the vehicles were parked and the times the tickets had been written argued strongly that these events did not have the least thing to do with the assassination of the country's prime minister. In addition he'd received papers on the matter from both the narcotics squad and the secret police.

I don't understand how I managed, even at that time, thought Lewin as he closed up his old boxes and placed them in a pile of their own to spare his back.

After that he started doing what he had promised Holt and Mattei he would do. Simply finding the investigation files he needed for his work kept him occupied far into the evening. He was not able to leave the police station until ten o'clock. He took the subway home to Gärdet. Hesitating a moment outside the 7-Eleven store in the block where he lived, he went in and bought a sandwich and a bottle of mineral water. When he stepped into his apartment everything was as usual. What awaited him was yet another night of loneliness and the next morning yet another day with the same substance. A series of nights and days that never seemed to end, thought Lewin as he finally fell asleep.

7

Anna Holt had no intention of sitting in the Palme room. Not at a wobbly card table they'd brought in themselves with barely enough room for the computers Lisa Mattei had set up for them. So Lisa, with the help of those same computers, located the documents Holt needed for her review of "Palme assassin" Christer Pettersson. Finally they carried the material over to Holt's office themselves, where she intended to read in peace and quiet. A total of ten binders, only a small portion of the material on Pettersson. At the same time, those portions, according to Mattei, ought to cover the essentials about the suspect up to the indictment in May 1989, the sentence of life imprisonment in Stockholm District Court a few months later, and how all this had been turned on end when a unanimous court of appeals released him in November of the same year.

As Holt disappeared with her burden she noticed a worried glance from Jan Lewin. In Lewin's world, files of that type were not something you stuck under your arm and simply walked away with. Not least the kind that were stored in the Palme room. Files that were removed should be signed for on a special list, returned as soon as you were done with them, and checked off on the same list. Date, time, signature. True, all his colleagues did the same as Holt, but this was also the sorry explanation for why meticulous individuals such as himself often had a terrible time finding the documents they needed for their work.

Pity that Jan is so anxious. He's actually very good-looking, thought Holt as she and Lisa disappeared through the door, headed toward the peacefulness of Holt's office.

"Is there anything else I can help you with?" asked Lisa Mattei as she set the binders down on Holt's desk.

"That's plenty," Holt said. "You've got a few things to do yourself."

"I pulled this out for you," said Mattei, giving Holt a plastic folder she'd carried squeezed under her arm.

"What's in there?" asked Holt.

"A few interesting dates on Christer Pettersson plus his police and court records. I'm sure you'll find it in one of the binders too, but an extra copy is never a bad thing if you want to make your own notes. Otherwise there's nothing special about most of it as I'm sure you already know. But sometimes it's good to have exact dates and so on."

"When did you find time to do this?"

"Did it as soon as I knew what Johansson wanted to talk about."

"But that was before we decided I should look at Pettersson."

"One of us had to do it," Mattei observed, shrugging her shoulders. "That much I could figure out anyway," she said, smiling.

"Thanks," said Holt. Dear, dear Lisa, she thought. She's got more in her head than the rest of us in this place combined.

When she finally shut the door, Holt cleared her desk of everything else. Placed her binders within comfortable reach, took out notebook and pen, leaned back in her not at all uncomfortable desk chair, took out the plastic folder about Christer Pettersson that Mattei had given her, and finally put her feet up on the desk. All in accordance with the general advice and life tips that her boss so regularly shared with his co-workers when he was in the mood.

According to Lars Martin Johansson, the "Genius from Näsåker," as co-workers who didn't think he could "see around corners" called him when they were sure he couldn't hear them, this was the most ideal body position for engaging in "more demanding reading." The feet and legs should be placed high in relation to the head in order to facilitate the flow of blood to the brain, and the very best choice was lying on a comfortable, sufficiently long couch equipped with the necessary number of pillows.

It was also important that it not be too warm in the room where the couch was. According to Johansson, who would usually make reference here to a major sociomedical study from Japan, including the names of the authors, this type of reading demanded approximately the same temperature as for the storage of fine wines.

The first time Johansson had expounded on this burning issue was when they were sitting in the bar toward the end of a nice staff party a few years earlier.

"That sounds really cold," Holt objected.

"Depends on what you mean by cold," Johansson snorted. "It should be cold around you. Then you think your best. It should be just cold enough that your noggin feels clear but without having to freeze your rear end off."

"Well, I thought wine should be stored at about fifty degrees."

"That depends," said Johansson evasively. "But it can't be more than sixty degrees in the room. For reading, that is," he clarified. "If we're talking about sleeping it should be a lot colder."

"Too cold," said Holt, shaking her head firmly. "Much too cold for me. Couldn't even think if it were that cold in my office." Wonder whether his poor wife is an Eskimo? she thought.

"Yes, I might have guessed that," Johansson observed, and no more was said about it for the rest of the evening.

I don't suppose I can even think about opening the window on a day like this, sighed Anna Holt, glancing at the sunshine behind the drawn blinds. She could also forget about a couch of her own. In any event Johansson hadn't implemented any concrete measures in that direction, and he was the only one at the entire bureau, of course, who had a sufficiently large, comfortable couch. According to well-informed sources he used it exclusively for his regular midday slumber. So far no one had seen him reading on it.

That man is like a large child, thought Holt. She sighed again and started reading the papers on Palme assassin Christer Pettersson that Mattei had given her.

.   .   .

Christer Pettersson was born on April 23, 1947, in Solna. He had passed away less than three years ago at the age of fifty-seven, on September 29, 2004. He showed up for the first time in the Palme investigation's material on Sunday the second of March 1986, less than two days after the assassination of the prime minister.

By then Jan Lewin and his colleagues who were responsible for the internal investigation were done with their first compilations of previous violent crimes that had occurred in the vicinity of the intersection of Sveavägen and Tunnelgatan, where the prime minister was shot. It was an extensive list that included thousands of crimes and more than a thousand persons. One of them was Christer Pettersson, who sixteen years earlier, in December 1970, had gotten into a quarrel with a man unknown to him down in the subway, only fifty yards from the place where the prime minister was murdered. Pettersson chased the man up to the street, where he finished the discussion by stabbing his victim through the heart with a bayonet he was carrying. Within the course of a week the police had arrested him, and in June the following year he was convicted of homicide and sentenced to a closed psychiatric ward.

To be sure, it was not the first time he'd run afoul of the Swedish legal system. In the court records there were notations on several hundred crimes, from the first time in 1964, when he was seventeen years old, and up to his death. The final notations were made in the crime registry during the summer of the year he died. Pettersson had spent almost half of his adult life in prisons, mental hospitals, and rehabilitation centers for addicts. Based on what was known about his criminal activity there was a strong element of violence. At the same time there were no notes indicating that he made use of a firearm, either before or after the murder of the prime minister. No signs either of any political or ideological motives. Pettersson's violence seemed to have been vented on persons in the same social situation as himself or who were expected to maintain control of people like him. Men he'd argued with or robbed of money and drugs, women he'd known or lived with, whom he'd also assaulted. Plus police officers, watchmen, store security guards.

Ordinary theft and shoplifting charges dominated his criminality in terms of numbers, and the particular crime victim who appeared most often as the complainant in his record was the state liquor store. That was also how he acquired three of the four nicknames that the police had noted, "Hit-and-Run," "Dasher," and "Half Bend."

Pettersson would go into the liquor store, order a bottle of vodka, schnapps, or cream liqueur, snatch the bottle as soon as the clerk set it down on the counter between them, and without further ado "run" or "dash" out of the store. A "half bend" was the body movement the liquor store employee was expected to execute when he pulled out the half-bottle of aquavit that for practical reasons was often stored under the counter near the cash register and that seemed to be one of the most common orders in Pettersson's life.

Against this background his fourth alias was even more astonishing. Pettersson was also known as "the Count." A title he often emphasized to his acquaintances. A real "count."

Why he was called that did not appear in the police papers, but for Holt the mystery was already solved by the precise Lisa Mattei. Under an asterisk in the margin she'd made the following note in her neat handwriting: "CP born and grew up in Bromma. Middle-class home. Father self-employed. Mother a housewife. Dropped out of high school. Went to drama school for a few years. In his association with like-minded in the same situation often presented himself and his background as considerably finer than was actually the case."

Heavy drug user, professional criminal of the simplest type—all these were known facts, thought Holt, but it wasn't what she knew that made her feel less comfortable after the introductory reading. Already on day three, Sunday, March 2, 1986, he ended up on a list among thousands of similar types because of a knife murder that had happened sixteen years earlier. After that none of her colleagues seemed to have given a thought to either him or his doings for more than two years. Only during the summer of 1988 did they start to investigate him, and in December the same year he was arrested.

Why just then? thought Holt. And why in the name of God did it take so long?

8

Without lowering the level of either her precision or her objectivity, Mattei nonetheless tried to facilitate her task. Using her computer, she pulled out all the summaries and analyses in the Palme material. Then she organized them in chronological order to get an easy understanding of what information was deemed so important at a certain point in time that it required special consideration.

Because the material was a bit thin for her taste, she then used the various registries in the investigation to extract a selection of documents that she pulled out and leafed through to see what they were about. Approximately every tenth document couldn't be located, because it had ended up in the wrong binder, the whole binder had gone astray, or the document had simply been lost.

Wonder if Johansson is aware of that? thought Mattei.

Then she carried out a number of simple, volume-related estimates of how much work her previous colleagues had expended on various working hypotheses or investigation leads. All those "tracks" as the first investigation leader, police chief in Stockholm Hans Holmér, had chosen to call them, even though the word had a completely different, very specific criminological meaning.

There were lots of Holmér's tracks, thought Mattei. But almost none of the usual clues. No foot- or fingerprints, no fibers, bodily fluids, or abandoned belongings that might lead to a perpetrator. Obviously no DNA, for that didn't even exist in the material world of the police when the prime minister was assassinated. All they had were the two revolver bullets that had been put to use the night of the murder, and the circumstance that it was ordinary people who found them at the crime scene and turned them over to the police had not made the burden easier to bear.

By means of a number of documents that could be ascribed to the various tracks, within a day Mattei had already formed a reasonable understanding of what her fellow officers had been doing for twenty years. The various tracks had appeared and vanished. As in a winter landscape, where certain track marks are more common than others.

First in and first out was the person who to start with was called the "thirty-three-year-old" in the media, but shortly thereafter appeared under his given name, Åke Victor Gunnarsson. In the first days after the murder the police received a number of tips about Gunnarsson. He possessed a reasonable likeness to the description of the perpetrator, was said to own a revolver of the type the perpetrator had used, to have contacts with an organization hostile to Palme, and to have expressed himself hatefully about the murder victim on several occasions. Last but not least he had been in the immediate vicinity of the crime scene at the time of the murder, and in the hours afterward he had been running around in the area, behaving strangely to say the least.

Less than a fortnight after the murder, Wednesday the twelfth of March, he had been arrested. A week later he was released, and after another two months, on May 16, 1986, the prosecutor decided to close the preliminary investigation on him.

During those two months a number of things happened that concerned Gunnarsson and in time filled half a dozen thick binders in the Palme investigation's files: technical investigations of his residence and his clothes, interviews with relatives and witnesses, photo arrays, diverse expert statements, as well as a major charting of his background and way of life. After that there had been mostly silence about him for several years. Freed from the suspicion of having assassinated the prime minister, he emigrated to the USA in the early nineties, and it was only when the American police made contact in January 1994 and reported that Gunnarsson had been found murdered—shot several times and dumped in a wooded ravine in the wilds of North Carolina—that he once again landed in the headlines.

It proved to be an ordinary drama of jealousy. That the perpetrator on whom Gunnarsson set horns was also a policeman was in some way consistent, considering the life Gunnarsson seemed to have lived. The investigator in the Palme group who was responsible for the preliminary investigation of Gunnarsson had a hard time handling his disappointment in any case. In his world it was still Gunnarsson who had murdered Olof Palme, and only a few years after Gunnarsson's demise he published a book in which he tried to prove it.

Mattei found a copy stuffed into one of the binders, with a personal dedication: "From the author to his colleagues in the Palme room," and when Lewin left the room to get coffee for them both she took the opportunity to slip the book into her handbag to read in peace and quiet as soon as she got home.

Six bulging binders on Åke Victor Gunnarsson, but nothing compared to the material that dealt with the so-called Kurd track, or PKK track, which evidently occupied almost two hundred police officers full-time during the first years of the Palme investigation.

The idea that the PKK, Partiya Karkerên Kurdistan, or Kurdistan Workers' Party, could have murdered the prime minister seemed to have made a deep impression on the leadership during the first week of the investigation. The original material came from officers with the secret police who had reason to be interested in the organization in a completely different context. During the two preceding years, PKK had been behind a total of three murders and one attempted murder in Sweden and Denmark, crimes aimed at defectors from the organization, but apart from a certain superficial similarity in approach, it was almost a mystery why they also would have attacked the Swedish prime minister.

PKK was known for murdering defectors and infiltrators in their own ranks. Not for attacking Western politicians and least of all the prime minister of Sweden, a politician and a country that was kindly disposed to the Kurdish liberation struggle and had offered political asylum to a large number of Kurdish refugees.

During the latter part of July 1986 the investigation leadership decided that PKK "with high probability was behind the murder of the prime minister." Several meetings were held on the topic, and in one of the many binders Mattei found detailed minutes from the investigation leadership's own management team, in which their conviction was put on paper.

During the following six months the Kurd track, or PKK track, would also constitute the so-called Main track. All according to the top boss's own terminology, and for Lisa Mattei it was a mystery in a factual sense. Regardless, at that time, twenty years ago, all their resources had basically been directed at this track, and the whole thing ended with a real bang.

Early on the morning of January 20, 1987, investigation leader Holmér conducted a major operation. Twenty-some Kurds were seized, several house searches were made, and many things were confiscated. Already after a few hours the prosecutors started releasing the majority of those whom the police had deprived of liberty, all the confiscations were revoked within a few days, and the two individuals who were arrested were released after a week.

It was a scandal. Holmér was fired as investigation leader and resigned as police chief. The responsibility for the investigation was turned over to the prosecutor, and the National Bureau of Criminal Investigation was given the task of supplying him with the police officers needed to take care of the practical aspects. The Kurd track had suddenly simply ended. All that remained twenty years later were almost a hundred binders of papers plus a number of boxes that held things that were hard to stuff into binders.

Sigh and moan, thought Mattei, even though she seldom thought that way.

But there were other things too. All the crazy tips, for example. Another hundred binders and thousands of tips, mostly about particular perpetrators who could have murdered Olof Palme. This was also the essential reason that the investigation's list of such persons—suspects of all kinds, provided on various grounds, pointed out with no grounds, the result of pure premonitions and vibrations in the informant's head—amounted to almost ten thousand named individuals. In the majority of cases the reports went straight into the binder without the police showing the least interest in them.

Let's sincerely hope it's not one of them, thought Mattei self-righteously.

Remaining were all the tracks that had the good taste to fit into a smaller number of binders. Often one or two were enough for these tracks, and the maximum was five. It was also here that there seemed to be political, ideological, or more generally visible ambitions. Here were leads that concerned South Africa, the Iraq/Iran conflict alias the Iran/Iraq conflict, the "Middle East including Israel," "India/Pakistan" alias the "Indian weapons affair" alias the "Bofors affair."

Here were other leads that dealt with various "terrorists" or "violent organizations" all the way from the Baader-Meinhof Gang, the Red Brigades, Black September, and Ustaša to the crew-cut talents in KSS, Keep Sweden Swedish, and the old disgruntled socialists who were said to form the backbone of We Who Built Sweden.

Here too were organizations and individuals who should have known better or at least shown mercy to the victim. Government security agencies in the Balkans, in South Africa and various dictatorships and banana republics, as well as the USA's own CIA. Military personnel and ordinary Swedish police officers, various intimates, acquaintances, and former work and party comrades. There was even a subfile that dealt with members of the victim's own family.

The family track, thought Lisa Mattei. For some reason she thought of her mother, who had worked as a police superintendent at the secret police for more than twenty years.

Here there was literally something for everyone, and as far as the factual basis for the political speculations was concerned, Mattei believed it seemed consistent enough. Mysterious informants who claimed to have a secret past, various revelations in the media, former TV journalists with psychiatric diagnoses plus all the regular nutcases who figured in the public debate. Otherwise little or nothing.

The most concrete contributions Mattei found were the travelogues that various Palme investigators had turned in over the years. Assuming that the clues led in the direction of warmer regions and the season was right, a number of leads had been investigated on-site.

Unfortunately and in all cases without result, but at least the foreign colleagues seemed to have taken good care of their Swedish visitors.

It's always something, thought Lisa Mattei.

Most of all, however, it was all about the "Palme assassin" Christer Pettersson. During two periods of several years combined, the investigation seemed to have been mainly about him. It began the summer of 1988 and ran through to the end of the following year, when he was freed by the Svea Court of Appeal. Then there was a period of relative calm lasting several years, up until 1993 when preparations were made for a petition for a new trial to rehear the acquittal decision.

The petition was submitted in December 1997, and in May of the following year a unanimous Supreme Court rejected it. Three years ago Pettersson himself had departed earthly life, and regardless of what he might have had to bring to the investigation, he took it with him to the grave.

The Palme investigation's material had been packed up in boxes for years. For several years before that, a dozen investigators in the group were primarily occupied with completely different tasks. Once a week they would meet, have coffee, and talk about their case. About things that had happened before, about old colleagues who had died or retired, about Christer Pettersson, who was still the most common topic of conversation at the table.

And soon they'll all be dead, thought Mattei, who was only eleven years old at the time when Sweden's prime minister was murdered.

9

Despite all that had happened on Thursday, Johansson was still looking forward to a quiet weekend. His exemplary clear and unqualified denial on all the major TV stations ought to have made some impression even on the nitwits working at the country's largest newspaper.

His message seemed to have taken hold in the other media. They'd stopped calling to ask about the Palme investigation anyway. Not so at *Dagens Nyheter*. On Friday morning his digestion was already disturbed at breakfast by a long editorial with the thought-provoking title "Police Force in Decline." Obviously unsigned, as usual when things were really bad.

Must be one of those angry women who work there, thought Johansson.

If matters were as the head of the National Bureau of Criminal Investigation maintained—previous experience had taught the writer that nothing someone like Johansson said should ever be taken for granted, least of all when it concerned the assassination of Olof Palme—the situation was obviously even worse than the newspaper had feared.

The Palme investigation had simply been closed down in secret, even though it concerned perhaps the most important event in postwar Sweden. The case files were packed up in boxes in silence, and the investigators assigned to solve the case had been working on completely different matters. Highly placed prosecutors and police officers had apparently intended to hide this police fiasco in their own basement.

Soon the murder of Olof Palme would pass the statute of limitations. After that the case files would be classified as secret for many years. On that point *DN* had no doubts whatsoever. The only obvious, definitive conclusion was that it was high time for the government to appoint a new review commission with representatives from all parties in parliament and citizens who had the confidence of the general public. The choice of a chairperson was also a given according to the newspaper, namely the chancellor of justice who, according to Johansson and his colleagues, had made a name for himself by his constant lamentations over the police department's deficient diligence, sense of order, and morals.

A fate worse than death, thought Lars Martin Johansson, and he was thinking about himself, not the prime minister who was the victim of an unsolved murder that disturbed Johansson's sense of order.

When he arrived at work it was time for the next variation on the same theme. According to his secretary, Chief Inspector Flykt "insisted" he had to see his boss immediately.

"Okay," he said. "You can send the SOB in."

Chief Inspector Flykt did not seem happy. He was even noticeably nervous, his face flushed beneath the otherwise becoming suntan.

"Sit yourself down, Flykt," Johansson grunted, nodding curtly at his visitor's chair. Comfortably curled up in his own chair, his hands clasped over his belly, wearing a heavy facial expression. Stop behaving like a fucking first-time offender, he thought.

"What can I help you with?"

Problems, according to Flykt. Two different problems, although there was a connection between them of course.

"I'm listening," said Johansson, picking at his left nostril with his large right thumb in search of unbecoming strands of hair.

· · ·

The people at *Dagens Nyheter* were obviously refusing to give up. Despite the boss's exemplary clarifying denials, they were still lurking in the bushes. Flykt had personally noticed clear signs.

"Of course," said Johansson. "What did you expect? We'll just have to live with it. Rooting out who let their mouths run loose is out of the question. I guess you know that as well as I do?"

Obviously not. Flykt knew that too, but the situation was both worrisome and—

"Forget about *DN* now," interrupted Johansson. "They'll get tired of this as soon as they find some other place to spread their usual dung. What was the other thing?"

"The other thing?" said Flykt with surprise.

"You had two problems," Johansson clarified. "What's the other one? The one that was supposed to be tied up with the first one? That's what you said a minute ago if I remember correctly."

Of course, of course, and the boss would have to be patient with him if he seemed a little confused. The thing was that for the past twenty-four hours he and his colleagues had been subjected to a veritable bombardment from the various informants and private detectives who had made up their primary workload since the Supreme Court had rejected the petition for a new trial against Pettersson.

In later years most of them seemed to have calmed down, but Johansson had managed to bring them back to life again.

"Yes, that is, not you, boss, but that unfortunate article in *DN*," said Flykt. "Right should be right," he added for some reason.

"The usual bag ladies who send dog shit and old bullet casings they maintain they've secured at the crime scene," said Johansson, grinning.

"Yes," said Flykt. "And all the messages of course."

According to Flykt the switchboard had been pretty much jammed. In addition letters were pouring in, and officers careless enough to give out their cell phone numbers were being texted. The mailroom had called to complain. With loads of parcels coming in, their bomb and shit indicators were on overdrive. The internal security department had already issued ten reports related to threats against the officials who were forced to take care of the misery.

"You'll have to excuse me," said Johansson. "But I still don't understand the problem." Throw away the shit and blame the post office if worse comes to worst, he thought.

Flykt's problem was very simple. He lacked the manpower to record, register, evaluate, and analyze this new flood of tips. Normally there were twelve investigators including Flykt, as well as his secretary and another half-time assistant. Right now there were fewer than that. Half of the force was on vacation or had comp time off. Two were at a course in Canada. Three were in the Canary Islands to help with the identification of the Swedish victims of a big hotel fire that had happened ten days earlier. Remaining were Flykt himself, his secretary, and a female colleague who was on half-time sick leave for mental burnout.

"Suggestions?" said Johansson, leaning forward and training his eyes on Flykt. "How do you want me to help you?" Whine, whine, whine, he thought.

Flykt took a run at it. Just a random idea. Could Holt, Lewin, and Mattei possibly take care of the registration until his own personnel returned to the building and could take over?

"Absolutely not," said Johansson. "How would that look? They're doing an administrative overview of your procedures for data handling. How could they get involved in your investigative work? That woman at the prosecutor's office wouldn't be happy if she could hear you now, Yngve."

"You have no other suggestions, boss?"

"Throw the shit away," said Johansson. "Blame it on the post office if anyone complains."

The rest of Johansson's day passed in a relatively normal, dignified manner.

Right before he was to go home Mattei requested admittance, and because Johansson was lying on his office couch and had already started thinking about what he would have for dinner, he was basically his usual contented self when his secretary sent her in.

"Sit yourself down, Lisa," said Johansson, indicating the nearest chair with his arm. "How are things going for you anyway?"

"You mean with the administrative overview of the Palme material," said Mattei.

"Exactly," said Johansson. "Have you found the bastard who did it yet?" Clever girl, he thought. A little like Nancy Drew.

No. Mattei had not found the perpetrator. On the other hand she had a reasonable understanding of why no one else had either. Besides, she was basically done now with what the case files contained.

"In general terms," Mattei clarified. "The direction and structure itself, if I may say so."

"So you say," said Johansson. You little string bean, he thought.

"I thought about trying out an idea on you, boss."

"Shoot," said Johansson.

"I was thinking about proposing a small sociological investigation," said Mattei.

True, Johansson had nodded, but Mattei noted the faint shift in his gray eyes.

A small sociological investigation in which she simply interviewed the officers who for all those years had been involved in the hunt for Palme's murderer. Those who were still alive and could be talked with. She would simply ask them about who they thought had done it and why the investigation went the way it did.

"You don't think this is waking a sleeping bear?" Johansson objected, suddenly recalling the morning's editorial.

On the contrary, Mattei responded. If the assignment really consisted of creating better procedures for processing this gigantic amount of material, then that necessarily required some kind of overarching assessment of it. Who would be better suited to express an opinion on the matter than the ones who'd been doing the job all these years?

"I see what you mean," said Johansson with a drawl.

"Personally I'd be flattered if I were in their shoes," she added.

Not you, he thought. Not me either. But almost all the others.

"Sounds good," said Johansson. "I'll buy it. Say the word if you need help with anything practical."

10

Johansson's first week after vacation ended just as well as it had begun, and he decided to forget all the nonsense in between. On Friday evening he procured leave from socializing with his wife to have dinner instead with his best friend, now working at the county investigation bureau in Stockholm as acting head of investigations, Chief Inspector Bo Jarnebring. The Greatest of the Old Owls.

"That works perfectly," said Pia. "I have to check in on Dad if we're going away for the weekend. Say hi to Bo and don't drink too much."

"I promise," Johansson lied.

Johansson and Jarnebring met at the "usual place." The Italian restaurant five minutes' walk from his apartment that had been his favorite place for over twenty years. He was a frequent guest, a generous guest, an honored guest, but also one who had left his mark. For several years now he could have his favorite aquavit from his own crystal shot glass, of which he'd brought over a dozen. And enjoy various Italian variations on old Swedish classics like anchovy hash, potato pancakes, and grilled herring besides.

"You look fit, Lars. I think you may have lost a few pounds," said Jarnebring, as soon as they'd dispensed with the introductory greetings and sat down at the usual table in a secluded corner where, according to established police custom, they could talk in peace and keep an eye on anyone coming and going.

"Depends on what you mean by a few," said Johansson with poorly concealed pride. "According to the bathroom scale we're talking double digits."

"You're not sick, are you? I got a little worried when I read the paper the other day and saw you'd appointed a new Palme investigation. Thought you had a little touch of Alzheimer's."

"I'm as healthy as a horse," said Johansson. "Now, if you'd seen me on TV—"

"Nicely done," said Jarnebring. "I saw it. You're your usual self. Administrating away so that everything's just so. Say the word when you want a real job and I'll put in a good word for you down at the county bureau."

"We'll cross that bridge when we come to it," said Johansson with a streak of melancholy in his voice.

Johansson abandoned that subject to talk instead about more essential things. The menu that he and his Italian restaurateur had jointly composed, in honor of the evening.

"Because we haven't seen each other all summer I thought we should do a thorough job," said Johansson. "The whole program, and I'll pick up the tab. Do you have anything against that?"

"Is the pope a Muslim?" said Jarnebring.

The whole program. First two deft waiters spread out the little smorgasbord that was a necessary prerequisite for having both beer and aquavit. A deplorably neglected part of the otherwise outstanding Italian food culture, but at this particular place set to rights long ago by Johansson.

"Nothing remarkable, a few mixed delicacies, that's all," Johansson explained with a deprecating hand gesture. "Those mini-pizzas on the plate over there—"

"No bigger than my thumbnail," Jarnebring interrupted. "Without the black lines though."

"Exactly. Small pizzas topped with Swedish anchovies and chopped chives, and baked with Parmesan."

"Is the pope Catholic?" said Jarnebring.

"Then we'll have sardines in a marinade of garlic, mustard, capers, and olive oil."

"The bear shits in the forest . . ."

"That ham there," said Johansson. "It's not Swedish or Italian. It's Spanish. It's called *pata negra*, blackfoot ham. Free-range hogs that wander around eating acorns until they're slaughtered, salted, and dried. The world's best pork if you ask me."

With the fragrance of Sierra Madrona's green-clad mountains, thought Johansson, picking up the scent with his long nose. He would never dream of saying that. In male company, between real policemen there were certain things you never said, and who was he to worry his best friend unnecessarily.

"Damn good pork, if you ask me," Johansson repeated, raising his full shot glass.

"Cheers, boss," said Jarnebring. "Shall we drink or shall we talk?"

When after his second shot Johansson described the impending entrée, Jarnebring expressed a certain hesitation. It was the only time during the evening, and it was mostly out of old habit.

"I thought we'd have pasta as an entrée," said Johansson.

"Pasta," said Jarnebring. Is Dolly Parton suddenly sleeping on her belly? he thought.

"With diced grilled ox filet, mushrooms, and a cream and cognac sauce," Johansson tempted.

"Sounds interesting," Jarnebring agreed. Dolly must be sleeping the way she always does, he thought.

Three hours later they had finished off the usual. First they talked about their own families and everyone near and dear. Ordinarily that part would be finished in five minutes, so that the rest of the evening could be spent discussing all the idiots they had encountered, regardless of whether they were fellow police officers, hoods, or ordinary civilians. Not so this time, because Jarnebring suddenly started talking about his youngest son and what it was like becoming a dad when you were over fifty and had decided long ago not to have any more children. That this in particular was probably the greatest thing that had ever happened to him. Despite all the crooks he'd arrested over the years.

Must be the good pasta that has brought out a new, gentler side of dear Bo, Johansson thought.

"So suddenly there you are with two new little rascals. The boy then. Yes, and the girl of course," said Jarnebring, shaking his head thoughtfully. "The boy's no slouch. Let me tell you, Lars."

"But his big sister," said Johansson divertingly. "How are things going for her?"

"You mean little Lina," said Jarnebring with surprise. "The spitting image of her mother, if you ask me."

Depends on what you mean by little, thought Johansson. Must be fifteen by now. He and Pia never had any children. It hadn't turned out that way, he thought. For various reasons he didn't want to talk about, and then he changed the subject.

"Speaking of crazy colleagues," said Johansson, "I ran into your dear police chief the other day."

After a while they left the restaurant and trotted home to Johansson's for the usual concluding session. Halfway there they ran into four younger men who came toward them four abreast on the sidewalk with expectation in their eyes. Jarnebring stopped, looked eagerly at the biggest one, and when he saw that he recognized Jarnebring the rest was pure routine.

"How's it going, Marek?" Jarnebring asked. "Planning to get yourself killed?"

"Respect, boss," said Marek with frightened eyes, stepping ahead of his friends onto the street.

"Take care of yourselves, girls," Jarnebring grunted.

We're too old for that sort of thing, thought Johansson, putting the key into his door and seeking the peace and safety on the other side. Wrong, he thought. You've always been too old for that sort of thing. Bo is who he is and he'll always be that way.

"Tell me about Palme," said Johansson ten minutes later when they were sitting in armchairs in his large study. Jarnebring with a respectable whiskey toddy and the bottle at a comfortable distance. He himself with a glass of red wine and a bottle of mineral water. At his age you had to take care of yourself, and apart from the obligatory introductory shot, because he would never give that up, these days he was content with beer, wine, and water. Plus the occasional cognac, to help his digestion. Though not Jarnebring, of course. He was who he was. With a physique that defied human understanding and seemed completely unaffected by alcohol.

I wonder why he drinks, thought Johansson.

"Tell me about Palme," he repeated. "You were there when it happened."

"You want ideas about how to put all the binders on the shelves? Personally, I usually set them with the spine out. Then I paste little labels on them so that I can tell what's in them," Jarnebring teased.

"Forget about my binders," said Johansson.

"It went to hell," said Jarnebring. "If we'd done it the usual way of course we would've caught the bastard. If those of us who usually took care of it had been able to do it the usual way," he clarified. "If we had not had a lot of crazy lawyers telling us what to do. You certainly would have found him if you'd been involved from the start. You wouldn't have needed more than a month or two. But I guess you had your hands full with your binders as usual."

"So who did it?"

"Who the hell knows," said Jarnebring, shaking his head. "But it wasn't Christer Pettersson. I knew him, by the way. Don't know how many times I dragged that asshole to jail over the years. May he rest in peace," said Jarnebring, raising his glass.

"He seemed crazy enough anyway," Johansson objected.

"Christer Pettersson was crazy, with a certain degree of sanity. For example, he was never so crazy that he tried to attack me the times I arrested him. He knew, you see, that he would get a sound thrashing and he never got that crazy. He drank and did drugs, carried on and was generally disorderly. Fought with smaller, drunker companions and his ladies. Though it wasn't more than that, and he didn't understand firearms. Besides, I think he liked people like Palme. It was people like you and me he didn't like."

"The one who shot Palme was a skilled shooter," said Johansson. Wonder what Palme would have thought about Christer Pettersson, he thought suddenly. A social outcast? A person who only happened to end up on the outside? Through no fault of his own?

"The one who shot, yes," said Jarnebring. "He was just as good a shot as you or me. Forget all our colleagues who complain that it's no big deal to shoot someone a few inches away—but in that case how could he miss Lisbeth Palme when he shot at her? Forget all that bullshit from everyone who's never shot at anyone in a crisis situation, when people move around and start jumping and running like dazed chickens as soon as it goes off."

"I see what you mean," Johansson agreed.

"The bullet that strikes Lisbeth Palme goes in on her left side, passes between the skin and her blouse, the whole way along the back, level with her shoulder blade and out on the right side. If you miss like that you're a damn experienced shot. If she'd just twisted her upper body a tenth of a second later he would've clipped off her back. So he could really shoot. I'm a hundred percent sure he was convinced he'd shot her through the lung, and because he also knew that was enough, with interest, he was content to get out of there."

"She falls down on her knees beside her husband," said Johansson.

"Sure," said Jarnebring with emphasis. "First he shoots Palme. Hits him from behind in mid-step, and he falls flat on his face on the street. He had a bruise the size of a silver dollar on his forehead. In the next second he aims at Lisbeth, targeting the middle of her back, but just as he fires she twists her body to see what happened to her husband who has suddenly fallen headlong in front of her feet. She hasn't even seen the shooter behind her.

"So all that about Pettersson, you can just forget. Cheers, by the way," said Jarnebring. "There's way too much talking at this party, if you ask me."

It was definitely not Christer Pettersson. Completely wrong type, according to Jarnebring. Just as wrong as that nonsense about the Kurds, those guys would eat out of the hands of someone like Palme. Or the "thirty-three-year-old" for that matter.

"Usual fucking pathological liar," Jarnebring summarized.

"So who did it?"

"Someone very familiar with the area, good physique, experienced shot, presence of mind, sure of himself, full control of the situation, sharpness and the capacity to resort to violence when it was time. Ice-cold devil. Not at all like Pettersson, because he would be jumping around yelling for a while, then waving his arms if his opponent seemed small and harmless enough. If he'd tried to kill Palme he would have started by doing a war dance around him, and then he would have done the wave and given him the finger afterward. But this perpetrator didn't do that. He did what he needed to do, calmly and quietly, and then he just left."

"I hear what you're saying," Johansson agreed. "An ice-cold devil who only needs to pull a trigger to be able to shoot another person from behind. Not the least like Christer Pettersson."

"Could be me. The one who put Palme out of business, that is," said Jarnebring and grinned.

"No," said Johansson. "I don't think so, despite all the rest, because I do believe that."

"Someone like me then," Jarnebring persisted.

Not you, thought Johansson. Not someone who is only bigger and stronger than everyone else and never lost a fistfight. Another type, someone who can just pull the trigger and suddenly change from person to executioner, he thought.

Although he'd actually thought that the whole time, so they didn't talk about it anymore.

Wednesday, October 10.
The bay outside Puerto Pollensa on north Mallorca

After an almost ten-minute run, two nautical miles from the harbor and even with the cape outside La Fortaleza, Esperanza corrected course twenty degrees port in the direction of the tip of Cap de Formentor. To port and starboard is land, the steep cliffs of north Mallorca, almost impossible to ascend from the sea. Straight ahead is only the sea. The same sea that awoke after a calm night and breathes with a slowly heaving swell. The sea. Esperanza. The sun quickly climbing up the pale blue wall of sky. The haze letting up. Then the sea under Esperanza. Just as deep as the spiny heights in the reflecting water. The keel, hull, plating, the five feet between that carries her over the deep below her. Alone on the sea. Esperanza, a beautiful boat with a beautiful name.

11

Seven weeks earlier, Wednesday, August 22.
Headquarters of the National Bureau of Criminal
Investigation on Kungsholmen in Stockholm

"Our colleague Flykt has a valid excuse," said Johansson, smiling at Holt, Lewin, and Mattei. "He suddenly has a lot of tips to take care of.

"I thought you could start, Jan," he continued. "Tell us ignorant people what happened that unfortunate Friday evening the twenty-eighth of February 1986."

"I've written a little memo about it," said Lewin with his obligatory, cautious throat clearing. "It's in your e-mail. You have it in front of you too. I suggest we take ten minutes so you can all read it in peace and quiet."

"Excellent," said Johansson, getting up. "Then I can get coffee for us and take the opportunity to stretch my legs."

Johansson seems pleased and satisfied, thought Holt. Suspiciously pleased and satisfied, she thought, taking Lewin's memo out of the plastic folder in front of her. What's this? she thought. Twenty pages of text plus another ten pages with some kind of index at the end. The latter listed almost two hundred individuals, with full names and social security numbers, each name accompanied by one or more reference numbers.

"The witnesses who were interviewed about the various sections as reported in my memo," Lewin explained, having evidently noticed her wonder. "The numbers reference the interviews in the Palme material where the information is reported."

"I see," said Holt and nodded. What's wrong with Jan? she thought. He's not the type who tries to call attention to himself. Pull yourself together, Anna, she thought, starting to read.

"Prime Minister Olof Palme (hereafter designated OP) left his office in the government building Rosenbad (address Rosenbad 4) approx. 18:15 on Friday, February 28, 1986. As far as is known—no information of a different import has been reported in the investigation—he walked the shortest route home to his residence at Västerlånggatan 31 in Old Town.

"OP passes through the main entry to Rosenbad, turns left down to Strömgatan approx. 55 yards, then turns left up Strömgatan to Riksbron approx. 66 yards. After that OP turns right and, on foot, passes Riksbron, Riksgatan, and the bridge across Stallkanalen up to Mynttorget, a total of approx. 220 yards. From Mynttorget OP continues up Västerlång-gatan in a southerly direction, approx. 270 yards. He arrives at his resi-dence about 18:30 or right before that. The total walking distance of just over 650 yards corresponds to an approx. ten-minute walk at a normal pace, and this time period is thus compatible with the times and other circumstances as stated above.

"OP walked home alone and does not appear to have spoken, or had other contacts, with anyone during that time. Right before 12:00 the same day he explained to his bodyguards that he would not need them anymore that Friday. His two bodyguards state in interviews that he told them he was going to spend the afternoon at his office and the evening and night in his residence together with his wife, Lisbeth Palme (hereafter designated LP), and that therefore he would not need them anymore that Friday.

"One of the bodyguards then contacted his immediate superior at the secret police bodyguard squad by telephone, who in an interview states that he, 'based on what the surveillance object himself stated, ordered them to suspend guarding for the remainder of the day.'"

.   .   .

Classic Lewin, thought Lisa Mattei. Jan Lewin—hereafter designated JL—she thought, and to cover her smile she held her right hand over her chin and mouth in a meditative gesture before she turned the page and continued reading. Lewin hadn't noticed. He seemed completely absorbed in his own text.

"OP spent the time between approx. 18:30 and right after 20:30 in his residence together with his wife, LP. No other persons were present or visited them during that time. OP spoke on the phone with three individuals, party secretary Bo Toresson, former cabinet minister Sven Aspling, and his son Mårten Palme (hereafter designated MP), and had dinner with his wife, LP. It was also during this time period that the Palmes decided to go to the cinema that same evening. After the conversation with MP it was decided together with MP and his then girlfriend (later wife) to see the film *The Mozart Brothers* (directed by Suzanne Osten) at the Grand cinema on Sveavägen, situated approx. 350 yards northwest of the scene of the crime at the intersection of Sveavägen and Tunnelgatan. This decision was only made at approx. 20:00 according to what has emerged in the interviews with LP and MP.

"Right after 20:30 OP and LP leave their residence on Västerlånggatan in order to go on foot to the subway station in Old Town. OP and LP turn left on Västerlånggatan and then right on Yxsmedsgränd. The total walking distance between the residence and the stairs down to the subway station is approx. 275 yards, and the estimated time expenditure approx. three–four minutes . . ."

It must be angst, thought Holt. Only strong inner anxiety can explain this manic interest in details. She was forced to change her way of reading. A whole page of text and our victim isn't even on the subway in Old Town yet, and damn you, Jan Lewin, she thought. Then in six short sentences she summarized a full two pages of Jan Lewin and located the Palmes in their seats at the Grand.

"Gets on the subway in Old Town approx. 20:40. Rides three stations and gets off at Rådmansgatan approx. 20:50. Enters the cinema right before 21:00. Talks with their son and his fiancée. OP buys tickets for him and LP. In their seats in the theater approx. 21:10," Holt noted on the back of one of Lewin's many papers.

"The screening was over right after eleven o'clock, and once they were out on the street the prime minister and his wife talked with their son and his girlfriend for a few minutes. Then they went their separate ways. The Palmes in the direction south toward the city center on the west side of Sveavägen and now the time is approximately a quarter past eleven. The temperature is twenty degrees Fahrenheit, wind speed of six to seven meters per second, and many people are moving about. A number of witnesses observed the prime minister and his wife. They walk at a rapid pace, side by side, he on her left side, closest to the street. At Adolf Fredriks Kyrkogata, the cross street before Tunnelgatan, they cross to the other side of Sveavägen. Stop a minute or two at a display window and then continue in the direction of the city center. This side of the street is deserted for the most part.

"As they pass the intersection to Tunnelgatan, with only a few yards left to the stairs down to the subway, the perpetrator suddenly appears behind their backs. He raises his weapon, and with only a few inches between the mouth of the barrel and his victim he fires the first shot at Olof Palme. It hits him in the middle of his back, at the level of his shoulder blades, and the prime minister falls headlong onto the sidewalk. His wife sees him suddenly lying there, looks at him, the murderer fires his second shot at her just as she twists her body and sinks down to her knees beside her husband.

"Now the time is twenty-one minutes and thirty seconds past eleven. Give or take ten seconds, for it will never be more precise than that, and in any event a fact of minor significance considering what just happened. The murderer observes the two on the sidewalk for a few seconds. Turns around and disappears into the darkness on Tunnelgatan."

.   .   .

And out of the story, thought Anna Holt. The only reasonable explanation must be that he followed them when they left the cinema. When they crossed Sveavägen at Adolf Fredriks Kyrkogata, the cross street before Tunnelgatan, he went on ahead of them, crossed the street, took a short cut ahead of them and waited at the next corner. It's no more conspiratorial than that, she thought. Despite all the pages à la Jan Lewin with all conceivable conditions, reservations, and alternatives.

Where does all this anxiety come from? she thought suddenly. A good-looking guy, slim, in good shape, true, over fifty, but he looks at least ten years younger, and when he's with the rest of us he behaves completely normally. Polite, maybe a little too reserved, but completely normal in contrast to our beloved boss, the Genius from Näsåker, thought Anna Holt. An attractive man harboring very strong inner anxiety. Why is that? she thought.

12

Johansson returned to them after twenty minutes, and what he had really been doing was unclear. It couldn't have been getting coffee, because his secretary had just brought it in. It was somewhat strange. As soon as Holt was done reading and pushed the papers aside, he suddenly came in and sat down, in just as good a mood as when he left them, judging by the expression on his face. I guess he *can* see around corners, she thought. From the couch in his office where he was probably lying down the whole time.

"Okay," said Johansson. "Thanks, Jan. A model of clarity," he added. And way the hell too long, he thought.

"I have a number of questions, so Lisa it would be good if you could take a few notes for us. And please pass the coffee around," he continued, nodding at Holt. "Where was I now?"

"You have some questions," Holt reminded him. How can it be that I suddenly recognize myself? she thought.

"Exactly," said Johansson. "It's the movie theater. When did he decide that, actually, and how many knew that he was going out to gad about town in the middle of the night on a Friday after payday, among all the drunks, glowworms, and common hoods? To me he seems almost a little suicidally inclined. What do you say, Lewin?"

"Well," said Lewin, squirming uncomfortably. "I've gotten an impression that his security awareness was significantly greater than has been generally thought, and according to the interviews this was decided very late. About eight o'clock in the evening. According to the interviews with his wife and son, that's how it supposedly went in any event," he said.

"The colleagues at SePo then," Johansson persisted. "Did he say anything to them?"

"Not according to the interviews," Lewin replied. "According to the interviews he states that he would spend the remainder of the day at his office and the evening at home in his residence together with his wife. Not a word about going to the movies or any other errands in town either for that matter."

"Were they asked that question?" said Johansson.

"It doesn't show up in the interviews," said Lewin. "It may be because they're in summary, of course, and no one thought to include it in the transcript." I would have asked that question anyway, considering what happened, he thought, but of course he hadn't. Not twenty years later and considering that his colleagues at that time hopefully thought like he did.

"But that's not the way it works if someone like him is going to the movies," Johansson persisted. "Think about it now. He and his wife must have talked about it, don't you think? I mean, someone like him must have had lots to do, and going to the movies isn't something you think of right before it's time to go, is it?"

"I don't really understand where you're heading, boss," said Holt. Maybe it's your view of people, she thought. You and your own little world populated by drunks, glowworms, and common hoods.

"What I mean is simply the following," said Johansson. "Assume that he'd said something along those lines. That he and his wife perhaps wanted to take a short swing into town and see the family but that he wanted to be left in peace for once. Not have a lot of police officers from SePo staring over his shoulder. Now, if he'd said something like that, or only hinted at it or left the possibility open, is it likely, considering what happened, I mean, that the ones who had responsibility for him would mention that particular detail in an interview? Do you understand what I mean, Anna? That it wasn't only drunks, glowworms, and common hoods that someone like him had reason to be worried about?"

"You mean that someone at SePo would have let the cat out of the bag and it reached the wrong ears," said Holt. Sometimes you're a little creepy, she thought.

"It wouldn't have to come from there at all," said Johansson, shrugging his shoulders. "He had lots of co-workers he talked with all the time. That special adviser he had as a henchman, for example, who sat in the same corridor in Rosenbad and was mostly occupied with various security issues. All his buddies at work. What are you and the little woman thinking about doing this weekend? We might see a movie. Maybe have a bite to eat in town. I see then. Well, you know how these things go," said Johansson. "That's how we humans are. We talk about things all the time. I never met Palme, but I get the idea that's how he was when he was comfortable and feeling good. A cheerful companion who talked about this and that with people he trusted."

He's probably completely right, thought Mattei. However you confirm that twenty years later.

"So you mean that such knowledge might have reached the wrong ears rather late, that it wasn't particularly precise, and that the planning of the murder came after that," said Mattei.

"Exactly," said Johansson. There's no limit to how far that little string bean can go, he thought. She's also female, so she'll probably get a thirty percent discount in the bargain.

"A slightly more spontaneous and modest conspiracy theory," said Holt, who sounded saucier than she intended.

"That's what I'm saying," said Johansson, who did not seem to have taken offense. "You should know, Anna, that I have nothing against conspiracy theories. The problem with most of them is only that they're so over-the-top conspiratorial, not to mention completely flat-out wrong, which in turn stems from the fact that the people who think them up are seldom operating on all cylinders. A quite different point is that when someone like Palme is murdered—I'm not talking about celebrities like John Lennon—then the usual explanation is a conspiracy in his vicinity. It's seldom anything remarkable. But even so it is a conspiracy, with more than one person involved who has special knowledge of their victim. The solitary madman is only the second most common explanation. True, it is almost as common, but if we take those two alternatives away then there's almost nothing left. Not all conspiracies are crazy.

There are plenty that are reasonable, logical, and completely rational, if it's the execution we're talking about."

"None of the witnesses who were questioned are said to have made any observations that indicate that the Palmes might have been under surveillance when they left their residence in the evening," said Lewin. "During and after the cinema, on the other hand, there are several witnesses who observed at least one mysterious man who was in the vicinity of the Grand cinema and the Palmes and may have followed them. But I understand what you mean, boss," he added quickly. "Assuming that the surveillance was sufficiently competent, such a person might have avoided detection."

"Exactly." Johansson emphasized with a satisfied nod. "A horrifying number of years ago when I was working as a detective down in Stockholm we had a saying—"

"See but don't be seen," Holt interrupted, having also worked in the detective squad with the Stockholm police. With the legend Bo Jarnebring, Johansson's best friend.

"So you know that, Anna," said Johansson. "Think about it," he added suddenly. "There was another thing—"

"But wait now," said Holt. "Assume that it is as you say. Why didn't he shoot them earlier in that case? In some dark alley in Old Town. Not on the subway, maybe, because there were lots of people and it would be basically impossible to escape from there."

"Maybe he never got an opportunity," said Johansson. "It might have been that a patrol car glided by on a cross street and that was enough for him to change his mind. Or someone approached. Or he simply didn't have time."

"I think he saw them by chance as they went into the theater, or perhaps even when they left," said Holt.

"Personally I don't believe in chance." Johansson shook his head. "That he would have seen them as they came out of the theater I don't believe for an instant. A crazy hooligan who hates Palme beyond all reason and happens to be walking around with a loaded revolver in his coat pocket the size of a suckling pig. That just such a person would get such an opportunity? No, I don't believe that."

"If he saw them before the movie started he would have had two

83

hours to arrange that detail with the weapon," Holt persevered, who didn't intend to give in. "There are also several witness statements that can be interpreted in that direction—that at least one mysterious figure remained in the vicinity of the Grand cinema while the Palmes were sitting inside."

"Possibly," said Johansson, shrugging. "Although I don't think much of the mysterious man and those particular witnesses. Regardless of whether it was Christer Pettersson or any of his brothers in misfortune these people might have seen."

"Okay," said Holt, raising her hands in a deprecating gesture. A final attempt, she thought.

"Let's assume it is as you say," she continued. "A completely different and more competent person than someone like Christer Pettersson, not a solitary madman, that is, has found out that the victim and his wife will leave their residence to go to the movies . . ."

"Yes, or out on the town in general terms," Johansson interjected.

"He follows them from their residence in Old Town, for various reasons doesn't get the chance before they are inside the cinema, and there are lots of people there so he can't do anything there. Instead he waits for them until they come out. Follows them, takes the opportunity to get ahead of them when they cross to the other side of Sveavägen, places himself in ambush and shoots them in the intersection at Tunnelgatan."

"Couldn't have put it better myself," said Johansson.

"But why in the name of sense does he choose to do it in such a stupid place?"

"Best place in the world if you ask me," said Johansson. "Otherwise we wouldn't be sitting here. The bastard went up in smoke."

"I hear what you're saying," said Holt. I wonder how many times our various colleagues have sat and bickered about this case? she thought.

"Good," said Johansson. "Which naturally leads us to the next question. Where did he go? I think we can all agree that he didn't go up in smoke."

13

The perpetrator had not "gone up in smoke."

He had "half run," "trotted," "lumbered," or "jogged" down Tunnelgatan in the direction of the stairs up to Malmskillnadsgatan. The word choice varied in the different witness statements, but the majority were at least in agreement on the essentials. In total there were almost thirty witnesses who had seen him, the entire act, parts of it, or what happened right afterward.

How the perpetrator runs down Tunnelgatan. On the left side of the street, seen from Sveavägen. How he runs "straddle legged" between the sidewalk and street. How he puts the weapon into the right pocket of his jacket, or coat, as he runs.

Nor did he have any choice. On the right side are construction site trailers, so he can't get out there. There's no use thinking about running out on Sveavägen because there are swarms of people and cars and there's no place to go. Down on Tunnelgatan, apparently deserted, and in any event no one who can threaten him, into the darkness, up the stairs and away. He already knows all this, and he also knows that as an escape route it can't be better.

"How long does it take, Lewin," asked Johansson, "running at a leisurely pace down Tunnelgatan from the crime scene and up the stairs to Malmskillnadsgatan? At a leisurely pace?"

"You have that on page seventeen in my memo, boss," said Lewin, starting to leaf through the pages.

"Refresh my poor memory," said Johansson. Preferably today, he thought.

It was a full sixty yards from the crime scene over to the stairs. Then fifty yards on the stairs up to Malmskillnadsgatan. A total of more than a hundred yards with a change in elevation of more than forty-five feet. At an easy running pace, according to the reconstructions that had been done, it would take between fifty and sixty seconds.

For someone like me, assuming I dash for all I'm worth, thought Johansson, who preferred to walk when he went out to get some exercise.

"And if you're running for all you're worth?"

"Max thirty seconds for a person in good shape," said Lewin. "According to our witnesses he ran rather slowly at first, but how fast he was running when he got to the stairs we know less about. There we have only one witness, and his testimony is not completely unambiguous. There's also some uncertainty about how much the witnesses actually might have seen. Other than that he was running up the stairs, for on that point at least our main witnesses seem rather sure."

"Perhaps I should add," said Lewin after a careful glance at his boss, "that we have no technical observations. True, there were patches of snow and ice on the sidewalk, the curb, and the street, but no footprints or other clues were secured that might give us an estimate of his stride."

"No, that wasn't done," said Johansson, leaning back and clasping his hands over his stomach.

"Admittedly the head of the tech squad and a couple of his co-workers were on the scene about an hour after the murder, but considering the situation that then prevailed at the crime scene it was decided not to carry out any such measures. They were judged to be futile.

"So they went home instead. To the little woman and a warm house, because it was Friday night after all," Johansson observed. Damn lazy asses, he thought.

"Yes, unfortunately they did," said Lewin. "The thing about him running straddle-legged, trotting a little, there are three different witnesses who describe it that way."

"Yes," said Johansson.

"I think he did that to keep from slipping," said Lewin. "But we haven't secured any clues to confirm that."

It was completely incomprehensible, he thought. Just leaving a crime scene unattended like that. But who was he to criticize his colleagues in the tech squad, considering that he'd been lying in his own bed at home and as usual hadn't been able to fall asleep until two o'clock in the morning. He had been awakened before six the next morning when his immediate supervisor called and reported that the prime minister had been murdered the evening before, and now it was a matter of embracing the situation and reporting immediately for duty.

"So what happens next?" asked Johansson.

According to Lewin the following happened.

The perpetrator ran diagonally across Brunkebergsåsen with a few dodges along the way to mislead anyone following.

"This was the initial understanding among the police about the perpetrator's escape route," said Lewin. "This was decided on rather early. After having shot the prime minister, he runs down Tunnelgatan, up the stairs to Malmskillnadsgatan, continues straight ahead across Malmskillnadsgatan, and on down David Bagares gata. After about a hundred yards on David Bagares gata he veers off to the left onto Regeringsgatan and thus disappears in a northerly direction. Where he goes then is less clear, but according to the prevailing understanding he must have veered off to the right after another hundred yards of double time on Regeringsgatan and taken Snickarbacken down to Smala gränd. After that he emerged on Birger Jarlsgatan at the corner by the park, Humlegården that is. It's about five hundred yards from the crime scene, and at the pace he's moving he ought to have managed it in about three minutes."

"So how do we know that?"

"We have five different witnesses," said Lewin. "In a kind of chain of witnesses, if you like, although the various links are a little iffy. Whatever, that's the escape route that was already decided on within a week, and that's also the one the officers who did the crime analysis and perpetrator's profile seem to have accepted. The alternatives are countless of course within five hundred yards from the crime scene. But . . ." Lewin shrugged his shoulders.

A chain of witnesses with five links, and just like all other chains it was as strong as the weakest link.

First there were a number of witnesses who had seen him disappear down Tunnelgatan. All were touchingly in agreement about this, and that escape route was also the only one imaginable, considering how it looked at the scene. After only forty yards he disappeared from their field of vision and all that was left is the chain with five links.

The first witness in the chain, a man in his thirties, is the only one who claims to have seen the perpetrator run up the stairs to Malmskillnadsgatan. That it was the perpetrator he had seen he also realized because he had heard the two shots and understood at least part of the course of events.

The perpetrator ran up the stairs, taking two steps at a time. At the top of the stairs, at Malmskillnadsgatan, he stopped for a moment. To get oriented, catch his breath, or see if he was being followed. This is according to the suggestions the witness himself stated at the initial interview. Then the perpetrator disappeared from the witness's field of vision.

The witness then followed him. In the interviews he makes no secret of the fact that he was extremely upset and was not in any great hurry. When he himself comes up onto Malmskillnadsgatan, he encounters the second witness, a woman, and asks her whether she has seen anyone running.

She had. She'd seen a man who disappeared down onto David Bagares gata in the direction of Birger Jarlsgatan. She hadn't seen much more than that, however, and when the first witness looks down the same street he in any event doesn't see the man who had run up the stairs.

When the perpetrator rounds the corner of David Bagares gata and Regeringsgatan, according to the third and fourth witnesses, a woman and a man, he literally ran into witness number three. The perpetrator comes running from behind, the woman hears someone coming, turns her head, and slips. The perpetrator runs into her, and she yells a few insults at him. The perpetrator takes no notice of this but instead continues running and disappears almost immediately out of their view.

The fifth and final link in the chain was the one who aroused the greatest public attention and the one about whom Lewin himself was most doubtful. A woman, who in the media came to be called "the Cartoonist," had observed a mysterious man in Smala gränd, approximately fifteen minutes after the murder and hardly five hundred yards from the scene of the crime. The man is walking hunched up with his hands in his pants pockets, and when he discovers that the fifth witness is looking at him—obviously without her having any idea what has happened to the prime minister—he looks "terrified," turns around, hastens his steps and disappears in the direction of Birger Jarlsgatan and Humlegården.

Regardless of all the doubtful aspects in connection with the observation itself, the suspect had however made a deep impression not only on the witness but also on the leadership of the investigation. A phantom image was made of him, which was published in the media the week after the murder, and which according to the leadership of the investigation depicted a man who "possibly could be identical with the perpetrator."

"Although hardly anyone believes that anymore," said Lewin. Personally I never did, he thought.

"A nosy question," said Johansson with an innocent expression. "That woman our perpetrator supposedly ran into when he rounded the corner at David Bagares gata and onto Regeringsgatan. The one who shouted insults at him. What was it she shouted?"

"Look out you fucking gook," said Lewin with a shy glance in the direction of Anna Holt.

"Gook," said Johansson. "What did she know about that sort?"

For some reason Jan Lewin seemed embarrassed by the question.

"She is extremely definite on that point. That was what she shouted at him. Her exact choice of words and the reason for it, she maintains, according to what she says in the interview, was that he looked like a— quote—'typical gook'—end quote. To answer your question. Well, I get the impression that she has a definite understanding of how such a person looks in any event. Her story is also corroborated in the interview with the man who accompanied her."

"She did of course get to look at the pictures of Christer Pettersson, everyone's Palme assassin," said Johansson.

"Yes," said Lewin. "Though as I'm sure you know, boss, that wasn't until the fall of 1988. It took over two years before Pettersson became a central figure in the Palme investigation." It's Anna he's after, thought Lewin.

"And?"

"No," said Lewin, shaking his head. "She didn't recognize Pettersson."

"Now when you say it," said Johansson, "I have a faint recollection of that interview. Isn't it the case that in response to a direct question of whether it was Christer Pettersson who ran into her, she answers approximately . . . that in that case she wouldn't have shouted 'fucking gook' at him?"

"Yes," said Lewin. "Something like that. I don't recall her exact words. But that issue is brought up. It's there on the tape. Not in the transcript, because that part of the interview has only been summarized."

"So what would she have said instead?" interrupted Holt, looking at Johansson. Sloppy of me to miss that interview, but that's not Jan's fault, she thought.

"She thinks Pettersson looks like a typical Swedish drunk, a genuine Swedish bum. Definitely not a gook," Johansson observed.

"Which conveniently leads us to the next item on the program, namely Christer Pettersson, and if I've understood things correctly you have a good deal to say about that, Anna," he continued with an innocent expression.

"Yes, I do have a few things," Holt agreed. She had decided to play along and put a good face on it.

"Then let's do that," said Johansson. "But first I would like to propose a leg stretch of about fifteen minutes. I have to make a few calls."

14

Holt and Lewin went to Lewin's office so they could talk undisturbed.

"I owe you an apology, Anna," said Lewin.

"For what?" asked Holt. You have to stop apologizing, Jan, she thought.

"I saw the material about Pettersson you brought with you. It was that documentation that was the basis for the indictment against him, and that witness that the perpetrator ran into, the one who shouted at him, she's not in there."

"It's really not your fault," said Holt. "Just a nosy question. Are there other witnesses like her who weren't included when Pettersson was indicted?"

"It was done the way it's always done, I guess," said Lewin. "You include what supports the indictment and the rest you choose to overlook. It's a real mess." Lewin looked at her gloomily. "When the suspicions about Pettersson came out in the media and he became a national celebrity, suddenly a lot of information came in about him. He'd been seen all over the area. At times I've thought that in this case there are witnesses about literally everything and everyone. Pointing in all conceivable and inconceivable directions."

"But from the beginning," said Holt. "If we stick to Christer Pettersson."

"From the beginning," said Lewin, nodding meditatively. "Well, none of the witnesses to the murder identify him in particular. Not so strange perhaps, because the majority are ordinary, decent people who don't know people like him. As I said, the first pictures of him were not shown to the witnesses until the fall of 1988, two and a half years after the fact.

Several of them then claim to see a certain resemblance with Pettersson, but it's nothing more than that. Not then. In connection with the new trial, additional witnesses emerged who claimed to have seen Pettersson in particular, persons in the same situation as he was, the kind who know him, and it was at this time that several of the earlier witnesses seem to have decided that it probably was Christer Pettersson they'd seen after all. With one exception. The only one who pointed him out the first time she saw him was Lisbeth Palme. It was at that famous, or should I say infamous, lineup on December 14, 1988." Lewin slowly shook his head.

"I'm sure you remember it," said Lewin.

"Yes, sure," said Holt. "But I'm listening. What's your understanding of that?"

"Well, first she says, Lisbeth Palme that is, that it's easy to see which one is the alcoholic. That good-for-nothing prosecutor told her before the lineup that the suspect was an alcoholic. Then she says, well, it's number eight, he fits my description, the shape of his face, his eyes and his shabby appearance. As you know, Christer Pettersson was number eight in the lineup."

"Just how sure do you think she was?"

"Well, I don't know. First there's that unfortunate statement from the prosecutor. Then there's the lineup video itself. It's a strange story. Pettersson undeniably stuck out. Compared with the others he looked really shabby. Unfortunately. I don't really know."

"The evidence is not as strong as pointing someone out," said Holt.

"Could have been better, of course," said Lewin.

"I have one more question," said Holt. "If you're able?"

"Of course," said Lewin, smiling and nodding.

"Why did it take so long before anyone started getting interested in Pettersson? It was more than two years. Even though he was on the list of people of interest only two days after the murder, and even though a number of tips about him came in during the spring of 1986. I noticed that a routine interview was held with him at the end of May 1986. He was asked what he was doing on the evening of the murder. But it was never more than that. Not until two years later did it get going in earnest."

"That's a good question," Lewin agreed. "But I'm afraid there's no good answer. Maybe the investigators had other interests those first two years."

"So what do you think?" said Holt.

"In the worst case it's as simple as that he wanted to make sure he ended up there," said Lewin.

"You have to explain that," said Holt.

"Yes, strangely enough the media seems to have missed this, but the fact is that only a few months after the crime, tips started coming in that Christer Pettersson was running around town and maintaining, or hinting, both saying and hinting, that he had shot Olof Palme. There were tips from various persons in his vicinity, and more and more as the reward got larger."

"But nothing was done about it then?"

"No," said Lewin. "I guess they were completely occupied with other things judged to be more interesting. He wasn't alone in running around bragging that he was the one who shot Olof Palme either. There were several with the same background doing that. But as I said it took awhile before he was taken at his word—not until the summer of 1988. Then they started checking what he was up to. They discovered he was at an illegal gambling club in the vicinity of the crime scene the same evening Palme was murdered. That his dealer had an apartment on Tegnérgatan in the vicinity of the Grand cinema. One thing leads to another, and suddenly it's all about him. It's a strange story."

"So what does he say about it in the interviews? That he himself supposedly ran around saying that," said Holt.

"He denies it categorically, flatly denies it," said Lewin. "The police didn't make a big deal of it either. Probably considering their informant. Their informant was one of those types Pettersson associated with. By the way, it's time we return to our dear boss," said Lewin with a glance at his watch.

"Depends on what you mean by 'dear,'" said Holt.

"Okay then," said Johansson, looking expectantly at Holt as soon as she sat down at her usual place. "Now we'll hear the truth about Christer Pettersson."

"I don't think I can promise that," said Holt. "But I promise to say what I think." You should get a taste of your own medicine, she thought.

"I'm listening devoutly," said Johansson, sinking back in his chair with his hands clasped over his stomach.

"It was Christer Pettersson who shot Olof Palme," said Anna Holt.

"Without further ado, just like that," said Johansson.

"Of course," said Holt. Call it what you want, she thought.

"You don't have the desire to be a little more, well, specific?" Johansson had lowered a few more inches in his chair.

"Of course," said Holt. "I've even written a little memo about it." She took a plastic sleeve from her binder, opened it, and passed out a letter-size piece of paper. First to Johansson, then Lewin, and then Mattei. One page with five points, and less than one line written for each point.

"A model of brevity," said Johansson after a quick glance at the paper. "I'm listening," he said, nodding at Holt. I must have overestimated Holt or else she just wants to mess with me, he thought.

15

The first point on Holt's list had the heading "Perpetrator Description."

According to the eyewitnesses, the perpetrator must have been at least six feet tall and between thirty and fifty years old. He was wearing a dark, longish jacket or short coat, reaching halfway down his thigh. His movement patterns were described as "clumsy," "loping," "limping," "rolling," "like an elephant."

"That agrees pretty well with Pettersson if you ask me," Holt summarized.

"Yes, this is a really amazing description," said Johansson with an innocent expression. "By the way, what do you think about those witnesses who describe the perpetrator as being as nimble as a large bear, as someone with powerful, controlled movements, who gave an impression of agility and strength as he ran away, who took two stairs at a time when he ran up the stairs to Malmskillnadsgatan? Not to mention our gook witness, the only witness who had physical contact with the perpetrator. Or everyone outside the Grand who'd seen a lunatic with an intense gaze. Or that small-boned artistic type our so-called Cartoonist saw down at Birger Jarlsgatan. The man in the first phantom picture. The woman who was supposed to be some kind of artist in civilian life. Do you want me to continue?"

"That's enough," said Holt, smiling. "Some of that information may also be consistent with Pettersson."

"The face, the hair?" Johansson looked even more innocent.

"Apart from Lisbeth Palme, none of the witnesses has been able to provide any such information," said Holt.

"No, exactly," said Johansson. "Sometimes our murderer is wearing a cap and sometimes he's bareheaded, and when you look at the times it seems he was seen simultaneously. With Lisbeth I think it's so bad that she never saw the perpetrator. I think he was standing in her dead spot, pardon the expression, at an angle behind her."

"I intend to come back to Lisbeth Palme," said Holt. "Now let's move on to the next point. Point number two."

"I'm listening," said Johansson.

At the time before the murder Christer Pettersson had been in the immediate vicinity of the crime scene. According to what he himself had admitted, he'd been at the illegal gambling club called The Ox up on Malmskillnadsgatan.

"So he's been there at least," said Holt. "Then we have other witnesses who saw him at the Grand cinema. By the way, one of his dealers had an apartment on Tegnérgatan."

"Everyone in the country's dealer at that time, Sigge Cedergren," said Johansson. "Nowadays no longer among us, and just like all the other drugged-out nutcases from Grand—more and more certain of their story the more years have passed since the murder. 'Cause at that time they didn't have much to say."

"Granted," said Holt. "But there is a logic to it. There are actually good prospects that he might run into Olof Palme completely by chance. He used to hang out in those parts, and it wasn't to go to the movies and see *The Mozart Brothers*."

"On that last point we're in complete agreement," said Johansson. "Personally I think the perpetrator ends up at the Grand and then by and by at the crime scene because his victim leads him there. I think he followed him from Old Town, and it was no more coincidental than that."

"I hear what you're saying," said Holt. "My third point," she continued, holding up her paper. "There are several pieces of information to the effect that Christer Pettersson at least periodically had access to a revolver of the type used in the murder. Among others from Sigge Cedergren, who is said to have lent him one like that."

"A gun that he and the others near and dear in Pettersson's circle of friends think up ten years or so after the murder. Which they denied at first, and then remembered, and then took back again. In that context there are two completely different things that struck me," said Johansson.

"Yes?" asked Holt.

"That there isn't a smidgen about Christer Pettersson using a firearm during his more than twenty-year criminal career before the murder. Not afterward either. There's only Cedergren's and the others' mixed memories ten years after the assassination of Palme."

"The second thing," said Holt. "What was the other thing that struck you?"

"That I'm hell and damnation convinced that our perpetrator is both a practiced and a skillful shot with so-called single-hand weapons, pistols or revolvers. Pettersson wasn't. He hardly knew front from back on a revolver."

"The perpetrator is a skilled shooter? Even though he misses Lisbeth Palme from a distance of three feet?"

"Believe me," said Johansson. It was meaningless to sit and argue with a woman about this, he thought.

"I hear what you're saying," said Holt. But I still don't agree with you. I can shoot too, she thought.

"I'm beginning to sense we're not in agreement," said Johansson. "This fourth point? That Lisbeth Palme supposedly pointed out Pettersson. I assume you know what happened when she did that?"

"Yes," said Holt. "I still think she makes a strong identification."

"Why in the name of God?" said Johansson with some heat. "First there's that crazy prosecutor who raves about the perpetrator being an alcoholic. Then there's that so-called lineup that would be a pure Santa Claus parade if one of them wasn't limping around in beard stubble, running shoes, and a dirty old sweatshirt."

Holt had been struck by two other circumstances. That Lisbeth Palme became noticeably upset when she saw Christer Pettersson.

"She got agitated, scared simply," said Holt.

"What would you have expected?" Johansson snorted. "The way he looked on that video?"

"Then she spontaneously points out that the perpetrator did not have a mustache. Pettersson had a mustache on the lineup video, but according to the investigation he didn't have one at the time of the murder."

"But sweet Jesus," said Johansson. "A type like Christer Pettersson, do you think he shaves every day? He probably has a mustache every other week if you ask me."

"There's another thing I've wondered about," said Holt. "The reason that the court of appeal rejected Lisbeth Palme's testimony was, in part, what you've said just now: all the errors committed in connection with the lineup."

"Obviously," said Johansson. "How the hell would it have looked otherwise?"

"Assume that it had been Lisbeth who was murdered and that Olof Palme had survived. That he was the one who testified and had to be involved in the same worthless lineup she had to go through. Assume that he pointed out Christer Pettersson and did it in exactly the same way that Lisbeth did. How do you think things would have gone in the court of appeals then?"

"Then Pettersson probably would have been convicted. Even courts make mistakes."

"You have no other observations in that connection," said Holt.

"No," said Johansson. Could it be so bad that Holt and little Mattei have been plotting a gender perspective? thought Johansson. Though she seems innocent enough, he thought, glaring acidly in Mattei's direction.

Holt's fifth and concluding argument was that Christer Pettersson corresponded well with the description of the perpetrator in the profile that their colleagues at the national crime bureau had produced in collaboration with experts at the FBI.

"In the profile the perpetrator is described in the following way," Holt began.

"This concerns a solitary perpetrator with primarily chaotic and psychopathic features, an intolerant, disloyal, and merciless person who is governed by impulses and whims. A disturbed person who has a hard time maintaining normal relationships with other people. Who in a superficial sense may appear self-confident, but who is both conceited and affected. A person lacking an inner compass. He is not interested in politics but probably harbors considerable hatred for society and its representatives. A solitary person living a failed life. Who has had poor contacts with his own family since childhood. It is completely ruled out that he would have participated in any conspiracy, whether large or small."

"Imagine that," Johansson snorted.

"Yes, imagine that," said Holt. "He is thus about six feet tall and relatively powerfully built. He is right-handed and not in particularly good shape. He was probably born sometime in the 1940s, and he has some experience with firearms. He lives alone, has only sporadic contact with women, and probably has no children of his own. He is probably poorly educated and has no job. If he has had a job it has been for short periods and involved unskilled tasks. He has bad finances, lives in an apartment with low rent, and has a low standard of living. He is probably known to the police for previous criminal offenses of a less serious nature. He lives, works, or for other reasons has often spent time in the vicinity of the crime scene and the Grand cinema."

Holt glanced up from her papers and looked at Johansson.

"The same man who according to the same profile, correct me if I'm remembering wrong, was not supposed to have had any contact with the mental health system. Who is not a serious abuser of either alcohol or narcotics," said Johansson. "So it can't have been Sigge Cedergren in any case, Pettersson's spigot and official purveyor, whom the perpetrator would visit to buy dope," said Johansson. "Maybe he was going to the movies after all?"

"I hear what you're saying," said Holt. "Ninety percent of this is still about Christer Pettersson, although—"

"Ninety percent? I really wonder about that," Johansson interrupted. "A person who according to the profile might possibly have committed minor crimes against property, but never killed anyone with a bayonet, never robbed or assaulted or threatened a lot of people. Pettersson was in various jails and nuthouses for over ten years for that very reason. Not to mention all the years he did for drug offenses and all the other shit he was up to. Plus the fact that he'd been drinking and doing drugs on a daily basis practically since he was a little boy."

"You think this speaks to Christer Pettersson's advantage," said Holt with an innocent expression.

"Right here I actually think it does," said Johansson. "Do you want to know what I personally think about the perpetrator?"

"Gladly," said Holt. I really do, she thought.

"For one thing, I believe he had help. Nothing remarkable, but I think he had some contact or contacts. Before he went to work."

"Okay," said Holt.

"This is a well-organized, alert perpetrator. He is in good physical condition. Strong. He has no criminal record, and he's not an abuser. He has both authority and presence, and he seizes his opportunity on the wing the moment he gets the chance. He has considerable personal experience where resorting to violence is concerned, and he is a very skilled shot, right-handed. The weapon he uses is probably his own, and in any event he didn't buy it on the cement down at Sergels Torg. He's very familiar with the area, has a driver's license, car, good residence, and good financial and other resources. In short he has all the qualities required for him to be able to disappear without a trace, even though it should be impossible considering the way in which he did it."

"In other words, he's the exact opposite of the profile," Holt summarized.

"No," said Johansson, shaking his head. "I'll buy the fact that he hated Palme. That psychological drivel about him and his upbringing leaves me cold. He's an evil person. Sure. Normal people don't shoot someone like Palme from behind, regardless of who they vote for."

"We're in agreement there," said Holt.

"Forget about that now," said Johansson. "Someone like that shouldn't be running around loose. He should be in prison for life, and if I could choose I would boil the bastard for glue."

"That last part I won't sign on to but otherwise we're in agreement," said Holt.

"Good," said Johansson, getting up quickly. "We'll meet in a week. Same time, same place. Then I want a name."

"Our boss seems to have taken this case to heart, " said Lewin as he and Holt left the meeting.

"It's not his commitment I'm questioning," said Holt.

"I understand what you mean," Lewin agreed. "The major problem with this particular case is that it's completely impossible to just sit down and read your way to the truth. Like I already said, regardless of what you think or believe, you can always find testimony to support it."

"You're thinking about that female witness who called the perpetrator a gook bastard," said Holt. "Careless of me to miss her."

"No," said Lewin. "I was actually thinking about a completely different witness. Although she disappeared from the process early on. Removed from the investigation. Her testimony was judged to be uninteresting. I actually saved a copy of it. I have it in my office if you're interested. I never did anything about it. It never happened," Lewin observed, sighing.

"I'd be glad to read it," said Holt.

"Sure," said Lewin. "You'll get it. Although perhaps I should warn you ahead of time: This is far from a problem-free witness."

"She has all the usual problems that witnesses aren't allowed to have? The kind of witnesses that our boss calls nutcases, glowworms, and bag ladies?" Holt looked inquisitively at Lewin.

"Of course," said Lewin. "But in this particular case that's not the problem."

"So what is it?" said Holt.

"The major problem arises if you get the idea that what she says adds up," said Lewin as he opened the door to his office. He held it open for Holt and made sure to close it behind them.

"So what do you mean?" Holt repeated.

"You can only hope that she's mistaken," said Lewin. "Here it is."

Lewin opened a binder he'd taken out of his well-organized book-shelf, removed a thin plastic folder with papers, and gave it to Holt.

"You're welcome to it, Anna. You're certainly braver than I am," said Lewin.

"So what happens if what she says is correct?" said Holt while she weighed the thin folder in her hand.

"Then there are problems," said Lewin, looking at her seriously. "Major problems."

16

The day after the second meeting, Lisa Mattei concluded her small sociological investigation. She had interviewed thirteen old Palme investigators, all of them men of course, of which six were retired, three
were still working in the Palme group, and four had left for other assignments within the agency. Combined, her thirteen older colleagues had
devoted almost a hundred years of their professional lives to searching
for the perpetrator who just over twenty years earlier had assassinated
the prime minister.

None of them seemed to have any problem with her explanation for
wanting to talk with them. On the contrary, almost all of them thought
it was an excellent idea. That it was high time someone did something
about the mountain of papers that nowadays were mostly collecting
dust. Several of them had also gone directly to what the actual purpose
of her visit was, without her even having to ask.

"It's an excellent idea. I saw your boss Johansson on TV when he read
the riot act to those journalists. That's a real cop for you. Not one of
those paper pushers with a law degree. We've known each other since
our time in the detective unit down in Stockholm, and if there was anyone who had the right feel for the job it was Lars Martin. Though he was
just a young kid at that time. You can tell him from me that he can carry
everything that's not about Christer Pettersson down to the basement,
and I guess the simplest thing to do would be just to burn it. You can tell
him that too, while you're at it. He's never been a coward. I'll be the first
to testify to that . . .

The Kurds. It was the Kurds who shot Palme. Those terrorists within their so-called revolutionary workers party, PKK. I and many of our colleagues realized that right from the start, so all the piles of paper the group collected later are really not our fault, and now it's too late to correct that mistake. The really big scandal is that we never got to finish our case. The politicians and the journalists took it away from us, for political reasons. It was the journalists who put the pressure on, and the prosecutors who couldn't stand up to them, and the politicians just chimed in as usual. Even though Palme was a Social Democrat and we have a Social Democratic government. What they did to our first investigation leader, Hasse Holmér—he was county police chief in Stockholm as I'm sure you know, and I say that mostly because it was before your time—it was a pure scandal if you ask me. He got fired simply because he refused to let a lot of politicians and newspaper people run the investigation . . ."

"Sounds like an excellent suggestion. Start by subtracting everything that deals with those Kurds. They had nothing to do with the assassination of Palme. It was thanks to him that people like that could come here. Palme was pro-immigrant, and I have nothing to say about that per se. When people got riled up about him it was usually for other reasons that mostly had to do with his personality. I don't believe someone like Christer Pettersson could have done it either. He was just too mixed up to manage a thing like that. Probably barely even knew who Palme was. Besides he's been dead now a few years, so that alone is enough to take him out of the Palme case. Then there were all those political speculations about Iran and Iraq and India and the Bofors affair and South Africa and God knows what. I think, even if it were that way, that's nothing we police can do anything about, is it? Besides, I don't believe in it. I think the explanation is much simpler. Some ordinary citizen who got tired of Palme and his politics and maybe even believed he was working as a spy for the Russians. Quite a few did at the time, I'll tell you. Someone who simply took matters into his own hands when he happened to run into him by chance outside the Grand on Sveavägen . . ."

There was an ongoing pattern in what Mattei heard. An expected pattern. You believed in what you had worked with or in any event what you'd worked with the most. On the other hand, you seldom set much store by anything you hadn't been involved in investigating. On one point, however, with one very surprising exception, they were in agreement. All except one of those asked categorically rejected the so-called police track, and the one who believed in it the least was the investigator who at various times had devoted five years of his life as a police officer to trying to find out what his colleagues had actually been up to when Palme was murdered.

"I promise and assure you," he said, nodding seriously at his visitor. "All those leads that the media inflated all those years. Once you sit down and figure out what it's really about, at best it's pure nonsense. I say at best because far too often there was real ill will on the part of a lot of extremists and criminals who fingered our colleagues."

There's still a certain something about old murder investigators, thought Mattei as she got into her service vehicle to leave the little red-painted Sörmland cottage where the last of her interview victims now enjoyed his rural retirement. Where she had been offered coffee and rolls and juice and cookies. Especially the retired ones, she thought. Retirement loosened the tongue and gave them both the time and the desire to talk about how things really were. Especially when they could do so for a younger female colleague who seemed both "quick-witted and humble."

If they only knew, Mattei thought. Although it was mostly pretty harmless, and most of them were good storytellers at least. There was only one she dreaded meeting, and during that meeting she mostly sat gritting her teeth while her small tape recorder whirled and her interview subject expounded about Olof Palme and everything else under the sun.

Chief Inspector Evert Bäckström, "legendary murder investigator with thirty years in the profession and considered by many the foremost of them all," according to the anonymous source that was frequently quoted in *Dagens Nyheter*'s most recent article about mismanagement at the national crime bureau. This in combination with the Swedish Envy was also, according to the same source, the only explanation for why just over a year ago the head of the National Bureau of Criminal Investigation had banished said Bäckström from the National Homicide Commission to the Stockholm police department's property investigation squad.

"So that genius from Lappland needs help clearing up Palme," said Bäckström, while leaning back in his chair and scratching his belly button through the biggest gap in the Hawaiian shirt that stretched across his stomach.

"No, that's not how it is," said Mattei. "We've been given the task of doing an overview of the registration of the material in the Palme investigation, and he was interested in your viewpoints. How the various parts of the material should be prioritized."

"Sure, sure, like I believe that," said Bäckström with a crafty look behind half-closed eyelids. "Imagine that, look over the registration."

"I understand you were involved in the initial stage and that it was you, among others, who ferreted out the thirty-three-year-old, Åke Victor Gunnarsson."

"That's right," said Bäckström. "I was the one who found that little piece of shit, and if I'd just been allowed to run the case, then I would have seen to it that we got to the bottom of it. Instead some older so-called colleague came in and took over. Someone who'd licked his tongue brown up the backside of the so-called police leadership. If you're wondering about all the question marks that still remain around Gunnarsson, then he's the one you should go to. Not me."

"Is there any particular track you think ought to be prioritized?" said Mattei to change the subject.

"Paper and pen," said Bäckström, nodding encouragingly. "So you have something to take notes with," he explained as he put his own ballpoint pen in his right ear to remove some irritating deposits of wax.

"In the material there's quite a bit you can carry down to the basement," said Bäckström, viewing the outcome of his hygienic efforts and wiping the pen on the desk blotter. "Start by taking out all the old ladies. Motive, modus operandi, and all conceivable perpetrators that are old ladies, whether or not they wear trousers. I won't go into what I thought about the so-called victim, but an old lady would never have managed to take the wrapping off Palme in that way. Not even an old lady like Palme," he clarified. "It was a competent bastard who was holding the ax-handle that time."

After that Bäckström talked for almost an hour without letting himself be interrupted. About conceivable perpetrators, motives, and methods.

According to Chief Inspector Bäckström, for the most part everyone, that is to say completely normal Swedish men like himself, had a motive to assassinate the prime minister. The driving force—according to his definitive, professional experience—also would be stronger the more you had to do with the victim. At the same time the good thing about that was that the frequency of old ladies, regardless of whether they wore pants or skirts, was especially high around someone like Palme, which in turn provided more opportunities to do a thorough cleanup in all those papers.

"Tell me who you associate with, I'll tell you who you are," Bäckström summarized. "There's a lot worth considering in our old Bible."

"I interpret this to mean that you don't believe in the often stated hypothesis of a solitary madman who by chance happened to catch sight of Olof Palme outside the Grand cinema," Mattei alertly interjected.

Pure nonsense, according to Bäckström. First, you didn't need to be crazy to have good reason to shoot Palme. On the other hand, secondly, you had to have "a fucking lot of spine," and thirdly, it would naturally be the very best if you were sitting on a little inside information about what someone like Palme was up to.

"Forget about Christer Pettersson and all the other drunks," Bäckström snorted. "Gooks, drunks, and common hoods. Why should they attack Palme? He was the type who supported them. What we're talking about is a guy with first-class knowledge of the situation, primo sense of locale, handy with the rectifier, and a fucking lot of ice in his belly."

"You mean, for example, a police officer or military man or someone with that background?" asked Mattei.

"Yes, or some old marksman or hunter. Or maybe that Gilljo even. Only author in this country who's worth the name, if you ask me," said Bäckström. "Besides, he's actually there on the lists of conceivable suspects. We got a fucking lot of tips about him. So take a look at Johnny Gilljo if you don't have anything better to do. I believe more in someone like him, or a military man, than in another police officer," Bäckström summarized, nodding. "I mean, me and the other cops could always hope we would get the chance to arrest him when he was drunk," he clarified. "Small consolation is still consolation, even when the general misery is at its greatest. As it was while Palme was alive."

"Arrest Palme for drunkenness?" Mattei asked, sneaking a glance at her tape recorder to be on the safe side.

"The most common wet dream among our colleagues at that time." Bäckström grinned, and for some reason looked at the clock. "Now you have to excuse me, Mattei, but I have a few things to do too."

"Of course," said Mattei, getting up with all the desired speed. "I really must thank you for participating."

"A few more things," said Bäckström. "For the sake of order. I see that this is a confidential conversation, and I assume that what I've said stays between us."

"As I said by way of introduction, all interview subjects are anonymous."

"Like I believe that," said Bäckström with a sneer.

"There was something else you wanted to say," Mattei reminded him as she put away the tape recorder, paper, and pen in her bag and closed the zipper.

"You don't need to greet the *surströmming* eater from me," said Bäckström.

"I promise," said Mattei. "You don't need to worry."

"I never worry," said Bäckström. "It's not my thing."

.   .   .

Lisa Mattei's little investigation had taken five days, and she had drawn her conclusions even before she started. The material in the Palme room was the result of these colleagues' work, and with two exceptions they believed in what they'd done.

The support for the police track was limited to Bäckström's general musings, and the material collected was not particularly extensive.

The great exception was the so-called Kurd track, for which the police investigations generated even more paper than for Christer Pettersson. In round numbers, two hundred man-years for a year, and it turned out an enormous number of binders. One investigator out of thirteen was left who believed in what was there, and surely the proportion wouldn't vary much with all the hundreds she hadn't contacted.

In the evening after the final interview she stayed at work until late and wrote a short memo about what she had come up with. Two pages, in contrast to Jan Lewin's twenty-five. Then she e-mailed it to Johansson. Only to Johansson, because she thought it was his business to decide whether anyone else should read it.

What do I do now? thought Mattei as she shut off her computer. It needs to be something quite specific, and it's time I had a talk with my dear mom, she decided.

17

As usual, Johansson arrived first at his office. The hour before his secretary showed up he would usually use to have an extra cup of coffee in peace and quiet, read his e-mail, and do all the other things he never had time for during the rest of the day.

A model of brevity and well written, thought Johansson as he read the memo Mattei had e-mailed him. That little string bean is hardworking too, he thought. According to the date and time the memo had arrived in his mailbox shortly after eleven the night before.

But the memo was hardly exciting, because he already knew everything that was in there, he thought. So all hopes were dashed from the start that any of the old owls would have a new, exciting, concrete lead to offer.

Although you knew that too, thought Johansson and sighed. The remaining consolation was that at least one of the older colleagues seemed to be thinking along the same lines as he was. A minor conspiracy in the victim's vicinity and a highly capable perpetrator who took care of the practical aspects.

Must be Melander, he thought. Melander had been his and Jarnebring's mentor when they started at the central detective squad in Stockholm more than thirty years ago. Wonder how the old geezer's doing? he thought just as Anna Holt stepped in through his open door, knocked on the doorjamb, and showed her white teeth in a smile.

"Knock, knock," said Holt. "Isn't that what you always say when you barge into someone's office?"

"Sit down, Anna," said Johansson, nodding toward his couch. "What are you doing at work this time of day?" She's actually a really nice-looking lady, he thought. On the thin side, perhaps, and a little tedious sometimes, but . . .

"Have to hurry along," said Holt, shaking her head. "Just a quick question."

"Shoot," said Johansson.

"If you'd shot Palme, run down Tunnelgatan and up the stairs to Malmskillnadsgatan, which way would you have gone after that?"

Mercy, thought Johansson.

"I have three options," he answered. "I can go left on Malmskillnads-gatan toward the park by St. Johannes Church, I can cross the street and go straight ahead, as it is alleged that the perpetrator did, continue straight across Brunkebergsåsen that is. Or I can turn right on Malm-skillnadsgatan in the direction of Kungsgatan."

"So which way would you have gone?"

"Personally I would go right," he said, nodding in emphasis, "take the stairs down to Kungsgatan, melt in among all the others walking there, and then disappear down into the subway."

"Why?" said Holt.

"Because it's best," said Johansson.

"Thanks," said Holt. She nodded, smiled, turned on her heel and left.

Wonder what she's after? thought Johansson, and though it was said he could see around corners, he had no idea that Holt too had shared his speculations for almost a day now. Wonder if little Mattei has shown up yet? he thought suddenly, looking at his clock. Worth a try, he thought, entering her number.

"Sit down, Lisa," said Johansson, indicating the chair on the other side of the desk.

"Thanks, boss," said Mattei, doing as she was told. Be on the alert, Lisa, she thought.

"Thanks for the e-mail," said Johansson. "A model of brevity. And well written," he added.

"Thanks," said Mattei. "Although I'm afraid there weren't any new ideas."

"No," said Johansson. "But neither of us thought there would be. Speaking of new ideas, by the way, I'd hoped maybe you would have some."

Sink or swim, thought Mattei, and if it were to sink and go completely down the toilet it would still be a point in her favor if Johansson knew about it in advance.

"I actually have an idea," said Mattei. "I don't know, but—"

"Go on," said Johansson, nodding encouragingly.

"I was thinking about what you said at our last meeting. About the Palmes going to the movies. I share your understanding, boss. I think he might very well have talked about it before, and that his plans might have been known among his co-workers, and that the people at SePo might also have heard talk of it."

"So now you're thinking about having your mother invite you and a now retired head of personal security to dinner and let all the good food and drink take care of the rest," Johansson observed. That girl can go as far as I have, he thought.

"Roughly like that," said Mattei. He can see around corners, though I already knew that, she thought.

"How long has she been at SePo now? Your mother, that is," Johansson clarified.

"Since I was in preschool," said Mattei. "Almost thirty years. Now she has a position as director of constitutional protection. She's retiring next year." My mom will be a retiree, she thought.

"Although you can't really say that kind of thing," said Johansson, who had been operational head of the secret police himself before he wound up at the national bureau. "I have the idea that she was with personal security too?"

"In the eighties, actually. She was there for several years, including when Palme was assassinated. She was responsible for the queen and the children in the royal family," said Mattei. "If I dare say that." What else would a woman be doing at that place? she thought.

"To me you can say anything whatsoever," said Johansson with an authoritative expression. "It stays in this room, as you know."

"So she knows Chief Inspector Söderberg well. He was the one who took care of the government and Palme, as I'm sure you recall. He's always had an eye for my mother." Who didn't at that time? she thought.

"Of course," said Johansson. "Who hasn't? She's an elegant woman, your mother. Though Söderberg has never really been himself since the murder of Palme," he added. I guess it would be strange otherwise, he thought.

"He seems to have taken it extremely hard in the beginning," said Mattei. "Although the last time I saw him, at my mom's sixtieth birthday dinner by the way, he was lively and happy. So what happened when Palme was murdered he certainly remembers in detail."

"Sounds good," said Johansson. "That's what we'll do," he said, nodding. "Say the word if there's anything practical I can help you with.

"Oh, and there's one more thing," said Johansson, who was suddenly struck by a thought. "Which one of the old Palme investigators was it, by the way, who had the same good idea as I did?"

"I really can't say that," said Mattei, shaking her blond head unusually firmly. Good Lord, she thought.

"I'm still listening," Johansson repeated.

"Not even to the boss," Mattei persisted. "I've promised all of them anonymity. You can get a list of the ones I've interviewed, but I can't go into what this one or that one said."

"I understand," said Johansson. "How's Melander doing, by the way?" he added with an innocent expression. "We worked together at the bureau ages and ages ago."

"Good," said Mattei. "He said to say hello, by the way." You didn't manage that corner, she thought.

"I can imagine that," said Johansson contentedly.

18

What does he really mean? thought Holt, when she had returned to her office the day before and started reading the papers Lewin had given her.

There was a total of ten pages, and at the top was a tip form that had been filled out on Saturday the first of March 1986, the day after the murder. That day a young woman succeeded in getting past the Stockholm police department's seriously overloaded switchboard and evidently made such a strong impression on the officer who took the call that he asked her to come down to Kungsholmen so they could hold an interview with her.

The interview with the young woman, Madeleine Nilsson, born in 1964, took place at the duty desk on Kungsholmen late on Saturday evening. The interview was transcribed in summary and took up no more than one letter-size page. It had been done by an officer unknown to Holt, someone by the name of Andersson, who sent it on to the homicide squad for any follow-up and other actions.

"Nilsson states the following in summary. She spent Friday evening at a pub down on Vasagatan where she saw acquaintances with whom she had a beer. Nilsson does not remember the name of the place, but states that it is diagonally across from the Central Station in the direction of Kungsgatan.

"After her companions went their separate ways about 11:00 p.m. she made her way on foot in the direction of her residence at Döbelnsgatan

31. She took Kungsgatan in an easterly direction, crossed Sveavägen, and then took the stairs on the left side of Kungsgatan up to Malmskillnads-gatan. Then she continued on Malmskillnadsgatan and Döbelnsgatan north home to her residence where she arrived at about 11:30 p.m.

"About halfway up the stairs from Kungsgatan to Malmskillnads-gatan she encountered a solitary man walking at a rapid pace down the stairs toward Kungsgatan. Nilsson is uncertain about the time but thinks it was about 11:20.

"The man was about six feet tall, broad-shouldered, neither heavy nor thin. He gave the impression of being in good condition and did not seem intoxicated in any way. He had short dark hair, and Nilsson estimates his age at about 35–40. The man had no head covering, was dressed in a half-length dark coat or longer jacket with turned-up collar, plus dark pants (but not jeans). Information about his footwear is lacking. Nilsson cannot talk about his appearance in more detail as the man held his hand in front of his face, as if to blow his nose, as he passed her. At the same time she has a general impression that he was good-looking with regular features, dark eyes, and short dark hair.

"During the walk between the intersection of Sveavägen and Kungs-gatan and her residence on Döbelnsgatan, she has not made any further observations of interest. She states in conclusion that according to her definite understanding it was calm in the city. She saw only a few people during the walk on Döbelnsgatan, and none of them acted strange in any way. When she was walking on Döbelnsgatan she encountered a police bus that drove in the direction of Malmskillnadsgatan. The bus was driving at a moderate speed and without flashing lights or sirens. She remembers this because they blinked the headlights at her."

I see then, thought Holt. So far everything seemed well and good, apart from the fact that the investigation's chain of witnesses had suddenly broken already at the second link. If this does add up, she thought.

Wednesday the fifth of March, the week after the murder, another inter-view had been held with Madeleine Nilsson at the homicide squad in

Stockholm. A dialogue interview that was seven pages in transcript. The interview leader was also named Andersson, unknown to Holt, but judging by the first name a different Andersson than the one the witness had met at the duty desk a few days earlier, and with a completely different attitude toward her.

First she had to repeat the same story she had told a few days earlier. Then she was asked whether she could provide the name of the individuals she had been with at the pub on Vasagatan. She didn't want to do that, and she didn't want to talk about why either.

The subsequent questions were straight to the point and left no room for any doubt whatsoever as to what direction the interview had taken.

What had she really been up to down in City on Friday evening the twenty-eighth of February?

She'd been doing what she already said. Nothing more, nothing less.

Had she in reality been in the block around Malmskillnadsgatan to "pick up a john"?

Or to "buy a few downers"? Or maybe even a few "uppers"?

She did not even want to comment on this. She had been doing what she said. Nothing more, nothing less. She had called the police because she wanted to help them. If it was going to be like this, she didn't want to cooperate anymore.

After a few more questions on the same theme, the interview was concluded. The handwritten notes that her interview leader made on the interview transcript also meant the end of witness Madeleine Nilsson.

"Witness Nilsson is not credible. Appears in the police record under five different sections (theft, fraud, shoplifting, narcotics offenses, etc.). Is a known addict and prostitute."

The chief inspector at the homicide squad who reviewed the various witness statements specifically related to observations of the perpetrator drew the same conclusion about the value of her testimony. According to the photocopy of his decision to withdraw the witness's statement from the file, the story lacked "relevance." "It is most likely that the witness passed the scene before the murder of OP."

His signature was completely legible, and Holt knew very well who he was. When she first starting working with the detective squad in Stockholm, a few years after the assassination of Palme, she had run into him on numerous occasions. One of the old legends at the homicide squad, Chief Inspector Fylking. Nowadays both retired and deceased.

What does he really mean? thought Holt, and the person she had in mind was her colleague Jan Lewin who had prepared the final paper in the thin bundle. Typewritten, neat, like everything that came from Lewin, it had been prepared on Friday the twenty-eighth of March 1986, exactly four weeks after the murder. Astonishingly brief considering it came from him. Only six points on a normal letter-size sheet. Signed by then criminal inspector Jan Lewin with the homicide squad in Stockholm, and in all essentials he seems to have been the same man then as he was now.

In principle what was there was as unimpeachable as it could ever be, considering the circumstances. Even the quintessence of what the police actually knew about what had happened. The problem was Lewin's exactitude. All these places where the actors found themselves, preferably stated to the nearest yard. All these points in time when they were at a certain place, if possible noted to the second. All movements and everything else humanly possible that the perpetrator and the witnesses were doing in between. Obviously calculated in yards and seconds. The pedagogical value was zero, the reading pleasure nonexistent, and it took Holt more than fifteen minutes before she managed to force her way through the Lewinian thicket of words and finally understand what was there.

The first point in his memo was comprehensible enough. The next four were harder to read, but his opening said most of what needed to be said: "(1) Sweden's prime minister Olof Palme was murdered at the intersection of Sveavägen and Tunnelgatan on Friday the twenty-eighth of February 1986, at approx. 23:21:30."

I see then, thought Holt. Lewin has set the time according to Witness One. He's the one who gets to start the film when the perpetrator flees, and with that you can forget about all the other clocks, whether they are fast or slow.

Witness One had been walking on Tunnelgatan in the direction of the crime scene when he heard the first shot and at the same moment he was clear about what was happening thirty yards further down the street. Then he hides himself—in the protection of darkness, the trailers, the piles of construction material, and all the other debris piled on the right side of the street—while the perpetrator "jogs past" to his left at a distance of no more than a few feet. Only when the perpetrator has passed, and for a moment disappeared from the witness's field of vision, does he peek out from his hiding place and see the perpetrator run up the stairs to Malmskillnadsgatan, stop for a moment at the top of the stairs, and then disappear from his view.

According to what Witness One says in the first interview, the first of many that the police would hold with him during that time, he then waited "about a minute" before he left his relative safety and followed the perpetrator. Carefully, carefully, first Tunnelgatan up to the stairs, then the stairs up to Malmskillnadsgatan. According to Lewin this had taken him "an additional sixty seconds."

The conclusion was clear enough. Witness One shows up at the same place where he saw the perpetrator disappear "not until about two minutes after the perpetrator." The perpetrator is *putz weg*. The only thing Witness One sees is Witness Two, and she is the one who is asked whether she has seen "a man in a dark jacket run past." She has. "Just now" she has seen "a dark-clothed guy" run right across Malmskillnadsgatan and down David Bagares gata.

The problem is that she shouldn't have seen him, considering that he would have passed by two minutes earlier.

In Lewin's own words: "Considering Witness Two's position when she observed this man, the fact that she states in interviews that she was walking in a northerly direction the whole time, across the bridge over

Kungsgatan and in the direction of the stairs down to Tunnelgatan, and her purely physical possibilities of making the observation as she claims to have done, her observation can thus be made at the earliest thirty seconds before she runs into Witness One farther down on Malmskillnadsgatan, that is, about one and a half minutes after the perpetrator already ought to have left the place in question."

It was the same with the witness Nilsson, according to Lewin. Hardly a minute before Witness Two came up onto Malmskillnadsgatan, Nilsson passed the stairs from Tunnelgatan and disappeared out of view, to the left down on Döbelnsgatan, in the direction of her residence at Döbelnsgatan 31.

The perpetrator? The perpetrator is far away. Yet another minute earlier, the witness Nilsson would have met him en route down the stairs from Malmskillnadsgatan to Kungsgatan. About sixty yards to the right of the stairs up from Tunnelgatan to Malmskillnadsgatan and moving in a direction that was completely different from what everyone except Lewin seemed to think.

In the sixth and final point in his memo Lewin reported his conclusions in an at least somewhat understandable way compared to the line of reasoning he had taken to arrive at it.

"It cannot be ruled out that the man whom the witness Nilsson encounters on the stairs down to Kungsgatan is the perpetrator. This however rules out that the man whom Witness Two saw running down to David Bagares gata is identical to the perpetrator. On the other hand, the fact that Witness Two actually saw a man who did this appears highly probable considering the testimony of Witness Three, who was run into by a man about fifty yards further down the same street, as well as Witness Four, the man accompanying Witness Three, who confirms the information in the interview with Witness Three. That this man, who had been observed by witnesses Two, Three, and Four, would be the perpetrator seems less probable, however, considering that he shows up on the scene one and a half minutes too late."

Finally, thought Holt.

. . .

"Have a seat, Anna," said Jan Lewin five minutes later, smiling and nodding at the vacant chair in front of his desk. "It's been less than an hour," he said, looking at his watch. "Long time, no see, as the Englishmen say."

"I've always been a little slow," said Holt. "We girls are a bit slow on the uptake, as you know."

"I've never thought that," said Lewin. "With you and Lisa it's more likely that you get things more quickly than most of us."

"Well, I get the point in any event with the help of what you wrote. What I don't really understand, on the other hand, is why you prefer witness Nilsson ahead of our old colleagues' entire witness chain? Can't it be as simple as Fylking thought? That Nilsson might have met someone on the stairs down to Kungsgatan, but that the meeting took place before Palme was shot?"

"Sure," said Lewin. "Of course it might be that way. The problem with that is it doesn't solve the problem for us."

"Take it one more time. I think I get it, but explain anyway. I'm a little thick, as you know," said Holt.

"The problem with the man whom Witness Two claims to have seen running down to David Bagares gata is that she sees him much too late. Now I don't recall exactly what I arrived at back then, but I seem to recall that it was about one and a half minutes. If it was the perpetrator she saw, she ought to have seen him one and a half minutes earlier, and considering where she was then, it's a good stretch from the stairs up from Tunnelgatan, then she can't have seen him. It's out of the question that it's the perpetrator she's seen running across Malmskillnadsgatan. That's the very point. Or the major catch in the investigators' line of reasoning if you like."

"I'm with you then," said Holt. "I understand how you're thinking."

"A lot can happen in one and a half minutes in such a limited area," said Lewin. "If you walk at a brisk pace you can manage a hundred fifty yards in one and a half minutes. If you trot or jog, then you'll manage two hundreds yards or more."

"Okay," said Holt. "Let's take this in order. Who did Witness One see down on Tunnelgatan?"

"The perpetrator," said Lewin. "On that point I have no doubt at all. Never had any."

"Witness Two then," said Holt. "Who is it she sees cross Malmskill-nadsgatan and run down to David Bagares gata?"

"Someone other than the perpetrator," Lewin observed. "Someone who's a minute and a half behind the perpetrator in our timetable."

"But wait now," said Holt. "If he's not the perpetrator, why is he behaving so strangely? According to Witness Two he was running as he passes her. You yourself write that it's the same man who runs into Witness Three farther down on David Bagares gata."

"Quite certainly so," said Lewin, nodding. "In this area, if we're talking about the blocks above the crime scene, around Malmskillnadsgatan, David Bagares gata, Regeringsgatan, the closest blocks in other words, there are, according to what we ourselves arrived at, more than a hundred persons who were moving about on the street at the time in question, that is, when Palme was shot. How many of them, considering the time and place, wanted to avoid having to talk with people like you and me at any price? Way too many, if you ask me. Let's not forget that this was the classic red light district in Stockholm and that there were also lots of ordinary criminals and addicts hanging out there."

"An alternative hood," said Holt. "He may not have shot Palme, but he realized that something bad has happened on Tunnelgatan down by Sveavägen that he doesn't want to be dragged into."

"About like that." Lewin nodded. "Perhaps you recall that in the interview with Witness Two she also says that not only was he running away—"

"I remember," Holt interrupted. "She saw that he was pushing something down into a clutch bag that he was trying to stuff into the pocket of his coat."

"Exactly," said Lewin. "This made a deep impression on many investigators. In other words, it was thought that this might be a small weapon case or a weapon bag and that he was trying to hide his gun."

"Sounds pretty likely," said Holt.

"I don't think so," said Lewin.

"Why not?"

"Three reasons," said Lewin. "First, we're talking about a revolver.

Almost fourteen inches long from the heel of the butt to the mouth of the barrel. One that scarcely fits in a coat pocket. Besides, if you put it in a rectangular case, then you need really large pockets, at a minimum.

"Second," he continued, "for that very reason, bags or bag-like cases for revolvers in particular are extremely unusual. With pistols it's a different story. There are small bags you can put them in. There were such bags for our service weapons at that time, our Walther pistols."

"I remember," said Holt. "I've used that kind of case myself." Including at a royal banquet or two, she thought.

"I suspect why," said Lewin. "Then I'm sure you also know that your weapon took up only half as much room as the revolver with a seven-inch barrel that was probably used to shoot Palme."

I see what you're thinking, thought Holt.

"And the third? Your third reason?"

"The time when he does it," said Lewin. "If it's the perpetrator she's seen, he's still only a hundred yards from the crime scene, and that's hardly the moment to be putting your weapon in a bag. A bag that means he won't have time to use the gun if he needs to and that what he has in his pocket becomes twice as bulky and even easier to find if he were to be stopped and searched. But I believe in the bag," said Lewin. "That's just the kind of observation that witnesses very seldom make up."

"So what would he be doing with the bag?"

"To me it sounds like one of those small handbags that many addicts used to store their equipment in. Their needles—so as not to risk sticking themselves, which can easily happen if you just put them in your pocket—a bent spoon for mixing and heating, a candle stub, a plastic bottle of water to dilute the dope with, a box of matches or a cigarette lighter, perhaps even a stamp envelope with leftover dope. Well, you know what I mean."

"I know exactly what you mean," Holt agreed. Someone who was hiding to shoot up at the absolute worst place in the city, she thought.

"You don't think it could have been an accomplice?" she continued. "The man whom Witness Two saw when he ran across Malmskill-nadsgatan? Someone waiting in the background to cover the shooter's retreat, maybe?"

Lewin squirmed.

"I've had that thought," he said. "But I still don't think so."

"Why not?"

"If he's further down on Tunnelgatan, in the background so to speak, then Witness One should have observed him as he was walking up Tunnelgatan. Though sure, this is maybe mostly a feeling I have, that he doesn't have anything to do with the case. Someone who only ended up at the wrong place at the wrong time. That's what I think."

"Let's go back to what you said about the times," said Holt.

"Okay," said Lewin.

"Another possibility naturally is that our first witness, Witness One in the chain, is considerably faster than you think," Holt objected. "Maybe he only waits twenty seconds, not a minute, after he's seen the perpetrator disappear up on Malmskillnadsgatan. Maybe he doesn't need a minute to run up the stairs. Maybe he runs just as fast as the perpetrator. Maybe he's up on Malmskillnadsgatan only one minute after the perpetrator. He's twice as fast as you think, Jan."

"In that case he's showing a large measure of modesty in the interviews that were held with him," Lewin observed. "But regardless of whether he was twice as fast, that doesn't solve the problem either. He's still half a minute too late up on Malmskillnadsgatan."

"For it to fit together in terms of time," he went on, "he has to run after the perpetrator at full speed as soon as he sees him disappear up Malmskillnadsgatan. Not hesitate a second to be on the safe side. Run full speed down Tunnelgatan and up the stairs. Say he manages this in thirty seconds. Then his story at least nearly jibes with the observations that Witness Two claims to have made."

"But not with his own testimony, because I've read that," said Holt, shaking her head. "Apart from the fact that in that case it would have been a pure suicide attempt on his part."

"No, he's really not trying to play the hero when he's questioned. He makes both a credible and a sympathetic impression on me," said Lewin, nodding in agreement.

"So all we've managed to do so far is get rid of the entire chain of witnesses," Holt concluded. "Without even needing to rely on the witness Madeleine Nilsson. She may still have passed by before the murder, and the man she met doesn't need to have anything to do with the case."

"Absolutely," said Lewin. "On the other hand, I was skeptical of the reconstruction of the perpetrator's escape route from the very beginning. I couldn't get the times to agree, as you understand."

"Did you talk with the other investigators about this?" Holt asked.

"No. I was too busy with other things. All the parking tickets and old suicides as you may recall," said Lewin.

"You wrote a memo about the case only four weeks after the murder. You must have thought a great deal before that."

"Approximately fourteen days before that," said Lewin. "Madeleine Nilsson contacted me a week or two after the second interview with her. We met and talked. Then I sat down and tried to redo the reconstruction of the perpetrator's escape route that our colleagues had made and that by then was already the established truth."

"You held an interview with Nilsson," Holt clarified.

"If you can call it an interview," said Lewin, shrugging his shoulders. "She wanted to meet me, we met, had a cup of coffee, and talked about what had happened."

"But why did she want to meet you?" asked Holt. This is getting stranger and stranger, she thought. Lewin of all people goes out for coffee in town with a known prostitute and drug addict.

"I knew her," said Lewin. "She was a good person who lived a very sad life."

"You knew her? How?"

"I got to know her a few years before the Palme assassination. It was in connection with an investigation. A female acquaintance of Madeleine's, in the same situation as Madeleine, had a so-called boyfriend who beat her black and blue and ended up trying to slit her throat. She got away, fortunately, but she was scared to death and refused to talk with us. Though not Madeleine. She not only showed up and testified against her friend's boyfriend. She also managed to talk sense into her so for once the charges held up in court. He got six years in prison for attempted homicide, felony procurement, and a few other things, and was released after serving his sentence."

"You think that Nilsson actually encountered the perpetrator on the stairs down to Kungsgatan?"

"Yes, actually," said Lewin. "It's highly probable that she did. I see no time-related problems, and she was definitely not the type who would lie or try to make herself interesting. She was a good person, honorable, talented, pleasant, always stood up for others. Considering the life she lived, I also believe she was very observant about just that sort of thing."

A good person who lived a sad life, thought Holt.

"You didn't speak with any of the investigators about this? After you talked with her, I mean," she said.

"I brought it up with Fylking," said Lewin. "Partly because it was his area, partly because he was my immediate boss, both in the Palme investigation and in ordinary cases."

"So what did he think?"

"He didn't think the way I did," said Lewin, smiling again for some reason. "At the same time he was friendly enough to point out, and it was very unusual coming from him, that regardless of which of us was right, it was completely uninteresting because the top officials in the investigation leadership—that was his own expression—had already decided."

"Is she alive?" asked Holt. "Is there any sense in interviewing her again?"

"There certainly would have been," said Lewin. "As I said she was an excellent individual. She died of an overdose about a year after the Palme assassination. In September the following year, if I remember correctly."

"I see then," said Holt, sighing faintly. "So our chain of witnesses already breaks between the first and second link. Instead we have witness Madeleine Nilsson, who has been dead for at least twenty years."

"Yes," Lewin agreed. "Though if it's Christer Pettersson we're thinking about, I'm afraid our witness chain broke off even earlier."

"Witness One," said Holt with surprise. "The one who seems so sensible. So what was wrong with him?"

"I don't think there were any major faults with him," said Lewin. "Possibly it was the case that our dear colleagues forgot to ask him the obligatory introductory question."

"The obligatory question," said Holt with surprise. "You mean whether he knew or recognized the perpetrator?"

"Exactly. But that doesn't seem to have been done. Instead they went directly to the perpetrator's appearance. He was never asked whether the perpetrator was anyone he knew or recognized."

"So you mean that Witness One is supposed to have known Christer Pettersson?" What is he saying? thought Holt.

"Witness One did not know Christer Pettersson personally," Lewin clarified. "On the other hand, he knew of him and knew who he was. Not least by appearance, because they lived in the same neighborhood out in Sollentuna. He had seen Pettersson on numerous occasions during the last few years, several times a week sometimes. Pettersson was the type that all normal people in the area took detours around."

"So when did he report that?" This is getting stranger and stranger, thought Holt.

"Toward the end of the summer of 1988. More than two years after the murder. When our colleagues in the investigation had become interested in Christer Pettersson. Then Witness One was questioned again. At that time pictures of Christer Pettersson were shown to him, among other things."

"So what did he say?"

"That's when he admitted that he knew Pettersson. Not least by appearance."

"And?"

"No," said Lewin, shaking his head. "This rang no bells in his head. He hadn't recognized the perpetrator as Christer Pettersson when he ran past him on Tunnelgatan ten seconds after the murder. Neither had the famous lightbulb come on at any time over the next two years during which he'd seen Pettersson in the neighborhood where he lived. And it seems like it should have. If it had been Pettersson who shot Palme."

"So how does he explain that?" said Holt.

"That the perpetrator and Pettersson were not especially alike," said Lewin. "In other words, he thinks he would have thought of that, and in that case naturally he would have contacted the police. Witness One is a completely ordinary, honorable person. Not the slightest shadow on him, if you ask me."

"How many are there who know about this piece of information?"

"A few, among those who count," said Lewin, shrugging his shoulders. "And now you too," he said, smiling faintly. "For the usual reason that it's not something that was talked about very much. Among other police officers."

"Among other police officers," Holt repeated, and for some reason it was Johansson she could see before her.

"Among other police officers," Lewin confirmed, and to be on the safe side he carefully cleared his throat as he said it.

19

As soon as Lisa Mattei left Johansson, she called her mother, Linda Mattei, one of the superintendents at SePo's department of constitutional protection, located in the building next to her daughter—"the secret building"—in the big police headquarters at Kronoberg. She was exactly twice Lisa's age. Apart from the fact that they were both blondes, they did not look particularly alike. Linda Mattei was a big, busty blonde. When she was a young police officer, she had been a "real bombshell" among her male colleagues. These days, and for almost twenty years, she was "still a very elegant woman," according to the same sources.

Her daughter, Lisa, was a thin, pale blonde. According to Johansson, like a young Mia Farrow. Lisa took after her father in appearance. Apart from the hair color, of course.

Her father, Claus Peter Mattei, had come to Stockholm and the Royal Institute of Technology as a young chemistry student in the late sixties. Short, thin, and radical, dark with intense brown eyes and almost a political refugee from Munich. He'd left because it was no longer possible to live there if you were a young person who thought and felt the way he did. In the strange world in which we live he and Linda fell madly in love, had a daughter they christened Lisa, and divorced a few years later when the differences between them became too great to be papered over by a love that steadily lessened.

What remained was Lisa. Apart from the hair color, recognizably like the father she seldom saw since he'd left her. He was the same father who for a long time now was different from the one who had left Lisa and Sweden. Still short, dark, and thin. His gaze was now melancholy and insightful in the way appropriate for every proper German investor with a PhD in chemistry and a job as research head of one of the Bayer group's larger companies. Repatriated to his childhood Munich, he was a humanist, a conservative liberal, of course an opera lover, a wine connoisseur, and a philanthropist too.

The mother, Linda, and her daughter, Lisa, had lunch together at a restaurant a comfortable walking distance from the big police building. Lisa's suggestion. A bit too expensive to entice their colleagues and thus discreet enough for anyone who wanted to talk undisturbed. Sliced beef with onions for Linda, seafood salad for Lisa, mineral water for both of them, the introductory mother-and-daughter exchange, and as soon as they started eating Lisa made the same suggestion she had to Johansson, and because Linda was her mother she also talked about why.

"Johansson," said Linda Mattei with a frown. "You have to be a little careful with that man. Is this something you've cooked up together?"

"My idea, but he bought it right away," said Lisa Mattei. "Best boss I've had. The best police officer I've met. You know he can see around corners?" Almost always, she thought.

"Yes, I've heard that. Ad nauseam," said Linda Mattei, who did not seem particularly pleased. "You haven't fallen in love with him?"

"But Mom," said Lisa, shaking her head, "he's twice my age, at least. Besides, he's already married."

"They usually are," Linda Mattei observed. "Which seldom seems to hinder them."

Though Lisa is probably not Johansson's type exactly, thought Linda Mattei. Even though I'm her mother.

"Nothing like that," said Lisa Mattei. "But what do you think about the idea itself?" I wonder if they've ever been together. Dear mother and Johansson.

"I promise to call Söderberg," said Linda Mattei, and then nothing more was said about it.

After her second meeting with Lewin, Holt started grappling with the witnesses from the crime scene. She had meticulously read each and every interview with the thirty witnesses to the murder itself. As well as the half a dozen who might have seen the perpetrator as he fled from the scene. Plus the dozen or more who several years later recalled that in any event they had seen Christer Pettersson right before and right after the murder. Plus the hundred others the police chose to disregard.

For example, Madeleine Nilsson, who for some reason ended up on the same computer list as the two teenage girls who admitted at the second interview, a week after the murder, that they had made it all up. True, they had been to the movies on Kungsgatan, but when the screening was over they ended up at a club down at Stureplan. They had not walked past on Sveavägen just as Olof Palme was shot.

Young punks, thought Holt with sudden vehemence, because just reading through all the papers had taken her almost a full day. She'd come up with no answers, only new question marks. And the big question mark, which Lewin had put in her hands, was just as big as before.

She could live with Lewin's calculations in principle. Perhaps something completely unexpected had happened to the perpetrator as he stood up there on Malmskillnadsgatan and no one saw him. Maybe he'd stood there only a minute or so before he finally collected himself and ran down David Bagares gata, where he saw Witness Two coming toward him further up the street. If that's really how it was, then suddenly the times were neat and tidy and there were no longer any broken links in the chain of witnesses. Although considering Witness One and his knowledge of Christer Pettersson, or Witness Three and the "fucking gook" who actually shoved her, it could hardly have been Pettersson who stood there collecting himself before he ran on to the next link.

Thought Anna Holt, sighing deeply.

Johansson's intuitive observation—dead sure and incomprehensibly spot-on—she could live with too. True, Johansson was almost always right, but now and then he was wrong, and in some isolated instance he might even have been completely out-in-left-field wrong. The few times Holt reminded him of this he grinned and shrugged his shoulders. If you were going to say wise things, it was also necessary to say something really stupid, and handled correctly that was an unbeatable way to learn something new, according to Johansson.

The problem was the improbable alliance between Lewin's monomaniacal calculations, his anxiety-driven exactitude, and Johansson's merrily unrestrained intuition. An angst-ridden accountant teamed up with a male fortune-teller, and to hell with both of them, thought Holt. To hell with Lewin, who was almost always right but hadn't been man enough to stand up for what he believed when he had the chance twenty years ago. To hell with Johansson, who was almost always right despite his big ego, his self-centeredness, and all his vices. But if both of them believe it, the bad thing unfortunately is that it's true, thought Holt. So what do you do about it? she thought. Shrug your shoulders, act like it's raining, and go on with your life?

Linda Mattei called her daughter within an hour after they'd finished their lunch.

"This evening at seven o'clock," said Linda Mattei. "Björn is going away fishing for the weekend. He was supposed to meet a former colleague down in Strömstad and be there all next week. But because it's Johansson who's insisting, there's probably some urgency too, and he had nothing against coming here as soon as this evening."

Rapid response, thought Lisa.

"He must have a little crush on you, Mom," she teased. "As soon as you call he comes rushing over."

"Certainly," said Linda Mattei. Who doesn't, she thought. The problem was that they were all considerably older than she was.

"What will you be serving?" asked Lisa.

"No salad anyway," her mother answered. "Be sure to arrive on time, by the way."

Just about the time Linda Mattei's two guests were sitting down at her neatly set kitchen table, Anna Holt decided to bite the bitter apple and visit a crime scene more than twenty years old. Embrace the situation. What alternative do you really have? thought Holt in the taxi on her way into town. It was another completely ordinary evening, nothing on TV, no movies she wanted to see, no friends or even acquaintances who had called and wanted to see her. Definitely no guys, despite the fact that there was more than one to choose from, and none of them should have any reason to complain. Not even her only child, her son, Nicke. He could be reached only by voice mail on his cell phone, where she would hear a message announcing with youthful naturalness that he didn't have time right now but feel free to try again later. He doesn't even need money anymore, thought Holt and sighed.

Holt spent over two hours in the neighborhood around the scene of the crime. Followed the perpetrator along the trail and even did so in the various walking styles described by the witnesses. She leafed through her bundle of old crime scene photos, paced out distances, pressed on her stopwatch, walked, jogged, and ran at full speed. She did everything the witnesses said the perpetrator or they themselves had done. Finally she considered the various alternatives and boiled them down to two conclusions.

Lewin was probably right. If it were the perpetrator Witness Two had seen, then she'd seen him much too late. The only possibility—it was unclear why and highly improbable—was that in that case he had stopped on Malmskillnadsgatan above the stairs to Tunnelgatan and that he stood there for approximately one and a half minutes. Why in the name of God would he do something that stupid? thought Holt.

Johansson was definitely right. There were no objections to his hypothetical line of reasoning. Other than that it was hypothetical, of course. The escape route he proposed was decidedly the best if you wanted to get away from the scene undetected. Up the stairs from Tunnelgatan to Malmskillnadsgatan, turn right, sixty yards' brisk walk, and then down the next set of stairs on the same street. The one that led from Malmskillnadsgatan down to Kungsgatan.

It was Friday after payday, and all the people walking down there were unaware of what had happened only a few hundred yards away. All the restaurants, cafés, cinemas, all the stairs down to the subway, and it could hardly be more safe than that for a perpetrator who had just shot the prime minister in the street. Times Square, Piccadilly, or Kungsgatan in Stockholm, if it was about hiding yourself in the crowd it was all the same, thought Anna Holt. An ice-cold soul who knows the area, without mercy and with no butterflies in his stomach. I only wonder whether Johansson read the interview with witness Nilsson, she thought.

The former chief inspector with the secret police bodyguard squad, Björn Söderström, had not felt better in a long time, and considering that it actually should have been a completely ordinary day, this was completely incomprehensible. First an unexpected invitation to dinner at home with a still very elegant woman he had known for almost thirty years and who had been a real bombshell when she started with the police.

Then there was the eighteen-year-old malt whiskey that she offered almost as soon as he stepped inside the door. Things having come that far, the whole thing appeared to be signed, sealed, and delivered. If it hadn't been for her daughter, of course. She seemed both quick-witted and well brought up, but nonetheless her appearance was a surprise because her mother had not said a word about her when she had called and invited him a few hours earlier.

"Cheers and welcome, Björn," said Linda Mattei, raising her glass. What one won't do for one's only child, she thought.

"I'm the one who should thank you," said Söderström. "It's not every day an old bachelor like me gets an invitation like this." The daughter is certainly here only as a cover, he thought hopefully.

"Nice to see you, Björn," Lisa Mattei concurred. "I don't know if you remember, but we are actually former colleagues too."

"Of course I remember," said Söderström heartily. "You were one of those youngsters who came over with Johansson when he became operations head with us. It was you and Holt and a few others, if I remember correctly. Now he's put you on Palme, if I understand things right. I saw something in the newspaper the other day."

"He's asked us to look over the registration of the material," said Lisa Mattei.

"It's about time that something happens," Söderström said. "I can promise you, Lisa, that you've ended up with the right man, because what I don't know about Olof Palme isn't worth knowing."

What do you say if you're a girl and just had a shot of aquavit? thought Lisa Mattei. Nothing, she thought.

You smile shyly and nod.

It's already ten, thought Anna Holt, looking at her watch. Time to go home and get your beauty sleep, she decided. Then she walked down the stairs from Malmskillnadsgatan to Tunnelgatan and out onto Sveavägen. Taxis went by there all the time, and considering the sparse traffic she ought to be home in her apartment on Jungfrudansen in Solna, brushing her teeth, in twenty minutes, she thought.

It had gone faster than that. Holt hardly managed to set foot on the sidewalk down on Sveavägen—two yards from the place where a Swedish prime minister, just shot in the back, had fallen headlong onto the street—before a patrol car from the police in West Stockholm braked and stopped alongside her. The older officer who sat next to the driver rolled down the window and nodded toward the backseat.

"If you're going home, superintendent, it's fine to ride with us," he said.

"Nice of you," said Holt. She opened the door to the backseat and sat behind the driver. It's a small world, she thought, because she recognized the older officer almost immediately.

"We're going back to the police station," he explained. "Coming from an appointment down at Grand Hôtel, and you live up on Jungfrudansen if I remember correctly."

They had not driven more than fifty yards from the country's most famous crime scene of all time before he started talking.

"I was there," he said. "I was working at the Södermalm riot squad, and we were the second patrol at the scene. According to one of all those know-it-all chief inspectors, we were supposed to have been getting out of the bus three minutes after he was shot. The victim, Palme that is, was still on the scene, and at first I didn't understand who it was, but I could see it was bad. People were screaming and pointing, so me and the other three officers ran down Tunnelgatan and up the stairs, and there was another couple standing and waving, pointing down to David Bagares gata. I ran so hard I could taste blood in my mouth, and you should know, Holt, at that time I didn't look the way I do today."

Then more police streamed in. The Norrmalm riot squad, several patrol cars, at least two detective units and one from narcotics.

"After ten minutes there were at least twenty of us searching the blocks around Malmskillnadsgatan. We tried to bring a little order into the general chaos. What were we doing there? 'Cause the man who shot Palme must have been halfway to the moon by then."

"I thought Christer Pettersson lived a good ways north of the city," said Holt.

"Pettersson," said the officer, shaking his head. "If only it had been that good. No, this was probably a guy of a completely different caliber, if you ask me."

"So you say," said Holt. Seems like Johansson has his own little fan club, she thought.

Former chief inspector Björn Söderström had not felt better in a long time. First this unexpected invitation from a very elegant former colleague who had the good taste besides to invite her young daughter. Also a former colleague, but above all a very delightful young woman. Then the malt whiskey, and all the good food. Food that an old bachelor like himself was certainly not treated to every day. First he ate pickled herring with chopped egg, dill, brown butter, and potato. A cold beer and an even colder shot of aquavit. The steaming carafe on the table promised more if he desired.

"Well, this I have to say," said Söderström, raising his glass. "This sort of thing doesn't happen every day for an old bachelor like me. You ladies ought to know that."

"It was really nice that you could tear yourself away, Björn," said Lisa Mattei with a well-mannered smile. The way to a man's brain goes through his stomach, she thought. Just like all other animals.

"Cheers, Björn," said her mother, raising her glass to the topmost button of the cleavage that had made her famous in the corps forty years ago. What one won't do for one's own daughter, she thought.

Fifteen minutes later Holt's colleagues let her off outside the building where she lived. Her older colleague, who had been there when Palme was killed, followed her to the entryway.

"The corps has probably never taken as many lumps as after the assassination of Palme. The Swedish police department's own Poltava," he summarized as he held open the door for her. "Imagine all the misery we would have avoided if the regular old colleagues from homicide had been in charge of it. Ask me about it. I don't know how many years those crazies on TV went on and on about the police track and alleged that it was me and the colleagues in the riot squad who were behind the murder of the prime minister."

"Yes, I've seen that," said Holt, shaking her head. "Thanks for the ride," she said, extending her hand and smiling.

Because you really have, she thought a minute later as she was standing in the hall of her apartment. If she hadn't counted wrong there were at least a score of leads in the Palme case files relating to him and his closest associates with the Stockholm police riot squad.

This must be the best completely ordinary day in my life. Or in any event the best I can remember, thought former chief inspector Björn Söderström, sinking his teeth into one of his absolute favorites, an ample grilled entrecôte with garlic butter, served with root vegetables au gratin and a good Rioja to top it off. Raspberries, whipped cream, and vanilla ice cream for dessert. He declined the port wine, too sweet for his taste, but that wasn't important, for half an later hour he was sitting in a comfortable armchair in his colleague Linda Mattei's living room with coffee and an excellent cognac.

. . .

Wonder where he went after that? thought Holt as she stepped out of the shower. First down to Kungsgatan, but then where? If he really was as skilled as Johansson seems to think, then he'd have to go to some secure location, she thought. Clean up, get rid of the clothes and all the annoying traces of gunpowder, hide his weapon. A secure location, because we all want to go to such a place whether we're ordinary madmen or professional killers, she thought. An ordinary person or an ordinary madman would surely go home. But this kind of character? Where does he go? A hotel room, a temporary apartment? Best to ask Johansson, she thought, sneering at her own mirror image. Then she brushed her teeth and went to bed.

"It was the worst day of my life," Söderström sighed. "So I can tell you I remember it in detail."

"I wasn't more than eleven when it happened," said Lisa Mattei, "so I guess I mostly don't remember anything. But I've understood from the papers that I've recently read that a lot of people asked how it happened that Palme didn't have any security that evening."

"Well," said Söderström, with an even deeper sigh, "I've asked myself that too a number of times. He's probably the only one who can answer that. He was no easy security object, but he was one very talented and, for the most part, nice guy. The boys who took care of him, he almost always wanted the same officers, so that was Larsson of course, and Fasth. Sometimes Svanh and Gillberg and Kjellin, who had to step in when Larsson and Fasth couldn't. The boys liked him, pure and simple. So I think I can say that none of them would have hesitated to take a bullet for his sake if it had turned out that way." Söderström nodded solemnly, taking a very careful gulp considering the seriousness of the moment.

"I understand that he was a troublesome surveillance object," Mattei coaxed, setting her blond head at an angle to be on the safe side.

"He had his ways, as I said," said Söderström. "If he'd had his way I think he would have dropped us. He was very careful about his private life, if I may say so."

"That particular Friday—"

"And that particular Friday," Söderström continued without letting himself be interrupted, "he said to Larsson and Fasth that they could take off at lunchtime. He would stay at the office until late, and then he intended to go straight home to the residence in Old Town and have dinner with his wife. A calm evening at home in the bosom of the family, as they say. So they didn't need to be worried about him. Although Larsson, he knew what to expect of the prime minister. He joked with him a little and said, . . . Can we really rely on that, boss? . . . or something like that . . . he said . . . Palme wasn't the type to be offended by that sort of thing. As I said, he and the officers liked each other plain and simple. I can vouch for that."

"A calm evening at home," Mattei clarified.

"Yes, although when Larsson was joking with him then, the prime minister said he wasn't planning any major undertakings in any event. That was exactly what he said. That in any event he wasn't planning any major undertakings. He and the wife had talked about going to the movies, but there was definitely nothing decided, and they had also talked about seeing one of their sons over the weekend. That must have been Mårten, if I remember correctly, for the youngest one was in France when it happened, and where the other one was I don't honestly remember. His son Mårten and his fiancée, that was it. But nothing definite there either."

"But he did say that perhaps he would go to the movies with his wife?"

"To be exact he didn't rule it out. But the likely thing was that he would sit at home all evening with his wife," said Söderström, taking a more resolute gulp. "When he said that, Larsson joked with him and said that if the prime minister were to change his mind he had to promise to call us at once. So he promised that. He'd been in a good mood, he often was actually, and there was no threat that was current, but in any event he said that if he were to change his plans he would be in touch. He had a special number to our duty desk, as I'm sure you know. A number he could call anytime day or night if he needed to."

"But he never did," said Lisa Mattei.

"No," said Söderström. "He didn't. The movie came up at the last moment. I guess he thought it wasn't worth the trouble. In that respect he was really not especially hard to deal with."

"But you know that at least there were such plans," said Mattei.

"Of course, Larsson called me right afterward and told me. Said what happened. That he and Fasth had been demobilized, so to speak, and that the security object would be at home during the evening. Possibly that he might go to the movies with his wife or see his son, but that nothing had been decided yet."

"What did you do then?" asked Mattei.

"I went to bureau director Berg, my top boss," said Söderström, "and told him what had been said. I think I can say that in a professional sense I wasn't very happy about that sort of thing."

"What do you mean by that?"

"If I'd been in charge, Palme would always have had security," said Söderström.

"Berg then? How did he react?"

"He wasn't happy either," said Söderström. "He was extremely concerned about Palme's . . . well, that bohemian side of his. He said actually that he would call his contact at Rosenbad—that was Nilsson, the special adviser on security issues; if I'm not misinformed he's still there—and ask one more time if we couldn't get somewhat clearer instructions. If there was a change in plans Berg promised to contact me immediately so I could reorganize."

"So what happened then?" said Mattei.

"He never called," said Söderström, shaking his head.

"Berg never called?"

"No," said Söderström, who suddenly looked rather moved. "He never called. Right before twelve o'clock, about midnight that is, the officer who was on duty with us called and told me what had happened. That was the absolute worst moment of my entire life."

Right before Holt fell asleep, in the brief moments between trance and sleep, she thought of it. Suddenly wide awake, she sat bolt upright in bed. It's clear—that's the way he did it, she thought.

20

On Friday Holt had e-mailed Lars Martin Johansson and attached the interviews with witness Madeleine Nilsson, Lewin's memo, and a written summary of the same matter. Where did the murderer go after he shot Palme?

She had not heard a peep from Johansson. After the weekend she ran into him by chance in the police station dining room, quickly led them both to the most remote table, and without any frills asked what he thought about what she'd written.

Considering what he'd said earlier, Johansson appeared strangely uninterested. He'd read the material from Holt. The interview with Madeleine Nilsson was new to him. What could he do about it more than twenty years too late? In principle he agreed with her of course. But what could he do about it more than twenty years too late?

"I also noted," said Johansson, "that you think our perpetrator went down to Stureplan on Kungsgatan and took the subway east. To the fine neighborhoods of Östermalm and Gärdet, to which regular hoods like Christer Pettersson would never dream of going."

"More or less," said Holt.

Considering the story up till then, if he had been following his victim, he could not set out in a car of his own. It didn't seem likely that he had an accomplice who picked him up either, considering that the whole thing happened before the age of cell phones. He had to manage by himself, and because he was logical and rational, he headed in the wrong direction. The right direction for him but wrong for everyone who was searching for him. He avoided the blocks around City that would be crawling with police officers right after the murder, both down in the subway and up on the street.

"The problem was that they weren't doing that," said Johansson, sighing. "The few who were there were running around like decapitated chickens up around Malmskillnadsgatan."

"But he didn't know that," Holt objected. "They ought to have been down in City, and if you're rational then you are.

"It was the other night," Holt explained. "Suddenly I happened to think about what Mijailo Mijailovic did when he'd murdered Foreign Minister Anna Lindh."

"Instead of heading down to City and risking running into all the officers there, he walked calmly and quietly down to Strandvägen and Östermalm," said Johansson, nodding.

"There he took a taxi, which then took him all the way home to the southern suburbs where people like him usually live," Holt observed. "He did the exact right thing. Regardless of how crazy he might have been."

"I don't believe in any taxi in this case," said Johansson, shaking his head. "All the regular taxi drivers were checked, and if he'd taken an unlicensed cab the reward would surely have enticed the driver who picked him up."

"I agree with you," said Holt. "Besides, I think he returned to Östermalm or Gärdet because he left from there," she said. "It's worth trying in any case," she added.

"Sure," said Johansson and sighed. "Stockholm must be crawling with tips if you just go looking."

What's happening? thought Holt. What's happened to Johansson?

"Lars," said Holt. "I don't recognize you. What happened to embracing the situation?"

"It's actually your fault, Anna," said Johansson, and suddenly he looked like usual again.

"Tell me," said Holt.

"The witness Madeleine Nilsson," said Johansson. "I got extremely depressed when I read what she said. It was during the first twenty-four hours in Sweden's largest murder investigation that she said it, and today it is twenty-one years and six months since she said it. Naturally I can't swear it was the perpetrator she saw, but in any case I wouldn't have dismissed her like that prize fool of a fellow officer did. Assume that it turned out it was as she said?" Johansson gave Holt an assessing glance.

"I'm still listening." Holt nodded.

"I won't put on airs," said Johansson, "but in that case I can promise you that Bo Jarnebring and I and all the other officers from that time, the ones who knew what they were doing, the ones who had done it all the times before, we would have rooted out the bastard."

"I see what you mean," said Holt.

"Damn that Lewin," said Johansson with sudden vehemence as he stood up suddenly. "Diligent as hell, almost absurdly meticulous, and an excellent head on his shoulders. What use is it to him if he's too cowardly to use it? Why the hell did someone like that become a cop?"

"Don't get worked up, Lars," said Holt. I understand what you mean. You're not particularly like Jan Lewin, and it's nice that he didn't hear what you just said, she thought.

"I'll try," Johansson muttered. "See you on Wednesday. Then I want the name of the bastard."

Police Superintendent Anna Holt, age forty-seven, devoted the weekend to physical exercise, and when she returned to her apartment on Sunday after a two-hour workout she faced the same alternative-free existence she had been lamenting all summer long. Is it my bathroom mirror there's something wrong with? Is there something wrong with me? Or is there something wrong with guys? thought Holt.

The most startling thing that had happened while she was running like a rabbit in the terrain around the police academy was that her son, Nicke, age twenty-four, had left a message on her voice mail.

For the past week Nicke had been in the archipelago with "the greatest woman in the whole universe." The life he was now living was "phat," and to top it off the greatest woman in the universe also owned the "coolest" place in the whole Stockholm archipelago. "What do you mean pool? Ma! We're talking pools here!"

Besides, her "pears," her parents that is, had had the good taste to head into town almost as soon as their only daughter showed up with her new boyfriend. "Can't describe it, really," said Nicke.

Pears. Wonder if the girl has a name, thought Anna Holt, scrolling to the next message for the answer.

"Her name is Sara, by the way," said Nicke, and that was that.

There is at least one person who seems to be happy, thought Holt, and without really understanding how it happened she phoned Jan Lewin at home and asked if he wanted to have dinner. Just a sudden impulse. A result of Johansson's outburst or simply that she had nothing better going on?

"Have dinner," said Lewin guardedly when he finally answered after the sixth ring.

"Dinner at my place," said Holt. "So we can talk in peace and quiet," she clarified. You know, dinner, that meal you eat before you go to bed, and if I said that I bet you'd die on the spot, she thought.

"Sounds nice," said Lewin. "Do you want me to bring anything?"

"Just bring yourself. I have just about everything," said Holt.

Because I do, she thought an hour later as she stood frying shrimp and scallops for the salad she intended to serve.

Wonder if she likes me? thought Jan Lewin as he exited the subway in Huvudsta.

"I've been thinking about one thing, Jan," said Anna Holt three hours later. You won't get a better chance than this, she thought. The first bottle of wine was lying in state in the garbage can out in the kitchen. The second was on the table between them, half empty. She had curled up on the couch, and Jan Lewin was sitting in her favorite chair and appeared both inexplicably calm and generally satisfied with existence.

"Well," said Lewin.

Not the usual throat clearing, thought Holt. Only a faint smile and a curious expression in his eyes. He should take care of those eyes. If he could just remove the fear from them, I would throw myself flat on my back, she thought.

"All those details you're so precise about," said Holt. So now it's finally said, she thought.

"You're not the first to wonder," said Lewin. No throat clearing now either, only the same faint smile. Same brown eyes, although without fear, without guardedness.

"Yes," said Holt.

"A year ago I actually went to a psychiatrist," said Lewin. "It was the first time in my life, but I was feeling so bad that I had no choice."

"This stays between us," said Holt.

"That doctor was an excellent person," said Lewin. "A very insightful person, a kind person, and if nothing else I learned a good deal about myself. Among other things, about the carefulness. The anxiety-conditioned carefulness that annoys all the other officers."

"Not me," said Holt. "I'm not annoyed by it. But I have wondered about it." Let me tell you, and it would be strange if I hadn't, she thought.

"I know," said Lewin seriously. "I know you don't get annoyed." Otherwise I wouldn't have come here, he thought.

"So what causes it?" said Holt.

"Do you want the short or the long version?" asked Lewin.

"The long one," said Holt. "If you don't think it's too trying, of course."

"It's trying," said Lewin. "Both the short and the long versions, but I can talk about it. Though I never have before." Never with another officer, he thought. "You'll get the long version," said Lewin.

Then he told her.

The summer that Jan Lewin turned seven and after he got his first bicycle, his father died of cancer. First he taught Jan how to ride, and when he finally could his father let go and died of cancer.

"It was as if the bottom went out of me in some strange way," said Lewin. "Dad took all my security with him when he disappeared."

Only Jan and his mother remained. No siblings. Only Jan and his mother, and because the bottom had fallen out for her too, her entire life revolved around Jan.

"It's not easy having a mother who does everything for you. That's probably the best way to get a guilty conscience about everything and everyone," Lewin observed.

Most likely that was also why he mostly felt relieved when she too died of cancer. Yes, it really was that way. He was mostly relieved. The bad conscience about her death had only come later.

Jan Lewin was twenty, just starting at the police academy, and Holt thought it was time for her first question. Why did he choose to become a police officer?

"I'm not sure," said Lewin. His father had a cousin who'd been a policeman. Not a replacement father figure, definitely not, but he'd been in touch on a regular basis, and he'd been there the times when he was really needed. He was a nice guy, Lewin summarized.

But most of all he talked himself red in the face about how Jan should become a policeman. It was the obvious occupation for every decent, honorable fellow who cared about right and justice and other people. Decent, honorable people who didn't wish anyone anything bad. Such as himself, or like Jan's mother, father, and Jan. Added to that, there was the camaraderie. Police officers always stood up for one another. Just like all those near and dear in a big, happy family.

"There were less than half as many of us at the police department at that time, but I bought the argument lock, stock, and barrel. Suddenly getting a family with seven thousand members who backed you up in all kinds of weather. That argument hit home with someone like me," Lewin observed.

"Then you discovered that not everyone in the family was fun to deal with," Holt put in.

"I guess it's like that in all families, and I discovered that the very first day," said Lewin. "The first thing I discovered was that almost all the people in the family were men, young men, and that not all of them were fun to deal with, and that basically none of them was like me."

"But you chose to stay anyway," said Holt. Why didn't you leave? she thought.

"Yes," said Lewin. "I was of course already me, so naturally I chose to stay. On the other hand, just quitting and telling them where to go, that wasn't me."

Jan Lewin stayed on. An odd character, but good enough at sports not to be bullied for the usual reason at that place and at that time. In addition, he was good to have around when there were tests looming in law and other theoretical subjects.

"Believe it or not," said Lewin, "I was actually a pretty good runner at that time and a passable marksman."

"Although you were best in the theoretical subjects," said Holt.

"Yes," said Lewin. "The competition was not exactly murderous. Not in the late sixties at the police academy in Solna," he said, suddenly looking cheerful.

"Our police instructor took a liking to me," he continued. "Already after the first course he came up and said that it had been years since he'd had such a promising student. Who do you think his last promising student was, by the way?"

"Johansson," said Holt. "Although according to the story I heard in the building, you should have been better."

"More precise," said Lewin, nodding. "The only thing our old teacher had to say against Lars Martin Johansson was that he had a bohemian nature. That he wasn't humble enough and wasn't even afraid to talk back. But what did it matter if you were like him?"

The years after school had simply rolled by, and Jan Lewin fell into line and followed along. His old teacher from the academy had not forgotten him. As soon as Lewin fulfilled the mandatory years with the uniformed police, his mentor called and offered him a position with the homicide squad in Stockholm, and it couldn't get better than that.

"It was not by chance that the homicide squad at that time was called the first squad, and the chief inspector with the first squad who dealt with murder investigations was C-I-1, chief inspector one," Lewin clarified.

"Those were the happiest years in my life actually," said Lewin. "We had a boss at homicide who was just as big a legend at that time as our own Johansson is today."

"Dahlgren," said Holt.

"Dahlgren," Lewin confirmed, nodding. "When he welcomed me and we had a so-called private conversation, he told me that he was the only one on the squad who had his diploma, from Hvitfeldtska second-ary school in Gothenburg to boot, and that he had noticed that now there were two of us. And even if Södra Latin in Stockholm couldn't compare to Hvitfeldtska, still, even more was expected from people like him and me than from the ordinary, somewhat simpler officers. Dahl-gren was a good person. He was educated, humorous, a very unusual policeman even at homicide. Which should have the best in the corps anyway."

Even so he took his own life, thought Holt. Because she didn't intend to say that.

"Even so he took his own life," said Lewin suddenly, "but maybe you knew that."

"Yes," said Holt. "I heard he got sick, was disabled, and as soon as he came home he took his own life."

"It was his heart. He couldn't imagine such a life," said Lewin. "Being a burden to others was inconceivable to him."

So it was better to shoot himself. Because regardless of how edu-cated and humorous he might have been, he was still the man he was, thought Holt. How damn stupid can they really be? she thought.

"Then I got my first big case," said Lewin. "I remember that. Just as well as I remember the summer when Dad died."

Now he looks that way again, thought Holt.

"It was 1978, in the fall," said Lewin. "I was barely thirty, and it wasn't common that such a young investigator got to run a murder investiga-tion, but that particular fall we were really busy. It was Dahlgren who decided it, and that's how it was, and if I had problems I could always come to him.

"Of course there were problems," Lewin continued, sighing. "Al-though of course I hadn't foreseen them."

A young Polish-born prostitute had been murdered in her studio in Vasastan. One of the major murders of that time, headline material in the tabloids. In a police sense it was cleared up and carried down to the basement the moment the prime suspect committed suicide.

"The Kataryna murder," said Lewin. "The victim was named Kata-

ryna Rosenbaum. I don't know if you're familiar with it? The perpetrator had treated her very badly. A very intense assault."

"I've read about it," said Holt. And heard about it, she thought. About
how Jan Lewin basked in police department glory.

"The one who was finally arrested, he was in prison for a few months,
and according to the tabloids he was of course the one who did it. He
was a man who knew her. They met at a restaurant, started a relationship; he didn't know she was a prostitute. According to him she said she
ran a secretarial agency. He was a completely ordinary man. Divorced,
true, but almost everyone was at that time. Had a child with his ex-wife,
a little girl, lived alone in a large apartment out in Vällingby, engineer,
orderly circumstances, good finances."

"From the little I've read it seems pretty clear that it was him," said
Holt.

"Yes, I actually believe that," said Lewin. "When he realized his new
woman was a prostitute, something snapped inside him and he beat her
to death. According to what I arrived at myself, at least."

"But the evidence wasn't sufficient and the prosecutor let him out."

"Yes," said Lewin. "Before my associates and I had time to have
another go at it, he took his own life. On Christmas Eve of all days,"
said Lewin.

"But that's hardly anything you can be blamed for," Holt objected.
"If you're a more or less normal person and you've murdered someone,
that's probably reason enough. To take your life, I mean."

"He doesn't think so," said Lewin, making a grimace.

"Excuse me," said Holt. What is it he's saying? she thought.

"Not when he visits me in my dreams," said Lewin.

"So what does he say?" asked Holt.

"That he was innocent," said Lewin. "That it was my fault that he
took his own life. That I was the one who murdered him."

"I can imagine what your psychiatrist said about that."

"Yes," said Lewin. "She was very clear on that point. It wasn't even
about him. It was about me."

"I agree with her," said Holt.

"I don't know," said Lewin. "But it helped to talk about it."

"It helped?"

"Yes," said Lewin. "Now it's been awhile since he visited me last. What do you think about a quick stroll, by the way? These therapy sessions can be a strain. My legs fall asleep."

"Sure," said Holt. "We can finish that when we come back," she said, nodding at the wine bottle on the table. Now he's smiling again. Maybe you should switch jobs, Anna, she thought.

Wednesday, October 10.
The bay outside Puerto Pollensa on north Mallorca

Just under an hour's run and the Volvo Penta marine diesel engine that is Espe-
ranza's heart has taken her twelve nautical miles out into the bay. Past Platja
de Formentor, Cala Murta, and the excellent fishing spots outside El Bancal
where you can catch sea perch, octopus, and skate almost year-round. Less than
a nautical mile remaining to the tip of the peninsula at Cap de Formentor and
then straight out in the deep channel toward Canal de Menorca. Heaving swell
with foam on top, a good deal deeper under her keel, parry with the rudder, soon
time to make the final decision and shift course. The sun like a flaming ball half-
way toward the zenith. High enough to burn off the haze and keep it 90 degrees
in the shade. A hot day even here where it is normally almost 70 degrees during
the day long into the fall. Other boats in sight and Esperanza is no longer alone
on the sea.

21

Six weeks earlier, Wednesday, August 29.
The headquarters of the National Bureau of Criminal
Investigation on Kungsholmen in Stockholm

"Flykt is no longer among us," said Johansson. "Tips are pouring in, so the Palme group has its hands full. We'll have to get by without him, and I thought that you, Lisa, could start," said Johansson, nodding at Mattei.

"Okay," said Lisa Mattei. "As I already told the boss, I saw Söderström last week. As I'm sure you know, he was the head of the bodyguards when Palme was assassinated."

"I'm listening," said Johansson solemnly, clasping his hands over his belly and sinking down in his own chair. The one that was twice as big as all the others around the table in his own conference room. The one that had neck support, arms, a foldable footrest, and built-in massage function.

Mattei reported what Söderström had said. That the prime minister, the day he was murdered, mentioned that he had tentative plans to go to the movies, or perhaps meet the family outside his own residence. Plans, Mattei underscored. The actual decision to go to the movies, and then kill two birds with one stone by also seeing their son Mårten and his fiancée, had been made only half an hour before Olof Palme and his wife left their apartment.

"I see then," said Johansson. "How many of the officers up at SePo were aware of his plans before he decided?"

"If I may add something before I touch on that," said Lisa Mattei, with a careful glance at her boss.

"Of course," said Johansson with a generous hand gesture.

"I've read the interviews with both his wife and his son. The decision to go to the movies was made that evening. What decided the issue was probably his conversation with his son about eight o'clock. He had, however, talked about plans to do that earlier the same day."

"Which of the colleagues at SePo knew about it, his plans, that is?" asked Holt.

"First the two officers who were assigned to him that day," said Mattei. "They were his usual bodyguards. The two colleagues the newspapers at that time always called Bill and Bull," said Mattei. "Criminal Inspector Kjell Larsson and Detective Sergeant Orvar Fasth. When at noon the prime minister told them he didn't need them anymore, Larsson called Söderström and reported how things were. Söderström went directly to his superior, bureau head Berg, and informed him; thus so far there are four people at SePo who were already aware of the whole thing at twelve noon."

"After that," said Lewin.

"Then it gets trickier," said Mattei. "Because Söderström might need to reorganize and send in two replacements for Larsson and Fasth, he informed the officer on duty during the evening. He in turn, at least this is what Söderström thinks, talked with the six guards on the on-duty list for the weekend. Another seven colleagues and now we're up to eleven," Mattei summarized.

"Which probably means the whole squad must have known about it by that time," Lewin observed.

"Not everyone," Mattei objected. "That's not what I think at least."

"Why not?" asked Holt. "Even at the time I was working there they had a break room."

"Certainly more than eleven." Mattei nodded. "Some of them must have said something to someone. But at the same time we have to be clear that this was not exactly a big sensation. The victim already had a history of similar behavior, if I may say so. Sometimes he simply wanted to be left alone." Who doesn't, she thought.

"Twenty," Johansson suggested with a slight wave of his right hand. "About twenty of our colleagues in the bodyguards knew that the prime minister had vague plans to go out and do something."

"Sounds about right," said Mattei. "In total there were thirty-eight officers working there at that time."

"Okay," said Johansson. "How many at the victim's office knew about it?"

"I've no idea," said Mattei, shaking her head. "My contacts in the government offices are still small, or more precisely, nonexistent. I've read the interviews with the people who worked there."

"So what do they say?" said Johansson.

"The question about possibly going to the movies was not asked at all."

"What kind of nonsense is that?" said Johansson. "It's clear they must have asked about that."

"No," Mattei persisted. "The closest you get is that a few were asked whether the prime minister said anything about leaving his residence that evening. That's not really the same thing," she observed.

Certainly not, thought Johansson.

"All three who were asked replied that he did not," said Mattei. "On the other hand, no one was asked about any plans."

"I do have a contact in the government offices," said Johansson. "He was around back then. I think I'll talk to him and then get back to you."

"The special adviser, later undersecretary, the government's éminence grise, the man without a name, Sweden's own Cardinal Richelieu," said Mattei.

"Oh well," said Johansson. "It's probably not all that remarkable. His name is actually Nilsson." So you're aware of him in any event, he thought.

"He was interviewed too," said Mattei.

"So what does he say?" asked Johansson.

"Nothing, basically absolutely nothing," said Mattei. "He simply has nothing to say. He actually says that. That's almost the only thing he says. Out of consideration for the security of the realm, he can't say anything. Out of consideration for the security of the realm he also can't explain why he can't say anything. It's completely meaningless. When he gets that routine question in the beginning about confirming that he is who he is, name and address and social security number and all that, he tells the interviewer to stop fooling around. Stop fooling around, next question, constable. Word for word, that's what he says."

"So what does the officer who interviewed him say?" asked Johansson.

"He apologizes. He's probably about to pee his pants," said Mattei.

"I'll talk to him," said Johansson with an authoritative expression. "Then I'll get back to you."

"About twenty at SePo, an unknown number at his office, but at least one—"

"Who's that?" interrupted Johansson.

"The special adviser," said Mattei. "Bureau head Berg confirmed that in his memos from the day of the murder. They're incorporated into the case files, and according to Berg's notes he discussed various security issues with him, including the prime minister's personal protection, at around three in the afternoon. What this concerned in concrete terms, according to Söderström, was the prime minister's plans to possibly go to the movies that evening."

"But the officer who questioned him still must have asked about his conversation with Berg," said Johansson.

"He did, too. But out of consideration for the security of the realm, blah blah blah, and next question, please. Amazing interview," said Mattei.

"What remains is the victim's family," she continued. "His wife, his son Mårten, and the son's then girlfriend. That makes three, and according to the interviews none of them talked with anyone else. Moreover, both the wife and the son seem pretty security conscious, if I may say so."

"Friends and acquaintances then," Johansson persisted.

"According to the interviews with former cabinet minister Sven Aspling and party secretary Bo Toresson, besides the son the only ones he talked with on the phone from home that same evening, he didn't say anything about this."

"They were asked the question anyway," said Johansson.

"Yes," said Mattei. "They were."

"So basically the whole world may have known about his plans, at least five or six hours before he even decided," sighed Johansson.

"A maximum of fifty persons, if you're asking me. Twenty at SePo, perhaps as many at his office, plus ten as a margin of error. Makes fifty tops," said Mattei.

It's always something, thought Johansson. The date and time of the masquerade at the Stockholm Royal Opera House in March 1792 were known by several hundred people months in advance. A hundred of them received written invitations two months before, and at least ten of those who were there had been involved in the assassination of Gustav III.

"High time for a little leg stretch," said Johansson, getting up suddenly.

22

After the leg stretch Holt declared that she no longer believed either in Christer Pettersson as the perpetrator or in the escape route that the Palme investigators had decided on early in the investigation. On the other hand, she did believe in the witness Madeleine Nilsson and even in Johansson's description of the perpetrator.

"You've finally seen the truth and the light," said Johansson.

"Call it what you want. I've changed my opinion," answered Holt.

"Although it took awhile, Anna," Johansson teased.

Mattei seemed to have taken on Holt's doubts. With all respect for Holt and Lewin's calculations, she was generally skeptical of witness statements. Essentially the only thing they had accomplished was to cast doubt on the earlier investigation's theories and promote a new hypothesis instead. Not an antithesis even, only a hypothesis.

"But we can't be any more certain than that," said Mattei. "A dramatic, muddled situation. Seconds here or there, that means nothing to me," she declared, shaking her blond head.

"Do you think there's any point in testing it then, our hypothesis, that is?" asked Johansson.

"Of course," said Mattei. "It's the only thing we have. We don't even need to prioritize. But it won't be an easy task finding our alternative perpetrator in the case files. Assuming that he's there. I can promise you that, boss."

"It doesn't seem completely hopeless though," Johansson objected. "A highly qualified perpetrator between ages thirty-five and forty-five, military, police officer, or someone else who understands this sort of thing, no criminal record, access to weapons, good financial and other resources, who has an inside contact in the government offices, with SePo or in Palme's family. To me it doesn't sound like a completely impossible task. Especially if you consider that he would have taken the subway to Östermalm or Gärdet when he'd finished the mission," he added, smiling at Holt.

"The problem is that you can't look for him that way," said Mattei. "It's not like on the Internet, where you can enter a number of search terms to limit the number of alternatives. The Palme case files are organized in a completely different way. Or according to completely different principles, to be exact."

"So what are those principles?" said Johansson, looking suspiciously at Mattei.

"It is highly unclear," said Mattei. "I don't even think they know themselves. It's said that the material has been organized by investigation lead file, but it's not searchable in the way you're talking about, boss."

"Investigation lead file," said Johansson with a bewildered look. I guess everyone knows what that is, he thought.

"Yes, and clearly different things are meant by that," said Mattei. "The most common lead is a so-called tip, which as a rule means that an informant has pointed to an individual; there are thousands of such tips. The next most common is an action that the investigators themselves have initiated, an interview, a search, an expert witness, basically anything at all. Even the sort of thing that the first investigation leader called 'tracks' in the mass media are stored as lead files. In a nutshell, it can be anything at all. Most of it seems to have been sorted in a spirit of fatigue. Everything is already so messy and immense that when something new shows up, they don't really know what binder to put it in. So it gets put in a separate binder. Literally speaking, that is. Would you like an example, boss?"

"Gladly," said Johansson. One lethal stab more or less makes no difference, he thought.

"I discovered the other day, for example, by pure chance, that the same tip from the same informant—it concerns the singling out of a certain individual as Palme's murderer—was registered in three different lead files. Considering the identity of the informant, and he is a very diligent one, I won't rule out that there are more leads than that. Same tip, same informant, same perpetrator who is singled out. At least three different leads, according to the registry."

"But why in the name of God then?" said Johansson.

"It came in at three different times, received by different officers. Because of the previous registration it couldn't be grouped with the earlier tip," said Mattei, shrugging her shoulders.

"What do you say, Lewin?" said Johansson. It sounds completely random, he thought.

"I'm inclined to agree with Lisa," Lewin said. "If you don't know which file to look in, then it's hard. That is, knowing what you're looking for doesn't help. You also have to know where to look. Apart from certain isolated exceptions."

"Like what then?" said Johansson. This is contrary to the nature of searching, he thought.

"The so-called police track is probably the best example. When the investigation started its work, SePo got the task of investigating all information that concerned the police. Almost all the officers who were singled out as involved in the murder worked in Stockholm, and considering that almost the entire investigation force was recruited from Stockholm it was considered inappropriate for them to investigate themselves, so to speak. So SePo got to do it, and the one good thing about that was that the material is collected in one place, most of it anyway. What it's like for anything that has come in later I honestly don't know.

"Okay," said Johansson. "I hear what you're saying. We just have to do the best we can. Work with what we've got." What the hell choice do we have? he thought.

"I think you know that, Lars," said Holt.

"Know what?" said Johansson.

"That we always do the best we can," said Holt.

"Excellent," said Johansson curtly. "Same time, same place, in a week."

"And then you want the name of the one who did it," said Holt. "Wasn't his name 'The Bastard'?"

"Watch it, Anna," said Johansson.

23

After their meeting Johansson took Lewin aside for a private conversation. What choice did he really have? What had evidently been an excellent, or in any case an energetic, idea fourteen days earlier had so far only produced five different results.

More than four hundred work hours for Holt, Lewin, and Mattei, who of course did not lack other tasks. Waste of police resources. That was the first.

The media also appeared to have put on high alert all the notorious informants who constantly made life miserable for this investigation. Flykt and his colleagues were not amused. That was the second.

Johansson had clearly ended up in the little black book at the editorial offices of Sweden's Largest Morning Newspaper. There had been a daily harvest of arrows against his bared chest, news articles about various improprieties at the National Bureau of Criminal Investigation, editorials on the police department's lack of efficiency, and most recently a cartoon with the heading "Remembrance of Things Past." Depicted was a very fat Johansson holding a leashed German shepherd with one hand while he shone a flashlight on something that suspiciously resembled an ordinary pile of dog shit. Johansson was not amused. That was the third.

What was left were things that had to do with the issue at hand.

There was the insight that the material to a large degree had already been lost. The old police article of faith that the perpetrator you didn't manage to find, despite everything, was there in the investigation might well be correct. The problem was simply that this time there were far too many papers that were far too unsorted for anyone to have a reasonable chance of finding him. That was the fourth.

At last the fifth. Fourteen days had passed and what had three of the country's very best detectives actually accomplished? On reasonably good grounds they had called into question the previously accepted opinion about the perpetrator's escape route. And they had offered only a new question mark in return.

There was the witness Madeleine Nilsson who had encountered a nameless, faceless man unknown to everyone on the stairs down to Kungsgatan. Before or after the murder? False or true? Regardless, the witness had been dead for about twenty years.

Lewin was a cautious general. If all generals had been like Lewin, there never would have been any wars. Lewin was nevertheless an excellent police officer. One of the very best. Okay, thought Johansson. Ask a direct question. If Lewin, in his peculiar way, even hints that this is futile, then you close it down.

"What do you say, Jan?" said Johansson. "Is this at all meaningful?"

"Don't know," said Lewin. "Easy it's not."

"Should we break it off and swallow the bitter pill?"

"Give it another week, by then we'll have made an honorable attempt at least," said Lewin. It must be Anna, he thought. She's still on my mind.

"Okay," said Johansson. What the hell has happened to Lewin? he thought. The guy seems to have had a change of personality.

"Sometimes you do things for good reasons but without really being clear about what those reasons are," said Lewin meditatively.

"That was nice of you, Jan, but this time maybe it's mostly about vanity," said Johansson.

"Let's give it another week," said Lewin, getting up, nodding, and leaving.

It's not just vanity, thought Johansson as his colleague closed the door after him. Of course he had personal reasons, that sort of thing is always present, but in this particular case it was probably more about the thirst for revenge than about vanity.

· · ·

The week before he went on vacation he had been at an international police chief conference at Interpol's headquarters in Lyons. These were recurring meetings that were aimed at people like him, whether they came from England or Saudi Arabia, Austria or Sri Lanka. Pleasant gatherings, to be sure, with plenty of time allotted for more informal activities. On the very first evening after the official banquet he and the usual colleagues from near and far gathered at the bar that was within walking distance of their hotel and which for several years now they considered their own regular bar in Lyons. There they had listened to the classic war stories. Everyone had something to contribute in the give-and-take, and naturally Johansson received the usual taunts for the same old reason. That the murder of his own country's prime minister had remained unsolved for more than twenty years constituted the most colossal failure in global police history. Regardless of what anyone believed about the role that Lee Harvey Oswald had played in the assassination of Kennedy in November 1963.

This time it was one of his best friends, the head of the detective department of the Metropolitan Police in London, who fired the first stone in the direction of Johansson's glass house. With an innocent expression, a friendly smile, and the nasal voice, vocabulary, and body language that people like him acquired at the breast at the family estate.

"How about the Olof Palme assassination? Any new leads? Can we look forward to an imminent breakthrough in your, quite surely, assiduous investigation? Satisfy our curiosity, Lars. Inform us ignoramuses in our professional darkness. Dispel all our worries."

The usual merry cackling, obviously. Toasts and sporting nods to take the edge off of what had just been said—no harm intended of course, comrades-in-arms, et cetera, et cetera—but in Johansson's case of little consolation, because the failure with the Palme investigation stuck in his head like a thorn.

For that reason too they always got the same answer.

With the Swedish police department's Palme investigation, things were unfortunately so bad that for years it had served as an example of the danger of a major murder investigation being cockeyed from the start. There was the fact that they had failed to seize the perpetrator at the scene of the crime or surround and arrest him in its immediate vicinity. That almost never happened when it concerned the murder of someone like the Swedish prime minister.

Instead there was an unknown murderer who disappeared in the darkness of the night. Police procedures and professional practices that suddenly seemed swamped by officers running in all directions. All the wild hypotheses and pure guessing games as a substitute for the persistent, penetrating, long-term detective work that was the structural part of every genuine police identity. Everything that held them up. The individual police officer just as much as the corps he served.

But certainly he and his Swedish colleagues had learned their lesson, and if they didn't believe him, all they had to do was to think back to the same Swedish police department's successful hunt for the murderer of the Swedish foreign minister a few years ago.

"A good piece of old-time footwork, if you ask me," Johansson stated in his now impeccable police chief English. "We learned our lesson. We did it the hard way. But we did it well."

His English friend and colleague nodded in assent and indicated his approval by slightly raising his glass of amber-colored malt whiskey. But he didn't want to let go, for if he'd understood things right the investigation was still active. Despite what Johansson had just said, and despite more than twenty years of failure.

"It's about embracing the situation," said Johansson sternly. "As long as the statute of limitations hasn't passed, we're going to keep at it." He hadn't said a word about the fact that for many years his investigators had essentially been occupied with other things.

"An obvious courtesy to a high-standing politician who was murdered," agreed his English companion, and obviously the only one imaginable or indeed appropriate, should anyone ask his opinion. Moreover a necessary measure to preserve political stability in every constitutional state and democracy. Despite the fact that police officers were actually above politics.

Possibly, nodded Johansson. Perhaps he hadn't thought about this because political theorizing left him cold. He hadn't even been involved in the investigation until much later, and then in the role of the government's technical expert in the various commissions that had been appointed. At the same time, if it was the police's failure that was to be explained, he wanted to underscore an observation he'd made, and from his listener's changed body language he understood that the occasion had arrived.

His well-mannered tormentor had obviously fallen into the trap, coming to a halt in Johansson's field of fire with his broad side toward the shooter. This was extraordinarily interesting and he wanted to hear more about it at once.

"It is essential for complicated police investigations to be run by real police officers," said Johansson as he smiled just as amiably, leaned forward, and patted his adversary on the shoulder.

According to Johansson's firm opinion, it was completely dangerous, not to say a guaranteed total fiasco, to turn such things over to all those attorneys and bureaucrats who populated the upper echelons of most modern Western police organizations nowadays, and this unfortunately had been done at the time when his own prime minister was assassinated.

"Touché, Lars," replied the colleague from New Scotland Yard, seeming almost more amused than the happy faces around him. Sure, it was no secret that he personally had not patrolled his way up through the corps that he now led. It was not until he turned fifty that he had risen from the judge's high bench in the criminal court at the Old Bailey to take his place in the executive suite on Victoria Street. For all that, the judge's seat he'd left for the police could be of use in that context. Especially as he worked mostly with finance and personnel issues and "would never dream of sticking my long nose in a murder investigation."

"You're the one who started it," grunted Johansson.

Then it continued as it always did; this time the acting police chief in Paris was talking about the city's problems with "all the statues of great

Frenchmen, the plentiful occurrence of pigeons, and not least the fact that the pigeons in Paris shit like crazy."

According to Johansson's French colleague, the Swedish Palme investigation was an extraordinary example of basically the only thing that the police could do. Failure or no. Actually Johansson and his Palme investigators played the same decisive role for the maintenance of Respect for Authority in Sweden as the fifty-some persevering workers with the municipal cleaning company in Paris, who tried to keep all the statues in the city free of pigeon shit.

"Respect for a great nation stands and falls with respect for the great leader," he said. He himself wanted to take the opportunity to make a toast to his Swedish colleague who, with indefatigable zeal and self-sacrifice, and without the least regard for his own comfort, had shouldered this task.

High time to call it an evening, thought Lars Martin Johansson as soon as the volleys of laughter subsided, and two hours later, as he was lying in bed in his hotel room, he made up his mind. Then he fell asleep. Just like he always did when he was at home. Lying flat on his back with his hands clasped over his chest. Quickly falling asleep while he thought about his wife and that he left her far too often for things that were actually unimportant and only stole their lives from them both.

24

"Has anything happened?" Johansson asked his secretary as soon as Lewin had left him.

"Things happen here all the time," she answered.

"Has anyone called?"

Just like always calls had been coming in the whole time. Not that the whole world wanted to talk with her boss, but a good share of those who were interested in the darker side seemed to experience a strong need to get in touch with him in particular. Just like always she'd taken care of these calls herself and given the person who called what he or she needed without having to disturb Johansson. With two exceptions so far on this Wednesday morning.

"That secretive character down in Rosenbad called, the one who never says his name."

"So what did he want?" The prime minister's own special adviser, Sweden's own Cardinal Richelieu, thought Johansson.

"Are you making fun of me, Lars?" she answered. "He wouldn't even spit out whether he would call again or if you should call him."

"I'll talk with him," said Johansson. "Who was the other one?"

"Probably nothing important," his secretary answered, shaking her head.

"He doesn't have a name either?"

"Well, he's called several times. Last Friday, actually, but because I didn't want to disturb the weekend for you I thought it could wait."

"Name," said Johansson, snapping his fingers.

"Bäckström," said his secretary and sighed. "He called the first time last Friday, and since then he's called another half a dozen times. Most recently just this morning."

"Bäckström," repeated Johansson skeptically. "Are we talking about that fat little creep I kicked off the homicide squad?" It can't be possible. That was only a year ago, he thought.

"I'm afraid it is. Chief Inspector Evert Bäckström. He demanded to speak with you personally. It was extremely important and enormously sensitive."

"So what was it about?" asked Johansson.

"He wouldn't say."

"Tell Lewin to call him," said Johansson.

"Of course, boss," said Johansson's secretary. Poor, poor Jan Lewin, she thought.

Johansson's secretary contacted Lewin by sending an e-mail via the police department's own variation of GroupWise, a system that was difficult to break into even for a talented hacker. Because Johansson's secretary was not the least bit like her boss, it was both a courteous and an explanatory message. Obviously formulated as a request. Would Lewin be so kind as to contact Chief Inspector Evert Bäckström, current position with the property investigation squad with the Stockholm police, and find out what he really wanted? This by request of their mutual boss, Lars Martin Johansson, chief of the National Bureau of Criminal Investigation.

What have I gotten myself into? thought Lewin. Only an hour ago, in a moment of weakness that had flapped past his top superior on weary wings, he had had the decision in his hands and a decent chance of putting an end to the whole charade. Now it was too late. Everything was as usual again and probably even worse. After taking three deep breaths he called Bäckström, and just as he'd feared he too was the same as always.

"Bäckström speaking," Bäckström answered.

"Yes, hi, Bäckström," said Lewin. "This is Jan Lewin. All's well, I hope. I have a question for you."

"Johnny," said Bäckström loudly and clearly, because he knew that Jan Lewin hated being called Johnny. "It's been awhile, Johnny," he continued. "What can I help you with?"

Lewin steeled himself. Really exerted himself to be polite, correct, and brief. He was calling on the boss's behalf. The boss wondered what Bäckström wanted and he had assigned Jan Lewin to find out.

"If he's so fucking horny about it I suggest he get in touch himself," said Bäckström.

"Excuse me," said Lewin.

"Now it's like this, Johnny," said Bäckström in his most pedagogical tone of voice. "If I were you," he continued, "I would seriously advise him to call me. I think it's in his own interest. Considering what he's up to," he clarified.

"I'm interpreting this as that you don't want to talk with me," said Lewin.

"As I said," said Bäckström. "If I were Johansson I would sure call Chief Inspector Bäckström. Not send you, Johnny."

"I'll convey that," said Lewin. "Anything else you want said?"

"If he really wants to put some order in Palme, then he can call," said Bäckström. "Now you'll have to excuse me. I have a lot to do."

What an exceptionally primitive policeman, thought Jan Lewin.

Regardless of anyone's opinion of the prime minister's own special adviser, he certainly could not be accused of being primitive. On the contrary, he was cultivated far beyond the limits of ordinary human understanding. Johansson called him on his most secret phone number and he answered immediately. Obviously without identifying himself because that, considering his mission and calling, was so to speak in the nature of things.

"Yes," said the special adviser with an inquisitive hesitation on the word.

"Johansson," said Johansson. "I heard you called, and naturally I'm wondering if there's anything I can help you with. How are you doing, by the way?"

"Lovely to hear from you, Johansson," said the special adviser with tangible warmth in his voice.

Actually he didn't want anything in particular. Just a simple "how are you doing these days?" to a good friend with whom he got in touch far too seldom. Personally he was just back from a well-deserved vacation, and as soon as he'd set foot on Swedish soil he was struck by the thought that he had to call his dear old friend Lars Martin Johansson.

"An almost Freudian symbolism," observed the special adviser, who seemed to have had vague presentiments of Johansson even an hour earlier, as he sat in the government plane en route from London to Arlanda, but it was only when he set foot "on the native soil that shaped us both" that the pieces fell into place.

"Nice of you to think of me," said Johansson. Talk, talk, talk, he thought. Otherwise the special adviser was feeling "really splendid, just as I deserve, and thanks for asking." He had obviously noted Johansson's friendly offer of unspecified help, but that was not why he'd called, but simply to invite Johansson to dinner. Socialize, eat a little and drink a little.

"What do you think?" said the special adviser.

"Sounds nice," said Johansson. "It will be a pleasure."

"What do you think about doing it as soon as tomorrow?"

"Suits me fine," said Johansson.

This preparedness, this readiness, this obvious capacity . . . regardless of all of life's changes . . . not to mention unforeseen and spontaneous invitations.

"I envy you, Lars." The special adviser sighed. "Imagine if I could always be the same. Shall we say seven-thirty at my humble abode in the Uppland suburbs?"

"Looking forward to it," said Johansson. Wonder what he really wants? he thought, and personally he also had a question to which he wanted an answer.

"What did Bäckström want?" asked Johansson as soon as he finished the call and got hold of his secretary.

"He didn't want to talk with Lewin in any event," she replied. "He wanted to talk with you. Lewin suspects that he has a tip about the Palme assassination. Bäckström called again just five minutes ago."

"In that case he'll have to take it up with Flykt," grunted Johansson.

"I actually suggested that," said his secretary. "I told him that if it concerned the Palme assassination, he should call Flykt."

"What did he say then?"

"He demanded to talk with you," sighed his secretary.

"The hell he will," said Johansson, feeling his blood pressure rise. "Call Flykt and tell him to shut the bastard up. Now!"

"I'll speak with Flykt," said Johansson's secretary. Poor, poor Yngve Flykt, she thought.

Flykt didn't send Bäckström an e-mail. All that stuff with IT and computers and networks and all the other electronic hocus-pocus that the younger officers were involved in was not his cup of tea. It was extremely overrated, if you asked him, and in any event he was too old to learn that kind of thing.

What was wrong with an ordinary, honorable telephone? The classic police resource when you wanted to get in touch with someone, thought Flykt as he dialed Bäckström's number. Bäckström answered the moment after the first ring.

"Hello, Henning," Bäckström hissed. "Where were we when we were interrupted?"

"I'm looking for Chief Inspector Bäckström, Evert Bäckström," Flykt clarified. "Have I—"

"Bäckström speaking," said Bäckström, sounding just like always again.

"That's good," said Flykt. "Then I've called the right number. This is Yngve. Yngve Flykt at the Palme group. Hope all's well with you, Bäckström. I heard you had something about Palme? I'm all ears."

"Do you have a paper and pen?" asked Bäckström.

"Of course," said Flykt sincerely, because he'd hit the record button before he phoned. "I'm taking notes," he lied. This is going like a dance, thought Flykt.

"Then you can tell your so-called boss that he can call me," said Bäckström.

"I understand," said Flykt. "But he has actually asked me to talk with you. This is my area, my and my colleagues' area, as I'm sure you understand."

"Well, that's too bad," said Bäckström. "So you can tell him I don't want to talk with you."

"Now I think you're being unjust, Evert," said Flykt. "If you have something to contribute, it's actually your duty as an officer—"

"Listen, Flykt," interrupted Bäckström, "I don't want to talk with you. I might just as well call the newspapers. I want to talk with Johansson."

"But why?"

"Ask Johansson," said Bäckström. "Ask Johansson if he has any ideas about that."

"He seemed completely out of control, if you ask me," said Flykt five minutes later.

"You have the call on tape," said Johansson.

"Of course," said Flykt. "First I got a definite impression that he thought it was someone else who was calling, some Henning . . . You don't think he may be in contact with that old celebrity lawyer? Henning Sjöström?"

"I can't imagine that," said Johansson. "Sjöström is an excellent fellow. He only defends pedophiles, arsonists, and mass murderers. Someone like Bäckström he wouldn't touch with a pair of tongs.

"It'll work out," he continued, shrugging his shoulders. "Just e-mail me the conversation."

"Obviously, boss," said Flykt. What do I do now? Best to ask a younger talent, he thought.

"Now let's do this," said Lars Martin Johansson fifteen minutes later, looking sternly at his secretary.

"I'm listening, boss."

"Prepare a memorandum on all previous conversations with Bäckström. As of now I want complete documentation when he calls again. When he's called five more times, inform me immediately."

"Understood, boss," said his secretary. Poor, poor Evert Bäckström, she thought.

25

After the meeting with Johansson, Holt felt a need to leave her office and the police building on Kungsholmen where her desk was only one of several thousand. Simply get out and move around. Work the way she had back when she was a real police officer. Talk with someone who'd been there and had something to tell.

Lisa Mattei had expressed doubt about Holt and Lewin's theory about the perpetrator and his escape route, and that was reason enough to check them one more time, two birds with one stone, and who better to talk with in that case than her older colleague from the uniformed police who'd driven her home from the crime scene a few days earlier. The one who'd been there when it happened.

The colleague was named Berg, and he was now with the uniformed police in Västerort. He had worked more than forty years as a policeman, would soon retire, and was still a police inspector. This could not be blamed on lack of contacts within the corps. His father had been a policeman, his uncle a legendary police officer, bureau head Berg, Johansson's predecessor as head of the operational unit of the secret police.

The fault was his own. For more than ten years, from the late seventies to the early nineties, he'd been one of the country's most investigated police officers. The department of internal investigations with the Stockholm police had been at him thirty or more times due to complaints of mistreatment and other excesses on duty. His own boss, Lars Martin Johansson, had even put him and his colleagues in jail twenty years ago. That time it concerned serious mistreatment of a retiree, which was supposed to have taken place in the holding cells at the Norrmalm district. Nonetheless, the outcome was minimal. Berg and his associates had been released every time.

The one who put a stop to his career—the one ultimately responsible for Berg's inability to gain the title of chief inspector—was his own uncle. The year before the prime minister was murdered, he had the secret police make a survey of extreme right-wing officers within the Stockholm police, and before long it became clear that his own nephew was playing a prominent role in that context. When the prime minister was assassinated six months later and the media started digging into the so-called police track, Police Inspector Berg was the individual officer most often mentioned in the various lead files that the Palme investigators were collecting. Never convicted. Indicted and released one time, but no more than that, and for the days his own boss had him held and jailed him, he was later able to collect sizeable damages.

The night the Swedish prime minister was murdered he'd been the third police officer to set foot on the crime scene.

Small world, and who could be better than him? thought Anna Holt.

When Holt got hold of her colleague Berg by phone, he suggested they meet at a café near the police station. Like Holt, he lived in Solna, and because he would be working the afternoon shift, getting together down by the station was best for him. Besides, there were never any people there at that time of day, and they had good coffee and sandwiches too.

"Iranians," Berg explained. "But nice people. They're the ones who've taken over the service sector nowadays."

"Nice of you to help out," said Holt half an hour later.

"It's cool," he said, smiling. "Had nothing better to do, to be honest. But there's one thing I want to say before we start."

"Of course," said Holt.

. . .

Then he'd expounded for five minutes about himself—by way of introduction, pointing out everything that Holt surely already knew—before he got to the payoff. He had not had anything whatsoever to do with the assassination of Olof Palme. He had been as surprised as everyone else. Just as dismayed as everyone else, believe it or not, and if there was anything he wished from his life, it was that he and his fellow officers who'd been there when it happened had succeeded in seizing the perpetrator at the scene.

"Just so we save time," said Berg, shrugging his shoulders.

"I believe you," said Holt. "I've never believed in those characters on TV and their police track." The fact that I do believe quite a bit of the other things I've read is hardly interesting right now, she thought.

"Nice to hear," said Berg, looking as though he meant what he said.

"There's a completely different matter I wanted to discuss with you," said Holt. "The reconstruction of the crime that our colleagues made at that time. I had a hard time getting the times to tally."

Then for five minutes she recounted her and Lewin's conclusions that Witness One must have been one and a half minutes behind the perpetrator when he came up from the stairs to Malmskillnadsgatan. And that Witness Two, simply for that reason, could not have seen the perpetrator run across the street "right before." On the other hand, she did not say a word about the witness Madeleine Nilsson. Holt intended to wait with that bit.

"If we assume that the murder was committed at 23:21:30," said Holt, "and that the perpetrator needs a minute to run down Tunnelgatan and up the stairs to Malmskillnadsgatan, then he's standing up there at 23:22:30."

"I know," said Berg with feeling. "The man who shot Palme must've had crazy good luck."

Then he recounted his memories of the same course of events, which Holt had devoted hours to reading about.

"According to the officers at central administration and all the know-it-alls, we got the alarm from Sveavägen almost exactly twenty-four minutes past eleven," said Berg. "I'll buy that, plus or minus the usual seconds here or there, 'cause it's always like that. The time is thus 23:24:00," he clarified. "Then we were at Brunkebergstorg right by the National Bank, we were coming from the north on Malmskillnadsgatan, so less than a minute earlier we'd passed the stairs up from Tunnelgatan. We must have missed the murderer by only thirty seconds. Palme is down on Sveavägen, a hundred yards to the right of us. He was shot only a minute and a half earlier, and we're driving past at a leisurely pace up on Malmskillnadsgatan and manage to drive another four hundred yards before we get the alarm. You can go crazy for less." Berg sighed and shook his head.

"So how fast were you driving?" said Holt.

"We were gliding," said Berg. "The way you do when you want to see all you can from a bus. Gliding down Malmskillnadsgatan at max twenty miles an hour. Calm and quiet out. It was cold and nasty too, I recall. People were trotting along with turned-up collars, hands in their pockets and shoulders hunched. We were sitting there in peace in our warm Dodge until all hell broke loose on the radio." Berg shook his head.

"What happened then?"

"Full speed as soon as we responded to the call," said Berg. "Gunfire at the corner of Sveavägen and Tunnelgatan, so there wasn't much more to ask. Blue lights, sirens, first a right from Brunkebergstorg down to Sveavägen and then five hundred yards straight north to the crime scene. I was the first man out of the bus, and the time must have been somewhere between 23:24:20 and 23:24:30. Would've taken us less than half a minute after we responded, so that certainly tallies," Berg said.

The riot squad bus had driven down Malmskillnadsgatan one and a half minutes after the murder, and thirty to forty seconds after the murderer stood at the top of the stairs and looked around before he disappeared from Witness One's view.

The officers in the Södermalm riot squad had not seen the perpetrator. They hadn't seen Witness One either, or observed Witness Two, and so far all was well and good, for they shouldn't have, thought Holt.

.

Witness One and Witness Two, thought Holt, but before she could ask him he had anticipated her.

"I see what's bothering you, Holt," said Berg suddenly. "You have the idea that the woman up on Malmskillnadsgatan, the one who's called Witness Two in that chain all the geniuses at the bureau were harping about, the one who says to Witness One as he comes up on the street that the murderer ran down David Bagares gata, you get the idea that it was someone other than the perpetrator she'd seen."

"Why do you think that?"

"That's what I thought as soon as the picture was clear to me," said Berg. "How else would it have fit together? Time-wise," I mean.

"But you never said anything," said Holt.

"Why do you suppose that is?" said Berg. "Assume that someone like me had gone to the fine colleagues at the detective bureau on Kungholmsgatan and said I thought they'd gotten a few things turned around. Something that major, I mean."

"I don't think they would've started cheering," said Holt. "What did you do when you got out of the bus down at the crime scene?" she continued.

"As soon as the situation was clear to me, this must have been ten seconds at the most, three of the others and I ran down Tunnelgatan. When we got to the stairs up to Malmskillnadsgatan a woman was standing up there, waving and shouting, so I ran up the stairs to the street. That was Witness Two, that woman, I realized later. It might have taken a minute at most for me to run from the crime scene up to Malmskillnadsgatan. As I said to you the last time we talked."

"So now the time is somewhere around 23:25:30, four minutes after the murder," Holt clarified.

"Something like that, yes," Berg agreed.

"So what did you do next," asked Holt.

"Continued in the direction shown by Witness Two," said Berg.

"Down David Bagares gata toward Regeringsgatan that is, and about fifty yards down the street I ran into Witness One."

"So what did he say?" asked Holt.

"Not much," said Berg. "It probably took a minute or so before I realized that he hadn't seen which way the perpetrator went. He only reported what Witness Two had said to him.

"If you ask me," he continued, "there's a thing or two rattling around loose in that part of the description. Such as, for example, that it's a hundred percent certain they'd seen the same person run past."

"Explain what you're thinking," said Holt.

Berg had talked with both Witness One and Witness Two. He was actually the first police officer to do that, and for once he hadn't been asked to write even a line about it. The officers from the bureau had taken over that aspect as soon as they arrived at the scene, and he had no idea what had happened to his brief, handwritten notes. He had just a vague memory, of some colleague from the duty desk who stuffed them in his coat pocket.

Berg had not conducted any interviews. He'd only stopped to talk with Witnesses One and Two for the obvious reason that he wanted to know as much as possible as quickly as possible to organize his initial search for the perpetrator.

"When Witness One comes up on Malmskillnadsgatan, he runs into Witness Two. Then he asks her if she's seen a character in a dark coat run past. I don't recall the exact wording, but I get the idea that Witness One asks her whether she's seen a guy in a dark coat who's run past. She replies that she has. Right before she saw a man in a dark coat run across Malmskillnadsgatan and down on David Bagares gata."

"Right before," asked Holt.

"I asked the same question myself as soon as I had the chance. It must have been maybe fifteen minutes later. According to her it concerned a male individual in a dark coat who twenty seconds at most before she got the question from Witness One had run across Malmskillnadsgatan and down on David Bagares gata. Otherwise she didn't have much in particular to offer. Nothing else about his clothes other than that she thought he had a small bag in his right hand that he tried to put in his coat pocket. She hadn't seen his face. She had an idea that he was maybe trying to conceal it from her as he ran past. Tall or short? Thin or husky? Stout or slender? Dark or light? Old or young? No definite perception about that either. Looked like all the other male individuals who were out that evening, I guess, if you were to summarize her observations. Apart from the fact that he'd acted suspiciously, of course. On that point she was more and more certain the more we talked. That he seemed nervous, hunted, tried to conceal his face and all that. Yes, Lord Jesus," said Berg and sighed. "What could she say otherwise? By that time there was a horde of officers crowding around her."

"Witness One then. What does he say?" asked Holt.

"He was right there the whole time up on Malmskillnadsgatan, and if I could have chosen I would have kept him and the other witness apart, but it was so damned messy that that didn't work. Before the officers from the bureau took over, the two of them must have stood talking with each other for close to half an hour. Witness One and Witness Two, that is."

"Did you make note of any differences between their descriptions of the man they'd seen?" asked Holt.

"Witness One was considerably more detailed. He'd heard the shot and seen the perpetrator with the weapon and realized what'd happened. A man in a dark jacket or coat, possibly bareheaded, possibly with a knit cap on his head, the kind Jack Nicholson had on in *Cuckoo's Nest*, sturdily built, rolling gait as he ran or trotted away, almost bearlike, maintained that he'd seen him put the weapon in his right jacket or coat pocket but nothing about a bag. He looked mean, that was what he said. About forty to forty-five years old. Older than the witness, in any case. Otherwise nothing."

"I see what you mean," said Holt and nodded. Now's the time to bring up Madeleine Nilsson, and how do I do that without putting words in his mouth? she thought.

"When you drive up Döbelnsgatan, past the stairs to Tunnelgatan at the start of Malmskillnadsgatan, the bridge passes over Kungsgatan and continues on Malmskillnadsgatan down to Brunkebergstorg where you get the alarm . . ."

"I follow you," said Berg, nodding.

"You didn't observe any other mysterious or suspicious persons?"

"Then we would have mentioned it," said Berg, shaking his head. "Definitely no one with a smoking revolver in his fist," he said.

"No one else?"

"Mostly ordinary Joes who were freezing. A whore or two, naturally, that's where they worked, and at that time there were lots of them. Certainly a few hooligans and addicts too, but no one up to anything."

"And if you'd seen someone like that?"

"Then naturally we would have stopped and frisked him or her. We always did that if we didn't have anything better to do. Otherwise we would blink at them, and I'll tell you, we had an uncannily good knowledge of people."

"Blink?"

"With the headlights," said Berg. "Just to let them know their presence was noted, if nothing else. Get them to realize we were keeping an eye on them."

"But you don't recall any particular person from that evening?"

"No," said Berg. "Then we would have mentioned it, like I said. It was not an ordinary evening exactly.

"Too bad you weren't involved from the start, Holt," he added, smiling at her. "There was one more thing, by the way. If you can stand listening, and it's really not at all about this. And besides, I want it to stay between you and me," he continued.

"If it's not about this, it will stay between us," said Holt.

"It's not," said Berg. "It's about your boss."

"Johansson," said Holt. "Fire away," she said. Not a second to lose, she thought.

"Just a piece of advice," said Berg. "As I'm sure you know, he and I have a history together that's not very pleasant, so I guess you have to take this for what it's worth."

"I know he put you in jail for a week twenty years ago." On not completely baseless grounds, she thought.

"Me and my colleagues," said Berg, nodding. "Then you also know that my colleagues and I were cleared of all suspicions and that we got damages for the time we spent in jail."

"I know all that," said Holt. "I know for example that you and many other colleagues in the uniformed police call him the butcher from Ådalen."

"It wasn't that he put us in jail. I'm sure I've put a few innocent so-and-sos in jail too. The name we gave him, he's earned honorably. I've never met such an ice-cold bastard in my entire life. A person who can kill you without hesitation if he thinks it's in his interest. Without even breaking a sweat. So whatever you do, Holt, watch out for that man," said Berg, shaking his broad shoulders.

"Now you'll actually have to explain yourself," said Holt. What is he saying? she thought.

"Yes," said Berg, "I will."

Then he told the story about his father.

Berg's father had also been a policeman, a regular patrol cop with the uniformed police in Stockholm. When Berg was a young boy in his teens his father had died on duty. While chasing a couple of car thieves he'd been forced into a ditch. It was the sixties, and there were no seat belts even in police cars. Berg's father was thrown headfirst through the windshield, broke his neck, and died on the spot.

"I really loved my father," said Berg quietly. "Despite all his faults, because both my mother and I knew he had them. It was because of him I decided to become a policeman. As soon as I got the chance I told everyone about my father and what happened to him and why I chose to become a policeman. I talked about what all my relatives had told me, and in our family there's no shortage of policemen, you should know. What all Dad's colleagues told me. That my father was a hero. That he actually sacrificed his life in his job as a policeman. For twenty-five years I believed that's what had happened."

The one who had opened Berg's eyes about his father was Lars Martin Johansson. Berg and his colleagues were being held for the third day.

Johansson and his co-workers conducted daily interrogations. Johansson spent most of his time with Berg, the one Johansson knew was the leader.

"I'm not particularly sensitive, but this you should know, Holt: It gets to you if you're a cop and suddenly you're sitting in the jail at Kronoberg," said Berg. "So on the third day I was actually pretty much done. Johansson and another officer had been attacking me the whole day, and if I'd only been able to keep my shoelaces or my belt I know exactly what I would have done as soon as they left."

"So what happened then?" asked Holt. Though I already sense it, she thought.

"A few hours later, after dinner, I was there on the cot staring at the ceiling and wondering how I could strangle myself with the blanket. Tear it in strips and all that—you get pretty inventive in those situations. There's no hook in the ceiling where you can hang yourself in that place, as I'm sure you know. Suddenly Johansson was standing in the doorway. He was alone, apart from a couple of jailers hiding out in the corridor. He had his overcoat on. I remember he said he was going to go out and get a bite to eat before he went home. He'd brought a little nighttime reading for me. He realized I had a hard time sleeping, that is. Then he threw one of those old investigation files at me. The ones with green cardboard binders that we had ages and ages ago. Then he simply left and there was a lot of locking and slamming before he and the jailers finally wandered off."

"At first I thought it was an interrogation with one of my colleagues who was in there too, and that he wanted to play us against each other, but that wasn't it," said Berg.

You're not feeling well, thought Holt. Right now you're feeling really bad, and you're not the least bit like the Berg I've read about, she thought.

"It was the investigation of the cause of death of my own father," said Berg. "With pictures and everything. From the scene of the accident, the autopsy photos, everything. The same investigation that Dad's colleagues had hidden down in the basement and that none of them had said a word about during all those years, and least of all to me or Mom."

Berg shook his head and took a short pause before he continued.

"What they'd told me and my mother wasn't correct. One day Dad put on his uniform and borrowed a radio car. He had been suspended from service because he'd shown up drunk at the station one evening the week before, but Mom and I knew nothing about that. Whatever," continued Berg, shaking his head. "He got into the radio car and drove out to Vaxholm. On the way there he consumed a whole bottle of straight vodka plus a quart of schnapps. More than a quart of alcohol. When he got down to the ferry landing in Vaxholm he waited until the ferry set out. Then he put the accelerator to the floor and drove right out over the edge of the pier. The car landed more than fifty feet out in the water, so before he drowned he really had driven his head through the windshield and broken his neck."

"So what happened then?" asked Holt.

"I went crazy," said Berg. "They had to strap me down and drug me. Took twelve hours before I came around enough that they could drag me back to my regular cell. The file was gone, naturally. Who do you think retrieved it."

"Have you told this to anyone else?" asked Holt.

"A few other officers," said Berg. "Without going into any details. It's history now." Berg looked at her and nodded. "Be careful with that man, Holt. He's not just pleasant and entertaining in that Norrland way. He has other sides that he can show when he feels like it."

26

After the conversation with Bäckström, Lewin sought the serenity of the Palme room. Mattei was already there, and she had clearly not been inactive. On the table in front of her was a tall stack of thick binders, and when Lewin came in she was leafing through one of them with her left hand as she typed diligently on her laptop with her right.

Eidetic memory combined with a very high capacity for multitasking, thought Lewin. A lovely young woman besides.

"Hi, Jan," said Mattei, smiling at him. "I had no idea there were so many certified crazies. I've already found over three hundred, and because I'm sure I've missed half of them there are going to be quite a few."

"But now they'll end up in a registry," Lewin observed. Wonder how many uncertified lunatics there are? Must be lots more anyway, he thought.

"There," said Mattei, shrugging her slender shoulders. "Some kind of list, in any case."

Nice to hear, thought Lewin, and for lack of anything better he took out his old box of parking tickets. Neatly packed, stored in one place, and probably completely uninteresting in fact. If our perpetrator is as well-organized as both Anna Holt and Johansson seem to think, he won't have parked illegally, he thought.

More than two thousand parking citations had been issued in the Stockholm area the day of the murder. A few hundred of them had been distributed in the finer parts of the city that were along the Red Line on the subway. Gärdet, Östermalm, Lidingö. Why was it called the Red Line? Considering who lived there, it really should be the Blue Line, Lewin philosophized as he leafed through the bundles of tickets, trying to think of what he was really searching for.

Vehicles in good condition, no clunkers, illegally parked in the hours before and after the murder around the various subway stations, thought Lewin. Twenty-one years later, for the most part all of the vehicles had gone to the junkyard several years ago, and all information about the owner or user had disappeared from all conceivable registries. Even if the murderer had a brand-new Mercedes when he shot Palme, thought Lewin and sighed.

For lack of anything better he had to rely on his old notations. Almost everyone who'd parked illegally had done so in the immediate vicinity of their own residence. Just as you would expect, and this was hardly instructive considering Holt's hypothesis that the perpetrator had relied on his own car for further transport.

Before Lewin went home for the day he also made a separate review of his own contribution to the so-called police track. Of the total of nineteen parking tickets pertaining to police service vehicles or cars belonging to individual police officers, three had been issued along the Red Line. One in Östermalm, one at Gärdet, and one in Hjorthagen at the final station in Ropsten. Besides one out in Lidingö, all the way on the other side of the bridge, five hundred yards from the final station.

Nothing strange about those either, thought Lewin as he put the bundles back in the box. The colleague out in Lidingö, for example. He lived in Lidingö, worked with the Lidingö police department, and his car had been illegally parked the whole weekend. According to information from his co-workers, this was because he had the flu and was in bed from Thursday evening until Monday morning.

Nothing strange about that either. When Lewin talked with one of the bedridden illegal parker's colleagues twenty years ago, he remembered that he'd called down to the station as early as Friday morning and asked one of the other officers to move his car. They could get the keys in his apartment up on Torsviksvägen. But it never happened. Suddenly there were more important things to do than deal with illegally parked vehicles.

There was a clear pattern in Mattei's material about more qualified crazies. The origin of the information was almost always a tip from various individual informants. Extremely few of the conceivable Palme assassins had ended up in the files on the basis of information the police had produced through their own detective work. The constantly recurring reason they ended up in the Palme investigation was that they all hated Olof Palme and had also talked about it to individuals in their vicinity. These individuals had then contacted the police, as a rule pretty soon after the prime minister had been murdered, and told about their strange friend, acquaintance, neighbor, co-worker, ex-spouse, partner, and so on, who had promised to kill him. Conspicuously often by shooting him, and always with a weapon to which they had legal access. Hunters, marksmen, reservists, gun collectors.

Their qualifications were not impressive either. To start with Mattei sorted out the cases of pure psychosis, known addicts, and professional criminals. What remained were several hundred odd, single men, often extremists, almost always with broken relationships, and usually with a bad name in their own neighborhoods. Almost exclusively men of Swedish origin. Immigrants—for example the "gook" who according to Witness Three supposedly ran into her on David Bagares gata—were a clear minority. This was about Swedish men. The kind you talked to only if you had to, so as not to rile them up unnecessarily.

"I'm a hundred percent convinced that it's Tore Andersson who murdered Olof Palme. On several occasions he's shown me a black attaché case with a revolver in it and said he was going to shoot Palme. The most recent time this happened was only a week before the murder, and I know he was in Stockholm visiting an acquaintance who lives on Söder, the same weekend Palme was murdered. And besides, he had definite information that Palme was spying on behalf of the Russians. Tore also corresponds well with the description of the perpetrator. He's rugged, about six feet tall, dark, and forty-four years old. Tore is something of a loner . . ."

"It was Stefan Nilsson who murdered Olof Palme. He has a definite radical right-wing image and is a very eccentric and exhibitionistic person. At the same time he's a so-called lone wolf, and as far as I know he's never been involved with a woman. He's forty-one years old, and in the hall to his apartment there's a closet where he stores a number of firearms. When Palme was here at a conference less than a year ago I know Nilsson visited the hotel where Palme was staying to try to find out which room he was in . . ."

"After much consideration I want to convey the following. I have a former boyfriend who, after being trained as a security guard, moved to Stockholm and got a job at a security company there. For the past several years he's said to have lived in Old Town right in the vicinity of the street where Palme lived . . ."

Mattei had a simple matrix she held them up against—about forty years old, about six feet tall, dark-colored hair without streaks of blond or gray, relatively sturdy body build, familiar with the area, familiar with the use of firearms, access to legal weapons—and at a rate of ten per hour she then put them aside.

In nine cases out of ten the lead file that her colleagues had prepared consisted exclusively of the tips they'd received. A letter, often anonymous, a telephone call, or even a personal visit to the police. Often a courier was used because the informant himself dared not risk appearing because the perpetrator would then immediately realize who had told on him. In nine cases out of ten it had never been more than that.

· · ·

In one case out of ten things had happened. The police had done searches on the person pointed out in various registries, interviews had been held with him and persons who knew him. On several occasions he had even been tailed. It was unclear why, because these individuals were oddly similar to a number of others on whom nothing more had been done than receive the tip, give it a serial number, open a new lead file, put the papers in a binder, and put the binder on a shelf.

What's the use of this? thought Lisa Mattei and sighed. The only consolation was that none of them seemed especially like the perpetrator that Lars Martin Johansson or Anna Holt had talked about. No acuity, no presence of mind or merciless capacity for practical action; not familiar with the area; no interesting contacts. What remained were chance encounters with the victim, where the probability was so slight that it could scarcely be calculated. The same chance that both Johansson and Holt had dismissed early on. Why in the name of heaven should a person who had lived his entire life in a small community in northern Värmland suddenly get in the car and drive four hundred miles one way to Stockholm, wander around the city, and quite unexpectedly run into the person he hated more than anyone in the world?

He'd been away that weekend. No one had talked with him before he left. When he came back on Sunday evening he was a different person. He made hints to people around him . . . he'd shown one of them his gun . . .

But you leave me cold, thought Mattei, putting him back in the same binder where he'd been the whole time.

27

Already by Thursday evening Bäckström had used up the grace Johansson had measured out to him. A quickly escalating activity in which Bäckström sounded more and more like Bäckström with every new call and expressed himself downright offensively in the last one. Pure telephone terror, and Johansson's secretary was not only sick and tired of him; she hated him deeply and heartily.

Now you've had it, you little butterball, she thought as she knocked on Johansson's door.

Now you'll get yours, you fat little slob, thought Lars Martin Johansson five minutes later. Then he called Holt and told her he wanted to meet with her immediately.

"So you mean to say he called Helena cunt-lips?" asked Holt ten minutes later.

"Sure," said Johansson. "We have it on tape. Along with all the other indecencies he spewed out."

"If he did that he'll be immediately removed from duty," said Holt.

"Sure," said Johansson, shrugging his shoulders. "Talk with our attorney if you need to. Do what you want with him. Boil the bastard for glue, if you want. But before you do it, I want to know what he wants, and when I know that I want him to stop calling."

"I'll arrange it," said Holt. "But before I do that there's another thing I have to talk with you about."

"I'm listening," said Johansson. "With excitement," he added.

"I talked with an old acquaintance of yours. Officer Berg who works with the uniformed police in Västerort."

"Depends on what you mean by acquaintance," said Johansson, who no longer seemed pleased. "The only Berg I know is dead. Erik Berg, his uncle. My predecessor at SePo and an excellent policeman. Not the least like that neo-Nazi he's unfortunately related to."

"I've read his file in the Palme material," said Holt. "But that wasn't what I wanted to talk about."

"You wanted to tell his version of what happened at the jail one evening more than twenty years ago," said Johansson.

"Yes," said Holt.

"You don't need to," said Johansson, shrugging his shoulders. "I've already heard it through the usual grapevine. If you're interested, on the other hand, I can tell you why I did what I did back then."

"That would be nice," said Holt.

"Sure," said Johansson, and then he told her why he'd visited Berg in his cell more than twenty years before, only six months before the prime minister was shot. Whatever that had to do with the matter.

The interrogation was on its third day. Berg had been confronted with a number of serious suspicions. He lacked all factual counterarguments. He was hanging by a thread, according to Johansson.

"The bastard was hanging by a thread, in brief, and earlier in the day he had mostly sat there and protested what a capable policeman he was and bragged about his dad and how much he'd meant to him and how he had had to sacrifice his life on duty and all that bullshit. I never met his father, but from what I'd heard I realized he was the spitting image of his son. Plus he drank like a fish. Lazy, incompetent, a bully, petty criminal, wife beater, drunk . . . and a policeman. We can't have it like that, Anna."

"But why did you show the investigation of cause of death to his son?" asked Holt.

"I'll get to that," said Johansson. "To show him that he could spare us that bullshit. To pull the rug out from under him. But it wasn't news to him. He'd known for a long time what had really happened when his dear dad closed up shop."

"Then there was no purpose in telling him that, was there?" Holt objected.

"Sure there was," said Johansson. "The purpose was to show that there were others besides him who knew. It hit home, if you ask me. If he could have chosen he would surely have admitted almost anything, just to avoid hearing that I knew the truth about his dad."

"I still think it was both cruel and unnecessary," said Holt.

"I hear what you're saying," said Johansson. "I don't think like you. Someone like Berg should never have become a policeman. Nor his dad either, and if I'd had anything better to hit him with than his hero of a dad of course I would have used that instead."

"You were never worried he might kill himself?"

"Not in the least," said Johansson. "Unfortunately he's not the type. He's the type who gladly kills other people. On the other hand, when it comes to himself he's both gentle and understanding."

"I think he's changed considerably, actually. I'm pretty sure he's a completely different and better person today."

"I don't believe that for a moment," said Johansson. "You, on the other hand, are a good person. An excellent police officer, a decent person. Too weak for someone like Berg, because you're a little too decent."

"What about you?" said Holt. "According to Berg—"

"I know," interrupted Johansson. "If you're wondering on your own account. Sure, I'm a consistent person. Good to the good, hard to the hard, and bad to the bad. Once upon a time when I was dealing with that sort of thing I was an excellent police officer too. One of the very best, actually. But if you're so worried about my character, I don't understand why you don't ask Lewin what he thinks of Berg."

"Lewin?"

"Your colleague Jan Lewin was around at that time. He was there and questioned Berg the same day that I visited him in jail later in the evening."

"But then he wasn't along," said Holt.

"No," said Johansson. "I would never dream of subjecting him to that, but if it's your meeting with that shitty little character Bäckström that's worrying you, I can take care of that myself."

"No," said Holt. "I'll arrange it."

"Excellent," said Johansson. "Find out what he wants and then you can boil the bastard for glue. Someone like Bäckström shouldn't be a policeman either."

What is going on? thought Bäckström. Here you try to help a lot of incompetent colleagues to finally put a little order in the Palme investigation and the only thing that happens is that they set police officers on you. Besides that nonentity who was his boss down at lost-and-found.

"Like I said, Bäckström, you will report immediately to Superintendent Holt at the bureau," said Bäckström's boss. This is the best day in a very long time, he thought. Finally a decent chance to get rid of that criminal little fatso his own boss had foisted off on him.

"If she wants to chat with me she can come here," said Bäckström. Fucking dyke, he thought.

"Like I said, Bäckström. This is not a general wish on my part. This is an order. You must report immediately to Police Superintendent Anna Holt at the National Bureau of Criminal Investigation," repeated Bäckström's boss. This is the best day of the whole summer, and I wonder just what he's thought up this time? he thought.

"Hello," said Bäckström, raising his hand in a deprecating gesture. "She can't give me any orders. I'm working in Stockholm. Has the national bureau taken over the Stockholm police district, or what? Have we had a fucking military coup?"

"Like I said, Bäckström. I'm the one who's giving you an order. I work here, in case you missed that. An order on duty. You must report immediately to Police Superintendent Holt at the national bureau." This is getting better and better, he thought.

"I promise to think about it," said Bäckström. "Now you'll have to excuse—"

"Go now, Bäckström," said his boss. "Otherwise I'm afraid you're going to spend the night in jail."

"Lay off. What for?" What the hell is this fairy saying? he thought.

"Johansson," said his boss. "Holt called on behalf of the boss." The butcher from Ådalen, he thought, and this was definitely the best day he'd had since he'd first met Bäckström.

"Why didn't you say that right away?" said Bäckström, getting up. Finally the Lapp bastard has understood his own best interest, he thought.

"Where's Johansson?" asked Bäckström ten minutes later, as soon as he sat down in the chair across from Holt. You skinny little wretch, he thought.

"Not here in any case," said Holt. "I'm the one you'll be talking with."

"I prefer to talk with Johansson," said Bäckström.

"I understand that," said Holt. "But it's like this," she continued. "You can talk with me and tell me what you want. If you don't want to we can go our separate ways and you will immediately stop harassing Johansson's secretary. If not, then we're going to file a complaint against you for unlawful threat, sexual assault, and official misconduct, so at a guess you'll be brought in for questioning later today."

"Lay off, Holt," said Bäckström. What the hell is that dyke sitting there saying? he thought.

"We have all your calls on tape," said Holt. "Our attorney has listened to them. According to him it's more than enough for a summons."

"What's in it for me?" said Bäckström. What do they mean by taping people secretly? That's criminal, damn it, he thought.

"Not much, I'm afraid," said Holt. "You're going to be reported as suspected of a crime, removed from duty, convicted of sexual assault, unlawful threat, and a number of other things. Believe me, Bäckström, I've listened to you on the tapes. Then you're going to get fired from the agency. The alternative is that you stop calling Johansson's secretary and tell me what you want to say. Maybe then I can convince Johansson not to file a complaint against you."

"Okay, okay," said Bäckström. "So it's like this. I've received a tip from one of my informants that concerns the weapon that was used when Palme was shot."

"That sounds like something you should talk about with Flykt," said Holt.

"Sure," said Bäckström. "So we can all read about it in the newspaper tomorrow."

"Hundreds of tips have come in about the Palme weapon," said Holt. "You know that as well as I do. What makes this tip so special?"

"Everything," said Bäckström with emphasis. "The informant's identity, to start with."

"What's his name?" said Holt.

"Forget that, Holt. I would never dream of exposing any of my informants. I'd rather go to jail. Forget about my informant. What counts is that the informant has the name of the man with the weapon," said Bäckström.

"Of the perpetrator?" asked Holt.

"Of the one who took care of the weapon," Bäckström clarified. "The spider in the web you might say." There, you got something good to suck on, you disturbed little sow, he thought.

"So give me a name."

"Forget it," said Bäckström, shaking his head. "You would never believe me if I told you."

"Try, Bäckström," said Holt, looking at the clock.

"Okay then," said Bäckström. "Blame yourself, Holt, but this is the way it is according to my informant, and who he is you can just forget. I know who he is. He's a white man. So forget about him now."

"I'm listening," said Holt. "Tell me what your anonymous informant has already told you. What he said about the weapon, who he's fingering, and how he knows it." A white man, thought Holt.

28

The special adviser lived in a palatial villa in the Uppland suburb of Djurs-holm, where the crème de la crème in the vicinity of the royal capital had the highest fat content. Twenty-plus rooms, 2,100 square feet, stone, wrought iron, brick, and copper. A hundred-yard-long asphalt driveway, an acre of lawn with shading oaks that weren't allowed to obscure the view. Not a vulgar waterfront location obviously, simply high and well-situated enough for morning sun and a clear view across Stora Värtan and Lidingö to the east. The special adviser would never have dreamed of swimming down in Framnäs bay where the IT billionaires and prop-erty swindlers held court.

Officially he didn't even live where he did. The villa was owned by his first wife—"clever as a poodle and faithful as a dog"—who had bought it thirty-five years earlier, only a few months before she was divorced from the man who had always lived there. Not a bad deal for a young woman who worked as a secretary at the military headquarters at Gär-det, earned 3,000 kronor a month at that time, and evidently didn't need to borrow a cent to execute the deal.

The special adviser himself was listed as living on Söder. A simple apart-ment with two rooms and a kitchen, and he was even in the telephone directory. Anyone who didn't know better could call there and talk with his answering machine or send a letter that would never be answered. The special adviser preferred a secret life, assembled of all the particular secrets that the truly initiated love to talk about, and he gladly contrib-uted his share.

The rumor was . . . that the special adviser was immensely wealthy. At the same time he lacked assessed property. He took no deductions, and his stated income agreed to the krona with the salary he had drawn from the government offices for almost thirty years. "I don't understand what people are talking about. I'm an ordinary wage earner. I've always been thrifty, but you don't get rich on that."

According to rumor . . . the special adviser had an art collection that would make the financier Thiel and Prince Eugen green with envy. "It's nice to have a little color on the walls. Most of this is actually on loan from my first wife." The same wife who'd moved to Switzerland thirty years earlier and was as quiet as a basenji. Immensely wealthy besides, according to the official information that the Swiss authorities unwillingly surrendered.

The rumor stated . . . that the special adviser had a wine cellar that, apart from the contents, could only be compared with Ali Baba's treasure chamber. "I appreciate a good glass of wine over the weekend and especially in the company of good friends. Because I'm extremely moderate of course I've accumulated a few bottles over the years."

The special adviser had been a member of the Social Democratic Party since he was a teenager attending high school. In his wallet he still carried his first party book, no photo, just his name, the party branch he belonged to, and old, handwritten receipts for the dues he'd punctually paid. "That's what characterizes us real Social Democrats. That we have both our hearts and our wallets to the left." He gladly showed the evidence that he carried in his left inside pocket, and presumably it was completely true.

According to the brief information in the *National Almanac, Who's Who,* and the *National Encyclopedia,* he was born in Stockholm in 1945, earned a doctorate in mathematics at Stockholm University in 1970, and was appointed professor in 1974. The following year he started as a technical adviser in the government offices ("technical adviser government offices 1975–76"), returned to the university and his professorship during the conservative administration of 1976–1982, then back as "special adviser at the disposal of the prime minister 1982–91," another pause during a three-year conservative administration when he worked as a visiting professor at MIT, back as "undersecretary 1994–2002." Since then he had evidently slowed down, "technical adviser in the government offices since 2002."

Finally a short recitation of his more important academic appointments: "Member of the Board of Directors of the Royal Academy of Science since 1990; Visiting Professor at MIT 1991–94; Honorary Fellow at Magdalen College, Oxford University, since 1980."

In the country where he lived there was no one like him—in any event there shouldn't be—and for a long time he had lived the myth that surrounded him. The special adviser, Sweden's own Cardinal Richelieu, the prime minister's top security adviser, the extended arm of power or perhaps simply power? In one of the few newspaper interviews with him he described himself as "a simple lad from Söder who's always been good at arithmetic."

Wonder what he plans to serve this evening? thought Johansson as the taxi stopped in front of the house where the man didn't live.

The special adviser received him under the crystal chandelier in the hall and in the most Mediterranean manner.

"Lovely to see you, Johansson," he said, standing on tiptoe, embracing his guest and marking two kisses on the cheek. "Let me look at you." He took a step back but without releasing his hand. "You look like the picture of health, Johansson," he continued.

"Nice of you," said Johansson, smiling as he coaxed his fist loose from the special adviser's damp grip. "You're doing well yourself, I hope?" Although you look awful, and what in the name of God have you got on? he thought.

. . .

The special adviser was just below average height. In school he'd been a chubby little boy who for obscure reasons had never been bullied. As an adult first corpulent, then fat, and nowadays truly obese. A rotund body, with spider-like arms and legs, topped by a good-sized head of thick gray hair that stood straight up and out at the sides over his large ears. His face was bright red in color, consisting mainly of forehead and a nose worthy of a conquistador. His eyes were large and clear blue, well entrenched behind heavy eyelids and bulging cheeks, the imposing nose, a round pouting mouth with moist lips like those of a small child, then a natural progression to the three flowing chins that sought shelter under the lining of his shirt collar. Taken as a whole he was clearly a person who must possess considerable inner qualities.

In honor of the day he was dressed in an improbable ensemble of green velvet. Baggy pants without creases, green jacket with shiny lapels, and held together with a thick braided silk cord that he'd wrapped around his body. Along with a tuxedo shirt with black bow tie and a pair of gold-embroidered velvet slippers.

"Thanks for asking," said the special adviser. "I feel truly excellent, exactly as I deserve. Like a pearl in gold. But you yourself, Johansson, you've become a real athlete lately. Soon you'll be looking like Gunde Svan, that skier—or was he a high jumper?—you know," he said with a slight wave of his left hand. "Shall we sit awhile and refresh ourselves while my dear housekeeper puts the final pieces in place?"

Then he made an inviting gesture and went ahead of Johansson across all the creaking parquet floors to the large salon where a small buffet was set out with mixed finger foods, a gigantic cut crystal vodka carafe, champagne, and mineral water in a table cooler.

Mostly beluga caviar, duck liver, and quail eggs, and why fritter away your short life on nonessentials? He still had free access to the beluga through one of his contacts "from the bad old days" who now ran an apparently successful contract operation in Kiev. The quail eggs he got from an acquaintance in the province of Sörmland, "a count and a land-owner interested in hunting," who also supplied him with pheasant, wild duck, grouse, and partridge. Plus all the "large game" of course. Such as moose filets, deer steaks, wild pig cutlets, and saddle of venison. His housekeeper shopped for the duck liver at the specialty food shops in the Östermalm market. On the other hand he'd stopped consuming goose liver. It was much too fat nowadays to be consumed in risk-free forms. Pure animal torture besides if you considered the source. He didn't drink beer anymore either, not good for either the stomach or the liver, and in the golden middle age in which he and Johansson were now living, they had to keep an eye on what they put away.

"Caution and precision should characterize temporal things as well," the special adviser summarized. "Water, vodka, champagne, and a little bite to eat with it. Cheers, by the way," he said, raising his full glass.

"Cheers," said Johansson. Talk, talk, talk, he thought.

After two sturdy shots, mineral water, a couple glasses of champagne, and ten or so small appetizers each it was time to sit down to a serious dinner. "No negligence this time," said the special adviser, shaking his flaming red face with emphasis. This evening he intended to compensate Johansson for previous frugal entertainments and treat him to "a really old-fashioned, bourgeois dinner." As soon as Johansson had accepted his invitation the special adviser had also conducted a number of "special reinforcement measures" to guarantee a successful result.

True, it was Thursday, but Johansson did not need to be troubled about either peas or pork. Much less pancakes with jam. The last time the special adviser had eaten such things was many years ago at a lunch at the defense department. Under silent protest, but unfortunately on duty and thereby without a choice. Before the end of this barbaric gathering he was already tormented by gas and for several days was confined to bed with tympanites, feverish and miserable, and if it hadn't been for the diet his considerate housekeeper had quickly established—plenty of Fernet Branca, boiled fish, light white wines, mineral water without bubbles—the situation might have ended very badly.

"How can the military be allowed to challenge our armed forces like that?" asked the special adviser with an indignant glance at his guest. According to him it was pure treason, and regardless of whether it was a crisis situation or not those responsible should be brought before a military court, convicted of high treason, and immediately executed. If the special adviser could decide, that is. Or even better, beheaded with a dull, rusty ax if they'd had the nerve to serve warm punch with the peas. Food that only barbarians could ingest, and according to the special adviser it was obviously not by chance that Hermann Göring was supposed to have been particularly fond of both peas and pork plus pancakes with whipped cream and jam. Not to mention warm punch.

Talk, talk, talk, and personally I think that sounds good, thought Johansson.

His host's reinforcement measures were clearly visible as soon as Johansson crossed the threshold to the dining room. The adviser's dining room table accommodated twenty-four guests, this too was a good old bourgeois custom, according to the host. Now it was set for two at one end of the table. The special adviser at the short end and his guest to his right. At a comfortable conversational distance without the risk of spilling on each other. On their plates were elaborate folded damask napkins plus printed menus, around them a parade of various cut crystal glasses and an improbable amount of silverware. Simply the host and his guest at a table for twenty-four and obviously only two place settings. But otherwise the table was completely set with a white linen tablecloth, candelabras, centerpieces, and flower arrangements.

In honor of the evening the special adviser's housekeeper had the help of a male steward in black tuxedo and a cook in full getup waiting in the background.

"Yum," said the special adviser delightedly, rubbing his fat hands together and sitting down as soon as his male reinforcement measure pulled the chair out for him.

Johansson had to seat himself, and it was probably his own fault. When his host's housekeeper hurried over to help him, he just shook his head deprecatingly and sat down. He quickly pulled in the chair and for lack of a straw reached for his napkin. I'm a simple boy from Näsåker. Hope she wasn't offended, thought Johansson. His mother, Elna, would never have dreamed of pulling out the chair for her husband or her seven children either as soon as they were big enough. On the other hand she often stood at the stove while the others ate. Here it was more complicated than that, thought Johansson, and when the day came that he wasn't man enough to seat himself it would probably be the end of most everything, he thought.

A nine-course dinner, different wines with every course, and already with the introductory consommé of lobster, finely shredded onions, and petits pois, the special adviser started the monologue that was his own variation on the cultivated conversation one was expected to carry on during the consumption of a bourgeois dinner. First of all however he spilled on himself. Just like happy children always have a habit of doing, and without even noticing it.

"I see you're admiring my tuxedo, Johansson," said the special adviser, sighing contentedly as he lowered the spoon and began his initial comments.

Despite the color it apparently had nothing to do with the French Academy. Such small societies for mutual admiration left the adviser cold. The French Academy was an ordinary, government-financed soup kitchen for various literary aesthetes who had never done an honorable day's work in their entire lives. As a mathematician he was above such things, and in his case it was far better than that. This was namely the particularly comfortable tuxedo that the special adviser would wear to dinner when he sat at High Table in the banquet hall at his English alma mater, Magdalen College, Oxford. Founded in the Middle Ages when most northern Europeans could barely express themselves comprehensibly, much less read, and obviously named for Mary Magdalene, the foremost of Jesus's female disciples.

"Mohdlinn, pronounced *Mohdlinn* without an English 'e' at the end," the special adviser clarified, pouting with enjoyment.

As Johansson perhaps didn't know, for many years his host had been an honorary member of this fine old college. Honorary fellow, first-class member of the faculty by virtue of his scientific merits in mathematics but also in the more philosophically oriented theory of science. Over the years there had been numerous prominent physicians, physicists, biologists, and chemists who had studied at Magdalen College, two Nobel Prize winners in fact, all of whom gratefully enjoyed the insights that were basically unique to the special adviser when it came to constructing intricate theoretical models and testing more complex empirical lines of reasoning.

"Speak up if I'm tiring you, Johansson," said the special adviser.

"Not at all," said Johansson. Better that than you drinking too much, he thought, and personally he intended to wait for coffee and cognac, when from experience he knew that his host would be in a more contemplative state.

Already by course number two—pilgrim clams with tomato, asparagus and Avruga caviar—his host had left the scientific world and taken a sidetrack. Magdalen had a particular quality that distinguished it from all other colleges, not only at Oxford but in the whole world, and that especially ought to appeal to a man like Johansson.

"We have our own deer enclosure," said the special adviser, smiling happily at his guest. "Think of it, Johansson. As an old hunter, I mean."

In the midst of the medieval main street in the world's foremost seat of learning, right behind the main buildings, walled in and along the river Cherwell, over three hundred years ago one of Magdalen's many benefactors had had a deer park constructed.

"Sounds like fallow deer," said Johansson.

"If you say so, Johansson," said the special adviser with the usual hand waving. "Those brown things with white spots on their sides. Some of them have horns," he clarified.

"Fallow deer," said Johansson. "Quite certainly fallow deer."

"Whatever," answered the special adviser, and in any event it wasn't the deer per se that was the point.

. . .

The point was better than that, and the special adviser did a proper job on all the details of the story while they enjoyed the third course, grilled king crab with veal sausage, grated potatoes, and a spicy sauce.

"Where was I now?" asked the special adviser as he wiped away a little sauce from his mouth and rinsed with an Alsatian pinot gris that was both refreshing and rich in minerals.

"The number of deer in the deer park," said Johansson, who was unwillingly getting interested in the subject.

"Exactly," said the special adviser, dabbing with his napkin. "As I've already suggested . . ."

The number of deer in the park should be, according to the donor's will, equal to the number of full members of the college. At the present time there were sixty fellows and honorary fellows, and in the park behind the main building there was thus exactly the same number of deer.

"So you have your own deer," said Johansson, raising his glass. A fat little rascal with a bad heart, gigantic head, short horns, and feeble legs. Approximately like the ones his children used to construct out of matches, pipe cleaners, and pinecones when they were little, he thought.

"Of course," said the special adviser, sounding rather conceited.

"But that's not all of it," he continued.

The story was even better than that, and all according to the original statutes. As soon as a new member of the college was inducted, the deer herd was increased by one deer. And if one of them died, the proctor—the students' own highest prefect—went out in the park and shot one deer, which was then served at the memorial dinner that was always held for the fellow who had taken leave of earthly life. The special adviser even claimed to have seen the proctor early one morning as he carried out this important task. Otherwise the deer were left in peace. Left to the pastoral peace that prevailed in the park at Magdalen College and in all the halls of learning.

"At the break of day, with the mist from the river sweeping into the park in its white veil, there comes the proctor in his long coat, his high black hat, with the worn-out shotgun in his steady hand. Imagine the shot, Johansson, that echoes out over the river Cherwell and the High Street," said the special adviser, sighing as voluptuously as the male protagonist in a novel by the Brontë sisters.

Although the dinner itself was nothing remarkable, he remarked. Just an ordinary English gentlemen's dinner, with venison steak, brown gravy, and overcooked vegetables. The wines on the other hand would usually be quite all right. A number of other benefactors had seen to that. The wine cellar at Magdalen was one of the foremost in Oxford. True, not like the one at Christ Church, with all those American Coca-Cola children, Arabian princes, and little Russian oligarchs, but quite all right, according to a connoisseur like himself.

"To be sure, English cuisine has little in common with this excellent filet of brill," Johansson agreed, having secretly peeked at the menu as soon as they'd made it to the fourth stage in the bourgeois dinner. Filet of brill with globe artichoke and étouffée of crayfish tail.

"Not to mention this phenomenal Meursault," the special adviser agreed, raising his large goblet of almost amber-colored wine. From his own cellar of course, and apart from the number of bottles completely in a class with the one served at Christ Church College, Oxford.

"There's one thing I don't really understand," said Johansson.

"You're much too modest, Johansson," said the special adviser.

"How you manage to keep the same number of deer as members of the college. If you only shoot them when someone dies," Johansson explained.

"What do you mean? Explain," said the special adviser.

Johansson's objections to the adviser's story, his explanations, the questions and counterarguments from his host, the entire discussion took up the remainder of their dinner, as new courses were continually brought in. Glasses were filled, raised, and lowered . . . the gooseberry sorbet to cleanse the palate, venison noisettes, chanterelles grilled in butter, roasted cauliflower, Cumberland sauce, cheese soufflé, Brie and truffles with apple jelly, cream cheese with plums, chocolate terrine, the concluding small pastries. New wines all the time . . . red from Burgundy . . . white from Bordeaux . . . from the Rhône and Loire . . . while an indefatigable Johansson—like a cavalry officer from the days of the Crimean War—rode ahead with the discussion of the special adviser's story about the deer in the park at Mary Magdalene's own college.

According to Johansson the whole thing was very simple. An enclosure with sixty fallow deer ought to reasonably include twenty or so fertile does, which in turn meant that you could count on twenty-some fawns around the end of June every year. If the enclosure had been there for three hundred years and you shot a deer only when a member of the college died, then the number of members of the same congregation ought to amount to several million by now, and as far as the more precise calculations were concerned, he would happily leave those to his host.

"You must have enormous recruiting problems every summer. All those new fellows who will suddenly be elected," said Johansson with an innocent expression.

There was really no question of that, according to the special adviser. He'd never really thought about how the exact details were solved. That the deer and their instincts would govern the selection of fellows was, on the other hand, inconceivable.

"What if a deer were to die? That sort of thing happens all the time," said Johansson. "How was that resolved? By showing a fellow the door or perhaps even expanding the proctor's assignment with the shotgun?"

This too was naturally ruled out, according to the special adviser who, however, promised to think about it.

"You are a real policeman, Johansson," he said for some reason.

"Of course I am," said Johansson. "Think about it, as we said."

. . .

Then Johansson thanked him for dinner with a few well-chosen words, and his host got up from the table so they could continue their conversation in the library in peace and quiet, have a cup of coffee, and perhaps a glass or two of the special adviser's downright remarkable cognac.

"Frapin 1900," said his host with a happy sigh. "Think how good we rich people have it, Johansson."

29

Over coffee they finally got to the point, and it was his host who raised the issue. For whatever reason, thought Johansson.

During his vacation, of which he had spent a week at Magdalen to ponder the larger questions in peace and quiet, the special adviser had understood, from the Swedish newspapers he'd still been reading, that his guest had apparently breathed new life into the old investigation of the assassination of his first boss, Prime Minister Olof Palme. Why, on the other hand, he hadn't understood. According to his firm opinion it was Christer Pettersson who had murdered Palme. Pettersson was now dead. In any event it was much too late in the day, time to wipe the slate clean, forget the whole thing and move on.

"Let bygones be bygones," he summarized.

According to Johansson a person should be very careful about believing everything that appeared in the newspaper. What he'd done was simply assign a few co-workers to look over the indexing of the material. That was all, and it was high time, by the way, that it was done.

"You don't think it was Christer Pettersson who did it?" his host interrupted.

"Because it's you who's asking," said Johansson, "no. I never have."

"But why in the name of God then," objected his host. "Lisbeth actually singles him out."

"Even the best can make a mistake," said Johansson.

"You'll have to excuse me but the logic of what you're saying—"

"He doesn't feel right," interrupted Johansson, indicating by rubbing his right index finger against his right thumb. "If you want details I can ask one of my co-workers to give you a presentation."

"To me he feels quite right," said the special adviser. "Unfortunately," he added.

According to Johansson's host, Christer Pettersson was a step in a logical progression. A woeful progression to be sure, but nonetheless a logical one. First there was an eccentric aristocrat, with certain radical ideas for the time, who murdered Gustav III at an opera masquerade for the upper classes. Then a middle-class child who had gone wrong in life and grew up to be a drug-addled hooligan who shot his own prime minister on the street. In the midst of all the ordinary citizens. Now most recently a crazy Serb had cut down the country's foreign minister in the most bestial way when she was shopping for clothes at the city's largest department store among all the other prosperous middle-class female shoppers.

"What should we expect next time, Johansson?" asked his guest with a sorrowful expression. "The old orangutan from the Rue de Morgue? Or perhaps the swamp adder in Conan Doyle's story about the speckled band?"

"More of the opera masquerade, if you ask me," said Johansson. "There's no time for monkeys or adders. They're too unpredictable."

"Yet another solitary madman, if you ask me," said the special adviser. "Even solitary madmen can change the world, unfortunately. They do it all the time, actually."

Because they were still on the subject Johansson had a question of his own. More precisely, one of his many co-workers had a question for his host, and he had actually promised to ask him.

"She knows we know each other," Johansson explained. "She worked with me at SePo."

"Of course," said the special adviser. Johansson was free to ask him about everything. In contrast to all his colleagues, who he was now much too old and tired to bear talking with.

The prime minister's plans to go to the movies that evening more than twenty years ago. Just how known were they at his office in Rosenbad?

"I've already been asked that question," said the special adviser, smiling.

"I know," said Johansson. "I've read the interview. I also know that you spoke with Berg about the matter in the afternoon of the same day Palme was shot. Not much was said."

"How would that look, Johansson? If someone like me exchanged confidences with people like that? It's bad enough that they exchange confidences with each other, and I'm actually a little surprised that Berg, who was a relatively well-organized person for being a policeman, had the poor judgment to submit a memo about our secret conversation into the investigation. And what is it that suddenly causes me to sense the sweet odor of a so-called conspiracy in the vicinity of the victim?"

"We're that way, us cops," said Johansson. "We wonder about strange coincidences, write little notes to each other."

"Yes, I've realized that. Personally I keep such things in my head. My own head."

"Tell me about it," said Johansson. "You knew the victim. Personally I never met him. What was he like? As a person?"

A talented person. At the same time a person of feeling. An impulsive person. In a good mood a very charming, entertaining, and considerate person. In a bad mood he was a different person, and in the worst case his own enemy.

"I've understood that he was very talented," said Johansson.

"Oh well," said the special adviser. "He had that quick, superficial, intuitive gift. Verbal, educated, the right background. He had all that in abundance. Although the really difficult questions he preferred to avoid. The questions that don't have any definite answers. Or, in the best case, several answers, none of which is clearly better than the others. The kinds of questions that I, and you too, Johansson, are drawn to. Like the moth that's drawn to the kerosene lamp. Although what you want to know is actually something else," he added.

"What do you mean by that?" said Johansson.

"You're wondering if he had the habit of running around among his co-workers, asking them what movies he should see?"

"Did he do that?"

"When he was in the mood. As I already suggested. When Olof was happy and suddenly stood there in the doorway to your office and just wanted to talk a little, then you were happy too. Genuine happiness and not so strange perhaps considering who he was and considering who you were. One time he even asked me if I could recommend a film."

"So what did you say?" said Johansson.

"That I never went to the movies," said the special adviser. "That I thought it was an overrated diversion. The temple of the fearful. Wasn't that what Harry Martinson said? Besides, I thought it was inappropriate for purely security reasons for him to do that. If it really was absolutely necessary for him, I assumed he would inform those responsible for his security in good time. The secret police, myself, all the others affected."

"So what did he say?" asked Johansson.

"That I was a real cheerful little fellow," said the special adviser. "He was in a good mood that day."

"The day he was murdered then," said Johansson.

"The only time he asked me for movie advice I've just mentioned to you. That was long before he died. Then I think he never returned to the question. I know I would recommend the occasional ethnic restaurant to him. Sure. Could he have asked someone else? Perhaps. I don't know. I didn't even know that he had such plans the day he was murdered. I remember that Berg was nagging about that when we talked on the phone in the afternoon."

"But you didn't talk with the prime minister about it?"

"No," said the special adviser. "It never happened, but considering what did happen perhaps I ought to have done that."

Suddenly he's as clear as crystal, thought Johansson. Not a trace of all the wine he's poured into himself. Suddenly a completely different person.

During the remainder of the evening the special adviser quickly recovered his usual amiable self—given that he was in the mood—and, just as expected, the dinner degenerated in the pleasant manner that bourgeois dinners supposedly never deviated from in the good old days.

First they played billiards. The evening's host insisted. He demanded to teach Johansson how you played billiards. If Johansson refused, it wasn't the first time the issue had come up, the alternative was that Johansson teach him how to shoot a pistol and on the police department's own firing range besides.

"Believe it or not, Johansson, but when I did my military service I was actually an excellent rifleman."

Faced with this alternative Johansson had no choice. He played billiards with the special adviser, and even though it was the second time in his life he thrashed him soundly. The special adviser excused himself citing all the good wine with dinner and offering difficult-to-interpret statements about the obligations of being a good host.

Then they had a light supper in the special adviser's laboratory-like kitchen. Herring; crayfish; and Jansson's temptation, grilled sausages; small beef patties topped with fried eggs; a multitude of various kinds of schnapps; and an improbable selection of beers. Despite their health-impairing qualities and obviously solely out of consideration for his guest.

"I thought you would surely want a little pilsner before going to bed," said the special adviser, raising his foaming glass.

When Johansson was standing on the front steps with his hand extended to say farewell, his host anticipated him in the most Mediterranean manner. Got up on tiptoe, placed his arms on his shoulders, and gave him two moist kisses, one on each cheek. When the taxi drove away he was still standing there. With raised arms, the baggy green jacket pulled up over his belly. In his delicate boy tenor he'd given his guest a concluding homage in song. The choice of music quite certainly inspired by the instructive conversation they'd carried on during dinner.

"We'll meet again, don't know where, don't know when, but I know we'll meet again . . . some sunny day . . ."

30

What Anna Holt was up to was unclear. Lewin and Mattei on the other hand devoted the whole weekend to going through the investigation's material on more qualified perpetrators. So far, however, none of the individuals they had scrutinized was particularly impressive, measured by Johansson's standards. Mattei was also struck by the fact that the number of suspects of foreign origin was surprisingly small. Normally this number would be considerable, and haunting the back of her mind was also the testimony of Witness Three, the woman who shouted "fucking gook" at the man who'd run into her only two hundred yards from the crime scene.

Mattei was clear about why almost immediately. As so often before, it was due to the way the case files had been registered. The usual proportions obtained, but this time the perpetrators of foreign origin had been piled under common lead files with titles such as "German Terrorism," "PKK Track," "Middle East including Israel," "South Africa," "Iran/Iraq," "Turkey," and "India/Pakistan." Clearly the most common reason that an individual ended up in one pile and not another was the suspected perpetrator's ethnic origin, or more precisely the Swedish police's perception of his ethnic origin, but the exceptions were numerous and the logic far from crystal clear.

In the lead file that dealt with German terrorism, a number of Swedes appeared that SePo had surveyed in the 1970s and '80s in connection with the drama at the West German embassy and the plans to kidnap the Swedish minister for immigration Anna-Greta Leijon. It was also here that Mattei stumbled on the first spotlighted perpetrator who fit Johansson's template. A Swedish former paratrooper from Karlsborg who during the seventies was suspected of having robbed a number of banks in Germany along with some members of the Red Army Faction. What he had been up to later was unclear. Where he was, whether he was alive or dead, was also unclear.

On the other hand it was clear that he had attracted the interest of the Palme investigators. Along with thirty-some other named Swedish military personnel, he was also included in the so-called "military track." There were even two cross-references in the files to make it easier to find him. That was something that Mattei was not otherwise accustomed to finding in the course of her diligent reading.

Why he would have reason to murder Palme was, however, veiled in darkness.

So what do I do about you then, little old man? sighed Mattei, even though he must be almost twice as old as she was if he was still alive.

Serbs and Croats, Bosnians and Slovenes, Christians and Muslims all over the place, and even though they'd been at one another's throats since ancient times the Swedish police finally united them all under a joint lead file, "Suspected Perpetrators with Yugoslav Connection." Police logic left it at that, both in the Balkans and elsewhere in the wide world outside Sweden.

Basically every Yugoslav gangster who had been active in Sweden and had sufficient hair on his chest was also on the investigation's list of conceivable or even probable Palme assassins. The majority of them were ordinary felons, convicted for murder and robbery, blackmail, hired gun and protection rackets, and everything else that could provide a person with a decent income without having to stoop to ordinary wage labor.

Where committing violence against others was concerned they had an impressive list of credits. Aggravated and instrumental violence to enrich themselves. Their motives for also having murdered Sweden's prime minister, like the reasons that were provided, were consistently weak or nonexistent. Various anonymous informants, the classic means among hoods and bandits to rat out a competitor, old police prejudices pulled out of the archives where they'd been unexamined for years.

The oldest contribution to the "Yugoslav track" came from the

Swedish secret police and was already fifteen years old at the time of the assassination. Three terrorist actions from the early 1970s: the occupation of the Yugoslav consulate in Gothenburg in February 1971, the embassy occupation and murder of the ambassador in Stockholm two months later, the airplane hijacking at Bulltofta in Malmö in September of the following year. The perpetrators were in all cases Croatian activists involved in armed resistance against the Serbian administration of the Yugoslav republic.

In the extensive investigation, mixed reasons were given for why these terrorists could have murdered Palme. As individuals they were described as "fascists," "political extremists," "aggressive psychos," and "extremely violence prone." In addition they were "hateful" toward the prime minister and the Swedish government that had kept them locked up in jail for fifteen years. On the other hand as far as the law itself was concerned the evidence was nonexistent, the indicators weak and contradictory, the investigative results nil.

If they really had murdered Palme—"that they had very strong reasons to want to see Olof Palme eliminated and that this motive is one of the most convincing in the entire investigation"—then of course their categorical denial conflicted with their whole terrorist tradition, their worldview, and their own personalities. "It was the most ridiculous thing I'd ever heard," as one of them summarized their common attitude, when before an interrogation he was named as being suspected of complicity in the murder of the Swedish prime minister.

I'm inclined to agree with you, and because you've been in prison in Kumla the whole time it wasn't you at any rate who ran into Witness Three on David Bagares gata, thought Lisa Mattei, taking out the binder with the "Iran/Iraq track."

All due respect to the violent traditions of the Balkans, but what do we have here? she thought.

On March 5, less than a week after the murder, an anonymous informant called the Swedish secret police with a tip. The day before in the morning "on Riksgatan between the two parliament buildings" he had observed "a slightly balding man, about thirty-five years old, dressed in a brown coat, black pants, and black shoes." The man appeared to be "under the influence of something, behaved aggressively, and called out Olof Palme's name at least three times." According to the informant, he was "Iranian or possibly Iraqi," was named "Yussef, or possibly Yussuf, Ibrahim," and "worked as a dishwasher at the Opera Cellar," a few blocks away from the Parliament Building.

The secret police's searches had yielded no results. At the Opera Cellar there were "so many dishwashers and janitors of foreign extraction that the tip based on the description was of very limited use." It was thus not possible to locate any "Yussef, alternatively Yussuf, Ibrahim at the referenced place of business." The one who best agreed with the meager facial description, a Tunisian, first name Ali, had an alibi for the relevant points in time and was still filed in the "Iran/Iraq" binder despite his place of origin and despite the fact that the secret police had eliminated him over twenty years earlier.

Wonder how the informant knew his name was Yussef? thought Mattei and sighed. And only after another three hours of browsing and reading was it time for her to take yet another binder out of the pile.

Suleyman Özök, born on February 28, 1949, and thus thirty-seven years old to the day when the prime minister was murdered, had come to Sweden in 1970, trained as a mechanic, and at the time of the murder was working as a repairman at Haga Auto Body Repair on Hagagatan in Stockholm. According to the informant "only a stone's throw from the crime scene."

The informant had not demanded to be anonymous other than in relationship to the perpetrator about whom he intended to turn in information. Fourteen days after the murder he visited the detective bureau on Kungsholmsgatan in Stockholm and reported that he was "a hundred and twenty percent certain that Suleyman Özök had murdered Sweden's prime minister."

According to the informant, Özök was actually a secret agent for the Turkish military dictatorship and his work at the auto body repair shop was only a cover. His real mission was to keep the Kurdish refugees in the country under surveillance and if needed conduct "wet work" for his employers.

Özök was an almost notorious Palme hater, and the reason was the support that Palme and the Swedish government had given to the Kurds who fled from Turkey and sought asylum in Sweden. Özök had access to "at least one pistol and a revolver" that he had shown the informant on several occasions. Most recently, on Tuesday of the same week the prime minister was murdered, he had taken the revolver out of the glove compartment of his car, shown it to the informant, and on the same occasion said that over the weekend he "intended to celebrate my birthday in an honorable way by shooting that swine Olof Palme."

The same evening the prime minister was murdered the informant "by pure coincidence" happened to pass Tegnérlunden in Stockholm, "only a stone's throw from the Grand cinema," and then discovered that Özök's private car was parked on the street on the north side of Tegnérlunden. Because he did not know that the prime minister "was sitting watching a movie just then only a stone's throw farther down the street," he hadn't thought any more about it, but instead took the subway home to his apartment on Stigfinnargränd in Hagsätra, where he also spent the night.

When he turned on the TV the next morning he was in such severe shock that it took fourteen days before he managed to gather himself to the point that he could contact the police.

Apparently he had made a deep impression on them. Özök had immediately been categorized under the lead file that then still went under the designation "Turkey/PKK." The investigator presented the case to the prosecutor, who decided that Özök should be picked up for questioning without prior summons and that the police should do a search of his house in Skogås, his car, and his place of work.

The efforts were extensive. The outcome meager. No weapons had been found. The closest they got was some fishing equipment. Özök was an enthusiastic sports fisherman both in Stockholm's archipelago and in various lakes in the vicinity of the capital. In addition he liked soccer and had been a loyal Hammarby supporter for many years. Most of all he was upset at the police and their informant.

He had never had any firearms. Thus he could never have shown anyone any. He admired Olof Palme, a great man and politician. He had never expressed criticism of him. Much less threatened him. On the contrary, he had taken his side in a number of political discussions at his workplace, Haga Auto Body Repair. He had been a Swedish citizen for many years. He did not intend to return to Turkey even on vacation. Turkey was a military dictatorship. Suleyman Özök was a democrat, a Social Democrat to be precise, and a proud one. He preferred to live in social democratic Sweden despite the sorrow and loss after Palme. He had given up hope on his old homeland long ago.

Finally he had a message for the anonymous informant. If he did not immediately stop harassing him and his new woman, Suleyman would deal with the matter personally. On the other hand he did not intend to make a police complaint. In an auto body repairman's world there were more substantial, manly means, if such were required.

"You can tell him that if he even tries to touch my lady I'll stuff a welding iron up his ass," said Suleyman Özök to his interviewer, but it hadn't amounted to more than that.

From the concluding notation in Özök's file it appeared that "Suleyman has been engaged for some time to a former female acquaintance of the informant. Özök's fiancée works as a secretary at Stockholm University and lives in a service apartment at Teknologgatan 2, in the vicinity of Tegnérlunden. She does not appear in the crime registry."

Late on Friday afternoon Lewin and Mattei took a long coffee break at an Italian café in the vicinity of police headquarters and discussed their findings of the past week. They each had a café latte. Mattei threw all moderation overboard and feasted on some tiramisu while the ever-cautious Lewin was content to nibble at the biscotti with almond and nuts that came with his coffee. Despite the weekend calm, the beautiful weather, the cheerful atmosphere at the table, and the article of faith that they must always embrace the situation, it had been a conversation under a cloud of resignation.

Together they had reviewed—or at least read about—almost a thousand suspects who, in at least a formal sense, met their criteria of a qualified perpetrator. Upon closer consideration, few of them proved to fulfill these criteria, and what they all had in common was that nothing tangible argued for their having murdered the prime minister twenty years ago. There was a shortage of motives, and even if the police had found the means and opportunities they still would not have been able to find the motive, although hundreds of man-hours had been devoted to certain cases.

At the same time only a few of the suspects could be ruled out with complete certainty. The normal reason was that they were in a correctional facility at the time of the crime, not on the run or on leave or able to sneak out unnoticed. That it was certain that they had been somewhere else, sufficiently far away or with people who were reliable enough that the police could live with their alibis. In summary almost all were investigative question marks, difficult enough to straighten out back then, probably quite impossible to get straight today.

A contributing reason to the latter was that a strikingly large share of them were now dead. When the prime minister was shot, the median age of the men in the group that Lewin and Mattei were reviewing was just over forty. Today it was sixty plus among the sixty percent of them who were still alive.

There were unusual causes of death. Twenty of them had been murdered over the years. Compared with regular, decent folk this was a hundred times more than the expected rate. A hundred of them had committed suicide, a rate twenty-five times greater than it ought to have been. Another couple of hundred had died in accidents, of drug abuse–related diseases, or of "unknown" causes. That rate was ten times greater than normal. Finally fifty or so had simply "disappeared," and it was unclear where and why.

"I got the list from our CIS squad this morning," said Lewin, sneaking a look at a small piece of paper. "But you seemed so occupied by your reading I didn't want to disturb you."

"More than a third have died," Mattei summarized. "Instead of about seven percent, as in the normal population, I mean."

"I wonder what the mortality rate is among our informants and witnesses," sighed Lewin, as if he were thinking out loud.

The same as for those they singled out, thought Mattei.

"What do we do?" she asked.

Talk with Anna Holt about it. Look at the military and police track because they'd looked at all the rest anyway. Talk with Johansson. Explain to him that his idea of this variation of an internal investigation lacked any conceivable possibility of success. That it was simply too late. That it was time to wipe the slate clean. That what remained was simply the hope of some decisive lead.

"The one we'll never get," said Lewin, sipping his coffee. "Not a moment before the clock strikes twelve in any case," he noted, shaking his head.

"Oh well," objected Mattei. "There are still three years, six months, six days, and a little over six hours left," she said, looking at her watch to be on the safe side.

"Three years, six months, six days, six hours . . . and thirty-two minutes . . . if mine is running right," said Lewin, looking at his watch.

"Yes, and here we are, lazing around," said Mattei. You're overworked, she thought.

"I was thinking about continuing that over the weekend, lazing around, that is," said Lewin.

Then they went their separate ways. Lewin walked to the subway to return to his apartment at Gärdet. He meant to shop on the way. Mattei didn't have anything particular in mind, until she suddenly discovered that she was outside the entryway to her office in the big police building on Kungsholmen.

I guess you didn't have anything better to do, she thought as she passed the guard in reception, held up her police badge, and drew her pass card through the card reader in the entry passage.

Exactly three years, six months, and six days left, she thought after a quick look at her watch six hours later.

Then she opened the end paper of the last of the thirty-one individual files that were in the three binders that contained the Palme investigation's "military track." The one that concerned a baron and captain who ended up last in the alphabetically ordered list of brethren because he was registered under "v" as in "von" and not under his real surname. He was fifty-five years old when the prime minister was assassinated, and in an opinion piece in *Svenska Dagbladet* a year before the murder he had criticized the murder victim because he had neglected Swedish defense and had been much too indulgent to the great neighbor in the east. An officer and a gentleman, as well as an aristocrat, politically incorrect, and, in the eyes of the Palme investigators, possibly a latter-day Anckarström.

Ay, ay, ay, now it's really starting to heat up, thought Lisa Mattei. Then she had a serious attack of the giggles and was forced to hunt for a tissue to dry her tears and blow her nose.

31

Late on Friday afternoon—about the same time as Lewin and Mattei were taking their coffee break at a nearby Italian café—Superintendent Anna Holt looked in on her chief to report what she was up to. The secretary's office was empty and the door to her boss's office was wide open. Johansson was lying on his couch, reading a thick book with an English title Holt was not familiar with, by an author she did not recognize. He seemed to be in an excellent mood.

"Sit yourself down, Anna," said Johansson, waving his thick book in the direction of the nearest armchair.

"Thanks," said Anna.

"Well, well," said Johansson, changing to a semi-reclined position. "Because Bäckström has stopped poisoning life for Helena I realize you've battered that little fatty. What can I do for you in return?"

"It would be good if I could return to my normal work assignments," said Holt.

"Everything has its time, Anna," said Johansson, making a deprecatory hand gesture. "Tell me. What kind of bullshit did he want to sell us this time?"

"He got a tip a few weeks ago. It was Friday the seventeenth of August. The day after all the articles reported that we'd started up the Palme investigation again."

"Imagine that," said Johansson.

"Yes," said Holt. "I understand what you're thinking. The tip comes from one of Bäckström's own informants. This one seems to have turned in tips to Bäckström on a previous occasion and is according to him a very experienced and reliable individual."

"You don't say," said Johansson. "So he wants to be anonymous of course."

"Of course. Although Bäckström knows who he is. They seem to have known each other a long time, according to Bäckström, and he has no intention of giving out his name. Otherwise he sounds more or less as usual."

"Well, perhaps he's found his place in life. The police lost-and-found warehouse. If he didn't steal so much I would've made a parking garage guard out of him," said Johansson. "Did he have anything to offer?"

"It's unclear," said Holt. "I'm in the process of checking that part. But probably not."

"Surprise, surprise," said Johansson.

"Although he actually gave us a name," said Holt.

"A name? What kind of name?"

"Of that bastard you're always harping about," said Holt, smiling for some reason.

"So what's his name?" asked Johansson, sitting up on the couch, and now he was no longer smiling.

"Not a bad name, actually," Holt teased. "We'll really have to hope it doesn't add up."

Esperanza was not only beautiful to look at with her harmonious lines and well-balanced proportions. She was also well built, with keel stock, frame, and plating made of oak from the mainland where the oaks grow more slowly than here and give better timber. Built entirely of wood with blue-coated carvel-built planks, white-painted railing, and a teak deck. She was twenty-eight feet long and ten feet across. Softly rounded at the stern, slightly concave bows tapering toward the stern and room for a small cabin forward. The deck was a good size, with plenty of room for fishing tackle and diving equipment. She had a reliable engine too, a four-cylinder, two-hundred-horsepower Volvo Penta marine diesel, and a good-sized fuel tank.

A boat built for all types of weather and the vicissitudes of life. To moor in the sunshine on the smooth sea; to eat, drink, and socialize. To fish and dive from. To rest in or simply sit leaning back against the railing while you cooled your hands and arms in the reflecting water. But also strong and tenacious enough to make its way to the mainland on either the Spanish, French, or African side, as long as the winds kept below hurricane force. Or perhaps to Corsica, where the boat's owner had at least one friend he trusted unconditionally, and where there were many like him. To Corsica, three hundred nautical miles and a thirty-hour run northeast of Puerto Pollensa, where he could find a refuge for the remainder of his life if he needed it.

32

Bäckström was little, fat, and primitive, but if necessary he could be both sly and slow to forget.

Of the country's seventeen thousand police officers he was also the one who had the largest professionally adapted vocabulary, with hundreds of crude names for everyone he didn't like: immigrants, homosexuals, criminals, and regular Joes regardless of gender. In brief, everyone who wasn't like him, of which there were extremely few. Taken together these human qualities had made him famous within the corps he had served for thirty years. Detective Chief Inspector Evert Bäckström was a "legendary murder investigator" who, in contrast to most other legends, was active in one thing or another.

A year earlier he had been exiled from his natural habitat at the National Homicide Commission to the Stockholm police department's property investigation squad. Or the police lost-and-found warehouse as all real policemen, including Bäckström himself, called this final storage place for stolen bicycles, lost wallets, and strayed police souls.

Bäckström was a victim. Of unfortunate circumstances in general and evil plots in particular. But most of all of the Royal Swedish Envy. His former chief, Lars Martin Johansson, simply could not cope with Bäckström's successful battle against the constantly increasing and ever more serious criminality. When Bäckström solved an unusually complicated murder case of a young female police candidate from Växjö, Johansson wove a rope from all the strands of slander, put the noose around Bäckström's neck, and personally gave him the final kick.

Despite an unsympathetic, grudging, and flat-out destructive environment, Bäckström tried to make the best of his situation. Work as a property investigator offered interesting opportunities for anyone sufficiently alert to seize opportunity in flight. That wouldn't include his new colleagues, who were a deplorable congregation of unimaginative pietists who did not even realize that they were sitting with the whole bunch of keys to the gigantic treasure chest that contained "stolen," "misplaced," or simply "ownerless" goods. Something that Bäckström of course realized as soon as he crossed the threshold to his new place of work.

The most deplorable colleague at his new job was an old acquaintance from the time when Bäckström worked at the homicide squad in Stockholm, Detective Inspector Göran Wiijnbladh. Wiijnbladh had worked at the Stockholm police technical squad until 1990, when he took partial retirement and was moved over to what was then the lost property warehouse. He was a technician from the old tribe, and apart from six years of elementary school, less than a year at the old police academy, and a few weeklong courses for crime technicians, he had carefully avoided all theoretical digressions, firmly convinced as he was that the only knowledge worth the name was what had been obtained through practical work. It was this attitude that would prove to be his misfortune.

Wiijnbladh's major problem at that time was that his wife had betrayed him. This was relatively simple, in that she made up approximately ninety-nine percent of his total quantity of problems. It was worse that she did it quite openly, which considering the nature of the operation also conflicted with its fundamental idea. Worst of all, however, was that she preferred to do it with other police officers, and because this had been going on since the day after their wedding, there wasn't a department in the Stockholm police where one or more co-workers hadn't put horns on fellow officer Wiijnbladh.

In the autumn of 1989 Wiijnbladh decided to do something about this by poisoning her with thallium he had come across at work. During his preparations he happened to poison himself. He handled his thallium the same way he was accustomed to dealing with fingerprint powder.

He got microscopic quantities on his fingers and hands, suffered acute poisoning, and almost died to boot. When he came back from the hospital a few months later, he was only a splinter of his former self. Though he hadn't been particularly imposing to begin with.

The whole thing had been hushed up by police leadership. With assistance from the police officers union the event was transformed into a tragic workplace accident, which the parties then resolved on the best of terms. Wiijnbladh was given a half-time pension and a decent one-time compensation for employment injury, and the half of him that remained was moved to the unit that later that same year changed its name from Stockholm police lost property warehouse to the Stockholm police property investigation squad.

There he'd been for the past fifteen years, occupied with stolen art and stolen antiques. Why this area in particular, no one understood. He did not seem to possess any particular expertise in the subject, but because it seemed harmless enough he'd been allowed to stay there. In the very smallest room at the end of the corridor sat Wiijnbladh, browsing through all his binders of stolen and misplaced artworks. He would drink his coffee in solitude in the same room, and none of his co-workers really had any idea when he came and went. No one cared, and soon he would take retirement.

It'll be nice to be rid of that little half-fairy, thought Bäckström in his sympathetic way the few times he'd seen him sneak past in the corridors.

Although to start with he'd had some benefit from him.

About the same time Bäckström arrived at his new workplace, the squad got one of its biggest cases in many years. An eccentric Swedish billionaire, who'd had his official and actual residence in Geneva for ages, had a break-in in his "overnight apartment" in Stockholm. An ordinary, simple, ten-room apartment on Strandvägen where, according to information from the Swedish tax authorities, he stayed at the most a few times a year. "It's usually a week around Christmas and New Year's, and perhaps another week when I'm home to celebrate Midsummer or visit my children," the man had said. Probably this was also the reason that it took almost a month before the Stockholm police became aware of the extent of the crime.

On Pentecost Eve, Saturday the third of June, the police command center received an alarm from Securitas of a crime in progress on Strandvägen. The reason that help was being requested from their government-financed competitor was that their own response vehicle happened to run into a bicyclist in Östermalm, approximately half a mile from the scene of the crime. In addition this was urgent, because the frightfully advanced alarm system that had been installed a few years earlier was completely convinced that the thief was still at the crime scene—according to the same system he appeared to be alone.

The police seldom got such an opportunity to rap their private-sector competitors on the knuckles, and in the general delirium unfortunately the officers in the radio car that arrived first forgot to turn off both the blue lights and the siren as they braked outside the entryway. The perpetrator had been scared off, and when the apartment was finally entered it was empty. The thief had sneaked out through the kitchen entry, across the back courtyard, and out to the street on the other side of the block. No one was arrested, but the outcome was good enough because it appeared that he hadn't managed to make off with anything from the overnight apartment, which could best be described as an "art museum" according to the technicians and experts from the property investigation squad who were called to the scene. This was also the information that the security company gave the customer when he was called at home in Switzerland.

Break-in at the apartment. Now taken care of by additional protective measures. Break-in interrupted. The thief had departed from the scene and it seemed that he hadn't taken anything with him. No technical clues had been secured. Perpetrator unknown. Only three weeks later, when the crime victim showed up to celebrate Midsummer—"have some pickled herring, a shot or two of aquavit, listen to Evert Taube, and watch the sun go down behind the dear old outhouse"—had they realized the extent of what had happened.

The crime victim's attorney then contacted both the security company and the Stockholm police to report that the thief had not left as empty-handed as they had asserted. Despite the sirens down on the street, the perpetrator had managed to take with him a small oil painting by Pieter Bruegel the Younger, which the owner of the apartment had hung in his guest toilet to annoy guests who weren't as rich as he was.

The crime victim was a taciturn man, and neither his security company nor the police made a big deal of it. There was not a word in the newspapers, although the stolen painting had an insurance value of thirty million Swedish kronor. In the greatest possible silence an extensive investigation had begun. Even if clues were completely lacking and despite the fact that in principle the painting was unsellable.

Bäckström heard about it all as he sat in the break room. Personally he didn't work with art thefts. No paintings, no antiques, not even a pitiful little silver candlestick was allowed to cross his desk for some reason. He had been assigned more substantial things, and since the first day he had been fully occupied with an Estonian freight truck found abandoned in a parking lot up at Norrtälje. Upon closer examination it proved to contain almost two hundred stolen bicycles.

"Here's something for you to bite into, Bäckström," said his immediate supervisor as he set the investigation file on his desk.

"What the hell should I do with this shit?" said Bäckström, glaring acidly at the multipage list of stolen goods.

"How about finding the owners?" said his boss with a sneering smile. "Welcome, by the way," he added.

Now this is war, goddamn it, thought Bäckström, and how the hell do you go about telling two hundred bikes apart? Personally he didn't know anyone who needed a bike. The only people who bike are homos, dykes, treehuggers, and anorexics. Even the Chinese drive cars nowadays, he thought.

Now it's a matter of embracing the situation if you're not going to starve to death, thought Bäckström, and after some pondering he remembered a female acquaintance he'd met on the Internet. She worked as a dental hygienist in Södertälje and surely needed a bicycle. She was a real barn owl who always ran around in home-sewn clothes and gave him a batik T-shirt she'd dyed herself back in the day. If she deals in that kind of shit she probably bicycles too, thought Bäckström. Sitting and rubbing herself on some old saddle, and what the hell did a horndog like that have to choose from? he thought.

A few things as it turned out, as soon as he got hold of her by phone. For one thing her new fiancé, who worked as district chief with the local police in Solna, had given her a car of her own. For another she already had a bicycle. Third, she thought it was a strange coincidence to say the least that Bäckström had a bike to sell. Almost new, and cheap besides. Fourth, she was seriously considering calling Bäckström's boss and letting him know about this.

"What the hell do you mean by that?" asked Bäckström.

"My guy told me you got a job at the police lost-and-found warehouse," she replied.

"Hello, little lady," said Bäckström. "You don't think I'm so fucking dense that I'm trying to foist a stolen bike off on you?" Now it's a matter of damming the creek before the shit ends up in the river, he thought.

"Yes," she said, "I think you really are that dense." Then she just hung up.

Fucking cunt lips, and what the hell do I do now? thought Bäckström, but because he'd always had a lucky streak it worked out anyway. The very next evening he ran into an old acquaintance he'd gotten to know at his neighborhood restaurant: Gustaf G:son Henning, a very successful and respected art dealer who had offered Bäckström a thing or two over the years in exchange for simpler police confidences. Now seventy years old, slender and well-tailored with silver hair, a large apartment on Norr Mälarstrand, an office at Norrmalmstorg, he was a frequent guest on all the art and antique programs on TV. Among those who knew him he was called GeGurra, and the only mystery was that he would show up regularly at the humble greasy spoon on the wrong side of Kungsholmen that Bäckström frequented basically every day of the week.

When GeGurra was born his dear parents had christened him Juha

Valentin. Juha after his maternal grandfather, who had Finnish Gypsies on his side of the family and had great success, as both a rag-and-bone merchant and a scrap metal collector. Valentin after his paternal grandfather, who had been active in the amusement industry and among many things owned a traveling carnival and two porno clubs in Bohuslän back when the industry was new and a real Wild West for anyone who could help themselves. Juha Valentin Andersson Snygg, a name with both ancestry and obligations, and absolutely inconceivable for the hopeful young man who saw a future in the somewhat more elegant trade in art and antiques.

As soon as Juha Valentin became an adult he changed his name. To be on the safe side both his first names and his surname, which he chose according to the snobbiest prejudices to be found in the industry he intended to make his own. He also made an exciting addition as an homage to the most stuck-up of them all. Juha Valentin Andersson Snygg had been transformed to Gustaf G:son Henning in the civil registry and to the public, and to GeGurra among near, dear, and regular acquaintances. Juha Valentin belonged to a time long since past.

It sometimes happened that Gustaf G:son was asked what G:son really stood for. Then he would smile sadly before he answered.

"After old uncle Gregor. Though he's been dead for many years, as I'm sure you know."

It was also quite true. His mother, Rosita, had a brother whose name was Gregor who had died under tragic circumstances back in the fifties. The distilling apparatus in his trailer exploded, but he never got that kind of follow-up question.

The day after the failed bicycle deal, GeGurra had again shown up in Bäckström's life and in the usual way.

"Nice to see you, Inspector," said GeGurra, patting Bäckström on the shoulder. "Here you stand, philosophizing by the worn-out old bar counter."

"Really nice to see you, Henning," said Bäckström, who could also be formal if required. Fucking good luck I haven't ordered yet, he thought.

"Thank you, thank you. You're much too kind," GeGurra acknowledged. "Have you eaten, by the way?"

"Thanks for asking," said Bäckström. "I was just thinking about having a small bite." Birdseed and a glass of water, if it's my own wallet that decides, he thought.

"You know what," said GeGurra, "then I propose we take a carriage and drive down to the Theater Grill where we can converse in peace and quiet. And I'll pick up the check."

"I understand you've finally wound up at a well-laid table," GeGurra observed fifteen minutes later, raising his glass. "Cheers, by the way."

"Depends on what you mean by well-laid," said Bäckström, shaking his head. Twenty minutes ago he'd been at the bar in his squalid regular place. Now he was sitting in the most isolated booth at one of the city's deluxe restaurants. The personnel tied themselves in knots as soon as GeGurra appeared at the door. Large dry martini for GeGurra, malt whiskey and beer for Bäckström, each with a menu in hand. As soon as they sat their rear ends down and without Bäckström's host needing to say a word about it.

"You don't know anyone who needs a bicycle?" Bäckström added and sighed.

"In a rough game you should keep a good face," GeGurra observed. "Ask me, a simple guppy who shares the aquarium with sharks, piranhas, and ordinary jellyfish. When I see you, dear Bäckström, I get a definite premonition that considerably better times are approaching."

"You don't say," said Bäckström. You don't say, he thought.

"You see, I have a small problem I think you can help me with," said GeGurra, sipping his dry martini carefully.

"I'm listening," said Bäckström.

GeGurra had an old customer. For many years now he'd also been a good friend. It was often that way among friends of art. Great art collector, significant patron, living abroad for many years. A few months ago he'd had a break-in in his apartment in Stockholm. An old Dutchman that wasn't exactly free had been stolen. True, it was insured for its full value, but what did that help for a true art lover who didn't care the least about money and besides had more of that commodity than all his spoiled heirs could imagine running through for several generations to come. He wanted his painting back. It was no more difficult than that, and now he'd asked GeGurra for advice.

"What do you think, Bäckström?" said GeGurra. "What do you think are the chances that you and your new associates will succeed in clearing this up and making sure he gets his painting back?"

"You probably shouldn't ask me that," said Bäckström. "It's not my case."

"Sad, very sad," said GeGurra and sighed. "You don't think your associates will put this to rights?"

"Forget it," said Bäckström. If you don't believe me I can show you little Wiijnbladh, he thought.

"You wouldn't be able to check on how it's going?" asked GeGurra.

"It's not as easy as you think," said Bäckström. "There's a fucking lot of secrecy these days. You'd almost think you were working for a secret sect. If it's not your case, then you're screwed if you try to ferret anything out. Back in the day the insurance companies would buy back stolen paintings, but then a lot of fucking teetotalers and clean-living fools came in who made short work of that solution. As soon as some helpful bastard shows up with the painting, he lands right in jail. He can just forget about the reward money, and the insurance companies don't want to hear about such things anymore."

"My good friend has a Swiss insurance company," said GeGurra. "I can assure you that they have a completely different and much more practical attitude."

"Sure," said Bäckström. "Tell that to the one who's going to turn in the goods. He can only dream about the dough while he's serving four years in the can for receiving stolen goods."

"Think about it," said GeGurra. "While we have a bit to eat and a little schnapps so we'll think better."

"What's in it for me?" said Bäckström. Just as well to have it said, he thought.

"In my world no one goes empty-handed," said GeGurra with a

well-tailored shrug of his shoulders. "So what do you say we start with gravlax?"

The following day Bäckström took the opportunity as soon as Wiijn-bladh stumbled out the door at three o'clock. All was calm and quiet in the corridor. Not a single soul around because it was both payday and Friday and high time for all hardworking constables to visit the state liquor store before they went home to the little wife and let the struggle against criminality take a weekend rest.

Bäckström started by turning over Wiijnbladh's desk pad, and the only problem was that he'd taped the reminder slip upside down. Eight digits and eight letters written in shaky handwriting. As a personal code he had chosen Cerberus, and he was probably not the only one in the building to do so. Wonder if he's thinking about buying new false teeth, thought Bäckström as he entered the codes in his flash drive.

Then he logged in and printed out a copy of the investigation of the art theft on Strandvägen. Put it in his pocket, took a bracing walk from his workplace to GeGurra's residence on Norr Mälarstrand, and dropped it in his mail slot.

The following week he and GeGurra had a discreet meeting with a Swiss attorney and an English-speaking representative of the Swiss insurance company. It was clear that Bäckström would be able to arrange the retrieval of the painting if he could do as real policemen had always done. No problem, according to the insurance executive and the attorney. One wish remained on Bäckström's side.

"This meeting never took place and you gentlemen and I have never met," said Bäckström.

No problem with that either, and what the hell do I do now? thought Bäckström when he returned to work an hour afterward.

One week later the matter resolved itself. Even though it wasn't his case, Inspector Evert Bäckström received an anonymous tip by phone. A polite young man who did not want to say his name announced that there was a recently stolen car parked on Polhemsgatan outside the entryway to the large police building. Only a hundred yards from Bäck-ström's own desk, although he didn't say that. In the trunk was a stolen painting, and so the police wouldn't have to waste time, the vehicle had been left unlocked.

Bäckström went to his immediate boss and briefly explained what the whole thing was about. He said that if his boss so desired he would obviously follow up on the phone call and take a look.

"What I still don't get is why the informant called you, Bäckström," the chief hissed ten minutes later when they opened the back of the stolen car and saw the just-recovered painting by Bruegel the Younger. "This is not really your investigation."

"I guess he wanted to talk with a real policeman," said Bäckström, shrugging his fat shoulders. There's something for you to suck on, you little bureaucrat, he thought.

One week later Bäckström's boss gave him a new case to sink his teeth into. The department at the Swedish Economic Crime Authority that dealt with environmental crimes needed help tracing the original owner of fifty-some barrels of apparently toxic waste that the police in Nacka had found in an abandoned factory.

How do you tell such things apart? thought Bäckström. They're all the same anyway, he thought. A few days earlier he'd met GeGurra, who thanked him for the help, treated him to dinner, and delivered a plain brown envelope without return address plus a promise that more would be coming, *peu à peu*, as custom dictated, between discreet friends.

You really are a cunning little devil, GeGurra, thought Bäckström when after a good meal he returned to his pleasant bachelor pad on Inedalsgatan, only a stone's throw from the large police building. Even a half-fairy like Wiijnbladh had to make his contribution without having a clue about it.

Maybe I should buy new false teeth for the little poisoner, thought Bäckström as he mixed an ample evening toddy. The wooden kind, he thought.

. . .

Chief Inspector Evert Bäckström, legendary murder investigator in forced exile at the police lost-and-found warehouse. Gustaf G:son Henning, successful art dealer and known from TV. Inspector Göran Wiijnbladh, the police's own knight of the mournful guise. Three human fates that had turned out differently, to be sure, but that in less than a year would be joined in a way none of them could have foreseen.

33

Almost a year later, on Thursday, August 16, Bäckström was sitting at home in his apartment on Inedalsgatan, having a quiet evening highball. Fruit soda and Estonian vodka he'd bought from a fellow officer who worked with the coast guard and had a few contacts on the other side. Despite the monthly contribution from the good Henning, there had been many holes to fill. Since he'd acquired his new plasma TV with the giant screen, malt whiskey, at least for a time, had to be replaced by simpler fare. I hope it is a temporary problem, thought Bäckström, sighing contentedly. Turning on his new acquisition he almost choked on his drink.

Lapp bastard, he thought, staring at Johansson on the screen. Sitting there telling lies in that drawling Norrland way. Just like all the other Lapp bastards in a coma from too many dumplings.

That put an end to his evening repose. Even though he changed channels almost immediately and even though he tried to extinguish the smoldering fire inside him with another couple of substantial bracers. He didn't even have the energy to check his e-mail to see if anything new had shown up from that crazy female who preferred "real men in uniform" with "fixed routines and clear orientation" but who at the same time were not unfamiliar with "boundary-crossing activities."

How the hell does the little sow get that to fit together? thought Bäckström. And the only prospect he could think of personally was a royally drunk Italian customs agent he'd met at a conference a few years earlier.

I'll kill the Lapp bastard, thought Bäckström, and with these consoling thoughts in his round head he fell asleep almost immediately in his newly purchased Hästens bed.

The following day was like all other days at his new job. Old bikes, shithouse barrels, and for a week now half an office that a practical-minded entrepreneur had dumped on a wooded hillside on an old aristocratic estate twelve miles north of Stockholm. A lot of worn-out computers, wobbly desks, and dilapidated desk chairs. A method of disposal both practical and cheap if you couldn't make it to the dump, and what the hell did the police have to do with this? thought Bäckström.

Although he did realize it was the wrong wooded hillside. The fine people who lived on the estate had been extremely indignant and took the chief constable aside when he was at dinner with their old friend His Majesty the King. Already the next day the case was on Bäckström's desk. Serious environmental crime with highest priority from the highest police leadership and necessary assistance required from the lost-and-found warehouse's most experienced property investigator, that is, Bäckström.

"So I guess you'll have to borrow a service vehicle, Bäckström, and do a little investigating on the scene. Sounds like there's a lot of nutritious technical clues out there if I'm correctly informed," said his immediate boss as he gave him the assignment and set the complaint on his desk. "By the way, don't forget to take along a pair of rubber boots," he added thoughtfully. "The ground is supposed to be pretty damp this time of year."

The case had mostly been going nowhere, but Bäckström did his best to get things moving and was even invited to a restorative lunch by the crime victim himself when he interviewed him about the probable time of the crime. Basically whenever, according to the plaintiff, because these days he spent most of his time in his house on the French Riviera where fortunately he didn't own any wooded hillsides he had to worry about.

"Probably one of those bankruptcies," the landowner suggested, saluting his guest with his schnapps glass. "Unless you have any better ideas, chief inspector?"

"I'm thinking about having the whole pile of shit hauled to the tech squad," said Bäckström.

"Sounds like an excellent idea," his host observed. "I assume the police will cover the expense."

"Of course," said Bäckström.

His boss had not been equally amused. Especially not after his conversation with the head of the tech squad, but Bäckström stuck to his guns and if this was to be war, so be it.

"So now I'm suddenly supposed to forget about a serious environmental crime," said Bäckström indignantly. "Even though that fucking greenhouse effect will be the death of both old ladies and children. You have kids, don't you?" With an exceptionally ugly old lady, he thought.

"Of course not, Bäckström, of course not," his boss protested. "Yes, I have three kids so I understand exactly. What I mean is simply that perhaps we shouldn't expect that tech will treat this as a priority. You haven't tried to trace the things yourself?"

"Bookshelf 'Billy,' office chair 'Nisse,' and a lot of old broken computers that were bought over the counter ten years ago. Though I did find at least two hard drives among the other mildew, and if the boys at tech just focus on those I think we'll be home free," said Bäckström. That gives you a little something to suck on, you effeminate little binder carrier, thought Bäckström.

Then his old benefactor GeGurra called him on his cell phone and suddenly there was hope in his life again.

"Do you have time for dinner next week?" Gustaf G:son Henning wondered as soon as they were finished with the introductory courtesies. "I have a very interesting story, and I think we can be of mutual benefit and use to each other, if I may say so. Unfortunately I have a lot of work right now, so what do you think about the Opera Cellar on Monday at seven o'clock?"

"Of course," said Bäckström. "You can't give me a clue?" Now this is starting to look like something, he thought. That fucking office furniture they could almost lamentably shove up their rear ends if they asked him.

"Big things, Bäckström," said GeGurra. "Much too big to be discussed on the phone I'm afraid."

Wonder if they've pinched that old Rembrandt at the National Museum, thought Bäckström. The one with all those bastards sitting and boozing while they swore some fucking oath.

"Worse than that, I'm afraid," said Gustaf G:son Henning, looking at his guest seriously as they sat down in the usual out-of-the-way corner and each got a refresher while they studied the menu.

"What do you know about the weapon that was used when Olof Palme was shot?" he continued, as he nibbled carefully on the large olive that the waiter had set on a dish alongside his dry martini.

Goodness, thought Bäckström. Now we're talking.

"Quite a bit," said Bäckström, nodding with all the dignity that suits anyone who was there when it happened. Now the Lapp bastard will have to watch out, he thought. The honorable Henning was unquestionably a man who dealt in hard goods. Not an ordinary glowworm who let his jaw run on its own.

"Do tell," said Bäckström.

"I have a few questions first, if you'll excuse me," said his host.

"I'm listening," said Bäckström.

"They say there's a reward?"

"The socialist government put a price tag on the bastard. Fifty million tax free provided he's delivered in travel-ready condition."

"What do you mean by that?"

"Ready for further transport to the courts and our dear criminal justice system." Bäckström grinned, taking a gulp of his life-giving malt.

"What if he's dead?"

"Still fifty million if it can be proved that it was him," said Bäckström. "On the other hand, if you can only deliver the weapon he used, you'll have to be content with ten million," he continued. "Because we have the bullets from the crime scene to compare with, it's also pretty easy. If you find the right weapon, that is. Proving that it was the one that was used, I mean," Bäckström clarified.

"What would happen if you were to show up with the weapon? Or mentioned where your colleagues could find it?"

"I wouldn't get any money in that case," sighed Bäckström. "I am a cop after all, so I'm expected to do that sort of thing for free." On the other hand I would have guaranteed hell from the Lapp bastard and probably wind up in jail as thanks for clearing up his shit, he thought.

"What if the tip came from me?" asked GeGurra.

"Then you'd get pure hell," said Bäckström, nodding in emphasis.

"Anonymously then? Assuming I gave an anonymous tip?"

"Forget it," said Bäckström. "We're talking about the assassination of Olof Palme, so you can forget anonymity. Jail! That's where you'll end up. Out of pure reflex, if nothing else."

"Even if I can prove that I wasn't the least bit involved?" his host persisted.

"Then you can still forget about being anonymous. This is no ordinary lottery winnings we're talking about," said Bäckström. "Some of my fellow officers are as taciturn as a tea strainer. Give out more than you pour in, if you know what I mean."

"Sad," said GeGurra and sighed. "Personally I've done considerably larger deals than this without saying a word about either the seller or the buyer."

"Sure," said Bäckström. "It's a completely different matter, since I'm the one who's the cop in this company."

"Yes?"

"What do you think if I ask the questions and you answer?" said Bäckström.

"Of course," said GeGurra and nodded. "Then I'll tell you what I heard from an old acquaintance almost fifteen years ago."

"Wait now," said Bäckström, making a deprecating gesture. "Fifteen years ago? Why haven't you said anything until now?"

"It was as if it never happened," said GeGurra, shaking his head.

243

"But then I saw in the newspaper a week or so ago that the head of the National Bureau of Criminal Investigation apparently opened a new secret investigation. Because the crime will soon pass the statute of limitations, I thought perhaps this was the right time to speak out."

"Okay, I'm listening," said Bäckström. Talk about danger in delay, he thought.

Almost fifteen years earlier, an old acquaintance, who "was in the same line of work as Bäckström," told Gustaf G:son Henning about the weapon used to murder Olof Palme. Because he had kept a diary for many years, Bäckström could of course get an exact date for their conversation if he so desired.

"Why did he tell you that?" asked Bäckström. A fellow cop. That's the shits, he thought.

"He wanted to know what it might be worth if it was sold on the international art and antiques market," GeGurra explained. "People collect the strangest things, you know," he said, shaking his head. "A few years ago I sold an old pair of flannel pajamas that had belonged to Heinrich Himmler, the old head of the Nazi SS, as I'm sure you recall, for three hundred fifty thousand kronor."

"What kind of answer did he get? Your acquaintance, I mean."

"That it would probably be extremely difficult to find a buyer. Considering that it concerned a still unsolved murder of a prime minister. A million, tops, at that point in time. But that the potential price could obviously change radically as soon as the murder was past the statute of limitations, assuming the weapon was not criminally acquired, of course. The limitations period for receiving stolen goods is a bit complicated, as I'm sure you know. In any event, after the end of that period this would surely be a matter of millions."

"More than ten?"

"Certainly." GeGurra nodded. "Assuming that you find the right buyer, and I know several who would reach down pretty far to add a showpiece like that to their collections."

"The Friends of Palme Haters," said Bäckström and grinned.

"Yes, one of them, at least."

"Did he tell you anything else about the weapon?"

"Yes. Among other things he said that this did not concern a Smith and Wesson revolver as has always been maintained in the media. Instead it concerned a different, American-manufactured revolver, a Ruger. The model is called Speed Six and has a magazine that holds six bullets. Chrome, silver-colored, with a long barrel, ten inches I seem to recall he said, a .357 caliber Magnum. Wooden butt made of walnut with a checkered grip. In perfect condition. I remember I asked about that, by the way. That kind of information is important to someone like me."

"Did he say anything else?" said Bäckström. "Did he have any registration number on the weapon?" The model may actually correspond, he thought.

"Not that he gave me anyway. On the other hand the weapon was ready for delivery, in the event of a deal. It had been stored in a very secure place for a number of years."

"So where was that?" asked Bäckström.

"In the lion's own den," said GeGurra, smiling faintly. "Those were his own words. That it had been stored in the lion's own den."

"What did he mean by that?"

"I've no idea. But he seemed extremely amused when he said it."

"Did he say anything else?" asked Bäckström.

"Yes, actually. One more thing. Pretty strange story, in fact. According to what he alleged, the same weapon had been used for another two murders and a suicide. A few years before it was used to shoot the prime minister. I definitely remember that he said that. That this was a weapon with a long history. It had been used not only to shoot a prime minister who spied for the Russians, but also to clear away more ordinary riffraff. He expressed himself more or less like that, actually."

"Does he have a name?"

"Who?" said GeGurra, with a modest smile.

"Your informant. The one who was in the same line of work as me. Does he have a name?"

"Yes," said GeGurra. "But hardly a name that you discuss at a place like this. So you'll have to be patient for a few hours. I asked one of my co-workers to place a discreet envelope in your mail slot. The usual monthly amount for our old deal plus a little extra to defray your expenses in connection with what we've just discussed, which I hope can be our next project. Plus a slip of paper with the name of my old acquaintance."

"Sounds good," said Bäckström. "By the way, how did you get to know him?"

"Like most of the others," said GeGurra. "He bought a painting from me. A Zorn, actually."

"Goodness," said Bäckström. "That wasn't cat shit." Wonder what a colleague like that had worked out? he thought. Must have been better than the lost-and-found warehouse.

"A rather unusual Zorn," said GeGurra. "When the great painter of women was in his most exhilarated mood, his female studies could be rather penetrating, if I may say so. Not just skin, hair, and water. An unknown side of Zorn, or perhaps a side not readily discussed by art historians, but which suited my acquaintance's somewhat special taste. Like hand in glove, if you will."

"He painted her pussy," Bäckström concluded.

"The best-painted cunt in Swedish art history," GeGurra concurred with unexpected emphasis. "What do you say to an ample slice of meat, by the way, and a decent bottle of red?"

Bäckström remained sitting at the restaurant longer than he intended. He had yet another project to attend to. Besides an envelope that waited on his own hall mat.

GeGurra really is an old brick, thought Bäckström as he sat on his couch, counting up the monthly stipend, plus the to say the least generous incentive to support the new project. Although personally he wouldn't have given many kopeks for the name of the informant on the enclosed slip of paper.

What do you mean "colleague"? No way did that fairy manage to shoot Palme, and how did someone like that have the money for a Zorn? thought Bäckström, shaking his round head before downing an ample dose of Estonian vodka and fruit soda. Besides, there was definitely someone else he knew who always used to bang on about the fact that he had been a good friend of the same man.

Now who the hell was that? thought Bäckström, and never mind, for it would certainly come back to him. Must be that fucking Baltic vodka, he thought before he fell asleep. Like an eraser on an otherwise perfectly functioning brain like his.

34

On Thursday, August 31, contrary to habit Bäckström had been dutifully active the whole day, because there were big things going on. Not bicycles, waste drums, or worn-out office furniture. Likely this was a matter of future Swedish crime history that for once had ended up in the right hands and not with one of his more or less retarded fellow officers. For once it was also so expedient that he had access to all the information he needed in his own computer. Even the police lost-and-found warehouse had been mobilized in the hunt for the revolver used to shoot the prime minister. A hunt that had gone on for as long as the hunt for the murderer himself. Which had required tens of thousands of man-hours over the years and still with no results.

As early as Sunday, two days after the murder, the leader of the investigation at the time, Hans Holmér, held his first press conference, and the murder weapon had been the media headliner. The large conference hall at police headquarters, hundreds of journalists, packed to the rafters with people, TV cameras from all over the world, and a police chief who was positively quivering with desire to meet his audience. He leaned on his elbows, his upper body swaying like a boxer as he sat at a table on the high podium, silenced the audience with a hand gesture, and nodded seriously but nonetheless smiling toward the hall of attentive listeners.

After a well-considered stage pause, he held up two revolvers in front of him while he was met by a veritable cascade of flashbulbs, wave after wave of lights that streamed toward him, and personally he had never felt as strong as right then.

From that day on the investigation leadership had also decided that this "in all probability concerned a U.S.-manufactured revolver of the brand Smith & Wesson with a long barrel." Partly because this was possibly true, but mostly because this was not a time for provisos and reservations.

How could he be so sure of that? Bäckström thought, who knew better because he had been there from the beginning and was a real police officer in contrast to Holmér and all the other legal fairies who barely knew where the trigger was.

That it concerned a revolver and not a pistol seemed highly probable. The half a dozen witnesses who had seen it in the perpetrator's right hand described it exactly that way. Like a "typical revolver," "one of those Western pieces with a long barrel," or even like "the real Buffalo Bill thing."

Their observations had also been supported by the few technical clues that had been secured—or not secured—at the crime scene. No bullet casings had been found, and because pistols in contrast to revolvers eject the casing when fired, this argued for a revolver. The caliber of the two bullets found at the crime scene was .357 Magnum, and almost all guns in that caliber were revolvers. There were exceptions, such as the Israeli army's Desert Eagle service pistol, but these were uncommon and did not tally with the bullets that were found. The bullets at the crime scene were somewhat special and manufactured only for revolvers.

The first one had been found early in the morning after the murder. It was on the sidewalk on the other side of Sveavägen, about fifty yards from the crime scene. The second one was found a day later at lunchtime and was in the line of fire less than six yards from the place where the prime minister had been shot.

It had been possible to trace the bullets to the manufacturer. The make was Winchester Western .357 Magnum, metal piercing. Lead bullets supplied with an especially hard mantle consisting of a layer of copper and zinc, which therefore could also break through metal. The reason for manufacturing them was that the American highway patrol expressed a desire for a bullet that was sufficiently hard and resistant so that for example it could be shot through the engine block of a car.

How many had then been used was uncertain. At the same time this was of minor importance because the metal piercing bullets quickly became popular among regular Magnum shooters and especially among those engaged in so-called combat shooting, a practice in which a certain type of adult male runs around shooting at most everything from paper figures to empty gas cans.

Otherwise these facts were hardly instructive. Revolvers of the relevant caliber had been on the market for over thirty years before the Swedish prime minister was shot. Millions of specimens had been manufactured and sold over the years, and their owners had fired hundreds of millions of shots using the same caliber bullets. How many of these had been metal piercing was uncertain, but the largest manufacturer, Winchester Western, had sold millions of them in any event.

On top of all this, from the start there had been serious doubt about the two bullets that had been found because it wasn't the police who had found them but two members of that great group of detectives, the general public, who moreover were kind enough to immediately turn them over to the police. Among many journalists and ordinary citizens it was therefore suspected that these bullets were actually false leads planted at the crime scene to deceive the investigators.

Because both bullets had quite visible traces of the substances they had passed through, that is Olof Palme's clothing and body and Lisbeth Palme's clothing, that issue could have been solved almost immediately, if normal criminological procedures had been followed and these fiber and tissue traces had been secured before the bullets were cleaned to determine their caliber.

This had not been done. Wiijnbladh and his associates at the Stockholm police department's tech squad had put them in separate little plastic bags and sent them to the National Laboratory of Forensic Science in Linköping for "caliber determination." This was the only request that had been checked on the form that was enclosed with the plastic bags.

At the crime lab the request had quickly been satisfied. The two bullets were placed in a basin with spirits; cleaned of fibers, body tissue, and blood; and rinsed off under ordinary tap water. Whatever was washed off the bullets and remained in the basin was lost when the liquid was poured off and the bullets' caliber was measured with a micrometer.

Not until some years later were helpful physicists at the University of Stockholm able to straighten out the question marks that the police had created for themselves. An amiable professor of particle physics made contact with the police and reported that what ordinary people called lead could actually be very different things depending on what was added to it. Lead could have various isotope combinations, and when, for example, bullets were manufactured, lead was almost always mixed with various isotope combinations, resulting in bullets with different combinations of lead isotopes.

The professor therefore ventured to propose a simple scientific investigation: the isotope combination in the two bullets would be compared with the traces of lead it should be possible to secure in the victims' clothing, to see whether they matched.

This they did, and the technical investigation had taken at least a small leap forward. The two bullets that had been found were with "very high probability" identical to the bullet that killed Olof Palme and the one that grazed his wife, and the constant nagging about planted false leads could finally be set aside. And that was not all. By means of the bullets' isotope combination, it had also been possible to trace the lead batch from which they originated.

True, the batch included hundreds of thousands of bullets, which the Winchester Western had supplied to a number of countries, but only six thousand of them had ended up with gun dealers in Sweden. The deliveries had been made during the years 1979 and 1980, in good time before the assassination of the prime minister. It was hope-instilling enough as a lead file, but they never got any further than that.

What remained was the weapon that the police had never found, but a number of other experts had put in their two cents' worth. Far and away the most common weapons in the relevant caliber were Smith &

Wesson revolvers in various models and barrel lengths. Hence the first investigation leader's conclusion that "with the greatest probability" it concerned a Smith & Wesson revolver.

At the same time this was a conclusion that could be challenged on both statistical and forensic grounds. It was true that the traces from the barrel on both bullets did agree well with a Smith & Wesson, but at the same time they also agreed just as well with half a dozen revolvers of different manufacture, and taken together the latter made up a quarter of the world's combined stock of revolvers of the relevant caliber. The great consolation in this context was that the ballistic traces on the bullets did not correspond with the second most common Magnum revolver, the one manufactured by Colt—the legendary armory that was Smith & Wesson's foremost competitor on the market for Magnum revolvers.

What made Bäckström happy was that the traces on the bullets also agreed very well with revolvers that came from the third largest American manufacturer, Sturm, Ruger & Co. in Southport, Connecticut. Even the barrel length agreed with the weapons technicians' conclusions to a fraction of an inch. If the barrel had been shorter than that the bullets should have "mushroomed up" in back, and they had not.

This is going like a fucking dance, thought Bäckström. If he'd only been able to run this from the very start, it would most likely have been settled right off.

One small question remained. How to connect—with sufficiently high probability—the two bullets from the crime scene to the revolver that was used to shoot the prime minister. The technical report that Bäckström found in his computer was from 1997, and the anonymous expert who wrote it was doubtful on that point. Both bullets were "in pretty poor condition." They could be used for comparisons of various types of weapons and they had been good enough to rule out the hundreds of various weapons that had been test fired over the years. But this was not to say that they could be linked to the murder weapon with certainty in the event it was found.

What a fucking ditchdigger, thought Bäckström. Technology was advancing by giant leaps! He'd seen this with his own eyes, on his own TV, at home on his own couch. The hundreds of miracles that his associates on *CSI* delivered all the time just by tapping on their computers. If it didn't work out some other way, it probably wouldn't involve more than his taking the weapon with him and traveling over to the other real constables, on the other side of the water.

Las Vegas or Miami, thought Bäckström. That's probably the big question.

35

After having freshened up his knowledge of the Palme investigation's weapons track—most of it he already knew, and it was really no great art to figure out the rest—Bäckström proceeded to more active internal detection on his computer. The results had unfortunately been meager. He had found only two Magnum revolvers of the Ruger brand entered in the registry of stolen, missing, or sought-after items in his computer.

The first had been stolen in a break-in a few years earlier at the home of a Finn who lived outside Luleå and was evidently both a marksman and a hunter. During vacation "one or more unknown perpetrators had forced entry into the plaintiff's residence, broken open his gun case, and taken three sporting guns, a combo gun, three shotguns, and a revolver." None of the stolen weapons had been recovered.

The revolver was a Ruger caliber .357 Magnum, but that was also the only thing that tallied. It was blued with a short barrel and rubber-clad butt, and for once there was even a picture of it on the computer.

Lapp bastards and Finns, thought Bäckström. How the hell could you put weapons in the hands of such people? It was bad enough that they could go to the liquor store and buy all the booze they poured into themselves all the time.

The second case seemed to offer more hope. Two years earlier the Stockholm police had made a house search in an apartment in Flemingsberg. Living there was the girlfriend of a known thug who was suspected of an armored car robbery in Hägersten a few months earlier, and behind the refrigerator they found a Ruger brand Magnum revolver. It was a pure mystery, according to both the girlfriend and the suspected robber. Neither of them had seen it before, and the only explanation was probably that the previous occupant of the apartment had left it behind when he moved out. It would probably be simplest to ask him directly, but unfortunately they could not help out because they didn't know what his name was or where he lived.

The technical investigation had not produced anything either. The weapon could not be linked to any crime, nor to the people living in the apartment. It was not reported as stolen and was not in the registry of legal weapons. The prosecutor had written off the case, the revolver had been confiscated and was now with the Stockholm police department's tech squad, but more detailed information than that was not available on Bäckström's computer.

Worth a try, thought Bäckström, and called the tech squad. He explained his business to his fellow officer who took the call, and asked him to immediately e-mail a picture of the weapon in question.

"Have you changed occupations, Bäckström?" asked his colleague, who sounded pretty reserved.

"What do you mean changed occupations?" said Bäckström. What the hell is the bastard yapping about? he thought.

"I thought you dealt with used office furniture."

"Forget about that now," said Bäckström. "Do as I say."

"I promise to think about it," his colleague replied, and then hung up without further ado.

While waiting for the colleague at the tech squad to be done thinking and finally get his ass in gear and send him the photo of the revolver, Bäckström engaged in his own musings.

Three murders and a suicide, thought Bäckström. Apparently as some kind of spring cleaning in the circles of greater and lesser riff-raff. Perhaps more, even, he thought hopefully. The weapon had been knocking around for more than twenty years and could certainly have been used for one thing or another during that time. Perhaps by some secret organization of professional murderers? More or less like what went on with the Brazilian colleagues, who periodically did a vigorous weeding out in their own slum neighborhoods.

That part about the lion's own den sounded interesting too. Didn't all those camel riders, date stompers, and suicide bombers have a lion as a symbol for their secret society and terrorist activities? Hadn't the victim rubbed elbows with a lot of hook noses from Arabia, and everyone knew how it usually ended when you associated with that sort? This may have limitless ramifications, thought Bäckström. He would beneficially continue pondering at home in his cozy lair that was only a convenient stone's throw from his run-down office.

Still no e-mail from that fucking lazy ass at the tech squad, and because it would soon be three o'clock it was time for something better. Now if one of his so-called bosses was wondering about where he'd gone, he actually had a crime scene of his own he had to inspect. Furthermore it was in the vicinity of a real crown estate where fine people lived, even though apparently they made a habit of dining with that fool who was his so-called boss.

Duty calls, thought Bäckström. He entered code two, as in official business, on his phone and quickly and discreetly left the building for so-called external duty. On his way home he took the opportunity to go past the liquor store and replenish his supply of malt whiskey and shop for some mixed snacks at the nearby deli. Fifteen minutes later he was on his couch in front of the TV with a little highball within comfortable reach. After the first gulp the blessed malt had dispersed the Baltic haze.

Suddenly it came to him which of all his crazy colleagues used to brag that he knew that half-fairy who had evidently offered the most well-known murder weapon in crime history to his old acquaintance GeGurra.

It was that fucking Wiijnbladh, thought Bäckström, shaking his round head in amazement.

36

The following day Bäckström decided it was time to get cracking, which is why he started work in good time before lunch.

First he turned on the computer to go through his e-mail. Nothing from that lazy ass at the tech squad, even though the hottest lead in Swedish police history might very well be sitting at the tech squad getting cold.

How the hell can someone like that be a cop? thought Bäckström, sending yet another e-mail.

Then he called Johansson's secretary and asked to speak with her boss.

"Chief Inspector Evert Bäckström," said Bäckström. "I want to speak with the boss."

"He's not in," his secretary answered in a reserved tone. "What does this concern?"

"Nothing I can talk about on the phone," said Bäckström curtly. In any case not with you, you little cunt lips, he thought.

"Then I suggest you e-mail a few lines and mention what it's about."

"Not that either," said Bäckström. "I have to see him." Even her jaw must sit perpendicular, he thought.

"I will convey your message and ask if he has time."

"Do that," said Bäckström, hanging up before she had time to. What the hell do I do now? he thought. It was only eleven-thirty. Too early to eat lunch if you wanted to have a real pilsner with your food. Even too early to punch out of prison, because his so-called boss was roaming around in the corridor, like an eagle eyeing his meagerly allocated time.

Wiijnbladh, he thought suddenly. It was time to put the squeeze on that little fairy and see what he had to offer.

Not very much, it appeared. Wiijnbladh was on all fours under his desk, and it looked like he was searching for something.

"How's it goin', Wiijnbladh?" said Bäckström. "Are you inspecting the cleaning, or what?"

Wiijnbladh twisted in place, shaking his head and giving Bäckström a shy glance.

"My pill, I've lost my pill."

"Pill," said Bäckström. What the hell is he babbling about? he thought.

"My medicine," Wiijnbladh clarified. "Right when I was going to put it in my mouth, it fell on the floor, and now I can't find it."

"Have you thought about switching to suppositories?" Bäckström suggested. Try to stay alive until I've had time to talk with you, he thought.

That little half-fairy is completely gone, thought Bäckström as he closed the door on Wiijnbladh.

For lack of a better alternative he returned to his office. First he thought about calling a relative who worked at the police union and knew most everything about all his so-called colleagues. Upon further thought, however, he decided not to. Despite the blood ties that united them, his cousin was a little too curious and much too unreliable for Bäckström to dare approach him in such a sensitive matter.

Because it was now the stroke of twelve, with room for a quick walk between the police building and his usual lunch place a few blocks away, it was time to see about putting something in his craw. Especially as his own hawk had evidently changed territory. Best to take the opportunity to keep starvation away from your own door, thought Bäckström. He punched in code zero—as in lunch—on his phone and quickly left the building.

It turned out to be a short mealtime. Before two hours were up, he had returned to the building and still had time to purchase some invigorating breath mints en route. Though still no e-mail from the tech snail and nothing from the Lapp bastard either.

He must have his hands full with reindeer sorting, thought Bäckström.

Then the good Henning called and wondered how it was going. Because almost everything in Bäckström's life these days concerned keeping him in a good mood, he laid it on a little. It looked rather promising, Bäckström assured him. He reported that he was fully occupied with internal surveillance of both person and object.

"There are a number of interesting leads, actually," Bäckström observed.

"Anything you can talk about on the phone?" asked GeGurra.

Unfortunately not. Much too sensitive. On the other hand Bäckström himself had a question.

"You said he bought a Zorn from you. How did he come up with the money for that? That's not like anything policemen usually hang on the wall. Mostly things like those crying children, I would think," said Bäckström. Personally he also had one that he hung in the bathroom in his apartment. Right above the privy so the little crybaby could at least enjoy the Bäckström super-salami the few times they met.

"Rich parents," Gustaf G:son Henning said. "Both his mom and dad and then several generations back. The great mystery is perhaps that he chose to become a police officer. Not an ordinary police officer fortunately, but a policeman nonetheless."

"So what do you mean?" What do you know about real police officers? thought Bäckström.

"He seems to have had his faults, if I may say so. Rather special faults, if you understand what I mean."

"No. Explain," Bäckström persisted.

It was not something one discussed on the phone, and because he had customers waiting GeGurra suggested they be in touch after the weekend.

You stingy bastard, thought Bäckström. What's wrong with meeting and having a bite to eat?

. . .

Then he called Johansson again. It was already past two, and because it was Friday it was presumably much too late. Someone like Johansson had surely already slipped away from work.

"Bäckström," said Bäckström urgently. "Looking for the boss."

"Unfortunately he's not available," answered Johansson's secretary. "But I promise to convey your message as soon as I have a chance to talk with him."

"That's probably best," said Bäckström.

"Excuse me?"

Shit your pants, you little sow, thought Bäckström and hung up.

For lack of a better plan he punched himself out with a code four. A short business trip to look at the crime scene twenty miles north of the city, and as soon as he was at a safe distance from the building he went straight home.

In some respects the weekend was more or less like it usually was. Some decent boxing on the sports channels and at least one memorable match where a giant palooka hacked a banty rooster half his size down to chicken feed, and the ringside audience looked like they had a case of measles after the first round.

Just wonder if life can get much better than this, thought Bäckström with a happy sigh. Here you sit on your new leather couch with an ample whiskey and a cold beer while two blacks pound the shit out of each other on your own big screen.

The weekend's porno offerings had unfortunately been the usual. The endless bobbing, hopping, and moaning, and at last he got so sick and tired of it that despite all the malt whiskey he made a serious attempt to find something more interesting on the Internet. He did too. A red-haired babe from Norrköping who posted a tape of her own efforts on her home page. Cheap besides. Red-haired for real, judging by her mouse, and definitely a natural talent. Not to mention her dialect. Unbeatable, considering the lines, thought Bäckström, being the connoisseur he was.

On Saturday he had dinner at the usual greasy spoon, even though he now had the means to do much better. Just as usual it turned out to be too much of most everything, and basically he spent all of Sunday in his checkered bed from Hästens. In the early hours he'd had the company of an insolent little lady he had dragged home from the bar. Then she got as tedious as all the other hags his age, but because he was a decent fellow he gave her money for a taxi before he kicked her out. So he was finally able to sleep off a hard week. With revived energies he concluded the weekend with a long walk to a better restaurant down in City. Returned at a humane hour and went to bed early. Now damn it, thought Bäckström when at ten o'clock on Monday morning he was already back at work.

No sign of life from the colleague at the tech squad, and as a first measure he called the Lapp bastard's secretary to give her a little reminder. This time the bastard was sitting in a meeting and could not be disturbed. If possible she herself sounded even snippier than usual. Wonder if it's her mouse she talks with, thought Bäckström. Perseverance wins the day, he thought an hour later and called again. Although she sounded exactly the same, it seemed as though the message was finally about to get through.

First that weak dick Lewin had called. Evidently he had had to interrupt his archival studies down in the Palme room for his boss's sake. Bäckström made the session brief. Then Lewin evidently trotted over to Flykt and asked for help. Ass licker Flykt, of all people. A retarded golf player who had evaded honorable work for at least twenty years by hiding behind his fine murder victim. Bäckström was even briefer.

Then he called Johansson's secretary again to give her yet another little reminder. Called her on Monday, on Tuesday, and on Wednesday, when his bottle cap popped off and he told her a thing or two she needed to hear. The only result was that his own little office fool and so-called boss came charging into his office and threatened first one thing and then another, and then suddenly Bäckström was going to be granted the favor of meeting Anna Holt.

From weak dick to ass licker to that anorexic dyke whose ribs you can count through her jacket. We're taking giant steps here, thought

Bäckström as he put his best foot forward in the corridors that led to Police Superintendent Anna Holt.

Clearly he was the target of a conspiracy. They had recorded his calls in secret, and Holt threatened first one thing and then another. First he only intended to give her some general advice and tell her to stick her opinions up her anus, but because this still was about the murder of a prime minister he tried to make an effort and give her everything GeGurra had given him. Decent fellow that he was, case-oriented as he was too, and considering the great values that were at stake.

What the hell is happening with the police? thought Bäckström as he left her office. Where the hell are we headed, really?

37

Holt was not impressed by the little that Bäckström had to tell. It sounded too much like other weapons tips that had come into the Palme investigation over the years. For the sake of orderliness she had nonetheless done such checking as she could with the help of the case files. It took her almost two days. With the greatest probability two wasted days, she thought as she put the last paper aside.

During more than twenty years the investigators had received close to a thousand tips that entirely or partially concerned the weapon that was supposed to have been used to shoot the prime minister. In addition over six hundred .357 caliber Magnum revolvers had been test fired. Practically all of them Smith & Wessons and legally owned. Nothing of what had been done had yielded any results. A few tips had seemed promising, because it was always like that. None of them led the police closer to the weapon or the perpetrator who had used it. more than

All of this information was collected in over sixty binders. For once at least the majority of this information had been transferred to computers. What disturbed Holt was that the police's follow-up of the weapons leads almost exclusively concerned Smith & Wesson revolvers, even though right from the start it was clear that it was fully possible that the bullets could have been fired by half a dozen Magnum revolvers of different makes, and that the Ruger revolver was one of them.

The explanation seemed to be historical. As early as fourteen days after the first press conference, the investigation leadership decided to focus on Smith & Wesson revolvers, and what was a statistical estimate to start with turned into absolute truth and a direct order.

Holt was an excellent shot. She shot better than most of her fellow police officers. She could take apart and put together her service pistol blindfolded, but at the same time she was also completely uninterested in weapons and almost considered them a necessary evil that came with the job. Fortunately less and less often, in her line of work.

To be on the safe side she called a colleague she had met at a conference during the spring. He was a forensic technician and an even better shot than Holt. Weapons were his life's interest and his livelihood, but he still had left room for other things. The only time they met each other they wound up in the same bed the first night of the conference, and it had been really nice. The silence that followed afterward she had first explained by the fact that he worked at the crime lab in Linköping and she in Stockholm. That he probably fiddled with his beloved weapons both day and night. That perhaps he didn't dare call a colleague of such a high rank. Thoughts she had let go of rather quickly.

So I'll have to ask for a little positive special treatment, thought Holt, dialing his number.

Nice of her to call. So why haven't you called yourself? thought Holt.

Sure, the weapon that shot Palme could just as well be a Ruger of the model she described, as for example the corresponding model from Smith & Wesson. It wasn't really the weapon that shot Palme that we're after, but the person who used it, thought Holt.

Then she asked the decisive question.

"Assume that you found the right weapon. Would you then be able to link it to the bullets that were found on Sveavägen? With the certainty required in a courtroom?" she clarified.

"Well, assuming it's in the same condition today, then it ought to be possible."

"If we assume that," said Holt. Stored in the lion's own den and in excellent condition, she thought. At least according to the little fatso

Bäckström. Or more correctly stated, according to the little fatso's own anonymous, obviously completely trustworthy source.

"Today I believe that the probability with which you can testify is a little over ninety percent," he answered. "If you had asked me five years ago, I would have said it was at maybe eighty percent, and that's probably the bare minimum."

"How's that?" asked Holt.

"Both bullets are damaged. What's messed them up the most is that they got a little bent and twisted around their own longitudinal axis, if you understand what I mean. But today we have access to software that means that someone like me can reconstruct them to almost original condition in my little computer. So with a little luck, then—"

"Can you link them together?" asked Holt. I recall that you were extremely handy, she thought.

"Excuse the question, but it's not the case that—"

"Absolutely not. Forget that," interrupted Holt. "My top boss has asked me to go through the Palme material, and as I read through the weapons part it struck me that they seem to have almost entirely disregarded all revolvers that didn't come from Smith and Wesson."

"Yes, that was sloppy of them," he sighed. "In my job you have to be extremely meticulous."

"Thanks for your help," said Holt. Not only at work, she thought.

"If you happen to be in the area then perhaps we . . ."

"I promise to think about it," said Holt. Besides, I seem to recall that you have my number, she thought.

Guys, she thought as she put down the receiver. What is it that's actually wrong with them?

Bäckström was so wrong in all human respects that she couldn't even hate him. Could barely manage to dislike him. Preferably avoided thinking about him. A fat little guy who had certainly been bullied by his classmates from the very first day at school. Who was sufficiently thick-skinned and good at fighting to be able to pay back in kind. Who had almost never been liked as the person he really was. Who to be on the safe side responded by disliking everything and everyone.

Then there was Lars Martin Johansson. Who could be as merciless as their fellow officer Berg maintained. Whom she herself could dislike intensely until he said something or did something that hit her right in the gut. Even though she had never loved, hated, or even feared him. Johansson, whom she mostly disapproved of nowadays. Because he affected her and because she thought about him far too often. Because of his gray eyes that assessed most of what came into his vicinity.

Her very temporary lover she had just been talking with. This handsome, physically fit, and handy man who couldn't even manage to pick up the phone to call her. Who at the same time made no secret of the fact that he could imagine another encounter. Casual and without reservations. Just like all the firearms he took apart, put together again. And fired off.

Or Lewin with his complete presence and his shy gaze. Who seemed to have understood most of both his own and others' lives but would never dream of talking about it. Not since that time when he was only seven years old, had just lost his dad, and it was as if the bottom had gone out of him. If it hadn't been for those scared eyes. If only he had a little more of Johansson's unreflective self-confidence. If . . .

Oh for Christ's sake, Holt, thought Anna Holt. Pull yourself together.

On Friday Bäckström received an e-mail from his lazy, incompetent colleague at the tech squad. Not because he understood what Bäckström was after, but mostly because Bäckström had nagged him so much and he himself was a decent, helpful colleague who unfortunately had far too much to do. There was Bäckström's old office furniture, for example, that he and his colleagues still hadn't had time to tackle.

According to the picture of the revolver that he sent with the same e-mail, it was chrome, had a long barrel, and a butt of checkered wood, which might very well be walnut. Exactly like the weapon Bäckström was asking about.

According to the accompanying text it had been test fired the week after it had been confiscated. A search in the police registry had not produced anything. They had not been able to connect it with any previous crimes. It had not been found in the Swedish weapons registry of legally owned weapons. Nor was it on any lists of weapons that Interpol, Europol, or the police in other countries were searching for.

In order to possibly get an answer to the question of how it could end up behind a refrigerator in Flemingsberg, a routine inquiry had been sent through Interpol to the American manufacturer. Six months later an answer was received. The weapon in question was more than twenty years old. This was evident, in part, from the weapon's manufacturing number. In the fall of 1985 it had been sold, along with fifty other pistols and revolvers, to their German general agent in Bremen, in what was then West Germany. This was evident from the manufacturer's own delivery lists, which, according to federal and state legislation, they had to archive for at least twenty-five years. On the other hand if the Swedish police wanted to know more about the weapon's continued fate, it was the general agent in Germany who should be contacted.

Hell, thought Bäckström excitedly. It was probably so simple that they neglected to compare it with the bullets from Sveavägen simply because it was a Ruger and not a Smith & Wesson. What could you expect from Wiijnbladh and his old colleagues who couldn't find either their mouth or their ass when they were going to take the daily dose of medicine that they so badly needed? The same colleagues who would doubtless rob him of both the glory and the money if he gave them the chance.

The description of the weapon matched what GeGurra's informant had said to a T, and it was surely no coincidence that it had been delivered only a few months before it had been used. What the hell do I do now? And here it's a matter of thinking clearly, thought Bäckström.

A minute later he was already sitting at his computer writing a memo that to be on the safe side he dated the day before he met GeGurra. A little more than a week before he met Holt, and at least one full day before he talked with the tech squad. First a description of the weapon and then a little, but not unessential, addition given the money and the glory. The weapon number that the incompetent lazy ass at the tech squad had just sent him.

What remained was a credible explanation to his female colleague, who would have to carry him on her raised arms into police department glory. A little addition with a few personal, explanatory lines between colleagues.

Dear Holt. At my first meeting with my informant information also emerged in the sense that the informant could remember portions of the referenced weapon's manufacturing number. After exhaustive searches in the registry, I have decided that it is highly probable this must concern the revolver described in the attached memo. The complete manufacturing number is enclosed. According to my investigations the referenced weapon was confiscated in a house search in Flemingsberg on April 15, 2005. A copy of the initial report is enclosed. The weapon in question has since been stored at the technical squad in Stockholm where unfortunately they seem to have missed doing a ballistic comparison with the bullets that were secured at the crime scene at Sveavägen and Tunnelgatan on the first and second of March 1986. Considering the sensitive nature of the matter I assume that the information I am now giving you is covered by heightened confidentiality and that only I personally will be kept informed on an ongoing basis of the measures that the national bureau carries out. With best regards. Detective Chief Inspector Evert Bäckström

Now you've got something good to suck on, you skinny little wretch. Now make sure you take care of yourself, and kind uncle Evert will buy a pair of real knockers for you, thought Bäckström contentedly.

What remained was to figure out how the revolver could have ended up behind a refrigerator out in Flemingsberg with a common thug who had nothing but consonants in his surname, and who was only six years old when Palme was shot. That's worth thinking about over the weekend, and the old poisoner Wiijnbladh surely has a thing or two to contribute, thought Bäckström. High time to go home as well.

. . .

A few hours later, about the same time that Bäckström was deep in thought on his couch with a whiskey and a cold beer nearby, Anna Holt was going through her e-mail as a final task before she took off for the weekend.

Goodness. Now Bäckström has really gone crazy, she thought as she read his memo. Because she still intended to talk with her boss before she went home, she printed out a copy for him.

So Johansson too gets something good to suck on, thought Anna Holt based on a familiar example, as she turned off her computer.

38

On Saturday morning Mattei woke up in the overly large apartment on Narvavägen she'd been given by her kind dad. Personally she would have preferred to live on Söder, but her father just shook his head. Either Östermalm or nothing at all. He would have preferred to see her move home to Bavaria. The Bavaria that was the Mattei family's homeland. Not like Sweden, which was only a temporary stopping place on the way through life.

What's wrong with Söder, and what is it that happens to all old radicals? thought Lisa Mattei as she laced up her running shoes.

She ran her usual end-of-the-week circuit on Djurgården. It went better than expected, considering that lately she had started noticeably neglecting her exercise. It's like there's no reason to work out, thought Lisa Mattei as she stood in front of the bathroom mirror and squeezed her flat stomach. A pale, thin blonde, thought Mattei, shaking her head at her mirror image.

It had been three months since anyone had kissed her, and that had happened when she made her annual visit to her dad. Because it involved one of her father's many assistants, she could not rule out that dear old dad had ordered him to do it.

She got dressed. Had a late breakfast. Took a mineral water, an apple, and a banana and went to work. In reception there was a new guard, whom she didn't recognize. That much too common type, with a shaved head, bulging shoulders, and upper arms as thick as her waist. She nodded curtly, held up her ID, and made a beeline for the entry passage. Then he called out after her.

"Hello! May I look at that," he said, pointing with his whole hand at her ID.

"Mattei, national bureau," said Lisa Mattei, holding up the card about a foot in front of his eyes.

"Okay," he said, suddenly smiling. "I'm new here. Just been at a course for two days, and the only thing they talked about was what would happen to me if I let the wrong person in."

"It's cool," said Mattei. Smiled and nodded. Seems relatively normal even though he looks the way he does, she thought.

Stuck-up lady, thought the guard, watching her as she went in. That cool, blonde type that always played the leading role in his daily dreams of a better life. What would someone like that have to do with someone like him? A moonlighting student. Shaved head to conceal the baldness that had started to appear even in high school. Could bench-press four hundred pounds. A workout buddy had suggested he should moonlight as a guard. Better than student loans. Plenty of time to read. Get paid while he did it.

So now here he was. In the reception area of the big police building, of all places. On the basis of his appearance and even though he was in cinema studies at the university. They must have missed that on his application. Although there wasn't much time for reading. Not after all the instructions he had been given at the new employee training course. But what would someone like her do with someone like me? he thought.

The police track was the track that no serious thinking person believed in. That the police themselves didn't was both human and explicable. At the same time they were in good company. The special adviser had already expressed his condemnation a few years after the murder, when the issue was discussed in the mightiest of all secret societies, where people like him exchanged viewpoints and ideas with one another.

"The classic conspiracy theory is a thin fabric of poorly conceived ideas, personal shortcomings and ordinary, common slander as . . .

ersatzmittel . . . for factual circumstances," he stated in his introductory address. "Or plain nonsense, if you prefer that description," he added.

What was called the police track in the mass media was, in the Palme investigation's materials, the general designation for a number of tips, leads, and theories that individual police officers, groups of police, or the police as an organization in one way or another were involved in the murder of the prime minister.

In an objective sense—factual, or simply putative—to start with this was about three threads in "the thin fabric of conspiracy." Policemen who had been on duty during the night of the murder and appeared, or acted, in a strange way; police officers who harbored extreme political opinions, hated the murder victim, and for that reason also would have had motive to kill him; and the operational leadership of the police in Stockholm, who conducted their mission so badly after the murder that it must have been with intent or ill will.

After that the tips had poured in. About mysterious meetings between police officers, about policemen who said strange things, about policemen who did the Hitler salute and toasted that Olof Palme was finally dead, about policemen who had supposedly vowed to kill him years before he was actually assassinated. Policemen who were observed in the vicinity of the crime, policemen who had a violent past, who had a license for their own Magnum revolvers, policemen who . . .

It was the secret police who as early as the second day of the investigation were given the task of investigating the substance of all this. The reason was simple and obvious. Almost all the tips were about policemen who worked in Stockholm, the same police authority that also had responsibility for the investigation of the murder. Placing it with the Stockholm police department's own department for internal investigations was not an option either. The mission was far too extensive, and those affected much too close to one another.

The opinion of the leadership of the first investigation had been clear from the start, and to be on the safe side provincial police chief

Hans Holmér had yet another memorandum prepared. In reality there was no "police track" that could be investigated. The very thought of such a thing collapsed on its own absurdity. What remained was that it could not be ruled out that the murderer, or one of his accomplices, was or had been a policeman. Just as he might be a doctor, teacher, or journalist. There was thus no police track, as a simple logical consequence of what was stated in the memo. Just as there was no doctor, teacher, or journalist track.

Even though the police track didn't exist it ended up with SePo, sufficiently far enough away and sufficiently nearby. But so as not to bring chaos into the overarching detective organization, for once the secret police had to subordinate themselves to their colleagues in the open police operation. The leadership in the Palme investigation also led the investigation of the police track. That was who the secret police reported to. It was there that the final, conclusive decisions were made.

In concrete terms the police track encompassed about a hundred named policemen. All the way from the first investigation leader, the provincial police chief in Stockholm, whose alibi for the night of the murder was challenged, to the sort of colleagues who had generated complaints for assault on duty, because they had behaved offensively, expressed themselves disparagingly, or simply acted inappropriately in general.

All the way from the provincial police chief to those who had already been fired, quit voluntarily, or been well on their way to doing so when they wound up in the investigation. Because they'd had problems with their nerves, with alcohol, with wives, with finances. Problems that seldom came alone. Because they drove while drunk, beat up inmates in jail, stole from the till at work, threw a flowerpot at the wife's head, shot real bullets through a neighbor's window after a night of partying. Or simply kicked their dog.

Some seventy of them were identified, investigated, and in all cases removed from the investigation. Remaining were about thirty cases where the policemen who were pointed out could not be identified with certainty. Or even the kind of cases where it was extremely unclear whether the nameless "policeman" that was pointed out was actually the one he was alleged to be. Leads and tips that sometimes had been investigated, sometimes immediately set aside without further action. Tips, leads, cases, which in any event had not resulted in the slightest concrete suspicion that the policemen investigated had been involved in the murder of Olof Palme. In everything else imaginable, to be sure, what came out was hardly flattering to these men or the organization they served, but considered as murder suspects without any substance worth the name. Exactly as might be expected from a track that collapsed on "its own absurdity."

Mattei started by making a list of the policemen, arranged them in alphabetical order by surname, and with her customary precision studied the information alleged against them.

After two hours and a dozen names she opened her bottle of mineral water, drank half, and ate her banana. Another two hours and ten names later she had consumed the rest of the water, eaten her apple, gone to the restroom, and then stretched her legs by walking around the floor where her office was.

Say what you will, but life as a police officer can be unbearably exciting, thought Lisa Mattei as she returned to her binders and looked at a postcard of one of her former colleagues. After twenty years of work as a policeman he had resigned. A few years later he entered contemporary history as one of the heavy names in the police track.

The picture on the postcard was a full-length photograph of himself. According to his own information, he also took the picture. Same with the postcard which he, according to the investigation, personally produced and paid for. Civilian clothes, polyester trousers, sport shirt, sandals with brown socks. Summer or late spring in the early eighties. A middle-aged man with a beer belly and early-stage baldness standing at the Brandenburg Gate in Berlin doing the Hitler salute. He's on vacation. In a week he will return to Stockholm and his work as a police inspector with the first precinct in Stockholm City.

Intense guy. Almost as handsome as Bäckström, thought Mattei.

· · ·

Two hours later and halfway through the police track it was time for her to go home. Why should she do that? thought Mattei. The very best thing would probably be if she brought a cot into the Palme room and didn't leave before she had the name of "the bastard who did it" and earned a friendly pat on the shoulder from her boss. The same man who was supposed to be able to see around corners, but for unknown reasons avoided personally peeking around this particular one.

The guard from the morning was still sitting there behind the counter in reception, and as she passed through he again called after her. He appeared at least to have a decent memory.

"Hello! Inspector Mattei. May I ask you a question?"

You want to know how to apply to the police academy, thought Mattei, who'd had that question before from people like him.

"Sure," she said.

"You have to promise not to get mad," he said, suddenly not seeming equally sure of himself.

"Depends on the question," said Mattei guardedly.

"I was wondering if I could invite you to a movie?"

"To a movie," said Mattei, who had a hard time concealing her surprise. To watch your favorite, *Conan the Barbarian,* she thought.

"Almodóvar's latest, the one that opened last week," he clarified.

Almodóvar, thought Mattei. Wonder if he's working for *Candid Camera,* she thought.

39

Mattei declined. And regretted it as soon as the words were out of her mouth. She tried to save herself with the usual follow-up questions and explanations. New mistakes were added to previous ones; everything went wrong.

Almodóvar? Are you pulling my leg? thought Mattei.

"You like Almodóvar?"

Yes, Almodóvar had touched him. Almodóvar had taught him a few things about "ladies" that he hadn't been able to figure out himself. Latin ladies at least. Almodóvar was perhaps not his biggest favorite, but he was good enough that he had decided to see his film. Besides, ladies usually like Almodóvar.

"I'm studying film at the university. This is a moonlighting job," he explained, shrugging his broad shoulders.

Still not too late to change her mind. Wrong again.

"That would have been really nice," said Mattei. "The problem is that I have to work all weekend. So maybe I'll see you tomorrow," she added.

"My day off," he said, shaking his head and looking downhearted.

"It'll have to be another time," said Mattei.

"It's cool," he answered.

What would someone like her do with someone like me? he thought as she disappeared onto the street.

.   .   .

When Mattei arrived at her overly large apartment that had been given to her by her kind father, she was in a lousy mood. Hated herself, hated the apartment, hated dear old dad. First she pulled on her workout clothes and did an extra circuit. She returned pumped up but in an equally bad mood. Instead of stepping into the shower and simply letting the water run, she started cleaning. In a fury she picked up, loaded the dishwasher, vacuumed, and scrubbed. Almost ready to faint, but just as angry, she called out for a pizza, managed to get half of it down even though she hated pizza otherwise. Drank almost a whole bottle of wine with the pizza. Even though she almost never drank. Then she lay down on the couch and flipped among the TV channels. When she finally went to bed her stomach hurt. She wasn't even drunk. Just angry. What would someone like him do with someone like me? she thought.

Then she finally fell asleep.

She woke up with both a headache and an upset stomach. Showered, got dressed, swallowed milk of magnesia and mineral water instead of eating breakfast, went to work.

And there he was.

"I thought this was your day off," said Mattei, smiling to conceal how happy she was.

"I traded with a buddy," he said, suddenly looking embarrassed.

"Okay then," said Mattei. "But it'll have to be the late showing because I have lots to do."

"Sure," he said and nodded. "That's no problem. I'm working until six o'clock so that's cool."

Yes, thought Mattei as she disappeared through the entry passage.

Yes, he thought as he watched her disappear into the building.

40

Concentration, thought Mattei as she opened the binder that she'd made it only halfway through the day before. Everything has its time. What remained were just under fifty policemen, the names of thirty of whom she didn't even have and who were not necessarily policemen. Eight hours for them, she thought. Then go home, shower, change clothes, and, for once, powder her little nose.

Then Almodóvar with a man she had only talked to three times and whose name she actually didn't know. Who had his appearance against him but seemed completely normal and even nice. "Call and find out what his name is," she wrote on her notepad.

Then she returned to her list of policemen who had been observed in the vicinity of the crime, who had a violent past, their own Magnum revolvers, harbored extreme political opinions, or simply acted inappropriately in general. Police, police, police, thought Mattei and sighed.

A few hours later Anna Holt called and asked her to check a name of a former colleague for her.

"Because I assume you're at work," Holt explained.

"Nothing better for me," Mattei agreed. Although tonight I'm going to a movie, she thought.

"Can you see if he's in the material?" Holt asked.

"No," said Mattei. "I'm pretty sure he's not. Not named, at least. I have the list in front of me and he's not there. There are about thirty who are supposed to have said they were policemen, or where the informant alleges that they were policemen but where their identity is lacking. If you ask me he's not one of them either," said Mattei. That's just as well, she thought, because according to Holt he was supposed to have been dead for fifteen years, and no bells were ringing in her head.

"You think so," said Holt.

"Yes. He doesn't tally with the description of any of them. Why are you asking, by the way?"

"A tip," said Holt and sighed for some reason. "From our colleague Bäckström," she said, sighing again.

"That explains it," said Mattei. "Lewin told me he'd called," she clarified.

"On a completely different matter, since you're working on it anyway," Holt continued. "Can you see if there's anything about lions?"

"Lions, like in Africa?"

"Exactly," said Holt. "The lion's den, in the lion's den, where they live or hang out, that is. Lions, that is."

"I can try with a plain text search," said Mattei.

"Will that work?"

"Should. Most of this is actually entered on the computer."

"This comes from Bäckström too. If you're wondering."

"I'll call if I find anything," said Mattei and made another notation on her pad. "Check lion, lion/den, the lion den, the lion's den, in the lion's den."

The plain text search for "lion" produced twenty hits. All could be traced back to half a dozen colleagues who had been in South Africa on vacation during the eighties and the apartheid regime. Who met with colleagues, visited nature reserves, went on photo safaris, saw lions out in nature, and in addition said the word "lion" when SePo's investigators held tape-recorded interviews with them.

The same search for "lion/den" produced one hit among the previous twenty. A Swedish policeman who said that during his visit his South African colleagues had invited him on a real safari—"not the kind of shit where you only get to take pictures"—so that he would get an opportunity to "put a bullet in a lion." A favor that evidently had not been granted the others, and a shooting opportunity that "unfortunately" did not happen.

Searches on "lion/den," "the lion den," "the lion's den," and "in the lion's den" produced one hit. A small apartment on Luxgatan on Lilla Essingen in Stockholm that did not have the slightest connection with certain colleagues' choice of politically controversial vacation destinations.

What's this now? thought Mattei as she finished reading half an hour later. Then she called Holt back and reported her findings.

"One hit on the lion's den," said Mattei. "Or more correctly stated on 'the lion den,' not possessive," she clarified.

"Okay. I'm listening," Holt replied.

In the eighties there had been an informal association of policemen, a kind of social club, that called itself "Mother Svea's Lions." Ten or so policemen, all of whom worked with the uniformed police in City, the majority of them with the riot squad, and many of them also did UN service both in the military and as police officers. That was how the name had come about. During their foreign service they started calling themselves "Mother Svea's Lions." Even had their own T-shirts printed, in blue and yellow with a big-busted, lion-like woman and the slogan: Mother Svea's Lions.

"One of them apparently had a spare apartment out on Lilla Essingen that they used to call the Lion's Den. Two rooms and a kitchen. A hundred and seventy square feet. They apparently shared the rent, they all had keys to the apartment, and it was there they would congregate and have their so-called meetings. Our former colleagues at SePo even did a house search there a few years after the murder. On October 10, 1988. I'm sitting with the report in front of me, if you're wondering."

"So did you find anything?"

"No," said Mattei. "It's very meagerly furnished, if you ask me. Beds in both rooms but not much more, judging from the pictures."

"Sounds like a fuck pad," said Holt.

"You probably shouldn't ask me about that," said Mattei. "I've never had the pleasure," she clarified.

"I have," said Holt. "You haven't missed a thing. But that's probably not why they did a search." Little lady, she thought.

"No," said Mattei. "It was because of who had the keys to it."

. . .

The information that produced the hit on the computer was in an inter-view with police inspector Berg. Apparently also the informal leader of Mother Svea's Lions. In addition he was the particular policeman who, by dint of his history, appeared in most of the lead files in the so-called police track.

"I don't know if you remember, but he was one of the officers Johans-son put in jail in the fall of 1985," Mattei explained. "The material about him reads like a serial."

"I know who he is," said Holt.

"But there's nothing concrete on either him or any of his friends. It's the usual, a lot of previous reports for excessive force on duty, strange political statements, and private weapon ownership. Plus he actually has an alibi that's pretty good. His . . ."

"I know," Holt interrupted. "His riot squad was the second patrol on the scene when Palme was shot."

"The world is full of coincidences," said Mattei.

"It sure is," Holt agreed and sighed for some reason.

As soon as she hung up the phone rang again. On her landline that she had connected to her cell.

"Hi," said the voice on the phone. "This is Johan, Johan Eriksson down in reception. If you want I can pick you up. Otherwise I suggest we meet ten minutes before outside the theater. I've got the tickets."

"Outside the theater is fine," said Mattei. Even though her name and address were actually in the phone book, in contrast to the majority of her colleagues. Leading him to her own front door would be bringing him a little too close.

If he didn't look like he did you would almost get the idea that he was as courteous as a gentleman of the old school, thought Mattei as she deleted him from her reminder list. Although he sounded a little shy, of course, and gentlemen of the old school probably weren't, she thought.

41

On Sunday Holt was supposed to meet her son, Nicke, and his latest girlfriend. An hour beforehand he called and canceled. They had quarreled and he wasn't in the mood even to see his mom.

"You'll just have to talk with her," said Holt, and as she put down the receiver she suddenly felt much older than forty-seven.

The next call came after an hour and was initiated with a cautious throat clearing. Lewin, thought Holt. Now he sounds like himself again.

"Yes, hi, Anna, it's Jan. Jan Lewin. I hope I'm not disturbing you."

"No," said Holt. "You're not." Because as usual I have nothing else going on, she thought.

Lewin wanted to thank her for the other evening and invite her in return. Not at his place however—cooking was not his strong suit—but at a decent neighborhood restaurant up at Gärdet where he lived.

"Really good, actually," Lewin attested.

"Sounds nice," said Anna Holt, and regretted it as soon as she'd said it. I hope he isn't falling in love with me, she thought as she hung up.

When Mattei left the police building at six o'clock her movie companion had already gone home. To shower and slick back his nonexistent hair, she thought, laughing to herself when she saw his co-worker with the same lack of hair behind the reception counter. A little gruffer type, apparently, who nodded at her curtly.

"Have a nice evening, police inspector," he said, managing to sound surly.

"Same to you," said Mattei. The type that doesn't like women police officers, she thought.

Once she arrived home life got more complicated. She intended to rest for an hour first, but somehow that didn't happen. Instead she lay down and half watched TV and even called her dad. To get the time to pass, if nothing else. Immediately she regretted picking up the phone, but fortunately he hadn't answered. Her bad conscience meant the message she left on his answering machine was more tender than intended.

Lisa, what the hell? thought Lisa Mattei, who never swore. You have to stop behaving like you're fifteen years old.

It was a grown-up woman who got into the shower. Who then dressed herself carefully. Not too much, not too little. Discreet dress, low-heeled pumps you could walk in. Who powdered her nose and a number of other places as well. Who regretted the look immediately as soon as she saw the results in the mirror. Tore off the dress and pumps. Threw them in a pile on the floor in the bathroom. Replaced them with jeans, linen shirt, an old jacket, and loafers. Still the same skinny, pale blonde, she thought crossly. Still fifteen years old and right now not much time to play with. She could forget about walking to the theater. It would have to be a taxi, which of course was late, and when she finally got there she was a good ten minutes late.

There he stood alone on the sidewalk outside the cinema, and when he caught sight of her he looked so relieved that all that had happened before was uninteresting.

"I was almost getting worried that something had happened," he said. "I didn't have your number, so . . ."

"You know women," said Mattei, smiling and shrugging her shoulders. "I'm sorry. I usually keep track of the time, actually."

"It's okay," he said, brushing lightly against her right arm. He nodded and invited her to go in ahead.

Just like an old-time gentleman, thought Mattei. Although they probably never looked that shy, of course.

"Not a word about work," said Holt as soon as she sat down.

"You don't need to worry, Anna," said Lewin with the usual faint smile. "I talked with our colleague Bäckström a few days ago, so I've had my fill for the rest of the year."

"Red or white, meat or fish," he continued, handing her the menu.

Goodness, thought Anna Holt. What is happening? Lewin of all people.

"Vegetarian pasta," said Holt. "With a lot of tomato and basil and a little, little grated cheese. Mineral water and a glass of dry white Italian wine."

"Sounds good," Lewin agreed. "I think I'll have the same."

Now I recognize you again, Jan, she thought.

Then they talked about everything except work. Holt talked about taking some time off and going to a warmer place as soon as she got the chance. Even though she hadn't planned the slightest little trip, just as insurance against something she couldn't even name.

Then they talked about travels in general. Lewin mostly about the kind that never happened, but the way in which he spoke was completely bearable to listen to.

"I read a novel many years ago. Unfortunately I've forgotten both the title and the author, but it made a deep impression on me." Lewin shook his head, the same Lewinian smile. "A little too deep, perhaps," he said and sighed.

"Tell me," said Holt. You need to talk, she thought.

·   ·   ·

The novel whose title Lewin had forgotten was about a young French nobleman who decided to go to Africa at the end of the nineteenth century on an expedition. First he devoted an entire year to the most careful preparations. Exhaustively depicted in a couple of hundred pages. Then came the great day when he and his servant and attendants left the rural estate en route to the station for further transport to the great harbor city Marseilles, the boat to Africa and all the discoveries that still remained to be made in his life.

"Then he changed his mind and went home again," said Lewin. "Why should he go to Africa? He'd already made the entire journey in his own mind."

"Jan," said Anna Holt. "Look at me. That's a terrible story."

"I know," said Lewin, who suddenly seemed almost exhilarated. "But that's me."

Then they talked about other things, and when they went their separate ways and she was standing down in the subway waiting for the train home the evening caught up with her. He's in love with me, she thought. It's your own fault, and what do you do about it? she thought.

As soon as they were in their seats and the lights in the theater had been turned down, her old-fashioned gentleman, roughly twenty-five years old and a hundred kilos of muscle and bone, stretched, made himself comfortable, sank into his seat, and laced his large hands over his flat stomach. Then he uttered not a sound for ninety minutes.

Halfway into the film—as if by accident—he placed his right hand on the arm support between them. Mattei happened to graze against it as she tried not to rustle the bag of candy she otherwise never ate. Then he turned up his palm and she set aside the bag of candy and—as if by accident—placed her hand in his.

It was still there when they stepped out on the street. It had started raining, and Johan looked at her with almost childish delight.

"It's raining," he said. "That's the surest sign of all."

"The movie, what did you think?" he continued, squeezing her hand, very lightly, almost imperceptibly, simply like a signal from his own hand. Strong, tan, long fingers, with the veins on the back of the hand clearly visible.

"I don't really know," said Lisa Mattei, shaking her head. What film? she thought.

"If you're very strong then you have to be extremely nice," said Johan, looking at her seriously.

"What time do you start work tomorrow?" Mattei asked suddenly.

"I'm off," said Johan, shaking his head. "Like I said, I switched shifts with a buddy."

"Then I suggest we go to my place," said Lisa Mattei. "I have to be up early."

Wednesday, October 10.
Canal de Menorca outside Puerto Pollensa
on north Mallorca

In order to avoid the strong currents closest to land, the solitary man on board Esperanza *passed the point at Formentor by a good margin. Continued a good cable's length out in the deep channel, and now it was about time for him to decide. He could change course ninety degrees port toward Cala Sant Vicente on the north side of the island. It was twelve nautical miles, just over an hour's run, and only a few hours ago that would have been the journey's destination. With plenty of time and a breeze that cooled considerably better here, out on the open sea. But now it was too late, he thought. Then he entered the new course on his GPS. Two nautical miles north of the Citadel on Menorca and the destination straight ahead. Sixty nautical miles to Menorca, six hours' run if the good weather held. And then what? he thought. Yet another day and night at sea.*

42

Five weeks earlier, Wednesday, September 5.
Headquarters of the National Bureau of Criminal
Investigation on Kungsholmen in Stockholm

Two people were at the table in Johansson's conference room: Jan Lewin and Lisa Mattei. Johansson himself had just let them know he had been delayed half an hour due to circumstances over which he had no control. His secretary served coffee and homemade apple cake as consolation. On the other hand where Holt had gone she didn't know. Holt had not been in touch with Johansson's secretary. Possibly she had called Johansson, or vice versa, and otherwise she hoped they would enjoy the cake.

It was not that Anna Holt had overslept. When Johansson called her an hour before the meeting and reported that he would be delayed half an hour she was already at her desk. That left at least an hour and a half at her disposal, and plenty of time for a visit to the tech squad in Stockholm to look into the tip about the revolver that Bäckström had given her. Question marks that it would be beneficial to straighten out for the meeting with Johansson and the others so they could finally draw a line through Bäckström and move on.

The head of the tech squad was a few years older than she was. Almost twenty years ago they had been co-workers at the detective squad in Stockholm. A good professional relationship, but nothing else.

"Just a quick question," said Holt, sitting down in the chair in front of his desk.

"I can't even offer you coffee?"

"Not even coffee," said Holt, shaking her head. "This is about a weapons tip that came into the bureau from our colleague Bäckström," she continued, for the sake of simplicity handing over the e-mail that Bäckström had sent her.

"Bäckström," said her colleague and moaned. "What did we do to deserve this?"

"We're in complete agreement there, but what I'm wondering about is simply whether you test fired the weapon in question and made a comparison with the bullets from the Palme murder?"

"No," said the technician, shaking his head. "We've test fired it of course. On the other hand, we haven't made a comparison with the Palme bullets, for reasons that are easy to see."

"So why not?" said Holt.

"The weapon in question was manufactured in the fall of 1995. Nine years after the Palme murder. You can tell by the manufacturing number, by the way."

"According to Bäckström's e-mail it would have been manufactured ten years earlier. Fall of 1985," Holt clarified. "It says so in your associate's e-mail to him too."

"Typo," said her former colleague, smiling acidly. "I promise and assure you. The weapon in question was manufactured at Ruger's factory in the U.S. in the fall of 1995. A good nine years after the murder of the prime minister. If it had been manufactured in 1985 we would have made a comparison. It's pure routine these days. That stuff about only comparing the bullets to Smith & Wesson revolvers is history now. That's a sad story, in itself."

"Typo," said Holt. "The thing about the general agent in Bremen in the former West Germany is also a typo? That's what it says in the e-mail from your associate."

"Childish of him," said the head of tech and sighed. "He probably wants to mess with Bäckström as thanks for that container of old office furniture he sent us."

"I'm listening," said Holt.

Then the head of the tech squad recounted the story of the old office furniture and all the other peculiar inquiries from their colleague Bäckström they'd had since he started at property investigation. Earlier too, for that matter.

"You know how Bäckström is. If he's suddenly interested in a .357 caliber Magnum revolver, it can only be the Palme weapon. Or more correctly stated, the reward for the Palme weapon that our good friend Bäckström hopes to share with the so-called anonymous informant. As a policeman of course he can't get any money."

"I think like you do," said Holt.

"Sorry you were involved," said the head of the tech squad. "I'll have a talk with him."

"Not for my sake," said Holt. "But if you're going to anyway, you can say hello and thank him." So there, you little fatso, she thought.

When Lars Martin Johansson returned after forty-five minutes, not thirty as he'd told his secretary, all three of his co-workers were in place and though they'd been sitting a good while not much had been said. Everyone seemed to be doing something.

Holt made notes in a binder she had brought with her. Mattei was tapping off text messages on her cell phone. Lewin was leaning back without doing anything at all, but at the same time his thoughts seemed far away.

Maybe in Africa, thought Holt, sneaking a glance at him.

Johansson started talking before he entered the room.

"Here you sit," he noted and sat down. "What do you think about starting, Anna?" he continued. "Give us the latest news about that wretched Bäckström so that we'll have Lisa and Jan with us."

. . .

Anna Holt gave a brief description of the tip from Bäckström. She handed out copies of his e-mail to her colleagues and told about her visit to the tech squad. A typical Bäckström, but it wasn't his fault alone because their colleagues in Stockholm had evidently taken the opportunity to mess with him.

"In addition he gave us the name of a former colleague who is supposed to have had access to the weapon. I asked Lisa to check that, but he's not included in the case files."

"So what's his name?" asked Jan Lewin, sighing just as wearily as his colleague at the tech squad had an hour before.

"His name is Claes Waltin. Or was, correctly stated. He was a former police superintendent with SePo. Resigned from the secret police in the summer of 1988 to go into private business. Died in a drowning accident on north Mallorca four years later. According to Bäckström's anonymous informant, Waltin supposedly had access to the Palme weapon a month or so before he died," Holt summarized.

"And he's not in the case files," Mattei interjected. "I've checked and checked again."

"Strange," said Lewin, shaking his head. "I'm sure he must be in the material. Assuming we're talking about the same Waltin, of course," he added in his meticulous way.

"Not on my lists," Mattei persisted. "He's not there. Why do you think that?"

"I put him in the investigation myself," said Lewin. "So he should be there."

"You don't say," said Johansson.

"You did," said Holt at the same moment.

What is he saying? thought Mattei.

"I don't know if you recall it," said Lewin, "but at our first meeting three weeks ago I talked about all the parking tickets I had the pleasure of going through."

"Tell us again," said Johansson, lacing his fingers over his far from flat stomach and leaning back in the chair.

"The details I'll have to come back to, but in broad strokes it went like this," said Lewin, cautiously clearing his throat.

On the morning of Saturday the first of March, almost exactly ten hours after the murder, Police Superintendent Claes Waltin incurred a parking fine on Smedsbacksgatan up at Gärdet. The car was his own. A new five series BMW and not a common car among police officers. Lewin had sent a routine inquiry to the colleagues from SePo who had responsibility for the Palme investigation's police track and received a written answer after about a month.

"I remember that distinctly. It felt a little strange to ask them the question considering who it concerned," said Lewin. "Waltin was a high-ranking chief at the secret police. He was directly subordinate to the bureau director, Berg, who was in the investigation leadership and responsible for SePo's cooperation in the Palme investigation."

"I can imagine it must have felt strange," said Johansson. "So what did they have to say?"

"I don't remember the exact wording, but I got a written reply that basically said the vehicle had been used for an official duty concerning supervision of a person who was staying in the neighborhood at one of SePo's so-called secure addresses."

"That was generous of them," said Johansson. "Personally I would have been content to say that it was an official matter. That thing about supervision of persons who are at secure addresses isn't something you commit to paper."

"It must be there in the material," said Lewin, looking almost apologetically at Mattei. "A written request from me and a written reply from them. Must be there."

"Perhaps you were sloppy with the registration, Jan," said Johansson. "It can happen to the best of us."

"Not me," said Lewin, shaking his head.

"I'll check again and see if I've missed it," said Mattei.

"Do that," said Johansson. "You, Lewin, go through your boxes and, you, Lisa, go through the rest. Then Anna, you'll take care of the remainder of the Bäckström message so that I can finally get rid of him. That part about the weapon in question supposedly being used in a total of three murders and a suicide sounds undeniably hair-raising. If we don't count the prime minister that still leaves two murder victims and one who's taken his own life."

"Sounds like a typical Bäckström, if you ask me," said Holt.

"Or a typical murder-suicide, if you ask me," said Johansson. "The classic case where dad, who's a hunter and marksman, shoots his wife and only child and ends by shooting himself. Jealousy, alcohol, and misery. Much too common, unfortunately, but too common to be able to check."

"Noted," said Holt. Sounds like a typical Johansson, thought Holt. Whatever this has to do with an ordinary registration review, she thought.

After the meeting Johansson took Mattei aside.

"I have a little special assignment for you, Lisa," said Johansson. "I've got the idea that it's your department, if I may say so."

"I'm listening, chief," said Mattei. I have to call Johan, she thought.

"There is said to be a college at Oxford University called Mohdlinn College. Spelled 'Magdalen' without an 'e' at the end. Pronounced *Mohdlinn*."

"That's right," said Mattei. "Said to be one of the oldest and finest. Founded in the Middle Ages. Named after Mary Magdalene, Mary from Magdala. Who according to the Bible is supposed to have washed Jesus's feet on some occasion." Yet another exploited sister, she thought.

"Exactly," said Johansson with unexpected emphasis. "Then there was the rumor that they might have been involved too? Jesus and her, that is."

"More than what I know," said Mattei. Whatever this has to do with it, she thought.

"All the same," said Johansson. "There's another thing I'm thinking about."

"I'm listening, chief," said Mattei. Preferably today, she thought.

Then, without providing the source, he told about the deer enclosure in the park behind Magdalen College, that the number of deer in the enclosure should be the same as the number of members of the college. That when one of them died a deer was shot and was served at the memorial ceremony for the deceased.

"You know, one of those typical English gentlemen's dinners," Johansson clarified. "Venison steak with overcooked vegetables and brown gravy. Can you find out if this adds up?"

"Deer enclosure, number of deer in the park, if a deer is shot when one of the professors dies, what is served at the memorial dinner," Mattei summarized. Yuck, what awful food, and what in the name of heaven does this have to do with the assassination of Olof Palme? she thought.

"Brilliant," said Johansson, patting her kindly on the shoulder. That girl can go as far as she wants, and finally this is starting to resemble something, he thought.

43

When Anna Holt returned to her office she continued checking the information she'd received from Bäckström. First she tackled the various turns in the "Bäckström weapons track," and after an hour's general pondering and two brief phone calls, she was clear in detail about what had gone on.

First she talked with Bäckström's immediate boss. She explained the situation and asked for his silence. Then by virtue of his rights as a superior he went into Bäckström's computer and inspected what had gone in and out during the last few weeks.

Rather little that had to do with his job, as it appeared. On the other hand there were a number of contacts with the tech squad regarding a revolver. Two e-mails to Holt. Finally an e-mail that he had sent that same morning to a not unfamiliar art dealer. Incompletely deleted, as so often before. Brief and cryptic in content, but in any case not an official matter that belonged on Bäckström's desk. After that he called Holt back and reported his findings.

I see, thought Anna Holt as she hung up. The little fatso has tricked me.

About this Bäckström of course had no idea. When on Monday the same week he returned to work after his well-earned weekend's rest, he started the day by calling his old friend and benefactor Henning on his cell phone. There was a constant busy signal, and because Bäckström had a lot to do he sent an encouraging e-mail instead, which he then deleted and put straight into the wastebasket. Just a few encouraging, discreet lines, that the project was proceeding completely according to plan. Hardly informative for all his so-called colleagues whose only task evidently consisted of spying on him.

Then he devoted half an hour to general optimistic musings. The weapon he had basically already found, and what remained was to get a bit more meat on the bones as regards the probable perpetrator, former Police Superintendent Claes Waltin. Who by the way would have believed there was so much spine in that little half-fairy? Other than Bäckström, of course, thought Bäckström.

As an initial measure he called his relative at the police union who knew basically everything about all former and current members. Also about Police Superintendent Claes Waltin, even though he was not even a member.

"He was one of those stuck-up little attorneys who go around thinking he's a cop. He was a member of the union for law graduates," Bäckström's cousin explained. "Us old comrades in the corps were probably not fine enough for an asshole like that."

"What was he like as a person?" said Bäckström. Phenomenally good formulation, he thought. What was he like as a person? Suck on those words, he thought.

"As a person," said Bäckström's cousin. "That's a strange question. The bastard is dead. There's nothing about the dead that isn't good. Haven't you heard that? We hold strictly to that here at the association."

"But what was he like? As a human being? While he was alive, I mean." There it was again, thought Bäckström. Soon you'll be giving courses to those vultures on TV. Must be all the good Czech beer, he thought. Just bitter enough but still softly rounded off.

"He's supposed to have been fucking hard on the ladies. Really hard, if you know what I mean."

"Leather and chains," suggested Bäckström, who was not entirely unfamiliar with the subject.

"Leather and chains," Bäckström's cousin snorted. "That was only the first letter, if you ask me. That old ass whipper that they ran on TV, the one who's supposed to have shaved the mouse off of five thousand women before he beat them up . . ."

"Yes?"

"He could have sung in the church's boy choir, compared with Waltin."

"Tell me," said Bäckström.

His cousin was happy to. Over the years various members of the association, all on duty of course and in connection with so-called external surveillance, had made the most peculiar observations of former police superintendent Waltin. Peculiar places, contexts, and people.

"A lot of those clubs for sex and leather and homos and dykes and God knows what. Plus all the usual pickup spots where he basically seems to have camped out. Plus all the stories, of course. You haven't heard what he's supposed to have thought up with that crazy colleague Wiijnbladh's wife? The poisoner, you know. By the way, aren't you working at the same place nowadays?"

"What did he do with her?" interrupted Bäckström. I'm the one asking the questions here, he thought.

Quite a bit worth sucking on, thought Bäckström contentedly an hour later, when his relative unwillingly hung up the phone. Then Bäckström punched out for lunch, and by the second pilsner he got an idea that was well worth trying. One of those small hunches that are granted only to real policemen. But first of all it was time for a conversation with the old poisoner Wiijnbladh.

Wonder if they had a threesome, thought Bäckström. The leather boy, the poisoner, and that red-haired sow he never managed to kill. He should have chatted with Waltin and got a few tips, he thought.

I have to talk with Bäckström, thought Holt. But before that there were other things to deal with. So she went over to their own intelligence squad and asked them to produce a list of all murder-suicides during the period from the beginning of 1980 through the end of 1985. Hopefully nothing earlier; unlikely that it could be later, she thought.

"We don't have a special code for what the criminologists call extended suicide," said the analyst, shaking his head. "Besides, it's going to take awhile because this information is so old."

"Two murders and a subsequent suicide. Start with the police authority in Stockholm. The weapon must have been a revolver."

"Still going to take awhile."

"It's the big boss who wants this information," said Holt.

"I understand. I'll call you on your cell when it's done, and what I find I'll send on GroupWise."

"When can I have it?"

"Give me an hour, at least," the analyst sighed.

Wiijnbladh had gotten up off the floor since the last time. Now he was sitting at his desk thumbing through a gigantic art encyclopedia. In general he looked like always. Wobbly, shaky, weary. Small and hollowed out, with a noticeable lack of both teeth and hair.

"So how's life with you, Wiijnbladh?" Bäckström asked as he sat down. Wonder how much electricity would be saved in the building if you hooked a battery up to the son of a bitch? he thought.

"Alive, but not much more than that," said Wiijnbladh in a faint voice.

"I think you look fucking frisky," said Bäckström. You can easily make the finals in the world championships for shaking like a leaf, he thought.

"That's nice of you, Bäckström."

"It's nothing," said Bäckström. "By the way, I met an old acquaintance the other day. Known art dealer. He told me he sold a really fine painting to a former colleague a bunch of years ago. It was a Zorn, apparently. It struck me suddenly that I think you knew him. Police Superintendent Claes Waltin. Weren't you and he old friends?"

"A close friend," said Wiijnbladh, who already had something damp in the corner of his eye. "So sadly lost in a tragic accident. Great art collector. Had a most excellent collection of contemporary Swedish paintings."

"But how did he have the money for that?" asked Bäckström. "I mean, on a regular police salary you don't have the cash for a few Zorns, exactly." At the most a porno photo or two that you can take with your official cell phone, he thought.

"Very well off, very well off," said Wiijnbladh, twisting his skinny neck. "Very rich parents. Waltin must have been good for many millions in his prime."

"You don't say," said Bäckström. "It was a common interest in art that brought you together?"

Or was it that red-haired sow you were married to, who introduced him as her cousin from the country? he thought.

"That and a lot of other things," said Wiijnbladh, nodding mournfully.

"So what were those other things," said Bäckström. Your old lady, he thought.

"The former police superintendent was a high-ranking chief in the closed operation, as I'm sure you know."

"Yes," said Bäckström with a bewildered expression. So what? SePo doesn't investigate poisonings, he thought.

"On a few occasions I had the opportunity to help him and the closed operation in their important work," said Wiijnbladh, who suddenly looked as proud as a person can who has almost no teeth of his own left.

Jeez Louise, thought Bäckström. Did you mix thallium into the beet soup at the Russian embassy or what?

"Sounds extremely exciting," said Bäckström. "Do tell."

"Can't say anything," said Wiijnbladh. "Secrecy. Security of the realm, as I'm sure you understand."

"You can say something anyway," Bäckström persisted. "Of course it will stay in this room."

"I don't know about that," said Wiijnbladh plaintively. "Sorry, sorry, Bäckström, my lips are sealed by Swedish law. But I can say this much anyway, that I received a formal thanks from the highest leadership of SePo for my efforts. If you were to doubt what I'm saying, I mean."

Wonder just what the poisoner Wiijnbladh could have helped leather boy Waltin with? thought Bäckström when he returned to his office.

Other than the beet soup, of course. Just about time to go home, by the way, he thought. The time was approaching the magic stroke of three, and the day's toil and moil had long been over for a simple wage slave in the service of the police administration.

After an hour Anna Holt got an answer from the bureau's Central Intelligence Service. There was a case that tallied with her specification. A so-called extended suicide that occurred in Spånga on March 27, 1983. Less than three years before the murder of the prime minister.

The perpetrator was a painter. A widower, forty-five years old, hunter and sports shooter with a license for several weapons. He shot his sixteen-year-old daughter and her twenty-three-year-old boyfriend at home in his house in Spånga. After that he shot himself. The weapon had been confiscated. The crime was solved, but for natural reasons no indictment was ever brought.

Nothing more than that emerged from the information stored in the bureau's computer system. The complete investigation would be found in the Stockholm police archives. The weapon ought to be at the tech squad in Stockholm. Because those kinds of weapons usually wound up there, according to the analyst who had searched out the report.

That can't be right. Not if we confiscated the weapon in 1983. You can't find fault with the little fatso's imagination, thought Holt, looking at the clock. It'll have to be tomorrow, she thought.

44

For the third time in a month Lewin pulled out his old boxes from the winter and spring of 1986. The same boxes that contained every random piece of evidence that might be—at best—of doubtful value to the police.

On Saturday the first of March at 9:15 a.m., Police Superintendent Claes Waltin got a parking ticket on Smedsbacksgatan up at Gärdet. The car was his own 1986 BMW 535.

When he got the ticket it had not been parked there very long. According to the meter maid Lewin spoke with, she and her associate followed a special Saturday routine. They made two rounds in the area. First they made note of illegally parked cars, and when they returned between fifteen minutes and half an hour later for the second round, cars were ticketed if they were still there. Simple and practical, considering the grace period of at least ten minutes this gave the owners.

Considering that Waltin was parked in a spot requiring a disability permit, it couldn't have been there during the first round. Cars parked like that were ticketed immediately. Based on the address and the time of the ticket, it could hardly have been parked illegally before 8:45. All according to the meter maid, who was quite understanding.

Lewin bought her line of reasoning. It was logical and had the stamp of probability, and there was little that argued for this parking violation having the slightest relevance to a murder that had been committed ten hours earlier and several miles away. Nevertheless he had still sent a written inquiry on Monday, March 24, 1986, to his colleagues at SePo who were responsible for the police track.

The written response had not arrived for over a month. It was dated Tuesday, April 29, 1986, signed by an inspector with the secret police, brief in its wording and surrounded in certified secrecy. "The vehicle in question has been used on duty in the supervision of the object of protection who was staying at one of our addresses in the area."

In all likelihood both of these letters should be in one of Mattei's binders, Lewin thought.

"Have you found it?" asked Lewin an hour later when Mattei returned to their office with a sizeable bundle of computer lists under her arm.

"No," said Mattei. "Neither your inquiry nor their answer. There aren't even any notes in the ongoing registration."

"So how do you interpret that?" asked Lewin. "I mean, you're the one who's the computer nerd among us ordinary mortals."

"Nice of you," said Mattei. "Because I have a hard time believing you're the one who's been careless, I also think they received your question. Then for some reason they didn't register it. Sent a reply a month later with one of their own serial numbers, which to be sure is in their registry, but which refers to a completely different case and a completely different file."

"So what is this about?"

"I've managed to trace that file. It's in the case files and concerns an inquiry to Ryhov's mental hospital about one of their patients who tipped off SePo about a police officer in Gothenburg who is supposed to have murdered Olof Palme. Moreover, that lead file was already written off in May 1986."

"But—"

"It doesn't have the slightest to do with your case," Mattei interrupted. "If I were Johansson I'd say it's one of the most phenomenally wacko tips I've seen."

"Extremely peculiar," said Lewin. "So what do you think happened?"

"I think that someone set aside your question to them without registering it. Then the same someone presumably waited a month and then sent a reply with a serial number that references something else. If you had received a reply without a serial number, I'm sure you would have reacted."

"And the colleague at SePo who signed my answer? Inspector Jan Andersson. Could Waltin have persuaded him to do something like that?"

"Sounds highly unlikely that he would have succeeded in persuading someone to reply to a letter that doesn't seem to exist and supply the response with a serial number that refers to a completely different matter besides."

"Andersson, our colleague Jan Andersson. True, it's been over twenty years, but—"

"Dead," Mattei interrupted. "Died in 1991 of a stroke, and there doesn't seem to have been anything strange about the death. Worked with SePo and in the Palme investigation. Moreover he was the one who took care of the kind of matters relating to your question."

"This is getting stranger and stranger," said Lewin. "What do you think about all of this?"

"At best what's happened is that someone, in that case probably Waltin, committed at least two crimes to get out of a parking ticket."

"And in the worst case?"

"In the worst case, it's really bad," said Mattei.

Lewin devoted the rest of the day to unpleasant musings. He did not like the fact that one and the same person showed up in several places in the same investigation without there being a common reason for him or her to do so. A natural, human explanation. Not the kind that had already started to torment him.

Mattei continued as if nothing had happened. As of twenty-four hours ago there were other things going on in her head, and work had to go on as pure routine. First she prepared a page of reminder notes about the mysterious parking ticket that would certainly interest her boss. Then she went to work on the strange special assignment he had given her. Sent a friendly e-mail to the administrative assistant at Magdalen College in Oxford from her private e-mail address, signed by Lisa Mattei, PhD at the University of Stockholm to be on the safe side. And that is really me, she thought.

An hour later she got an answer. Goodness, things are moving fast, she thought.

Dear Dr. Mattei,
Thank you for your kind e-mail. It's a nice old tale, but I am afraid it's not true, and there's never been any actual evidence for it. I rather suspect that it's a legend that's been passed around by other colleges—and perhaps even colleagues. It's true that our deer herd is occasionally culled. However, this has nothing to do . . .

Good or bad and what is he really looking for? thought Lisa Mattei, and because it was Lars Martin Johansson, and urgent as usual, she called him on his cell phone.

"Lisa Mattei," said Mattei. "I have an answer to your questions, boss. I'm afraid the whole thing is a tall tale."

"Brilliant," said Johansson. "Come over at once, and I'll tell Helena to put on the coffeepot."

"Two minutes," said Mattei. And I'll tell Helena to put on the coffee-pot, she thought, shaking her head.

Lars Martin Johansson was on his thinking couch and waved at the nearest chair.

"I'm listening," he said.

Not the slightest sign of any coffeepot, fortunately, Mattei thought after a quick look around.

"According to the administrative assistant at Magdalen, a Mr. Edgar Smith-Hamilton, whose official title by the way is bursar, which means he's in charge of the change purse so to speak, there are presently thirty-two deer in the park behind the college, and they've had approximately that many for a number of years. On the other hand the number of fellows is considerably greater than that. More than a hundred, if you include honorary fellows. The deer park is over three hundred years old, but there has never been any rule that the number of deer must tally with the number of fellows. In the old days it seems to have been the case that there were considerably more deer than fellows, but for the past fifty years it's been the other way around."

"Phenomenal," said Johansson, glowing with delight. "Go on, Mattei. Go on."

Nor was it the case that a deer was shot when a fellow had died. On the other hand a certain amount of shooting was done for reasons of game management, as a rule after rutting, which happened in October each year.

"Although you know about that sort of thing better than I do, boss," said Mattei.

"Just a guess," Johansson smiled. "Do continue."

The part about the dinner didn't add up either. Dinners in memory of deceased fellows were held twice a year. One in early summer and one in late autumn. To be sure, exceptions had occurred, but then it was for very esteemed members of the college. Most recently a deceased Nobel Prize winner had been honored with a dinner, a theme day with lectures and seminars to discuss his scientific work, plus a Festschrift from Oxford University Press.

"So what do they eat?" asked Johansson eagerly.

"As far as the menus are concerned it does happen that deer from the park may be served at college dinners, but it's not a mandatory feature of the memorial dinners. Varied menu, in other words. Usual banquet food, as I understood it."

"I'll be damned," said Johansson, sighing contentedly from the couch.

"You're satisfied with the answers I got, boss?"

"Satisfied," said Johansson. "Do we celebrate Christmas Eve on the twenty-fourth of December?"

"Yes, that was all I guess," said Mattei, making an attempt to stand up.

"Just one more thing," said Johansson, stopping her with a hand gesture. "How did these rumors arise?"

"From what I understood between the lines it was a story that was tended very carefully by those most closely affected. Well, not the deer, that is."

"I'll be damned again," Johansson grunted.

Wonder if he's checking information in some old interrogation or what, thought Mattei as she left. Johansson was still Johansson, despite his highly suspect view of women, she thought.

45

On Tuesday Inspector Evert Bäckström was engaged in archival research.

The Stockholm police department's old central archive was in the basement of the big police building and it was there his sensitive nose had led him. Following a scent no stronger than a vague hunch. Impossible to be detected by all his nasally congested colleagues. Concealed from everyone except a seasoned old bloodhound like him.

Besides, he had good memories of this archive. When he had worked overtime at the after-hours unit in the eighties, it was here he would make his way for a moment of reflection and rest. It was necessary so as not to capsize in the tidal wave of common gangsters, lunatics, drunks, and glowworms that the half-apes in the uniformed police ladled in through the duty desk.

A memory from another time. Before computers took over the fine old handiwork. A time when all real constables sorted their thugs in neat hanging folders with cardboard tabs. Where every thug had at least one file, and where the most diligent would be rewarded within a short time with several. Arranged in endless rows by social security number. In different colors over time. Brown, blue, green, light red, red . . . and already by the change in color Bäckström understood early on what was about to happen.

The dear old central archive. The wellspring of police knowledge, where he himself had both slaked his thirst and refreshed his soul on numerous memorable occasions. This final safeguard and stronghold of knowledge, where literally everything you put your mitts on was collected and never discarded. Regardless of unverified suspicions, dismissal with prejudice, withdrawn indictments, verdicts of acquittal, and all the other nonsense that attorneys were involved in. The crook remained in the central archive. For all time. Once in, you never got out.

Of course he'd been right, he was always right. There he hung, dangling in his blue sixties file. Now I have you, you little leather boy, thought Bäckström, releasing Waltin from his hook.

A thin file with copies of old typewritten forms. Initial report, interview with the plaintiff, personal information about the suspect, interview with the suspect, summons to new interview with the plaintiff, dismissal with prejudice, no crime, and if it hadn't been for the central archive, Claes Waltin would have been lost to worldly justice for all time.

The night between April thirtieth and the first of May 1968, the twenty-three-year-old law student Claes Waltin had, according to the report, shoved a wooden candlestick into the vagina of a twenty-five-year-old woman who was a doctoral candidate in Nordic languages and supported herself working as a substitute teacher at a high school in the southern suburbs. They had met earlier in the evening at the Hasselbacken restaurant on Djurgården in connection with the students' traditional celebration of Walpurgis Eve.

Assuming that you believed her, the following was said to have happened.

Waltin had gone home with her to her residence on Södermalm. There he had first assaulted her sexually by forcing her to have anal intercourse. Then he bound her, put a muzzle on her, and inserted the candlestick into her genital area. When he was done with that he left.

An hour later the woman suffered severe bleeding, called for an ambulance herself, and was taken to the Söder hospital. There she remained for over a week. A female social worker visited her, got her to talk, and saw to it that she filed a police report.

A forensic examination had been made and damage to the entry to her vagina, vaginal walls, and portio vaginalis had been observed. In conclusion the forensic doctor observed in his statement: "that the observed injuries appear to have arisen through physical impact from a hard, oblong object inserted into the vagina"; "that the insertion of this object probably required considerable force"; "that the injuries do not contradict the description the patient has given"; "that at the same time it may have arisen in some other way through comparable physical impact"; "that it cannot be ruled out either that they are self-inflicted."

Not until a few weeks later was the young Waltin called for an interview with the police. He denied any form of assault against the plaintiff. They had met at the Hasselbacken restaurant, he had gone home with her, and it was on her own suggestion that they had had normal intercourse in which moreover she had taken the initiative.

An hour or so later he left her and walked home to his student apartment on Östermalm, because he would be getting up early the next morning. He had promised to visit his mother, who was sickly and needed regular checking by her only son.

In conclusion he also said that he was shocked and shaken by the horrible accusations he was being subjected to. He could never even imagine doing something like that and did not understand why the plaintiff said what she had.

A week later the plaintiff had been called to another interview. She never appeared. Instead she called the police and said that she wanted to withdraw her report. She never provided any more detailed explanation for this turnabout. A month later the prosecutor had written off the report. "The reported incident is not to be considered a crime."

Typical police chief candidate, thought Bäckström, rolling up the file and putting it in his jacket pocket. Much simpler than wasting your precious time at that copy machine that never worked. Gold, Bäckström, he thought, patting his jacket pocket as he came out onto the street again, and because it was both simplest and safest he went straight home.

For lunch he took a few things out of his own refrigerator, where these days there were a number of delicacies, had a cold pilsner, even allowed himself a little drop of liquor. Then he lay down on the couch so he could think in peace and quiet about an ordinary leather boy's motives for murdering a prime minister.

It must have been something sexual, thought Bäckström. The same motive, although a different modus operandi, so to speak. What remained was to link Waltin to his latest known victim. Perhaps they belonged to the same secret society of leather boys? Was it an ordinary little internal settling of accounts because they had a falling out over some little ass-whipping subject? It was about time that inspector Bäckström started smoothing out the perpetrator profile, he thought.

In the midst of these pleasant musings he must have fallen asleep, because when he woke up it was time for dinner.

One thing I know that never dies, and that is the reputation of a dead man, thought Bäckström when a while later he was walking at a slow pace to his usual place. That was straight talk. Not that liberal drivel about never speaking ill of the dead. It's enough if it's true, damn it, he thought.

46

For the second day in a row Anna Holt called her old colleague from the bureau who was now head of the tech squad.

"It's me again, Holt," said Anna Holt. "At the risk of being tedious, do you have two minutes?"

Holt was not the least bit tedious. She could call every day if she wanted. What could he help her with?

"This is about another revolver. The murder weapon in a murder-suicide that happened on March 27, 1983. A man who shot his daughter and her fiancé before he shot himself. Happened out in Spånga. The revolver was confiscated and is said to have ended up with you. You couldn't pull out a more detailed description of it, could you? It doesn't appear in the extract I got from our own CIS."

"Sure," said the head of the tech squad. "You don't have a number on the case?"

"Of course," said Holt. "I'll e-mail it."

"Just give me an hour," said her old colleague.

What am I really up to? thought Holt as she hung up.

This time it had taken only forty-five minutes. The weapon she was wondering about ended up at the tech squad the day after the murder/suicide. It had been test fired and compared with the bullets the forensic doctor had plucked out of the three victims. The results confirmed what had already been figured out. The murder weapon.

"Also a Ruger .357 caliber Magnum. The same as that revolver Bäckström was raving about. Although a somewhat older model."

"Would it be possible to take a look at it?" asked Holt.

"Unfortunately not," replied the head of the tech squad. "It's not here anymore."

"So where is it?"

"Nowhere, I'm afraid. According to our papers, it was here until October 1988. Then it was turned over, along with twenty or so other weapons, to the Swedish Defense Factories for scrapping. There are papers on that too."

"Scrapping," said Holt. "I thought you kept all the weapons you got in?"

Far from it, according to her colleague. They kept those weapons that were interesting from an investigative standpoint. Besides that they kept those that were interesting for ballistic comparisons in general.

"As you perhaps know we have a little weapons library up here at the squad. Over twelve hundred weapons, actually. Various types of weapons. Different brands in various calibers and models."

"So which ones do you send to scrap?"

Those that were in poor shape. Assuming they wouldn't be needed for any crime investigation.

"Mostly old rejects, actually. Sawed-off shotguns, drilled-out starter guns, all sorts of home-made contraptions. On the other hand, if we have several copies of the same weapon in good condition we usually don't scrap them. We apportion those out to colleagues around the country. Most tech squads have their own weapons libraries, and in Stockholm we confiscate more weapons than any other police authority in the country."

"So this one was in poor condition then," asked Holt.

"Ought to have been, answer yes. Although in itself it sounds a bit strange considering that the person who used it was evidently a marksman and had a license for it. They're usually very careful about their weapons. To say the least, if you understand what I mean."

"You test fired it," said Holt. "Are the bullets from the test firing still around?"

"Nope. I checked that. Probably due to the fact that we had a solved case right from the start. By now it would have almost turned twenty-five, so they probably threw it out in a spring cleaning. The copy of the report from the test firing should still be around, on the other hand."

Starts to sound more and more like a typical Bäckström, thought Holt.

"A completely different matter," said her old colleague. "Just a question out of curiosity. What I'm wondering—"

"I know exactly what you're wondering," Holt interrupted. "Before you ask, I wish I knew what this was about. I don't have a clue. Let me put it like this. I was given the task of following up a tip."

"I didn't think police superintendents dealt with such things."

"Neither did I," said Holt. Wonder if I can quote you, she thought. What am I really up to? thought Holt as she hung up.

If there's something you're brooding about, something that bothers you, something that worries you, then you have to talk about it. Share with someone you trust. Over and over again his female psychiatrist had repeated this. Like a mantra. If there's something that . . . It'll have to be Anna, thought Lewin.

"There's something that's bothering me," said Jan Lewin with a cautious throat clearing and an apologetic smile.

"Then you should talk about it. You know that perfectly well," said Holt, smiling at him.

"I thought so," said Jan Lewin. Then he told the—to say the least—strange story about Waltin's parking ticket.

"I understand exactly," said Holt. "I have something that's bothering me too."

"I'm listening," said Jan Lewin.

"So what do you think about this?" said Anna Holt. Then she told the hopefully not-so-strange story about the scrapped Magnum revolver.

"I know what those marksmen types are like," said Holt with unexpected emphasis. "I was married to one myself. They spend more time tinkering with their weapons than playing with their children."

"I get the idea that your ex-husband, our esteemed colleague with the uniformed police, is one of the agency's more distinguished marksmen," said Lewin.

"Exactly," said Holt. "Although there are more reasons than that, which we can talk about some other time. But you have to admit the whole thing is a bit mysterious."

"There must be an investigation," said Lewin, whose thoughts seemed elsewhere.

"Certainly," said Holt. "How are we helped by a lot of papers?"

"This was 1983," said Lewin, shaking his head. "It was another time then. When you were done with a major investigation, you would pack it up in a box and carry it down to the archive. It wasn't just papers that ended up in those boxes. It could be anything imaginable, like the victim's old diaries, photographs, threatening letters from the perpetrator, even the sort of thing the tech squad wanted to get rid of."

"You don't say," said Holt. "Personally I was a trainee with the uniformed police at that time, and it was papers that all the older officers warned me about. Whatever you do, see to it that you don't stir up a lot of papers you will have to fill out."

"I'll find the investigation," said Lewin, nodding and getting out of his chair. "As long as it's still there, I'll find it."

Of course he found it. It was there among all the papers. A bullet from a revolver that apparently had been scrapped twenty years ago. Shining like a gold nugget in a little plastic bag from the tech squad.

47

The box with the investigation was in a basement storeroom in the building where the old homicide squad in Stockholm had its offices during the eighties. Lewin himself had been in the building for a number of years and this was not the first time he'd gone down to the squad's basement storeroom to put away papers or search for them.

He had no recollection of the double murder from 1983. It had been much too simple a case for him and his associates at the first squad. Not even a murder investigation. Cleared up from the start. If it had been a murder investigation, he would have remembered it, even though during his almost thirty years as a murder investigator he had been involved in more than a hundred.

At the top of the box was a plastic sleeve with a number of newspaper clippings from the day after the murder. "Tragic Double Murder," "Family Tragedy," "Three Dead in Family Drama in Spånga." Toned-down descriptions of how a middle-aged man shot his teenage daughter and her boyfriend and then took his own life. Nothing about his motives. A family tragedy, quite simply.

In the binder with the preliminary investigation was the answer.

The perpetrator was a painting contractor. Together with a partner he ran a small painting company with five employees, with an office and workshop in Vällingby. Three years previously he had become a widower. After a long illness his wife had died of cancer. Remaining were the husband and a then thirteen-year-old daughter who soon after her mother's death began to have problems. Skipped school, ended up in bad company, started using drugs, was taken to a treatment center several times. That was how she met her boyfriend, seven years older, who was a known petty criminal and drug addict and already had several short prison terms on his record.

It appeared from the technical investigation at the father's house in Spånga that she and her boyfriend were evidently there to steal when the father suddenly came home and surprised them. In the hall by the front door there were a couple of paper bags. In the bags were, among other things, the mother's jewelry box, a pair of silver candlesticks, a few of the father's shooting trophies, a new toaster, and a couple of small paintings. In the stairway up to the second floor someone had dropped a TV and a video player. Farther down the hall, at the foot of the stairs, the boyfriend was lying flat on his face, shot through the head with one shot. The bullet was in the wall halfway up the stairs.

The technician in charge was an older colleague whom Lewin remembered well. A very meticulous man, known as a real nitpicker. With the help of various clues he had given a highly probable picture of the course of events.

The father comes home. Hears someone rummaging around on the second floor. Sneaks down into the basement. Retrieves his revolver from the gun case. Sneaks back up to the hall. The boyfriend is on his way down from the second floor, carrying the TV and the VCR from the father's bedroom. Tumult.

Most likely the boyfriend threw the TV and VCR at the father. When he tried to force his way past him in the hall, the father shot him in the head from a distance of about three feet. Basically, the boyfriend was killed instantly.

The daughter comes running from the kitchen on the first floor. Throws herself at her father, hitting out like a fury. The father drags her into the living room. Bloody tracks from his shoes, the boyfriend's blood. Throws her on the couch. Tries to hold her down. Another shot goes off. A contact shot that hits the daughter level with her left breast, passes through the heart and out, ends up in the back support of the couch. The daughter expires within the course of a minute or two in the arms of her father. Evidently he has squeezed her so hard that she had cracks and breaks in several ribs.

Then the father goes out into the kitchen, blood dripping from his shirt. The daughter's blood. Sits down on the floor with his back against the refrigerator and shoots himself through the head. Entry hole through the palate in the upper jaw. Exit hole in the back of the head. The bullet stops in the refrigerator door. The father dies instantly.

An elderly female neighbor in the house next door helped the police with the time-related course of events. The first shot. A woman who screams. The next shot, a minute or so after the first one. The neighbor who calls the police emergency number. The call that is taken at 14:25. Then the third shot. Five minutes after the second one. Only seconds before the first patrol car turns onto the street and stops fifty yards from the house.

The three dead who will soon have company of twenty or so police officers from the uniformed police, the detective bureau, and the tech squad. "Three Dead in Family Drama in Spånga."

Lewin's old colleague from the tech squad was named Bergholm. He had already retired by the late eighties but was still alive, hale and hearty. He lived on Hantverkargatan, a few blocks from the police building, and Lewin had run into him only a month earlier. Treated him to a cup of coffee and talked about old times.

A meticulous man, known as a real nitpicker, and when he was done with his investigation in Spånga he sent the crime scene report over to the homicide squad to be forwarded to the prosecutor. He had also sent along the report of the test firing, a photograph of one of the comparison bullets where the barrel grooves were marked with arrows. Along with a little plastic bag with one of the two bullets he had used for the comparison.

For the three bullets from the crime scene he had sent along three photos where he marked the grooves from the barrel with arrows the same way as on the photo on the comparison bullet. The three bullets from the scene of the crime, on the other hand, were still at the tech squad. The one he sent he had fired himself. One of two and a confirmation to the prosecutor that he had done his job.

Bergholm had also enclosed a handwritten message. If the prosecutor wanted he was welcome to keep the bullet. He had one in reserve for himself. If not, the prosecutor could send it back to the tech squad. If he had any questions it was okay to call.

A meticulous man, known as a real nitpicker, thought Jan Lewin.

The prosecutor, on the other hand, seemed to have been like everyone else, and the bullet had ended up in the box with everything else that was no longer needed.

Which perhaps was just as well, thought Lewin. He sighed and put the plastic bag with the bullet in his jacket pocket.

Then he sealed the box with tape and attached a handwritten note to it. At the top the date and time. Then a brief explanatory text. "Time as above the undersigned has gone through hereby stored preliminary investigation material. Removed certain materials from the tech squad in Stockholm to head of NBCI for further examination." Then he signed with his name and title. Detective Inspector Jan Lewin, Homicide Squad, National Bureau of Criminal Investigation. Finally he paper-clipped his business card on the cover of the box.

Jan Lewin too was a meticulous man and known as "a real accountant type."

"This isn't the least bit like the bullet Palme was shot with," Anna Holt observed with disappointment when an hour later she was sitting with the plastic bag in hand, inspecting Lewin's find.

"A different type of ammunition," said Lewin, who was well-informed as of a few hours ago with the help of Bergholm's old report. "This seems to be the type of bullet that competitive shooters prefer," he explained. "It gives clearer target markings. That's why it's completely flat in front. It punches a round hole in the target. If several hit close to one another, it's a lot simpler to see how many hits there are than if you shot with a regular bullet that tapers in front."

"Not the same ammunition," said Holt. "Not one of those metal-breakers that killed Palme?"

"No," said Lewin. "At the crime scene investigation in the house in Spånga an unopened and an opened box were found with the same ammunition you have in your hand. It was in the perpetrator's gun case in the basement. In the revolver that he used were three empty casings and three unfired bullets. Six shots, full magazine, same type of ammunition as in the boxes. Our colleague Bergholm used two of the three unfired bullets in the magazine when he test fired to get his basis for comparison. Better one bullet too many than one too few," Lewin observed.

"A bullet of a completely different type than the murder bullet that was fired with a revolver that went to the scrap yard almost twenty years ago," Holt observed. "What is it that makes me think this is more about Bäckström than about the murder of Olof Palme?"

"I hope it will be possible to find that out," said Lewin, shrugging his shoulders.

"You or me?" said Holt, smiling at him and rocking the chair she was sitting on.

"You," said Lewin, smiling back. "Definitely not me. You're the one who started it, Anna."

"Okay then," said Anna. What do I do now? she thought.

"I completely understand that I'm going to drive you crazy soon," said Holt when for the third time in three days she called the head of the tech squad with the Stockholm police.

"Not at all, Holt," he answered. "The fact is I was just thinking about you. Why doesn't she ever call, I was thinking."

"This time I'm afraid I'm forced to come over."

"Then you have to promise to have coffee with me."

"I promise," said Holt.

· · ·

Three calls in three days. That was bad enough, so Holt suggested they have coffee in his office. Besides asking for his silence.

"Then you've come to the right place, Holt," said her old colleague. "As I'm sure you recall, I'm the strong, silent type."

"I know," said Holt. "Why do you think you're the one I'm talking to?" I don't suppose he's trying to make a pass at me, she thought.

"There are a few things I hope you can help me with," she continued.

"I'm listening."

"For one thing, if there are any papers on the scrapping of this revolver that I've been nagging you about. If so I want a copy of them."

"There was a special form. You can get a copy of our copy. Anything else?"

"If there are any other traces of the weapon up here at the squad. It was test fired here in April 1983. I already have access to the report. I would still like to have a copy of the copy that must be in your files."

"Sure. No problem. As I already said, someone apparently cleaned out those old bullets, but the report should be here. May take awhile to find the right binder, but that shouldn't be any problem."

"I don't understand a thing, I'll be damned," said the head of the tech squad half an hour later when they finally found the right binder. "Seems like someone cleaned out the shooting report too."

"You're sure this is the right binder?" asked Holt.

"Sure," he said, turning to the first page. "Here you have the list of all the reports that should be in this binder. Here you have the registration number on the revolver you're searching for, date of the test firing in April 1983, and then colleague Bergholm's signature farthest out in the margin. The report should also be here but it's not. What I can give you is the copy of our request for scrapping. That exists. I've seen it myself. When you visited me the first time."

According to the copy of the request for scrapping, in October 1988 the tech squad with the police in Stockholm had sent a total of twenty-one weapons for scrapping to the Defense Factories in Eskilstuna. Stapled together with the squad's request was a confirmation from the Defense Factories in Eskilstuna that the task was carried out.

Judging by the list of weapons it was also about scrap. Sawed-off shotguns, old hunting rifles, a drilled-out starter gun, a home-constructed revolver, a butcher's mask, a nail gun. Possibly with one exception. A Ruger brand revolver, manufactured in 1980 judging by the serial number.

This is getting stranger and stranger, thought Holt when she saw the name of the colleague who had apparently sent off the tech squad's request.

Before Lewin went home for the day he returned to the homicide squad's old basement storeroom. This time he took the whole box with him. He returned to his office and locked it in his cupboard. He had not left the slightest trace behind him even though he was known for being extremely meticulous and very formal. *? doesn't make sense*

48

On Thursday morning Holt called Bäckström in to talk sense with him.

First she told him she had figured out what was going on with the revolver found behind a refrigerator out in Flemingsberg. That he got the registration number from the tech squad, that his colleagues had messed with him and given him the wrong year of manufacture, that he in turn had tried to fool Holt.

"You've tricked me, Bäckström," Holt summarized.

"I don't understand what you're talking about. There must be some misunderstanding," said Bäckström. What do you mean tricked? he thought. She was talking to him as if he were a young punk. What was she up to, really? Spying on him, apparently, not to mention those semi-criminal characters at the tech squad who had tried to swindle him.

"We've got to get some order in this now," said Holt. "I was thinking about having an interview with your informant."

"Forget it," Bäckström snorted. "My informant is sacred to me, and this old man has demanded to remain anonymous. Besides, he's not easy to get hold of."

"And why is that?" asked Holt.

"Lives abroad," said Bäckström curtly.

"I thought the art dealer Henning lived on Norr Mälarstrand," said Holt with an innocent expression.

What the hell is going on? thought Bäckström. Can cell phones be tapped? Has she sicced SePo on me?

"Don't know what you're talking about," said Bäckström, shaking his head.

"Then it won't do any harm if I talk with him," said Holt.

"Listen, Holt, if you really are interested in cooperation, and I sure would be if I were you, I suggest you take care of your business and let me take care of mine. What do you think about taking a peek at this, for example," said Bäckström, giving her the file he'd taken from the central archive.

"Where did you get this?" said Holt.

"Read it," said Bäckström. There, you've got a little something good to suck on, you little sow, he thought.

"I see," said Holt when she was through reading. "I still don't understand."

Holt must be stupid, thought Bäckström. Even for a hag, she must be uncommonly stupid.

"I'm in the process of refining a little profile of our perpetrator. Waltin, that is. I think, among other things, this may be interesting from the standpoint of motive."

"From the standpoint of motive?"

"You betcha," said Bäckström, nodding emphatically. "I think this may have been about something sexual."

"Excuse me," said Holt. "We're talking about the assassination of Olof Palme?"

"We sure are," said Bäckström with a shrewd expression.

"Explain," said Holt. "Who is supposed to have been involved with whom?"

"I get the idea that Waltin and that socialist may have had the same interests. If I may say so." She must be even denser than the densest hag, he thought.

"So why do you think that?" He must have a screw loose, she thought.

"It struck me that they were actually fucking alike. Those small, skinny upper-class types. Misty eyes. Moist lips. You know how they usually look. As if they're licking their lips all the time. There are these kind of secret societies for leather boys. I think that's where we should start rooting around. Both were lawyers, besides."

"I'll be in touch if there's anything," said Holt. I have to see to it that he gets some kind of help, she thought. Whoever it would be who could help someone like Bäckström.

"I've thought of one more thing," said Bäckström.

"I'm listening," said Holt.

"You know Wiijnbladh?" said Bäckström. "That crazy colleague who tried to poison his old lady a bunch of years ago. He and Waltin apparently were also involved."

"They're supposed to have had a relationship too, you're saying?"

Holt is completely unbeatable, even if she is an old lady, thought Bäckström. A cabbage is a Nobel Prize winner compared with Holt.

"Forget it," said Bäckström, shaking his head. Someone like Wiijnbladh has probably never screwed, he thought.

"There are other things," he continued. "He is supposed to have helped Waltin on a few occasions. What that was he didn't say, but it was apparently fucking secret. Supposedly got some distinction or medal from SePo as thanks for his help."

"As stated," said Holt, "I'll be in touch if there is anything." So Wiijnbladh is supposed to have helped Waltin, she thought.

As soon as Bäckström left, Holt called her acquaintance at the crime lab. She needed help from a weapons technician. Sensitive matter. On an informal basis. Just so you don't get any ideas in your head, old man, she thought.

"You can't be more specific?" he asked.

"I want you to look at a bullet for me," said Holt. "Make a comparison with another bullet."

"No problem."

"See you in two hours," said Holt.

Then she put the plastic bag with the bullet in her jacket pocket. She signed for an official vehicle, went past Lewin on the way, retrieved an old shooting report from the spring of 1983, and drove to Linköping.

"What do you want me to do with this?" her acquaintance asked two hours later.

"Compare it with the Palme bullet," said Holt.

"Goodness," he said, looking at her. Clearly surprised. "You're aware that this is a completely different type of bullet," he asked.

"Yes," said Holt. "What's the problem?"

"Several," he said. "How much do you know about firearms? About modern revolvers, for example?"

"Educated layman," said Holt. "Give me the essentials." No long expositions, thanks, she thought.

"Okay," he said.

Then he gave her the essentials. Without digressions. The bullet with which the prime minister had been shot was a .357 caliber Magnum. This meant that it had a diameter of 357 thousandths of an inch. The word "Magnum" meant that the bullet had an extra strong powder charge.

"That I already knew," said Holt.

The bore in the barrel on a modern revolver has elevations and depressions—lands and grooves—that run in a spiral through the barrel. Either to the right or to the left. Figuratively speaking you might say that the bullet is screwed along through the bore and that the lands and grooves then leave tracks in it. The purpose of getting the bullet to rotate is to give it a straighter trajectory.

"I knew that too," said Holt.

Different makes of revolvers have different such characteristics as a rule. A different number of lands and grooves with varying land width, groove direction, and groove gradient, where the latter determines how many revolutions around its own axis the bullet rotates over a given distance.

"I have spotty knowledge about this," said Holt.

"You see," he said. "Now we're starting to get close."

The bullet with which the prime minister had been shot had right-rotating lands with a width of about 2.8 millimeters and a groove gradient of about five degrees.

"I didn't know that," said Holt. "So what's the problem?"

The problem with the bullet she had brought with her was that it was of a different type than the bullet Palme had been shot with. Bullets were made of lead as a rule. Both Holt's bullet and the Palme bullet were lead bullets, and so far no problem.

"Lead is soft, as you know," he explained. "In order to protect the bullets from deformation and increase their penetration force when they hit the target, they are usually supplied with a protective coating of harder material. What's called a mantle."

"Of copper," said Holt.

"As a rule of copper or various copper alloys. Your bullet, for example, has a pure copper mantle. Harder than lead, to be sure, but far from as hard as the mantle on the bullets from Sveavägen. You see, it's made of an alloy of copper and zinc. It's very hard. Called tombak, by the way."

"The problems," Holt reminded him.

"The traces from the same barrel can vary, depending on the bullet. Your bullet has a softer coating. The traces from the barrel may be clearer than on the bullet with a harder coating. Traces that are not deposited on a harder bullet are perhaps deposited on your bullet, because it's softer."

"How do we solve this?" asked Holt.

"Give me the revolver, then I'll do a new test firing with a bullet similar to the one used on Sveavägen."

"There we have another problem," said Holt.

Without going into details, she told him that the only thing she had was the bullet she had just given him. Plus a report from the test firing done in the spring of 1983.

"Here's the report," said Holt, handing it over.

"The weapon type agrees. So far there's no problem."

"So what do we do now?" asked Holt.

"We work with what we have," said her acquaintance, nodding encouragingly. "I'll just retrieve the bullets from Sveavägen so we have something to compare to."

Retrieve the bullets from Sveavägen. Now this is finally starting to resemble something, thought Anna Holt.

. . .

In other respects what happened next was not particularly like what you might see in crime shows on TV about life on an American tech squad. He sat there at his comparison microscope, looked, adjusted knobs, hummed, and made notes. It took more than half an hour. Almost a whole episode of *CSI*.

"Okay," he said, straightening up and nodding at her.

"Shoot," said Holt. She pointed at him with her right index finger, curled it and fired, formed her lips to an O and blew away the gunpowder smoke.

"All the traces that are on the Palme bullet are on your bullet," he said. "This argues for the fact that they come from the same weapon. But," he continued, "in addition there are traces on your bullet that aren't on the Palme bullet."

Typical, thought Holt.

"So how do we explain those?" she asked.

"Because your bullet was fired three years before the bullets from Sveavägen, we can rule out that the traces originate from additional use of the weapon. The explanation is probably that the mantle on your bullet is softer."

"The probability that they come from the same weapon," asked Holt.

"What I said on the phone about ninety percent you can forget as long as we can't compare the same type of bullet. Seventy-five, maybe even eighty percent probability."

"What do you think personally?" she asked.

"I think they come from the same weapon," he said, looking at her seriously. "But I wouldn't swear to that in court. There I would say that with a probability of seventy-five percent they come from the same weapon, and that sort of thing isn't enough for a guilty verdict. Which despite everything we probably should be happy about."

"Even though all the traces that are on the Palme bullet are on my bullet," said Holt. Coward, she thought.

"The problem with those traces is that they are mostly so-called general characteristics," he said. "The kind that go with the type of weapon. As far as the characteristics of a particular weapon are concerned, through use, damage, and so forth on just that weapon, then it's not as clear. There are some like that, but none that are simple and unambiguous. On a completely different matter, by the way," he continued. "What do you think about staying and having dinner?"

"It'll have to be another time, unfortunately," said Holt. "What do you think about—"

"I know," he interrupted. He smiled and put his right index finger to his mouth. "Just don't forget about dinner."

As soon as she was in the car she called Jan Lewin on her cell.

"I'll be at work in two hours," said Holt. "You and me and Lisa have to meet."

"So it's that bad," said Lewin and sighed.

"With seventy-five percent probability," Holt replied.

Then she called her boss, Lars Martin Johansson, but although it was said that he could see around corners, he only sounded like the Genius from Näsåker.

"I hear what you're saying, Holt," Johansson muttered. "But you don't believe in all seriousness that little dandy Waltin shot Olof Palme?"

"Have you been listening to what I said?"

"How could I have avoided it?" said Johansson. "You've been talking nonstop for half an hour. My office," he continued, "as soon as you get back. Bring the other two with you too."

"I'll need a good hour," said Holt. "It's a hundred miles."

"One more thing," said Johansson, who didn't seem to be listening.

"Yes?"

"Drive carefully," said Johansson.

"That was nice of you, Lars," said Holt.

"Considering that you must have the bullet in your pocket," said Johansson. Then he hung up.

49

GeGurra is a real player, thought Bäckström, who was on his way to a late Thursday lunch at the Opera bar to which his benefactor had invited him. GeGurra always treated and he always treated generously. He was definitely a real player who sprinkled his manna over all the first-rate people in his vicinity. Like Bäckström, for example.

Something of an operator besides, thought Bäckström. With his silver-white hair, his shiny Italian suits. Never made a show of himself. He was simply there like an old-school mafioso. Not someone with a mouth that ran ahead of his brain, creating problems for himself and for others. A player and an operator, he thought.

A little like himself, actually. Most recently last week he had given a whole fifty-kronor bill to an unusually hopeless hag so that she could take a taxi to the subway for further transport to her wretched Tatar thermos in the southern suburbs. So that she would not lie in Bäckström's Hästens bed and make a mess of his existence. There was also all the advice and good deeds he had portioned out. Completely free of charge and even to complete vegetables like Anna Holt.

A bit like you, Bäckström, thought Bäckström. A player and an operator.

"How's the pea soup at this joint?" asked Bäckström as soon as he sat down and knocked back a little Thursday dram to prepare the way for his lunch.

"The best in town," said GeGurra. "Homemade with extra pork and sausage. Real meat sausage and that old-fashioned fat pork, you know. You get it in slices, of course, thick slices. On a separate plate on the side."

"Then it'll be pea soup," Bäckström decided.

"Do you want a warm punch with it?"

"A regular shot and a pilsner is fine," said Bäckström. Warm punch? Does he think I'm a faggot, or what?

"Personally I'll have the grilled flounder. And a mineral water," said GeGurra, nodding in confirmation to the white-clad waiter.

Fish, thought Bäckström. Are we homos, or what?

Nice place, thought Bäckström. It was basically empty as soon as the lunch rush was over and ideal for confidential conversations.

"How's it going?" asked GeGurra, leaning forward.

"It's rolling along. At a rapid pace, actually," he added so that GeGurra wouldn't get any ideas under his white hair.

"Starting to get the hang of that character Waltin," Bäckström continued, and then in brief strokes he recounted his finds down in the central archive.

"I almost suspected as much. Sometimes he expressed himself in a peculiar way, to say the least." GeGurra sighed.

"I get the idea this may have been something sexual," said Bäckström. Ask the woman with the candlestick, he thought.

"Sexual? Now I don't understand."

"Possible motives," Bäckström clarified, and then he also expanded on this line of reasoning.

"I won't get mixed up in that part," said GeGurra, shaking all his white hair almost deprecatingly. "How's it going with the weapon?"

Won't get mixed up with it, thought Bäckström. Who the hell does he think he is?

"Fifty million," said Bäckström, rubbing his index finger against his thumb. "The weapon is ten mill. In itself nothing to scoff at, but now we're talking fifty. If I find the weapon, then I find the murderer. There are more involved in this business than Waltin," said Bäckström, letting GeGurra have a taste of his heavy police gaze.

"You think you can find the weapon and you can also solve the murder?"

"You betcha," said Bäckström. "I have good leads on the weapon, and I've already found two of those involved. There are more, if you ask me."

"I'm assuming that I can be anonymous," said GeGurra. "I have to be kept out of it, as you understand. This sort of thing is not good for business."

"Of course," said Bäckström. And that part about fifty-fifty you can just forget, he thought.

A player and an operator, thought Bäckström as he sat in the taxi on his way back to work. Although not like me, he thought. A little too gay and a little too nervous when push comes to shove.

Thursday pea soup with extra pork and sausage, plenty of mustard, a couple shots and a large pilsner to get the system going. A few pancakes with whipped cream and jam on top and a real marvel for the little craw that was already rumbling like a blast furnace as he sank down behind his desk. Perhaps I ought to open the door so all the little thing finders out in the corridor get a chance to enjoy a really good lunch, thought Bäckström, who felt that a major fart was on its way.

He test fired carefully but it wouldn't come out until his own little half-boss suddenly knocked and came into his office. Now, you little binder carrier, thought Bäckström. Giving him the evil eye, he sank down in the chair, eased up on his left buttock, and tightened his well-trained diaphragm. A sizeable barrel and not an ordinary lousy six pack like all the gym queers.

A completely formidable and juicy one. One of Bäckström's best ever. A real orchestra finale. First a couple of noisy blasts with ass bassoon, a several-seconds-long solo on bowel trumpet, then a few concluding toots on anal flute.

"Is there anything I can do for you?" asked Bäckström, flexing lightly with both cheeks. There, you got a little something good to suck on, he thought. The little bastard looked ready to faint, and apparently he wanted to deliver a letter.

"Set it with the rest of the mildew," said Bäckström, pointing at his overflowing desk. "I'll get to it when I have time." Damn what a hurry he was in, he thought.

The letter was from the Stockholm police department's own female police chief. Just as skinny as that attack dyke Holt. Just as crazy as Holt, and certainly a sister in the same association of fairy and dyke constables.

Bäckström had received a summons to a gender sensitivity course that would start on Monday morning at nine o'clock and last the whole week. Police officials of the highest rank had noticed that Bäckström apparently lacked this mandatory feature in police training and intended to remedy the matter immediately. Accommodations were at some camp up in Roslagen. Not a request, but an order.

Now damn it this is war, thought Bäckström, tensing all his muscles from his navel on down.

50

After an hour and a half Johansson called on Holt's cell.

"I'm sitting in a line of cars up on Essingeleden," Holt explained. "See you in fifteen."

"I thought there were blue lights on that car," Johansson whined.

Most often cheerful, far too often furious. Surly sometimes, never whiny. Johansson must be worried about something, thought Holt with surprise.

If that's the way it was, there was no trace of it twenty minutes later as she stepped into his conference room. He was entertaining himself with Lewin and Mattei, and there were only happy faces around the table.

"Coffee," said Johansson, nodding at the tray. "I remember those times I was out in the field and drove like a car thief. Then I would always be in the mood for coffee afterward."

"I thought it was Jarnebring who always drove," said Holt.

"Bragging," said Johansson. "Can you give us a quick summary, Anna?"

Curious twists of fortune with a parking ticket. A scrapped revolver and a vanished firing report. Seventy-five percent probability that they had found something that would trigger an earthquake, and not just in the neighborhood where they were sitting. It was high time to turn this over to the chief prosecutor in Stockholm and the murder investigation that the government had appointed.

"One can certainly get the impression that Waltin ran around and cleaned up after himself, and with that this is not our area any longer," Holt concluded, supporting herself on the table and jutting her jaw for emphasis.

"We'll get to that later," said Johansson. "Now we'll play devil's advocate for a while. You start, Lisa."

That Waltin was involved was still far from proven, according to Mattei. On the other hand it was quite certain that he had died fifteen years ago. In a drowning accident on Mallorca. Dead for a long time, and the worst conceivable alternative for anyone who was searching for a perpetrator in a murder investigation.

That he would have shot the prime minister seemed completely unlikely. In any event, the witnesses' descriptions of the perpetrator did not match Waltin.

"Five foot nine. Barely taller than the victim. Slender and delicately built. Doesn't match," said Mattei. "Not with the witnesses and even less with the shot angle that the technicians describe. That points with high probability to a perpetrator who is at least six feet tall. Probably taller."

But there certainly were some strange circumstances. That was not to say that Waltin had to be behind them. Previous experience showed that even police officers who did not have the slightest thing to hide could clean away papers and technical evidence. Through ordinary carelessness, if nothing else?

"I think nonetheless that the vicissitudes of this parking ticket do point in a definite direction," Holt argued.

"Sure," said Mattei. "Or else there's just some kind of silly human explanation. Like that married man who preferred to remain in jail suspected of having killed his wife than admit that he was with her girlfriend when someone else murdered his wife."

"I've actually had one just like that," Johansson observed.

. . .

A series of strange circumstances. Particulars that didn't even work as indices. Much less a chain of indices that could link Waltin to the vanished weapon, and the vanished weapon to a perpetrator who could be linked to Waltin, in order to finally link them both to the murder of a Swedish prime minister.

"Seventy-five percent probability that our bullet comes from the murder weapon. That's what the whole thing boils down to," said Mattei. "That's not enough in court. Far from it," she added.

"Take this about the weapon," she continued. "A fundamental thought in the whole line of reasoning seems to be that someone, probably Waltin, is supposed to have come across a revolver from the tech squad in Stockholm. How could he do that? A high-ranking police chief at the secret police who was also an attorney. Who would someone like that have contact with at the tech squad at the Stockholm police?" Mattei looked questioningly at Holt.

"Wiijnbladh," said Holt. "It's alleged that Waltin knew our colleague Wiijnbladh, who was then working at the tech squad, and that he possibly could have come across the weapon through him."

"Excuse me," said Johansson. "Are we talking about that nutcase who tried to poison his wife?"

"Yes," said Holt.

"So how do we know that?" asked Johansson.

"According to Bäckström," said Holt and sighed.

"Perhaps we ought to attach Bäckström to our little group," said Johansson. "I'm listening," he said, nodding encouragingly.

"Sounds like Bäckström," Johansson observed five minutes later. "I'm really looking forward to seeing that medal that Wiijnbladh is supposed to have got from Waltin."

"Some form of distinction in any event," said Holt. "Whatever. What do we do?"

"We're going to do the following," said Johansson. He held up his right hand and ticked off the points with his fingers.

"First, we'll make a compilation of what we know about former colleague Waltin. Without waking any bears among his former co-workers.

"Second," he continued, "we'll interview Bäckström's informant, Wiijnbladh, and Bäckström himself, and we'll do it in that order."

"Then we turn it over to the Palme group," said Holt, who did not intend to give up. Not this time.

"If we have something to turn over, then we'll do that," said Johansson. We'll cross that bridge when we come to it, he thought.

Before they went their separate ways Johansson confiscated the bullet that Holt quite correctly had in the pocket of her jacket.

Who knows what he's planning to do with it, she thought.

51

Mattei had been forced to cancel a romantic weekend cruise to Riga to devote herself to the Palme investigation's police track. Even though Johan was seven years younger than she was, he handled his disappointment like a real man. He could imagine some very different cruise destinations if she were to have a few hours extra.

Now it's time to read thoroughly, thought Mattei, pushing aside thoughts of anything else. To really be sure that Waltin was not included in the material. At the same time find a conceivable contact for him. If he really was involved, he could not have shot the prime minister in any event. If he had an accomplice there was also a decent chance this man had the same background as Waltin.

It remained to find him, thought Mattei.

Anna Holt, Lisa Mattei, and Jan Lewin started their survey of Claes Waltin first thing on Friday morning. Their quarry had been dead for fifteen years, but that was not an insurmountable obstacle for people like them and the bureau's intelligence service. By Friday afternoon they had already put together a binder to add to the thousand that existed in the investigation.

Claes Adolf Waltin was born on April 20, 1945, and had died in a drowning accident on north Mallorca at the age of forty-seven, on October 17, 1992. He was born and raised on Östermalm in Stockholm. The only child of estate manager Claes Robert Waltin, born in 1919, and his wife, Aino Elisabeth, née Carlberg, who was four years younger. His parents divorced in 1952. His mother died in an accident in 1969. The father was still alive. Remarried to a woman ten years younger and living on an estate outside Kristianstad in Skåne.

Strange, thought Jan Lewin. What kind of parents name their son Adolf right before the end of the war in 1945?

"Did you know that Waltin was christened Adolf as a middle name?" said Lewin to Mattei, who was sitting on the other side of the table browsing through a sizeable pile of papers. "What kind of parents christen their son Adolf when he's born on the twentieth of April 1945? That's only a week or so before the end of the Second World War."

"Hitler's birthday," said Mattei. "His dad and mom probably wanted to give him a model in life. They were probably Nazis."

"Hitler's birthday?"

"Adolf Hitler was also born on April 20, in 1889. In the village of Braunau in Austria," said Mattei. In contrast to General Maternity Hospital in Stockholm, and for God's sake don't drag in a Nazi track as thanks for the help, she thought.

"Strange," said Lewin, shaking his head. "Very strange."

Sigh, thought Lisa Mattei.

Mattei had not found either Waltin or Wiijnbladh in the part of the Palme investigation's material that dealt with the police track. No signs either to indicate that they should have been found there but had been cleaned out. However you find that sort of thing, she thought.

For lack of anything better to do she also searched for Detective Inspector Evert Bäckström. Considering the life he had lived he ought to be first-rate material for the same track. But there were no traces of Bäckström. Other than under the second lead file and then in the role of interview leader. One of the Good Guys. However that might be, thought Mattei.

Waltin does not seem to have been a nice, decent guy, thought Anna Holt after she reread the old investigation that Bäckström had given her. The complaint written off as not a crime, according to the decision by the prosecutor. She had not succeeded in finding more of the same or that he had ever been charged with anything whatsoever. Waltin did not appear in the police department registry. Not even for a simple speeding infraction.

Mysterious, thought Anna Holt. The types that had that disposition tended to leave tracks behind them.

Claes Waltin had graduated in 1964 and completed his military service with the Norrland Dragoons in Umeå. In the fall of 1965 he began his legal studies at the University of Stockholm and allowed himself plenty of time. It took eight years for him to earn his law degree with mediocre grades. After that he applied to police chief training. Finished that in the appointed time, and in 1975 he was hired by the Stockholm police department's legal department as an assistant commissioner.

Two years later he changed jobs and started with the secret police. First as police superintendent, up until 1985 when he was promoted to chief superintendent and the second-in-command to SePo's operations head, the legendary Berg.

Three years later he suddenly resigned. Another four years later he was dead. At the age of only forty-seven, and completely healthy as it appeared, he suddenly drowned during a vacation on Mallorca.

On Mallorca of all places, thought Holt.

Johansson seemed to have devoted himself to something other than Claes Waltin. On Friday afternoon he had been at a meeting in Rosenbad, and after the meeting he ran into the special adviser, who quickly took him aside and into his office.

"Nice to see you, Lars Martin," said the special adviser, looking as if he really meant it. "By the way, I read your e-mail."

"About the deer at Magdalen College. Thanks for the last time, by the way," said Johansson.

"Life has taught me at least one thing," the special adviser observed. "Not only about the deer at Magdalen," he added.

"So what's that?"

"That even wise people like you often confuse the truth with what you think you know," said the special adviser, winking at his visitor. "Have you thought about that, Lars Martin?" he continued. "How often does the truth appear with a mask on her face and in clothing that she has not even borrowed but simply stolen from someone else entirely?"

"I thought it was the lie that wore a mask," said Johansson.

"The truth, too," said the special adviser, nodding seriously. "Not only do they share a room with each other; they share a bed in a lifelong relationship where the one's existence is a prerequisite for the other's survival."

"You're in one of your philosophical moods, I'm hearing." Is he trying to say something or is he just a bad loser? thought Johansson.

"Speaking of the truth," said the special adviser. "Do you have any desire to come to the Turing Society for our next seminar? As chairman of the society it would please me greatly to have such a wise and well-informed guest as you."

"What were you planning to talk about?"

"About the murder of Prime Minister Olof Palme," said the special adviser.

Claes Waltin had drowned during a vacation on Mallorca in October 1992. He was staying at north Mallorca's best hotel. He had stayed at the same place at the same time for a number of years. A week in October at the Hotel Formentor was his recurring fall vacation.

Every morning he would go down to the beach for a morning dip. At the hotel's private beach. Secluded from the hoi polloi and public view. The water was still about fifty degrees so there was nothing strange about that. For someone like Waltin and if you weren't a Spaniard, that is. Then it was far too cold. Besides he was up far too early in the morning. At the Hotel Formentor all the normal guests were asleep at that time of day. Hence Waltin could always swim alone.

At eight in the morning, this unchristian time of day for any civilized Spaniard, he passed the reception desk. Equipped with a bathrobe and towel and quite clearly en route to his daily morning dip, according to the two employees in reception that the Spanish police had talked with. Señor Waltin had been exactly as usual. A friendly greeting to the male reception clerk, for his female associate the smile and compliment she always got, regardless of who she was. Everything had been exactly as usual on that morning, the last known observation of Claes Waltin while he was alive.

Fourteen days later he was found. What was left of the former chief superintendent was washed up on the beach a few miles from the hotel. Natural death by drowning, according to the Spanish police investigation. They had not found any simple, unambiguous signs of murder or suicide in any event. What thus remained was natural death by drowning.

The Swedish secret police had made their own investigation. The drowning of a former high-ranking boss at a luxury hotel in southern Europe was not something that was taken lightly. Least of all as the medical examination Waltin had undergone only a month before showed that he was in excellent health. Apart from rather high liver function values he seemed to have been in the best condition, but despite this the Swedish investigators had still come to the same conclusion as their Spanish colleagues.

A purely accidental occurrence. Nothing the least bit peculiar about it, and it was only when his will was opened that things got strange. Really, really strange.

At four in the afternoon Lewin started looking at the clock and fidgeting. At first Mattei ignored him, but finally she showed mercy. Personally she intended to work the whole evening, and because she knew the considerate, loyal Lewin, she made his anguish brief.

"Before you go home, Jan," said Mattei. "I looked into that thing about Adolf for you."

"Adolf?"

"Claes Adolf Waltin," Mattei clarified. "His father, Robert, was evidently an organized Nazi during the war. Participated as a volunteer on the German side. From 1942 until the end of the war he was part of the Viking Battalion. That was an SS battalion made up of volunteers from Scandinavia. Swedes, Danes, Norwegians."

"How do you know that?" asked Lewin, looking at her doubtfully.

"Found it on the Internet," said Mattei. "He's included in Hermansson's dissertation on the Swedish volunteers in the Viking Battalion. Was decorated with the Iron Cross on three occasions. Advanced from regular soldier to lieutenant. Known right-wing extremist and nationalist far into the seventies. Disappears from the Swedish national movement about the same time his son started as a police officer."

"Peculiar, extremely peculiar," said Lewin, shaking his head.

Claes Waltin appeared never to have had any financial difficulties. A millionaire at the age of twenty-four since he inherited from his mother. A multimillionaire when he died and left behind the most peculiar will Holt had ever read. As an investigator with the police she had read a number over the years, but nothing even in the neighborhood of former chief superintendent Claes Waltin's last will and testament.

Either he was off his rocker or else it was worse than that, thought Holt.

The will had been in Waltin's safe deposit box at SEB. It was handwritten, and according to the police department's graphology expert Waltin was the one who wrote it.

All the money that Waltin left, and this was several million, was to start a foundation that would support research on hypochondriac complaints among women. This in memory of his mother, and the foundation would also bear her name. A long name: The Foundation for Research into Hypochondria in Memory of My Mother Aino Waltin and All Other Hypochondriacal Old Hags Who Have Ruined the Lives of Their Children.

What a little mama's boy, thought Holt.

Then it quickly got even worse, venturing far beyond the boundaries that normally applied when a will was prepared. The deceased had attached a long statement of cause that was to be incorporated into the statutes of the foundation according to the "donor's last will and testament."

343

"During my entire childhood my mother, Aino Waltin, was dying of most of the diseases known to medical science. Despite this she never honored her repeated promises of her imminent demise. Because it would not have been possible for me to sue her for ordinary refusal to deliver according to civil law, I finally saw myself compelled to put her to death myself by pushing her off the platform at the Östermalm subway station when she was on her way to one of her daily doctor's appointments."

No ordinary mama's boy, thought Holt.

The will had of course been contested by the closest survivor, Waltin's father. The district court took his side and found that the will should be invalidated because the testator was obviously not of sound mind when the will was written.

What remained was the peculiar fact that Lewin's mother had happened to fall down in front of a subway train at the Östermalm subway station, was run over, and died immediately. A pure accident, according to the police, probably brought about by one of her recurring dizzy spells, which one of her many doctors had reported. Dead by accident in June 1969. Her only son and heir was twenty-four years old, a law student at the University of Stockholm, and for him life went on.

There were many accidents in that family, thought Holt.

Puerto Alcúdia on north Mallorca

Esperanza was built at a small local shipyard in Puerto Alcúdia, still owned and run by Ignacio Ballester and his two sons, Felipe and Guillermo. The shipyard has been in the family for generations, and it has always specialized in the area's local fishing boats, illaut.

This particular customer, however, had special requests, which broke in part with tradition. Among other things he did not want the vertically pointing bowsprit that was mostly a joy to the eye, just like the dragon on the prow of a Viking ship, but at the same time good to be able to hold on to if you were boarding a swaying deck.

Ignacio talked about this with his customer, but he just shook his head. Besides, he said that the Vikings never had dragons on the prows of their boats. That was a latter-day Romantic invention, and if Ignacio didn't believe him he could always take Felipe and Guillermo, go to Oslo, visit the Viking Ship Museum, and see with their own eyes what Viking sailing vessels really looked like.

Ignacio gave in. The customer presumably knew more about this than he did, and the customer was always right, as long as it didn't affect the seaworthiness of the boats that he and his sons built.

He didn't want a mast either. He didn't intend to sail with Esperanza; instead he would rely on her engine. With a mast a ship rocked more than necessary, and the customer preferred a steady deck under his feet.

On the other hand he did want a number of other things that were not on a regular illaut. Ultrasound, of course, because it was necessary for anyone who dived in unknown waters and good for anyone who chose to fish instead. Radar was discussed, but they came to a joint decision to avoid that, because it would stick out too much and disturb Esperanza's lovely lines. The navigational equipment that was on board—compass, nautical chart, chart table, and reckoning—were fine according to Ignacio's customer, and a few years later he complemented it with a modern GPS system.

After a few more years Ignacio had to install a butane grill on board Esperanza. There was no better stove for meat, vegetables, fresh fish, or seafood. For Esperanza's owner, his guests, and idle, sunlit days at sea. The grill folded against the bulkhead to take up less room when it wasn't being used, and it was equipped with a stainless-steel cover that resisted weather and wind. The tank was hidden below the deck. Ignacio had to run the hose from the five-gallon butane container inside the wall of the bulkhead to keep the outside nice and clean.

After that not much remained to do on Esperanza. Every spring Ignacio drew her up on the slip, made the annual inspection, and scraped the bottom, which was necessary for all wooden boats and especially in these snail-infested waters.

Esperanza was a very beautiful little boat, and her owner had always taken good care of her.

52

Wednesday, September 12.
Four weeks remaining until October 10.
Headquarters of the National Bureau of Criminal
Investigation on Kungsholmen in Stockholm

The big boss's own conference room. At the table sit the usual four. Lars Martin Johansson, Anna Holt, Jan Lewin, and Lisa Mattei. Outside the window autumn has arrived after a long, hot summer that seemed like it would never end. Suddenly, surprisingly, without advance warning. Cut the temperature in half and struck with gale-force winds. Like a street robber pulling and tearing at the trees in the park across the street and throwing itself against the outside of the building.

"A question," said Holt. "Why does he leave SePo so hastily and strangely? Waltin, that is. According to my papers he is supposed to have applied for and been granted dismissal in May 1988 and left formally at the end of June the same year. He seems to have already left in early June. That's when he turned in his police ID, his keys, his service weapon and signed all the papers. The only thing I've produced is that he applied for and was granted dismissal by his own request."

347

"He had no choice," said Johansson. "The alternative would have been that he would be fired."

"Why?" said Holt.

"Okay then," sighed Johansson, looking like the former head of SePo he was. "Assuming that this stays in this room. Briefly and in summary. Lots of financial oddities and some real irregularities. Waltin was also head of the so-called external operation, where the secret police had, among other things, started a private company to use as a cover and control instrument. Waltin seemed to have mostly been interested in making money. The parliamentary auditors went crazy when they found out about it. Justice did an investigation and decided that the whole operation had been illegal from the start. Apart from Waltin's own efforts as an entrepreneur."

"So how has SePo solved that today?" said Mattei with an innocent expression.

"Excuse me," said Johansson. What is it she's saying? he thought.

"I'm joking with you, boss. Excuse me," said Mattei, who didn't seem the least bit repentant.

"Don't do it again," said Johansson sternly. What has happened with Mattei? he thought.

"I have a question myself, by the way," he continued after a moment.

Had they thought about Waltin's motive, if things were really so bad that he was involved in the murder of the prime minister? True, Johansson himself was no friend of motives. He considered them almost a source of entertainment for the judicial upper classes, and the sort of thing that real police officers seldom made use of when they tried to advance a murder investigation. In fact, or simply in his experience, the motives he had encountered during his life as a police officer were almost always obvious or crazy. Concerning Waltin, however, he could imagine making an exception.

"Possibly he had a role model," Lewin replied with a cautious glance at Mattei. "Lisa and I are looking at that."

. . .

Then he talked about Claes Waltin's middle name, the date he was born, and his father's background. Holt filled in with the story about his to say the least strange will, and his statement that he had murdered his mother.

"Absent father, dominant mother, idealizes the father, hates the mother, classic psychology," said Holt. "If you want more—"

"Thanks, thanks," Johansson interrupted. "That's good enough. I want something to sink my teeth in. Get to the bottom of this fellow. Trace his contacts. Find out who he associated with. How he thought, felt, and lived. Where he stood politically, who and what he loved and hated. What he read, what he ate, what he drank. I want to know everything about the bastard. His dad, by the way. How old is he now?"

"He'll soon be eighty-eight," Mattei interjected alertly, before Lewin had time to leaf through his papers.

"Find out if there's any sense in interviewing him," said Johansson. "If he was crazy enough to christen his boy Adolf at that point in time, it might very well be worth the bother. People like that usually like to hear their own voice. Who knows? Maybe he was the one holding the revolver. Frisky, happy retiree. Looked considerably younger than he was."

"I think you can forget that," said Holt. "He's too short, for one thing. Five foot eight according to his passport from that time."

"Good, Holt," said Johansson. "Embrace the situation. Give me the name of the bastard."

"Sometimes I get the idea that you have it," Holt objected.

"Not him," said Johansson, shaking his head. "Not Waltin. Give me the name of the bastard who did the shooting."

That evening after dinner Johansson and his wife, Pia, watched a film by Costa-Gavras. It was about a leading left-wing politician who was murdered by the Greek junta's police. Johansson had borrowed it from Mattei, who in turn had borrowed it from an acquaintance who was studying film. *Z—He lives on,* thought Johansson, and well worth watching, according to Mattei.

Personally he had a hard time concentrating. Probably because he would soon have bigger problems than any of the others. His suddenly, inexplicably happy co-worker who dared to test his democratic captaincy. What is happening? thought Johansson.

Pia, he thought. Soon he would probably have to talk with her. Although not now. Not now when they were curled up in their separate corners of the couch with legs interlaced, watching a film about a murdered politician while the wind picked up and howled against his very security there in front of the TV in the building where they lived. He and his wife and everything that his life was ultimately about.

"What is it, Lars? You seem worried."

"It's nothing," Johansson lied, smiling at her. "Just a bit much at work."

Then he leaned over, placed his arm around her and drew her to him. It'll work out, he thought. We'll cross that bridge when we come to it.

53

On Wednesday, September 12, Superintendent Anna Holt and Inspector Lisa Mattei held an interview with Gustaf G:son Henning at his office on Norrmalmstorg.

To begin with he had been both guarded and surprised, very surprised, almost unsympathetic. Courteous, to be sure, but mostly because they were women and despite the fact that they came from the police. Pretty soon they softened him up. Holt, at her most attractive with her clean features and white teeth, her black hair and long legs. Mattei, with her blond, innocent admiration for a mature man of the world. Gustaf G:son Henning was irretrievably lost. Despite his white hair, his tailor-made Italian suits, and his seventy years of experience of every form of human intrigue.

How nice, thought Anna Holt, smiling at him. So I avoid having to bring up Juha Valentin Andersson Snygg.

Then he told them everything he had told Bäckström. Speaking more and more comfortably and elaborately the longer the story went on. Exhaustively too and in detail, because he was asked those kinds of questions. A few times he even confirmed the date and what had happened with the help of his old diaries.

Mostly he talked about Claes Waltin. They had met at the restaurant. The old Cecil on Biblioteksgatan where well-off young men at that time would get drunk and socialize with women. A twenty-year-old Waltin and Henning, only ten years older. Told about their first business deal, when Waltin had just received his inheritance and was running around

351

with a lot of money burning a hole in a young man's pockets. About Waltin's early interest in pornography—"good pornography"—and about the painting he sold to him when he was barely "dry behind the ears."

"It was a small oil by Gustav Klimt, and it's probably the worst deal I've made in my entire life. Considering the price it would have commanded today."

About the years that followed. How they met, or talked on the phone, at intervals of a month or two. Did the occasional deal. Had numerous good dinners together. Talked about art, about the good life, even about women, actually, though personally he only reluctantly talked about women with other men.

"We were not close friends. More like acquaintances, in the positive sense. In addition we were neighbors on Norr Mälarstrand for many years, and we might run into each other on the street on a daily basis when we were both in town."

"Did he have any close friends that you know about?" asked Holt.

Not that he knew. No family, except his father whom he talked about occasionally. But a frightful lot of women. Beautiful women. Young women. Some very young. Perhaps much too young. He had seen that with his own eyes, not least when they ran into each other in the block where they lived. Claes Waltin with a new woman hanging on his arm.

"On some occasion I recall he said that was how he wanted them. Young, very young. He wanted to take them in mid-leap. His view of women left a great deal to be desired, if I may say so," Henning the art dealer observed, smiling paternally at Lisa Mattei where she was sitting in her blue pumps and with demurely crossed legs.

"A great deal to be desired, you say," said Holt.

"Yes," said Henning, shaking his head. "On some occasion I remember he asked if I was interested in a collection of photos and films. Privately recorded, somewhat rougher things, to say the least. I declined of course."

. . .

The revolver with which the prime minister was supposed to have been shot?

Besides what he had told Bäckström, and now them too, he had one thing he wanted to add. He had forgotten to tell this to Bäckström, but had thought of it when he was ransacking his memory.

"He showed me a picture of the revolver," said Henning.

"A picture?" asked Holt.

"It was an ordinary photograph. Color photo, enlargement, maybe eight inches by six, with the revolver on top of a copy of *Dagens Nyheter* from the first of March. The day after the murder. If I remember correctly, the headline was "'Olof Palme Murdered.'"

"Revolvers of this model usually have a serial number marked on the barrel. Do you recall whether you saw that?"

"No," said Henning, shaking his head. "I recall that it was shiny, metal-colored, that is. Had a long barrel and a wooden butt. With that kind of hatched grip. Checkered."

"Checkered?"

"Yes, that's what it's called. Probably walnut, according to Waltin. Like I said, I asked about that. And what condition it was in."

"Do you remember in what direction the barrel was pointing on the photo?" Mattei interjected.

"To the right, it must have been," said Henning. "The revolver was under the headline. On the photo that is. Parallel with the headline. With the butt to the left and the barrel to the right."

"You're sure of that?" asked Holt. With the serial number on the other side, she thought.

"Completely sure," Mattei repeated. May have been chance too, she thought.

"At least I have a definite recollection of that," said Henning. "Why are you wondering, by the way?"

"The serial number on a revolver of that model is on the left side of the barrel. Explains why you didn't see it," said Holt.

. . .

"But he said nothing about how he acquired it," Holt persisted for the third time, five minutes later.

"He said he had access to it," Henning clarified. "That it was in good condition. That it had been stored in a secure place. In the lion's own den. That's what he said. He was extremely amused when he told me that, so I'm quite sure about it."

"Waltin was quite certain this was the revolver that was used when the prime minister was murdered?"

"Quite certain," said Henning. "For whatever reason. I actually tried to joke about it and asked whether he was involved in some way, but he denied that. Then he said something to the effect that if I only knew what he had found out in his job, I would be able to live well on my silence the rest of my life."

"So how did you interpret that?"

"I knew what he worked with," said Henning, shrugging his shoulders. "I had no reason to believe he was pulling my leg. That wasn't the sort of thing he did. I got a definite impression that he could actually produce the revolver, assuming I could find a buyer and do a risk-free deal."

"So did you do that? Try to find a buyer?" Holt asked.

"No," said Henning. "Not really. There are certain deals that I would never do. I tried to say that to him too. In as refined a way as that sort of thing can be said."

"If I understand it correctly, this discussion went on only a month before he died," said Holt.

"Yes," said Henning. "It was pretty shocking when I found out what had happened. As I'm sure you understand. Not because I think he was murdered. I've never cared much for conspiracy theories. I thought that if anything maybe he had taken his own life."

"Why did you think that?"

"He was worn-out," said Henning. "Drank more than he could handle. Was careless about his appearance, even though he had always been careful about that. Waltin was always perfectly dressed. Tailor-made clothes. Had good taste. That he also had a self-destructive side I guess I was convinced of early on. But at the end, and now I'm talking about the last year before he died, there was something unrestrained about him. He said things a person doesn't say. Not normal people in any event. I know he was sick. He mentioned that he had problems with his liver, but personally I think that was about the alcohol. He drank too much, to put it simply. Way too much."

"Any examples? Of strange things he said."

"Yes," said Henning and sighed. "One evening when we were out having dinner, this must have been six months before he died, he delivered a long monologue about how he would like to stand on his balcony watching Rome burn, but because that wasn't possible he would have to be content with beating up and dominating any woman who crossed his path."

"So what did he mean by that?"

"I'm afraid he meant exactly what he said," Henning said and sighed.

"Anything else that you recall?" asked Mattei.

"He told me a few things about himself. Very vulgar things, actually, that no one would be particularly amused to hear. Personally I wasn't the least bit amused."

"Give me an example," said Holt, with a warning glance in Mattei's direction.

"When he was studying law at the university he seems to have started a peculiar society with a few of his fellow students at the law school. A somewhat strange name, to say the least. For their society, that is."

"So what was it called?" asked Holt.

"The Friends of Cunt," said Henning with an apologetic glance toward Mattei.

"The Friends of Cunt," Holt repeated.

"Yes," sighed Henning, "and it might possibly be excused as an eruption of youthful high spirits and general poor judgment, but that wasn't his point when he was telling the story."

"So what was his point?"

"That he'd been expelled," said Henning. "His three friends in the society expelled him. There were only four of them. A small society, I should think. Waltin was expelled by the others. For reasons I've already hinted at."

"That he beat women up before he slept with them," said Holt.

"More or less," said Henning. "And a few other things too."

"Such as?"

"That he would tie them up, among other things. Shave their pubic hair and that kind of thing. Photograph them after he'd tied them up."

"When was he expelled by the other members of the society?"

"Well. They had a party with a few young women they got hold of. At home with Waltin, if I understand it right. It evidently degenerated, according to the other members. Not according to Waltin. He was very amused as he was telling the story."

"These other members. Waltin didn't mention any names?"

"Sure," said Henning. "That was how he started in on this story. We started talking about one of them in a completely different context, and that was when he said he had once belonged to the same society."

"So what is his name?"

"A very well-known individual, I'm afraid."

"I'm listening," said Holt.

"Nowadays he's a member of parliament for the Christian Democrats," said Henning with a deep sigh.

"And his name is?"

"Let me think about that," said Henning, shaking his head. "This is forty years ago, after all," he added.

"We can discuss that before we leave," said Holt.

"Wonder who the other two were?" said Holt in the police car on their way back to headquarters.

"Our member of parliament perhaps remembers," said Mattei. "I mean, just a small society. He must remember anyway?"

"Shall you or I talk with him?" said Holt.

"I demand to be present," said Mattei. "Otherwise I'm resigning from the police."

"Let's think about it," said Holt and sighed. "It's not completely given that this has anything to do with the matter," she added.

"I think it probably does," Mattei objected. "If you're expelled from a society like that, it definitely has something to do with the matter."

"We'll think about it," Holt decided. Sometimes Lisa can be completely merciless, she thought.

Before Anna Holt went home for the day, she called up an old colleague she had met during her time at SePo. Nowadays he was regional head of the local police in a district outside Kristianstad in Skåne, where Claes Waltin's aged father owned a large estate that had been in the family for several generations.

"Robert Waltin. Of course we know him. Something of a local celebrity down here. Nosy question: Why do you want to talk about him?"

"For informational purposes, about another individual that we're looking at," said Holt. "He's not suspected of anything, but when I discovered how old he is I thought it was best to hear from you whether there was any point in trying to talk with him," Holt clarified.

"Depends," said her colleague. "What you want to talk about, that is. I'm sure you know whose father he was?"

"Former superintendent Claes Waltin."

"One and the same. So the apple didn't land very far from the pear tree. There doesn't seem to be anything wrong with the old man's mind. Still drives around in his old Mercedes spreading terror on the local roads. I've tried to talk with him about that. But it was completely meaningless. We tried to take away his driver's license, but we had to reverse ourselves on that."

"Do you have any suggestions? If I were to make an attempt?"

"Say that you've decided to investigate the murder of his son," said her colleague. "Then he's never going to stop talking. He's been harping about that every single time I or any of my associates has had contact with him because he's been driving like a lunatic, tearing down the neighbor's sheep fence, or suing someone for placing a manure pile upwind of his house. All the kinds of things that extremists do to promote neighborly harmony out here in the country. Then he always talks about all the shit we're involved in to avoid devoting ourselves to essential things.

For example, that the socialist administration murdered his son. That's what he calls them. The socialist administration or the socialist mafia."

"I get the sense that Claes Waltin drowned," said Holt.

"In that case you should be careful about saying so. He's an uncommonly repulsive old bastard," Holt's colleague observed. He was born in the district where he was now chief.

54

Bäckström was on the third day of his weeklong imprisonment. The camp to which he had been transported was a former summer camp for children up in Roslagen. A number of barracks-like buildings scattered on a forested hill above a wind-blown reed cove. Complete with a rotted pier and a broken rowboat shipwrecked on the embankment. Paper-thin walls in the buildings where they were staying. Iron beds made for poor children, with banana-shaped bedstead bottoms and old horsehair mattresses from the days of the Second World War. Beds that you had to make yourself. Beds that were lined up in hovel-like rooms you were expected to share with another brother in misfortune.

Although Bäckström had luck. He wound up with a colleague from the traffic police in Uppsala who seemed relatively normal and just like him had escaped all these years until yet another new female police chief sank her claws in him. Besides his roommate had had the foresight to hide a suitcase with beer and aquavit under a nearby outhouse before he registered at reception.

Once there you were lost. Bäckström realized this as soon as he came up to the counter and talked with the attack dyke running the check-in.

"Cell phone," she said, looking dictatorially at Bäckström. "All course participants must turn in their cell phones."

"I didn't think you could bring your cell phone with you," Bäckström lied with an innocent expression. "I mean, they are extremely annoying if you're going to be at a course and have to concentrate." Hope the piece of shit doesn't ring while I'm standing here, he thought. Especially as he'd stuffed it in his briefs as soon as he got on the bus they drove up in.

"You left your cell phone at home," said the receptionist, looking at him suspiciously.

"Of course," said Bäckström. "I mean, it's extremely annoying if you're going to be at a course and have to concentrate. A good initiative you've taken, I think." Now suck on that, you little sow, he thought.

"Did you bring along any alcoholic beverages?" asked the receptionist as she glanced at Bäckström's heavy suitcase.

"I don't drink alcohol," said Bäckström, shaking his round head. "Never have, actually. Both my mother and my father were strong opponents of intoxicants, so that's never been of interest to me. I had that with me from childhood, so to speak," added Bäckström, with a pious expression. "What I mean is that if you absorb such an important message while you're still a child, then—"

"Room twenty-two, second building to the left, second floor," the dyke interrupted, banging the key on the counter.

"Although I missed that bit with the phone," said his colleague after they had finished the introductory greeting ceremonies between old constables.

"Too fucking depressing, actually," he added. "I know a lady who lives only six miles from here, when for once I have the old lady at a safe distance."

"It'll work out," said Bäckström, pulling in his gut and fishing his cell phone out of his underwear. "Who the hell doesn't make mistakes? Personally I thought they had a bar at this place. I mean, who the hell runs a conference hotel without having a big fucking bar?" And my good malt whiskey, which I have in my little suitcase, I do not intend to share with some country sheriff from traffic in any event, he thought.

"Here they apparently do. The ones running the place seem to be some of those anthropologists. Did you see the menu?" His colleague sighed, shaking his head. "Vegetarian shit, all the way through."

"It'll work out," said Bäckström. "It'll work out. What do you think about a little checking-in shot, by the way? Then you can take the opportunity to call that broad you were talking about and ask if she has a younger girlfriend." Who wants to sample the Bäckström super-salami, he thought.

Sure. It had worked decently for three days. Despite all the fairies babbling uninterruptedly about gender issues and equality and how you became a liberated man and not just a useless prisoner of your own sex, and why someone who had a cat was a better person than the bastard who stuck to an ordinary dog.

Despite group therapy and relaxation exercises and a crazy old hag who held forth on Rosen therapy and human energy fields and following your inner voice so as to find the way to a higher consciousness, free from inhibiting male hormones and hereditary prejudices.

Despite the food, which was a real Christmas banquet for both guinea pigs and chaffinches with its groaning abundance of mineral water and salad and birdseed and nuts and cleansing root vegetables and unseasoned soy patties and fruit and hot water with milk and decaffeinated coffee for the most daring, who really wanted to get turned on before going to bed.

Bäckström had not betrayed his true sentiments and agreed with everything, and already during the first group discussion he had initiated the dialogue by firing off a juicy fart right in the chocolate kisser of the queer leading the discussion. Fridolf Fridolin, the Stockholm police department's own psychologist, as well as gender sensitivity manager at the agency. Small, round, and rosy, complete with a Manchester jacket and down on his upper lip.

"There's a lot of talk about equality and gender issues among our fellow citizens these days, but how serious is this, when we—"

"Fellow citizens?" Bäckström interrupted with raised hands. "Why do you say 'fellow'? Are all citizens supposed to be guys? Is that what you mean?"

"I hear what you're saying, Bäckström," said their discussion leader, smiling nervously.

"Bäckström," said Bäckström. "I thought we agreed that we should call one another by our first names, and personally I know for sure that during our introduction I said that my friends always call me Eve. Never Bäckström, never even Evert. My friends call me Eve," said Bäckström, nodding challengingly at his blushing victim.

"Excuse me, Bäck . . . Eve. Excuse me. Eve."

"I forgive you, Frippy," said Bäckström. "It was Frippy you wanted to be called?"

"Fridolf. It was my dad who—"

"Your dad," said Bäckström accusingly. "But you must have a mom too? What did she used to call you?"

"Little Frippy, although that was—"

"You're forgiven, Little Frippy," said Bäckström with a dignified expression.

On the evening of the third day things really went downhill. First the aquavit ran out. Almost, at least, for he had had the foresight to save a drop of his own. Then he and his colleague from Uppsala came extremely close to being caught in the act as they were sneaking home to the hotel after the usual evening orgy at the hot dog stand up by the highway. Once in the safety of the room he listened to his voice messages. GeGurra had called and cursed and sworn like a sailor. Not the least bit like a silver-haired elderly art dealer. More like an ordinary tramp, actually, and it was all apparently that dyke Holt's fault. As soon as he had been admitted to the gender sensitivity asylum, she had thrown herself on the old homo and evidently scared the shit out of him.

"You gave me your word of honor, Bäckström," GeGurra repeated on the voice mail. "I look forward to hearing what you have to say in your defense."

She's trying to cheat me out of the cash, and now it's a matter of being quick, thought Bäckström. He packed his little bag, put on a tie, wandered down to reception, pulled on the tie until his skull felt like it was going to burst, eased up on the tie so as not to die for real, and staggered into reception.

"I think I'm having a heart attack," Bäckström hissed, sitting down on the floor, staring at the dyke receptionist with round eyes and waving his hands in front of his very red face.

Then everything had gone like a dance. The dyke receptionist called the emergency number while she sponged Bäckström's forehead. To be on the safe side he had assumed a horizontal position on the floor. He was taken by ambulance to the emergency room in Norrtälje. Was admitted for observation overnight by a real Swedish doctor and not some quack in a violet turban. Private room, newly made bed, Finnish blonde who was apparently the night nurse and had a weakness for a real constable from the big city. She came in several times and chatted with him before he finally had a little peace so he could consume the last drops from the bottle he'd brought with him and get the beauty sleep he so heartily needed.

The next day he took a taxi home. Put on sick leave, with a referral to Karolinska in Stockholm to follow up on possible allergies, blood pressure, cholesterol levels, and a few other goodies that worried the dear doctor up in Norrtälje.

Now, Holt, thought Bäckström as soon as he closed the door and fetched a cold pilsner from the fridge. Now this is war.

55

"When did you intend to interview Wiijnbladh?" said Johansson as soon
as he appeared at the door to her office.

"Good morning, Lars," said Holt. "Yes, I'm doing just fine. Thanks
for asking. I was just meaning to call him and set a time. Jan and I will
hold the interview with him. It will have to be for informational purposes. How are you doing yourself, by the way?"

"For informational purposes?"

"Yes, otherwise how could we set it up? The part about the revolver
passed the statute of limitations several years ago. So we don't have a
suspect. Even if it were true."

"He's going to be picked up," said Johansson, glaring at her acidly.

"Excuse me?"

"I've spoken with the prosecutor. Brought in without prior notice.
House search at his residence and at his workplace."

"On what grounds then?" asked Holt. What's happening? she
thought. Has Johansson talked with the prosecutor? And in that event
what am I doing in this case?

"Premeditation for murder," said Johansson. "That's not prescribed,"
he added, nodding gloomily.

"Premeditation for murder? Wait now. Are we talking about the
prime minister, because in that case it's more likely complicity to murder that we—"

"We're talking about his former wife, whom he wanted to poison,"
interrupted Johansson.

"Neither Jan nor I intend to bring that up," answered Holt, shaking

364

her head. "There doesn't seem to even be a report in that matter, by the way."

"Now there's a report," said Johansson. "Which is why you shouldn't talk about it, but because that was the best the prosecutor and I could come up with, now there's a report. Before you ask, by the way, it was our usual prosecutor, if you're wondering, not that skinny woman who takes care of Palme.

"Do as I say for once," he continued. "See to it that we have him here within an hour. And try for once not to be too nice and understanding. That applies to both you and Lewin."

And so it turned out. One hour later Wiijnbladh was sitting in an interview room at the National Bureau of Criminal Investigation with Holt and Lewin. Very shaken up, and not understanding a thing.

"Why do you want to talk with me?" Wiijnbladh whined, licking his lips nervously.

"About your previous acquaintance with Chief Superintendent Claes Waltin," said Holt, taking pains to look both friendly and interested.

"He's dead, you know," said Wiijnbladh, with a confused look.

"Yes, I know that. But when he was alive it seems that he and you were good friends."

She got no farther than that, for suddenly Johansson opened the door and simply walked right in. With him he had two colleagues from the bureau's homicide squad. Rogersson, with his narrow eyes, and then that disgusting bodybuilder whose name I've managed to repress, thought Holt. Hardly by chance.

"My name is Johansson," said Johansson, glaring at Wiijnbladh. "I'm the one who's the boss at this place."

"Yes, I know who the boss is," stammered Wiijnbladh. "I don't think I've had—"

"I want the keys to your home, your pass card to the building here, your computer card, and the codes to your computer," Johansson interrupted.

"But I don't understand," said Wiijnbladh, shaking his head and looking almost imploringly at Holt.

"House search," said Johansson, holding out his large hand. "Empty your pockets, then I won't have to ask the officers to do it for you."

One minute later they left. Remaining were Holt, Lewin, and a terrified Wiijnbladh who was looking at Holt.

"I have to go to the bathroom," he said. "I have to—"

"Jan here will go along with you," said Holt, turning off the tape recorder. I should have listened to Berg, she thought.

He took his sweet time in the bathroom. Wiijnbladh apparently splashed his face with cold water, which seemed to have been of little help. Confused and absent. Doesn't understand what this is about, thought Holt.

"Now we resume the interview with Detective Inspector Göran Wiijnbladh," said Holt after she restarted the tape recorder. "Before we were interrupted we were talking about your acquaintance with former chief superintendent Claes Waltin with the secret police. Can you tell us how you knew him?"

"We were good friends," said Wiijnbladh. "But I still don't understand."

"How long had you known him?" asked Holt.

According to Wiijnbladh he had known Waltin since the early eighties. It started as a professional contact, but by and by it had turned into more of a regular friendship.

"I had the privilege of giving him a little general guidance in forensic issues," said Wiijnbladh, who suddenly seemed calmer. "But otherwise we mostly talked about art, actually. We had that interest in common,

366

and Claes had an excellent art collection. Really excellent, with a number of major works by both Swedish and foreign artists. On one occasion he asked me to look at an etching by Zorn to see if it might be a forgery."

"General forensic issues, you say," said Holt. "Did you ever talk about other things in that line, other than the sort of thing that concerned art forgeries?"

"What might that have been?" asked Wiijnbladh, looking at her.

"Firearms," said Holt. "Did he ask you about firearms?" Just as confused again, she thought.

"He asked me about everything imaginable. About fingerprints and various forensic methods for securing and analyzing clues. Claes, well, Claes Waltin that is, had a very strong interest in education. He simply wanted to learn more. Used to show up and visit me at the tech squad."

"Let's return to the subject of firearms," said Holt. "I've understood that in September 1988 you turned over a revolver to him that was stored in your so-called weapons library at the tech squad. It was confiscated in a case from March 27, 1983. A murder-suicide."

"I know nothing about that," Wiijnbladh stammered, his gaze wobbling between her and Lewin. "I know nothing about that."

Unfortunately you probably do, thought Holt. If I were to believe your eyes, then you do.

"But you must remember it anyway," said Holt. "In the fall of 1988, Claes Waltin asked you to turn over a revolver to him. This revolver, to be more exact," she said, handing over a photograph of the firearm that was used in the murder-suicide out in Spånga in March 1983.

"One of your former colleagues took the photo," Holt explained. "Bergholm, if you remember him. He was the one in charge of the technical investigation when the photo was taken."

Wiijnbladh did not want to pick up the photograph. Didn't even want to look at it. Shook his head. Turned away. Holt took a new approach and hated herself as she did it.

"I'm getting a little surprised by your answers," said Holt. "Either you gave a revolver to Waltin or you didn't. Yes or no, that is, and it's no more difficult than that. I and my colleague Jan Lewin here have reason to believe that you did. Now we want to know what your position is on this."

"I'm prevented from saying that," said Wiijnbladh.

"How can you be?" said Holt. "You have to explain that."

"With respect to the security of the realm," said Wiijnbladh.

"With respect to the security of the realm," Holt repeated. "That sounds like something Claes Waltin said to you."

"I had to sign papers."

"You had to sign papers that Claes Waltin gave you. Where do you keep them?"

"At home," said Wiijnbladh. "At home where I live. In the drawer to my desk, but they're secret so you can't look at them."

"I'll come back to that," said Holt. "In September 1988 you turned over the revolver that you see in the photograph sitting in front of you to Claes Waltin. We'll come back to why you did that, but before that I intend to ask you about a few other things we've also been wondering about. The tech squad's report from the test firing of that revolver is missing. Jan Lewin and I think you were the one who removed it. The second thing concerns a request you addressed to the Defense Factories for scrapping the same firearm. We do not think that the firearm was scrapped. How could it have been? You'd already given it to your good friend Claes Waltin."

"I know nothing about that," Wiijnbladh whimpered, staring at the floor.

"I want you to look at me, Göran," said Holt. "Look at me."

"What?" said Wiijnbladh, looking at her. "Why?"

"I want to be able to look you in the eyes when you answer," said Holt. "You must understand that anyway. You're a police officer yourself."

"But I can't answer, I just can't. If I answer I'm committing a breach of secrecy. It's in the papers I signed."

"The papers that Claes Waltin gave you and told you to sign?"

"Yes," said Wiijnbladh and nodded. "Although I can't say that either."

Finally, thought Holt.

.   .   .

"Do you have any questions, Jan?" said Holt, turning to Lewin.

"There are a couple of things I'm wondering about," said Lewin with a cautious throat clearing. "When you signed these papers, in connection with giving Waltin the revolver, this was in September 1988."

"I'm not allowed to say that," Wiijnbladh complained, shaking his head.

"I'm assuming that you were not aware at the time that Claes Waltin had resigned as a police officer."

"No, that can't be right," said Wiijnbladh, staring at Holt for some reason.

"Yes," said Lewin. "Waltin resigned as a police officer in June of that year. Several months before he got you to turn over the revolver, remove the test firing report, and prepare a scrapping certificate, which was incorrect on at least one point. Claes Waltin was not a police officer when you performed these services for him."

"That can't be right," said Wiijnbladh, shaking his head.

"So why can't that be right?" asked Lewin.

"I got a distinction. I got a medal too. From the secret police. As thanks for my efforts for the security of the realm."

"Which you keep in your desk drawer," Jan Lewin surmised.

"Yes. Yes. I've had it there the whole time."

Poor wretch, thought Jan Lewin.

56

"So you intend to come along to the poisoner's home, boss," said Rogersson, holding the car door open for Johansson.

"You betcha. I need to get out and move around," said Johansson.
"Although I intend to sit in front," he said. "Falk can sit in back, then he'll
have room."

"Thanks, boss," said Falk, grinning and holding open the right door.

"So we don't need any protective gear," said Rogersson as they drove
out of the tunnel to the police building's garage.

"Hell no," said Johansson, shaking his head. "Not us. What we're
looking for are some papers and some fucking medal the bastard is supposed to have received."

"From the pharmaceutical company," said Rogersson, grinning.

"If only it were that good," said Johansson and sighed.

For the past fifteen years Detective Inspector Göran Wiijnbladh had lived
in an assisted-living facility for early retirees in Bromma. One room and
kitchen with a small bathroom. Four alarm buttons to call for help, if
needed. One by the front door, which could be reached even if you were
lying on the floor; one in the bathroom between the toilet and bathtub.
One in the kitchen by the stove. One by the bed in the only room. It was
also equipped with an extension cord, in case he wanted to have it with
him when he sat at his desk or in the armchair in front of the TV.

The place was worn-out, musty, with a faint but unmistakable odor
of urine. On the floor in the bathroom was an opened package of adult
diapers. In the medicine cabinet were twenty-some vials and packages

with various medicines. An empty plastic denture case. Shaving razor, shaving cream, and aftershave. On the sink a plastic mug with a toothbrush and a tube of denture cream.

Poor devil, thought Lars Martin Johansson, continuing into the one room.

Rogersson stood rooting in the desk by the window while his colleague Falk dug through the contents of the small dresser that was against the short wall. On the nightstand beside the bed was a framed photograph of Wiijnbladh's ex-wife. The one who had left him almost twenty years ago when he happened to poison himself, although he only wanted to kill her.

"Is it this you mean, boss?" said Rogersson, holding up a plastic bag with a medal the size of a five-krona coin. "To Detective Inspector Göran Wiijnbladh in gratitude for meritorious efforts for the security of the realm," Rogersson read.

"I'm afraid it is," said Johansson.

"Was he some fucking war hero?" asked Rogersson, shaking his head.

"More likely the Man of Steel," Falk sneered, holding up a pair of white underwear. "A lot of rust in these briefs."

"Papers," said Johansson.

"Must be these," said Rogersson. "Some kind of receipt for a firearm and a mysterious letter of recommendation. From the gumshoes in the B building. Their stationery in any event."

"I'll have to see," said Johansson. How fucking stupid can you be? he thought.

57

Johansson returned to the interview room in less than two hours. This time he apparently intended to stay, because he was carrying a chair that he could sit on.

"The head of NBCI is entering the room," said Holt. "We interrupt the interview at—"

"Turn off that piece of shit," said Johansson, waving toward the tape recorder. "Now we have to have a serious talk, you and me, Göran," he said, nodding at Wiijnbladh. "You have nothing to worry about," he added. "So you can be completely calm. But first we'll have coffee," said Johansson, looking at Holt for some reason. "Black or with milk, Göran?"

"With cream, if there is any," Wiijnbladh stammered.

That man defies all description, thought Anna Holt. Wiijnbladh did not seem the least bit calm. Despite Johansson's assurances, she thought.

Then she got the coffee. What choice did she really have? And saw to it that Wiijnbladh got cream in his, and listened to Johansson while he talked to Wiijnbladh as if he were talking to a child.

"As perhaps you know, I was operations head of the secret police for a number of years," said Johansson, nodding at Wiijnbladh.

"Yes, that was before the boss . . . before you became head of the bureau," Wiijnbladh concurred.

"So what I'm saying to you now is in strictest confidence," said Johansson. "Before we leave I also want you to sign a confidentiality agreement. The usual, you know, on nondisclosure."

"Of course," said Wiijnbladh.

While the maid fetched coffee, the boys had apparently dispensed with formalities, thought Holt.

"As I've understood it, it happened in the following way," said Johansson in a leisurely manner, pretending to read from his papers.

Waltin had tricked Wiijnbladh. Abused his confidence. Blatantly exploited him.

"Let's get some order into the details," said Johansson. "What went on when the revolver was turned over?"

First Waltin had called him on the phone. At work. He remembered that distinctly. He needed to see Wiijnbladh immediately. It was a matter of the utmost importance. Wiijnbladh could not talk about it with anyone. He was not to contact Waltin. The matter was so sensitive that Waltin was forced to work outside the police building for a while. For that reason he could not be reached.

"I knew from before that he was head of the so-called external operation, so I assumed he was working on reorganizing that," Wiijnbladh clarified.

"So it was Waltin who came to see you?"

"He came up on the weekend. It was sometime in the middle of September. I was on after-hours duty, and he asked me to call as soon as I was alone at the squad so we could talk in private. So when my associates, who were on duty with me, had to leave the building I called him. On the secret number he gave me. I think it was a Sunday. Sometime in the middle of September. We had a suspected death out in Midsommarkransen. It turned out to be a suicide."

"And then he came over to see you?" asked Johansson.

"He came like a shot," Wiijnbladh confirmed.

Wonder how he pulls it off? thought Holt with reluctant admiration.

Once up at the tech squad Waltin explained his business. The secret police needed to take possession of a certain weapon from the tech squad. Why he could not say, other than that it concerned a story of the utmost importance for the security of the realm.

"He had a complete description of the weapon with him. Serial number and everything. And a photo too."

"Do you remember what it looked like?" asked Johansson. "Was there anything besides the weapon in the photo?"

"Just the weapon," said Wiijnbladh and sighed. "Photographed right from above against a white background where the usual measuring stick had been placed to show the size, and a tag with the serial number in the lower corner. I got the impression it had been taken by our colleagues at the tech squad at SePo. But naturally I didn't ask."

"What did you do next?" asked Johansson.

First Waltin checked that they actually had the weapon in question. They did. It was in a drawer in the weaponry library along with the bullet that had been used for the test firing plus a cartridge that had not been fired. Wiijnbladh gave him the revolver, the bullet, and the cartridge. Plus the report from the test firing.

"It was very important that all traces of the weapon disappear," Wiijnbladh explained. "That's why he wanted me to arrange a scrap certificate."

"No one at the Defense Factories wondered?"

"They weren't so careful at that time. Not like today," Wiijnbladh explained. "I put together some loose gun parts from revolvers. A cylinder magazine, a sawed-off barrel where the serial number was filed off, and a loose butt, among other things. We have a lot of that lying around. Then I put it in a bag and pasted on a regular tag with the serial number of the weapon that Waltin had signed for."

"Signed for, you say," said Johansson.

"I was forced to have some kind of receipt," said Wiijnbladh. "For my own account, that is."

"And it was then that he gave you this affidavit," said Johansson, pushing over one of the two papers he had found in Wiijnbladh's desk drawer.

"Now I realize this is a forgery," sighed Wiijnbladh, shaking his head. "This is terrible. But what should I believe? An affidavit written on SePo stationery. Signed and everything. I mean, what should I think? I even had to sign a special confidentiality agreement."

What should he believe? The following week he received a medal besides and a thank-you note from SePo signed by bureau head Erik Berg. Delivered by Claes Waltin personally in connection with an invitation to a "more formal" dinner in his apartment on Norr Mälarstrand.

"The delivery itself happened before dinner," Wiijnbladh explained. "Then the other guests came to the dinner itself. Although we didn't talk about my distinction of course."

"The other guests," said Johansson, sending a glance in the direction of Holt. "So who were they?"

"An old friend of Claes, he's dead now too, unfortunately, but I seem to recall that he was a very well-known business attorney when he was alive. Died only a couple years after Claes himself happened to drown. Then there was his old dad too. Very successful businessman at that time. Lived in Skåne, I seem to recall."

Before Wiijnbladh left he had to sign yet another confidentiality agreement. Johansson kept the medal, receipt, and the thank-you note. Partly because he needed them to be able to write off all suspicions against Wiijnbladh, and he had no objections.

Before Lewin accompanied him back to the lost-and-found squad, Wiijnbladh asked Johansson one last question.

"I sincerely hope it's not so bad that this has happened in connection with a new crime?"

"There's nothing that indicates that," said Johansson with a steady gaze and honest gray eyes. "It came up in connection with the inventory from Waltin's estate and we wondered, naturally, because he didn't have a license for it. By pure chance we found out some time ago that the weapon had originally been confiscated by our colleagues in Stockholm. The mills of justice grind slowly. Unfortunately," added Johansson and sighed.

While you continue to defy all description, thought Anna Holt.

58

"So what do you think about this?" Johansson asked the following day when he and his immediate co-workers had gathered for counsel and the mandatory coffee.

"What do *you* think?" asked Holt.

"If we take this in order and start with the so-called receipt, then it's a poor forgery and an even worse joke," said Johansson, holding up the receipt for the revolver Waltin had given Wiijnbladh.

"According to the letterhead, the receipt comes from SePo's tech squad," he continued. "Signed by employee 4711, who unfortunately has an illegible signature. A good photocopier and a little imagination. Waltin seems to have had access to both."

"The thank-you note from Erik Berg," said Holt.

"Apart from the fact that such things don't happen in the material world, the signature is decently composed. 'To Detective Inspector Göran Wiijnbladh . . . I wish to express in this way our gratitude for your meritorious efforts for the preservation of the security of the realm . . . Stockholm, September 15, 1988. Erik Berg. Bureau Head. Secret Police.' September 15, 1988, was a Sunday, by the way, but Berg worked all the time, so that's not the end of the world," said Johansson.

"The medal then," said Mattei.

"Manufactured by Sporrong's medal factory. It even says so on it. Copper plated. 'To Detective Inspector Göran Wiijnbladh in gratitude for meritorious efforts for the security of the realm.'"

"Have you had our technicians look at what was confiscated?" asked Lewin.

"Not really. I've done it myself. Out of concern for the security of the realm," said Johansson.

"So what do you think about this? Other than that our colleague Wiijnbladh is perhaps not God's gift to forensic science? What do you think, Lisa?" asked Johansson, looking at Mattei.

According to Mattei there were a number of different explanations. These led in turn to several different conclusions that covered a very broad span of conceivable alternatives.

"Such as?" said Johansson.

That this whole story didn't actually need to have anything to do with the murder of the prime minister.

"Seventy-five percent is actually only seventy-five percent, if we start with the bullet, for example," said Mattei.

"That Waltin only wanted to get himself a revolver in the cheapest way," said Johansson. "That he wanted to kill badgers and other vermin on his estate in Sörmland."

"Well," said Holt. "The second possibility is still that the revolver that Waltin acquired by trickery had been used to shoot Palme. Seventy-five percent is still three times greater than twenty-five, if I've understood this correctly."

"Two and a half years after the prime minister had already been shot?" asked Lisa Mattei with an innocent expression. "Between March 1986 and September 1988 it's supposed to have been at the tech squad in Stockholm."

"In secure storage. In the lion's own den," said Lewin for some reason. "If this was the one that was used, it must have been liberated for the murder of Palme and then put back."

"I'm an old man," sighed Johansson. "Too old for scientific seminars. Give me the most probable explanation. What do you say, Anna?"

"The revolver is the murder weapon," said Holt. "Waltin takes it from the tech squad before the murder. According to Wiijnbladh he would show up and visit him up at tech. That's when he probably seizes the opportunity to take the revolver. Gives it to the perpetrator. The perpetrator gives it back to Waltin after the murder. Waltin replaces it in the tech squad. There can hardly be any safer storage. When the worst has settled down and he's been fired, he fools Wiijnbladh into giving it to him. It is a trophy he wants to have, at any price."

"Another possibility is that right or wrong, he gets the idea that this is the murder weapon and that he uses deception to get it to sell to a collector. Not as many twists and turns now, not as complicated," Mattei objected. "Tallies well with Henning the art dealer's story."

"Now we're there again," sighed Johansson. "What do you think, Jan?"

"I agree with Anna," said Lewin.

"Your old parking ticket," said Johansson.

"Yes," said Lewin. "Waltin has the weapon in his possession. Don't ask me how. He gives it to the perpetrator before the deed. Takes it back the day after the deed. The perpetrator spent the night at one of SePo's secure addresses up at Gärdet."

"Not a bad conspiracy theory, Lewin," said Johansson.

"No," said Lewin. "So we really have to hope it doesn't add up."

When Holt returned to her office she had an unscheduled visit from Bäckström. He was sitting on her desk, and presumably trying to read the papers lying there.

"I'm furious," said Bäckström, glaring at her threateningly.

"Please sit down," said Holt.

Bäckström was not only furious. He was also disappointed. In Holt, in her associates, in all of humanity, actually. So disappointed that it had affected his health. He had been struck by a heart attack or possibly a minor stroke the evening before, spent the night at the ER, and now he was on sick leave. As soon as he recovered he intended to contact the union to get help with his complaint against the police administration in Stockholm, the bureau, and not least Anna Holt.

"I think you look spry, Bäckström," said Holt, who did not appear to have been listening.

"For a real policeman like me an informant's anonymity is sacred," said Bäckström indignantly. "You and Mattei have gone behind my back. Gustaf Henning called and gave me a good dressing-down, and you should know that I understand him. But I'm not the one who tricked him. You're the one who tricked me."

"You're worried about the reward," said Holt.

Not really. It was deceitful colleagues that bothered him. The general decline of the police force. A society on a fast track to destruction, a society where an honorable, hardworking person like him could no longer rely on anyone. That was the kind of thing that worried Bäckström. He had never counted on any reward for his drudgery. That's one thing he'd learned during his more than thirty years with the police.

"Who gave you the tip about the weapon? Who gave you the name of Waltin? Without me you wouldn't have squat. I was even the one who put you on the track of that secret sect of sex abusers. Friends of Cunt. You can count with your feet what they've been up to all these years. A society of perverse lunatics! You can hear it in the name, can't you?"

"It's ugly to read other people's papers without permission," said Holt, putting the interview with Henning in her desk drawer to be on the safe side.

"What do you have to say in your defense?" asked Bäckström, fixing his eyes on Holt.

"That I'm doing my job," said Holt. "In contrast to you, who are only running around sticking your nose in other people's business. Besides, you're supposed to be on sick leave. Go home and go to bed and rest, Bäckström. And stop reading my papers without permission," she concluded, fixing her eyes on him.

"War," said Bäckström, getting up out of the chair and pointing a fat index finger at Holt.

"War?"

"War," Bäckström repeated. "Now this is war, Holt."

59

After lunch Holt and Mattei took a flight to Kristianstad to hold an interview with Claes Waltin's elderly father.

"I had a visit from Bäckström," Holt reported. "He was sitting in my office when I came back after the meeting with Johansson."

"That horrible little fatso," said Mattei with feeling. "So what did he want?"

"Unclear requests," said Holt. "On the other hand he did declare war against us."

"In that case I'll ask Johan to give him a thrashing."

"Johan?"

"Johan," nodded Mattei. For the rest of the trip she talked about Johan, and she would have been happy if the flight to Kristianstad had lasted even longer.

Little Lisa is in love, thought Holt with surprise as they got off the plane.

Large estate in Skåne. Whitewashed exposed-timber house, complete with thatched roof, pond, and lane of birches.

So there are people who live like this, thought Anna Holt as their airport taxi stopped on the gravel yard in front of the main building at the "Robertslust" estate.

"The Waltin family has lived here at Robertslust for generations," their host explained when he'd led them into the "gentlemen's room" and seen to it that the "ladies" got coffee. Large desk, crossed swords on the wall above, suite of furniture in worn velvet with crocheted antimacassars on the chair backs, old portraits in gold frames, and a hundred years later life still went on.

A really cozy old place, thought Holt.

"Is it named after director Waltin himself?" asked Mattei with a friendly, inquisitive smile.

"Not really," snorted Robert Waltin. "It's named after the family ancestor, my great-great-grandfather, estate owner Robert Waltin. Originally the family had the estate as a summer place."

And you look like you've been here the whole time, thought Lisa Mattei. Mean old man, but far from harmless, she thought. Despite the skinny neck sticking up out of a frayed, oversized shirt collar. Certainly an expensive shirt from the days when Robert Waltin was in his prime. Those days were gone; now he seemed mostly interested in complaining about everything and everyone.

"The reason we're here is that we want to ask a few questions about your son," said Holt with a formal smile.

"It's about time. I've never believed in that so-called drowning accident. Claes was completely healthy. Swam like a fish too. I taught him myself."

Before he turned five and you left him to go to Skåne and marry your secretary, thought Holt.

"Taught him when he was just a little tyke and I was still living with that crazy woman who was his mother," said papa Robert. "Then he used to come here in the summer and we sailed and swam quite a bit, he and I. He was murdered. Claes was murdered. I've thought so all along."

"Why do you think that?" asked Holt.

"The socialists," said the old man, looking at her slyly. "He knew something about them so they were forced to murder him. He worked with the secret police. He probably knew almost everything about their illegal deals with the Russians and Arabs. Why do you think they were forced to shoot that traitor Palme, by the way?"

"Tell us what you think, director Waltin."

"Palme was a traitor. Spied for the Russians. It was no more complicated than that. Russian submarines had secret bases far inside our inner archipelago. It was a corrupt political leadership, in which the one at the top was simply a spy for the enemy. Who betrayed the class he came from besides."

"What makes you think that Olof Palme was a spy for the Russians?" asked Holt. Keep out of the way, she thought.

"Every thinking person understood that," said Robert Waltin. "Besides I got it confirmed early on, from a secure source. My own son. There were even papers about it with the secret police. Papers they were forced to destroy on direct orders from the highest political leadership. It's a terrifying story of abuse of power and treason."

Really, thought Holt, and now how do I get the old guy to change track?

"Really," Holt concurred. "It would be of great help if you would tell us about your son."

His dad was happy to do so. His son had been very talented. Had an easy time in school. Always best in the class. Good-looking besides. As soon as he was big enough he didn't have a quiet moment, because of all the women running after him.

"They were crazy about him. But he handled it with good humor. Was always polite and charming to them."

"But he never married," Holt observed. "Never had a family and children of his own."

"How would he have had time for that kind of thing," his father tittered. "Besides, I warned him. I knew what I was talking about. I was married to his mother, after all."

"The one who was killed in the subway?"

"Killed? She was drunk. She was drunk all the time. Had a couple bottles of port a day and stuffed herself with a lot of pills. She was drunk and she staggered over onto the rails, and there was no more to it than that."

Had he and his son seen each other regularly?

In the summers, of course. At large family occasions on his side of the family, to which he didn't need to invite his first wife. When their paths crossed, so to speak.

"We talked with another person, a colleague of ours," said Holt, "who had met you at home with your son at a dinner in the late eighties. In his apartment on Norr Mälarstrand."

"Was it that little policeman who helped Claes with some forgery that art Jew Henning palmed off on him?" the old man asked. "A wretched character who sat and apologized for his existence the whole time and could barely manage the silverware."

"That may be right," said Holt. And personally you're not much better than Johansson when it comes down to it, she thought.

"I remember that," said papa Waltin. "As soon as we were rid of that buffoon I asked Claes why in the name of God he associated with someone like that."

"So why did he?"

"He seems to have been a useful idiot. Lucrative, too, according to Claes. Despite his deplorable appearance."

"Did he explain why he thought that?" Holt persisted.

"He didn't go into that," said Robert Waltin, shaking his head. "As I remember it, my son said only that the most useful idiots were those who had no idea what they were helping out with. That this particular specimen had done both him and the nation a very great service."

Wiijnbladh and one other guest. Did he recall who that other person had been?

"Yes, I remember him well," said Robert Waltin. "It was one of Claes's old classmates. He too became a very successful attorney. A business attorney for some of our most successful companies. Was even on the board at Bofors for several years. He died only a year or two after Claes. His name has slipped my memory, but I seem to recall I sent a card to the widow after the funeral. An excellent individual. They studied law together, as I said, and then they were members of the same society."

Goodness, thought Holt.

"Society?" she said with an inquisitive smile.

"First they were in Conservative Law Students, but then there was some dispute with the board. This was at the time when the Bolsheviks were trying to take over our universities, so Claes and his good friend started their own society. Law Students for a Free Sweden, I think they called it."

"Law Students for a Free Sweden?"

"Something like that," said papa Waltin, shrugging his shoulders. "I don't remember exactly. There were a lot of organizations that my son was a member of at that time, in case you're wondering."

"Do you recall any others?" asked Holt innocently.

"None that I intend to talk with you ladies about," said Robert Waltin.

On the other hand he was happy to talk about his son. A two-hour-long exposition on all his son's good qualities and merits, which at last they were forced to put a stop to themselves because their taxi was waiting for them.

"I really must thank you, director Waltin," said Holt, extending her hand in farewell.

"If there is anyone who deserves a thank-you it's my son," said Robert Waltin.

"I've understood that," Holt agreed.

"Because he saw to it that traitor was shot," hissed Robert Waltin, turning abruptly and disappearing into the house where the family had lived for five generations.

"So the old bastard maintains that his son is supposed to have been involved in murdering Palme," said Johansson. "How does he know that?"

"Unclear," said Holt. "More a feeling, if I understood it right. In any event, those were his parting words."

"Feeling," snorted Johansson, and it was then he decided it was time he talked with bureau head Berg's old watchdog, Chief Inspector Persson. A real constable who had been involved back in the day.

60

Persson lived in Råsunda. In one of the old fin de siècle buildings just north of the soccer stadium. He had lived in the same little two-room apartment since he got a divorce in the early seventies and could devote himself to being a policeman full-time. The human being he had spent the most time with during his seventy years was the legendary bureau head Erik Berg, operations head of the secret police for twenty-five years. Johansson's predecessor in the position and Persson's boss for two-thirds of his police career.

Berg and Persson had known each other since their days at the police academy. They shared the front seat of the same patrol car for a couple years in the sixties. Front seat only; at that time the Swedish police drove around in black Plymouths with rumbling V-8s. Before all the Volvos and Saabs. In another era.

Then Berg moved on, studied law and ended up at SePo, where he quickly made a career. In 1975 he had been named operations head with the secret police; he was the one who in reality controlled the secret police operation. The same day he got his appointment, he called Persson and offered him a job as his henchman and confidant. His only confidant, which naturally went along with the mission.

An hour later Persson resigned from his position as investigator with the Stockholm police burglary squad. He started as a chief inspector with Berg and stayed for the next twenty-four years of his active career until he retired. The following year Berg quit, and shortly thereafter died of cancer. Persson was still alive and had no intention of dying. People like him didn't die.

"Nice to hear from you, Lars," he said when Johansson called him. "It's been awhile."

"What do you think about getting together and having a bite to eat?" Johansson suggested.

"It'll have to be at my place," said Persson. "I never go to restaurants with guys. Besides, I can't stand the damn music."

"What do you think about this evening?" Johansson suggested.

"Sounds great. Don't have anything better going on," said Persson. "What do you think about salted beef brisket with homemade mashed turnips and potatoes?"

"Sure," said Johansson. "I could go for that." Is there anything better? he thought.

"Then let's say seven o'clock," Persson decided. "If you want aquavit you'll have to bring it with you."

One never ceases to be amazed, thought Johansson a few hours later as he sat in the kitchen in Persson's small apartment while his host was just pouring a refill in their shot glasses. The eternal bachelor Persson, who was known at work for always having on the same gray suit, yellowing nylon shirt, and mottled tie, regardless of the season.

His place smelled of cleanser and floor polish, and it was as tidy as an old-fashioned dollhouse. Not much bigger either, and because Persson weighed four hundred pounds and was over six feet tall, it was like watching an elephant cruising around in a china shop. An elephant with the coordination of a ballet dancer, and as skilled in the culinary arts as Johansson's beloved aunt Jenny had been. In the good old days she'd been in charge of the bar at the Grand Hotel in Kramfors and supplied both lumber barons and gamekeepers with the good things of life.

"What is it, Johansson? Are you thinking about buying some furniture from me?" asked Persson, who had evidently noticed him looking around.

"Naw," said Johansson. "It's just that things are so orderly here. People like you and me aren't exactly known for that."

"I hate disorder," said Persson. "Ever since I was drafted. So speak for yourself, Johansson."

"I'm listening," Johansson nodded, refilling their glasses for the third time.

Persson had done his military service in the navy. After the mandatory ten months he had remained as an NCO for another few years before he mustered out and applied to the police. He was still a policeman, even though he was now a retiree.

"A cop is not something you become," said Persson. "It's something you are."

"If you're a real constable, yes," agreed Johansson. "Otherwise who the hell knows. Were you on a submarine when you were in the navy?"

"No," said Persson. "Why do you think that?"

"The orderliness of your stuff," said Johansson. "If you leave your jacket lying out on a sub, your bunkmate has to sleep on the floor. According to what I've heard at least."

"Yes," said Persson. "Pretty damned cramped, and that was probably reason enough for someone like me. Although I've been on board a few times. Had a tough time even then wriggling down through the tower. I've never been claustrophobic, but who chooses to live in a pair of tight shoes? I mostly stayed on land. Worked as an explosives technician out at the Berga naval base, taking care of the old mines that floated up after the war. In the late fifties and early sixties it might happen a few times a month that we had to go out to rescue some poor wretch who got the wrong catch in his net."

"Then it was crucial to have order around you," Johansson observed.

"I'd say so," Persson agreed. "If you went half a turn too far with the screwdriver, that might be the last thing you did. And if you had the wrong tools with you, it wasn't the time for trial and error."

"I can imagine that," said Johansson.

"You learn," said Persson, shrugging his shoulders. "Actually it's not any harder than fixing a block in the drain. It's in your fingers, once you've learned. It's the consequences that are a little different, if I may put it that way. The last fifty years I've mostly dealt with drains and electrical lines, to hold down the household budget, and I'm not one to complain. Besides, workmen make a terrible mess. They lie too. Never come when they promise. How the hell would that work if you have an old German mine tapping against the shell of your boat? Cheers, by the way!"

"Cheers," said Johansson.

After the food they loosened their belts and sat in the living room to have coffee and talk about what real police officers always talked about. About other real police officers, about those who never should have been police officers, and about hooliganism in general.

"I ran into Jarnebring down in Solna center a month or so ago. Asked him to say hi to you, by the way. He was his usual self, even though he's become a dad late in life."

"Jarnebring is Jarnebring," said Johansson with feeling. "Although maybe a little too much revolves around his little boy."

"It's easy for it to get that way," sighed Persson. "That's one of the reasons I decided never to have any of my own."

"What do you mean by that?" asked Johansson.

"You get attached to them," said Persson. "You never started a new brood either?"

"No, it didn't turn out that way," said Johansson. "The first two are grown now. I'm a grandfather twice over. It's a lot easier if you ask me."

"Yes, you see," said Persson, "I've always thought the business of raising kids was overrated. Most kids are completely incomprehensible. Speaking of overrated, by the way, how's life at the bureau? Can't be too much fun to wind up at that place if you've had the privilege of working at Sec."

"Five years at Sec was enough," said Johansson, shrugging his shoulders.

"Erik was there for twenty-five," Persson observed. "Till the cancer took him. For me he could just as well have stayed there for good."

"Though you quit before he did," said Johansson.

"Yes," said Persson. "The year before. But then he was already sick and I couldn't really take seeing what was happening to him. Not every day, at least. But we had regular contact all the way to the end. We saw each other several times a week, actually. And I probably phoned him every day.

"Are you getting Palme straightened out, by the way? It's about time," his host continued, looking at Johansson inquisitively.

"Why do you ask that?" said Johansson.

"Saw something in the newspapers a month or so ago," said Persson.

"The newspapers," snorted Johansson. "The Palme investigation doesn't look too lively, if you ask me."

"I guess it never has," said Persson. "That case was already on its back the first day."

"Though there is one thing I've been thinking about," said Johansson.

"You know what, Johansson," said Persson, raising his cognac glass. "I almost suspected as much."

"Waltin," said Johansson. "What do you think about Waltin?"

"Waltin," Persson repeated, looking at Johansson and shaking his head. "Now I'm almost getting worried about you."

"Why is that?" asked Johansson.

Waltin was a dandy, conceited, incompetent. He was also cowardly. Someone like that never could have shot Palme. Besides, he didn't match the description of the perpetrator. Anyone at all but not Waltin, and not to salvage his reputation. Waltin was certainly capable of coming up with almost anything that had to do with financial irregularities and everything else under the sun where he could make a pile at no risk to himself. At the secret police there had also been a lot of whispering in the corridors about Waltin's interest in women and the peculiar expressions this allegedly could take.

"Sure," said Persson. "I'm sure he beat up a lady or two. Several, even. He was the type who did that sort of thing. Did he shoot Palme? Never in my life. Why not? He wasn't the type. He was completely the wrong type for that sort of thing," said Persson.

"He doesn't need to have shot him," Johansson objected. "That's not what I'm saying, and so far we're in agreement. That doesn't rule out that he might have been involved in some other way."

"Now I'm almost getting a little worried about you, Lars," said Persson, shaking his head. "Is he supposed to have been part of a conspiracy, do you mean?"

"For example," said Johansson.

"He was too cowardly for that," said Persson. "Besides, he was too lazy to bother planning. Waltin was the type who took the easy way out. Preferably along with others who traveled the same way. Fine folk, with a silver spoon in their mouth since they opened their eyes. Who could that little snob have known who could have done something like that for him?"

"Don't know," said Johansson. "Do you have any suggestions?"

"If it's other police officers you mean, then you're out on a limb," said Persson. "None of us would have managed that sort of thing or even picked up someone like Waltin with tongs. Not us. Besides, there's something you should know. The colleagues who worked for the bodyguards at that time, they actually liked Olof Palme. I don't think they had any intention of voting for him. But they liked him as a person. Even though he could be pretty troublesome as a surveillance object."

"So who do you think shot Palme?" asked Johansson.

"Someone like Christer Pettersson," said Persson. "Some crazy, violence-prone devil who didn't care about the consequences. Took the chance when he got it. Someone a little more orderly than Pettersson, perhaps. There must be thousands of people like that. All the idiots with a closet full of firearms that we policemen gave them a license for."

"I hear what you're saying," said Johansson.

"Nice to hear," said Persson. "Do you want a good piece of advice along with it?"

"Advice from a wise man is always welcome," said Johansson.

"It's enough if you listen to an old man who's been around even longer than you," said Persson as he served them the last drops from the bottle of cognac Johansson had brought along.

"I'm listening," said Johansson and nodded.

"Drop the thing with Palme," said Persson with feeling. "That case was lost to us more than twenty years ago."

"Sure. If I could choose I would like to boil the bastard who did it for glue," said Johansson.

"Who wouldn't," said Persson. "The problem with us policemen is that we can't do that sort of thing, and in this case we don't even know who to put in the gluepot."

Drop it, thought Johansson an hour later as he sat in the taxi on his way home to Söder. If you just stop thinking about it, then at least you've gotten something done, he thought.

61

Claes Waltin's police biography was starting to get content and form. From the birth certificate to the certificate of death. From the announcement in *Svenska Dagbladet* and the picture of little Claes and his parents to the two investigations into his death by the Spanish and Swedish police that marked the end of his earthly life.

He had not been a shining light at school, as his father Robert Waltin had maintained. More like a rascal. The best schools but mediocre grades throughout. Except in behavior and neatness. He already had low marks for conduct in the second grade.

Only eight years old and even though he was going to private school. I wonder what kind of trouble he got himself into? thought Lisa Mattei.

During his time in the military he changed in an astonishing way. Waltin did his military service with the Norrland dragoons in Umeå, serving in an elite company, the army's mounted riflemen. When he mustered out as a sergeant after fifteen months it was with the highest marks in all subjects. Then everything returned to normal. It took him eight years to finish his law degree instead of the usual four.

Didn't Palme finish his degree in two? thought Lisa Mattei.

Waltin seemed to have had many things to occupy his time besides studies. Club activities, for one thing. As soon as he'd enrolled at the law school in Stockholm he became a member of the Conservative Law Students. He left them after only one year and asked to have his reasons added to the minutes. In short, the society was much too radical for his taste.

Along with a few like-minded students, he founded a new society, a breakaway faction that called itself Young Law Students for a Free Sweden. Complete with capital letters and everything, but as a society it was already dormant after three months.

In contrast, the small circle of four young law student friends who formed the Friends of Cunt Society were considerably more persevering than that. The society was established in September 1966, at the start of the fall semester, and remained active the rest of the decade.

Waltin appeared to have been a very active member. He was the society's "Treasurer" and "Wine Cellar Manager." He won the title of "Cuntmaster of the Year" in both 1966 and 1968. He was expelled in 1969 for reasons that had left no traces in the minutes and which, almost forty years later, it took the extremely competent detective inspector Lisa Mattei a couple of days to figure out. Without the help of one of the former members of the society, now in the Swedish parliament as a representative of the Christian Democrats and an esteemed member of the Parliamentary Standing Committee on the Administration of Justice.

Mattei asked Johansson for permission to interview the member of parliament but got a point-blank no in reply.

"I'm getting worried about you, Lisa, when you talk like that," Johansson answered, fixing his eyes on her. "Why do you want to talk with him? I assume you're aware he worked as a chief prosecutor before he wound up in parliament."

"To get some sense of Waltin's personality, his background. I think it's extremely interesting," Mattei objected. "I can imagine—"

"That's pure nonsense," Johansson interrupted. "A few snotnosed kids and upper-class students in the sixties who totally lacked judgment. What relevance does that have for your case? Forty years later. Why do you think Palme was murdered? Do you think it was an attempted rape that got out of hand, or what?"

"No," said Lisa Mattei. "I don't think that. But I do believe interviewing his old friend may give us something about Waltin as a person. Besides, it was barely twenty years later that Palme was murdered. This society was founded in the fall of 1966 and Palme was shot at the end of February 1986."

"Forget it," said Johansson, shaking his head and pointing with his whole hand toward the door to his office. "Don't contradict me," he said sternly as she got up and left.

Mattei had not forgotten. Johansson's way of treating her was a guarantee of the exact opposite. Quite apart from whether the issue was relevant or not. Besides, she'd had help from Waltin's father, without his being aware of it as he sat and bragged about his son's fine friends from high school and university, and about the one who was the finest of them all, the banker, financier, billionaire Theodor "Theo" Tischler.

May be worth trying, thought Lisa Mattei, and already an hour after the conversation with Johansson she had gotten hold of Tischler by phone and arranged a meeting the next day at his office on Nybroplan without asking Johansson for permission.

As an informant he was unbeatable and improbable. A little square bald man with wide red suspenders and very attentive eyes, who inspected her nonchalantly from the other side of his gigantic desk. The man who gave Tourette's syndrome a face, thought Lisa Mattei while the tape recorder in the breast pocket of her jacket whirred for all it was worth.

"Claes Waltin," said Tischler. "What has that pathological liar come up with this time?"

"I assume you know he died a number of years ago," said Mattei.

"That's no obstacle to someone like him," Tischler observed, and within five seconds he brought up the Friends of Cunt Society.

Tischler had not had any contact whatsoever with Waltin since the spring of 1969, when Waltin had spread a malicious rumor about Tischler among the women who constituted the society's foremost recruiting base: female nursing students from Sophiahemmet, the Red Cross, and Karolinska.

"It was there of course we got the most meat on the bone," said Tischler. "If it had been today I would have sued him because he tried to mislead the market. I had a miserable time before I could get back in the game."

"So what did he say?" asked Lisa Mattei.

"That I had a prick the size of Jiminy Cricket's," said Tischler, grinning.

Was there any truth to that? thought Mattei as she shook her blond head regretfully.

"Now you're wondering of course whether there was any truth to that," Tischler continued.

No truth at all, according to the informant. Just a wicked tongue; Waltin had done everything to prevent the future banker from becoming the rightful winner of the Cuntmaster trophy. Which was why Tischler had ganged up with the society's two other members and pooled their already considerable economic muscles to bring about the fall of the slimy rumor-spreader Waltin.

"A lie from beginning to end," said Tischler. "If you don't believe me I'll give you the names of a few of my old friends from the Sea Scouts, so they can tell you what I was called back then.

"All the scout leaders at that time were old queers and pedophiles, so we little boys were always forced to swim naked when we were at camp. That was when my buddies nicknamed me the Donkey," Tischler clarified.

"The donkey?" asked Mattei.

"I've been accused of many things but never of having been stupid," Tischler observed. "It wasn't the upper part of the donkey, by the way," he said, nodding in the direction of his crotch, which was hidden by his desk.

Was Waltin a sexual sadist?

Of course, according to Tischler. Yet another reason that he was expelled. Waltin hated cunt, hence his insatiable sexual appetite and the expressions that it took.

"He damaged the society's name and good reputation," said Tischler. "Clearly we couldn't have someone like that."

Was there anything else worth recounting about Waltin? Other than that he was a sadist?

For the next hour Tischler told in proper order about how Claes Waltin poisoned a dog, made himself guilty of arson, stole things from Tischler's childhood home, was caught in the act of masturbating with a picture of Tischler's own mother. Manufactured a revolver in shop class and already the next day shot a classmate in the rear end with the same weapon. Only a sampling from secondary school and high school, according to Tischler. Mattei was welcome to hear as much as she liked, if she could bear listening.

When Waltin first poisoned a dog and then burned down the dog owner's cottage, he was fifteen years old.

"Waltin's crazy mother owned a large estate outside Strängnäs. We used to go there sometimes, a few schoolmates, when we wanted to relax. Drink beer, play some good tunes, and squeeze the breasts of the local talent. Mother Waltin was always completely gone so things couldn't have been better. There were a couple of retirees living in an isolated cottage near there that Claes got worked up about. Among other things because they had a dog that ran loose, but mostly because they lived in such ugly poverty, so to speak. So he decided to change that."

"What did he do?" asked Mattei.

"First he treated the poor dog to rat poison wrapped in steak that their retarded housekeeper bought for little Claes at the Östermalm market. The dog ate, went home, lay down on the porch, and died. The problem was that his owners didn't understand a thing. They got another dog. So Claes was forced to take new measures. He snuck over there and set fire to their house while they were asleep. Fortunately they got out in time, but the house and all their possessions burned up. Then they moved."

"How do you know this?" asked Mattei. Because I'm guessing you weren't there, she thought.

"He bragged about it at school," said Tischler. "At first I didn't believe him, but the next time I was down there I could see what had happened.

Only the chimney was left on the shack. I already knew the pooch was dead."

Two years earlier Tischler and his family had themselves been the victim of classmate Claes Waltin and his unrestrained criminal tendencies.

"Presumably he'd stolen a key to our apartment when he was visiting me and decapitating my tin soldiers. One weekend when we were in the country he came in and stole a few things. Among other things he swiped a nude picture of my mother from a photo album. My dad had photographed her, when mom was swimming nude, and obviously the photo was private."

"But you continued to associate with him anyway," said Mattei.

"I caught him a year or two later in the dressing room in the gym, beating off over the photo of my dear mother. Before that we hadn't discovered anything. He seems to have taken wine and a little jewelry besides. But nothing that my parents missed."

"So what did you do? When you caught him."

"I hit him. Took back the photo. Smuggled it back into the photo album. Dad hadn't even missed it. That was a year or so before they separated. Claes asked for forgiveness. Told a long story about how horrible his mother was and that he loved my mother and so on."

"So you forgave him?"

"I've always been a very nice man," Tischler observed with a contented sigh. "Much too nice, perhaps. Everyone loved my mother, so I forgave him."

The thing with the revolver and the schoolmate who was shot in the ass hadn't damaged their friendship either. Besides, Tischler himself had been involved.

Waltin bought a starter gun in a sporting goods store. He widened the barrel in shop class and transformed it into a .22 caliber revolver. They stole small-bore ammunition from Tischler's dad, who was a Sunday hunter when he wasn't seeing all his women.

"I kept watch down in the shop room while Claes stood there and drilled," said Tischler. "On the other hand I wouldn't have believed he'd use it to shoot one of our classmates in the butt."

"So why did he do that?"

"The victim was a real character," said Tischler. "He's still a real character, by the way. In class we called him Ass Herman, Nils Hermansson. Maybe you've heard of him. He's the guy who swindles people out of their money by offering so-called ethical funds. Listen to me, little lady. Alcohol, tobacco, firearms, casinos, and whorehouses have always given the best rate of return. Both in the long and the short term, so watch out for those characters. We wanted to scare him after school. The coward ran away. Claes fired one shot in his butt. I think he was aiming at it. Nisse Hermansson has always had a big ass and a small head."

"So what happened to him?" asked Mattei.

"We actually helped him pick out the bullet. I guess we were curious too. Took the opportunity to take a closer look since we had the chance anyway. As I said he was called Ass Herman when we were in school. We pulled him into the school restroom and took a few emergency measures. Wasn't so bad actually. He was wearing a long jacket and thick pants because it was winter. The bullet had gone in less than an inch. He was bleeding a bit, but it was actually no more than that. Fortunately Claes's revolver was not as remarkable as he'd hoped. Nisse kept his mouth shut for once. Mostly complained about his coat and his pants, but we solved that for him. I had to go through Dad's pockets one more time. Once I found seven thousand-kronor bills he'd forgotten in the breast pocket of a tuxedo when he was out on a binge. A lot of money at that time."

Just an innocent boyish prank, thought Mattei.

"So there you have a small sampling. Say the word if you want more. There's as much as you like," Tischler concluded.

"I think I'm content for now," said Mattei, looking at the clock to be on the safe side.

"The trophy," said Tischler. "How could I forget that? Before you go you really do have to look at our old trophy."

· · ·

Tischler had taken the trophy with him when the Friends of Cunt Society eventually dissolved. He was completely within his rights, because he had been the society's financial backbone. Most of them were done with their degrees and would go on in life. Rumor-spreader Claes Waltin was already expelled.

It was a silver-plated trophy about twelve inches tall. Crowned at the top by the figure of a naked woman who was not the least bit indecent, more like the image of chasteness.

"An ordinary sports trophy. Girls swimming, if I were to guess. Claes bought it at Sporrongs, but they refused to make the engraving, so I had to arrange that with the help of an old goldsmith I knew. He used to put together a lot of knickknacks on the sly for my old man's various secretaries."

Wise of Sporrongs, thought Lisa Mattei when she read the text. At the top the name of the society in elegant capital letters: Friends of Cunt Society. Beneath that the name of the member who was "Cuntmaster of the Year": first Claes Waltin 1966. Then Alf Thulin, nowadays a conservative member of parliament and former chief prosecutor, whom she didn't have permission to talk to. He had won the title in 1967. Then Claes Waltin again in 1968. The man she was now talking to without asking Johansson for permission, in 1969. A long-dead business attorney, Sven Erik Sjöberg, in 1970.

"Cool thing, huh," said Tischler, grinning from ear to ear. "Do you know who this is, by the way?" he asked, pointing to the prize winner for 1967.

"Yes," said Mattei. "If he's the one I think he is."

"Always was a fucking hypocrite," said Tischler. "Looked hideous even back then, but he was completely phenomenal at getting the ladies on their backs. Wonder just how much he might give for this today?"

Wonder what he would give for it? thought Lisa Mattei when she was on the subway on her way back to the police building. And wonder just what Lars Martin Johansson would say if I asked to look at fund manager Nils Hermansson's ass? she thought.

Instead of asking for permission she wrote a summary of her conversation with Tischler, and before she went home she stopped by Johansson's office and asked him to read it.

"I thought we were finished with this issue," muttered Johansson.

"If you'll just read what Tischler had to say, boss. Before you send me down to the parking garage."

"Hell," said Johansson five minutes later. "This is not the usual nonsense. This is something different. I don't like that part about the poor dog and the arson and Ass Herman. We'll have to pull out those old witness statements from the shooting on Sveavägen. I want to know everything the witnesses say about the perpetrator's physical description. Then I want the technical report on the firing angle and the probable height of the perpetrator."

"I've already looked at that," said Mattei. "You can too, boss, but I don't think it's necessary."

"Why not?" said Johansson.

"It can't have been Claes Waltin," said Mattei, shaking her head. "Not a chance. He's way too short. At least four inches too short."

"Thanks, Lisa. I forgive you," said Johansson for some reason. She's like me, he thought. When she knows something and has that look, that's just how it is.

"One more thing, if you have time, boss," said Mattei.

"Of course," said Johansson. "Why don't you sit down, by the way?"

"Thanks," said Mattei.

When Mattei had gone through the testimony of the eyewitnesses about the murder on Sveavägen again, she discovered a circumstance that was possibly interesting considering the previous.

"Listening," said Johansson.

"I'm sure you remember the witness that Lewin called Witness One in the so-called witness chain. He's the one who hides among the construction site trailers on Tunnelgatan, sees the perpetrator run past, up the stairs—"

"I remember," Johansson interrupted.

"The first interview with Witness One was held on the night of the murder. Then he gave his physical description of the perpetrator. After that additional interviews were held with him over the following ten years. Even after the prosecutor's petition for a new trial was rejected. There are a total of eight interviews, besides the first one."

"Sounds reasonable," said Johansson. "What's the problem?"

"That he knew of Christer Pettersson," said Mattei. "They lived in the same area, and Witness One knew very well who Christer Pettersson was. Knew of him before the murder of Palme, knew what he looked like, knew what kind of person he was."

"But it wasn't Christer Pettersson he saw run past in the alley," said Johansson, smiling for some reason.

"No," said Mattei. "The first time he mentions Pettersson is more than two years later when he is interviewed about Pettersson in particular. Then he relates that he knew of Christer Pettersson."

"But that he wasn't the one he saw on the night of the murder."

"He's more careful than that," said Mattei. "First he says what he did about Pettersson, and then he explains that he did not associate him with the man who ran past. Neither spontaneously in connection with the observation or later when he bumped into Pettersson in the area where he lived. He thinks he ought to have recognized him if it really was him."

"Good, Mattei," said Johansson. "In contrast to the nitwit who held the initial interview with him, you have just done a little real police work. You have thereby earned yourself a little gold star."

"I was hoping for a big one," said Mattei.

"No way," said Johansson. "I've never believed in Pettersson. Wrong type. I realized that from the start, and the thing with Witness One I discovered myself almost twenty years ago."

"Thanks anyway, boss," said Mattei. So why didn't you say that? she thought.

"It's nothing," said Johansson. "That society," he said, nodding at Mattei.

"I'm listening," said Mattei.

"Do a search on the ones who were involved and see if you find them in the case files."

"Any particular reason?"

"No," said Johansson, shrugging his shoulders. "I just have a hard time with those kinds of characters."

In the evening when she and Johan were lying in her bed in the oversized apartment her kind dad had given her, she told him about Claes Waltin, without saying what his name was or why she was compelled to be interested in him. She only told everything she'd heard about him.

"Sexual boundary crossing," Johan observed. "There's a lot of role-playing in that area. But not in this case. This is something really bad. Genuine misogyny."

"Not boundary crossing," said Mattei, shaking her head. "To me he seems completely lacking in boundaries or perhaps free of boundaries. Not immoral, more like amoral. Completely free of morals. The only restraints he seems to have had were the sort that prevented him from being put in jail."

"That's not enough," said Johan, shaking his head. "We're talking about an evil human being. An evil and intelligent human being. Are you familiar with Patricia Highsmith's books about the talented Mr. Ripley?"

"So-so," said Mattei. "I haven't read any of them."

"I have a good film we can watch if you like. With Alain Delon in the lead role as Mr. Ripley. There are several, but this one's the best if you're interested in an evil psychopath. Not all psychopaths are evil, as I'm sure you know."

"We'll get to that later," said Lisa Mattei, stretching herself in bed. "Now we'll move on to something else, I think." Some regular fun that's only a little on the edge, she thought.

Mallorca, present day

Esperanza *was not just a boat. Esperanza was also an insurance policy that would protect him if something unwanted happened. Esperanza, which was strong enough, durable enough, to take him to the mainland on the Spanish, French, or African side. Or to Corsica where there were many like him, and at least one whom he trusted unconditionally. A constant reminder of the only mistake he had made in his life.*

Only fools trusted in fate. Only fools put their lives in the hands of someone else. Personally he had always been his own master. Always capable of mastering any unexpected situation and quickly regaining control over his life. Paddle your own canoe; his father had taught him that. He had lived that way too. Until the day he trusted another person and made himself dependent on him. Actually put his life in his hands. The only mistake worth the name in his entire life.

Naturally he had corrected that. Decided to do it as soon as he sensed that the one he was dependent on was starting to descend into his own self-inflicted misery and could no longer be trusted. The eternal observation, which even the hoods in Hells Angels had the good sense to adopt as their rule of conduct. That three people might very well keep a secret if two of them were dead. For him it had been simpler than that, because there were only two of them to start with. Then he solved his problem. Regained his solitude, took back power over his life, and the worry that at first remained he handled by having Esperanza built. As an insurance policy against the undesired and as a constant reminder not to repeat his mistake.

He did not even need to plan his rehabilitation. He avoided planning. The more carefully you planned, the greater the chance that you would meet with the unexpected, the uncontrollable, which meant that all your plans were suddenly turned upside down. He had simply done what he had always done. Had the goal before his eyes, a simple framework for action as support, waited for the opportunity and seized it in flight.

That was his strength. Seizing opportunity in flight. That was what he had done that morning he'd seen him on the beach below the hotel. Seized the opportunity in flight, because he was all alone, not a person in the vicinity and no need to wait any longer. He stood up in the boat he'd rented. Waved to him, watched him swim toward the boat, grasped his hand, helped him up on deck. Then he won back his solitude, his freedom. Afterward he decided to build Esperanza and never soil her with the sort of thing he had just been forced to do.

Nowadays he didn't even think about it. Not fifteen years later. Not now when everything was over and nothing else could happen to him. One time was no time for anyone who was his own master, and the other times when he had been alone from the start had never bothered him. He and Esperanza. A beautiful little boat, an insurance policy, a constant reminder.

62

Wednesday, September 19,
three weeks remaining until October 10.
Headquarters of the National Bureau of Criminal
Investigation on Kungsholmen in Stockholm

Their usual meeting was canceled on short notice. Johansson was otherwise engaged, and he let it be known by phone that he would be in touch as soon as he had time and no later than that afternoon. As far as the team's continued work was concerned, he still wanted the name of the bastard. Preferably immediately and no later than the weekend.

Holt and Lewin would finish the survey of Waltin. They agreed that Lewin should run the desk work while Holt would take care of the field efforts. She knew she needed to get out and move around.

Before Mattei returned to the Palme investigation's archive and the police track, she took care of Johansson's request and did a search on the four members of the Friends of Cunt Society, founded in 1966, dissolved, finished, dormant five years later.

First she typed in the names and social security numbers of all four members. In alphabetical order by surname: attorney Sven Erik Sjöberg, deceased in December 1993 after a long illness. Former chief prosecutor Alf Thulin, now a member of parliament for the Christian Democrats, member of the Parliamentary Standing Committee on the Administration of Justice and even mentioned in the media as a possible conservative minister of justice. Banker Theo Tischler, for many years now with a registered address in Luxembourg. Claes Waltin, former police chief superintendent with SePo, dead in a drowning accident on north Mallorca in the fall of 1992.

The rest was a matter of pushing the right keys on the computer, and a mere fifteen minutes later she sat with three hits on names and ten references to the investigation files that produced the hits.

Attorney Sven Erik Sjöberg had been interviewed on two occasions due to his possible connection to the "Indian weapons track" or the "Bofors affair." He had been a Bofors attorney for many years, even served on the company's board for a few years. He had not been able to contribute anything of substance to the investigation of the murder of Olof Palme. Besides, his personal opinion was that every such assertion—that the murder of the prime minister could have had anything whatsoever to do with the company's sale of artillery to the Indian government—was "completely ridiculous."

The deal stood on its own steady legs. The Bofors long-range 155 millimeter field howitzer was by far the best artillery piece on the market. It was no more complicated than that, and the Indians should simply be congratulated for making the best choice. If you wanted to inquire into things that concerned business secrets, military secrets, or secrets between two friendly nations, you would have to take that up with someone besides him. The Munitions Inspection Board, the Ministry of Defense, the Ministry for Foreign Affairs, the Swedish and Indian governments.

That part of the matter had then been concluded by the national prosecutor, who at that point in time was the formal leader of the preliminary investigation into the murder of the prime minister.

In connection with the usual summer vacations in the prosecutor's office, chief prosecutor Alf Thulin had substituted as one of the "Good Guys." In part for the colleague who had been leader of the preliminary investigation in the Palme case during the summer of 1990. After that he had returned as an expert and technical adviser in one of the many review commissions set up by the government. In the minutes from a meeting of the commission, which for unclear reasons ended up in a binder in the Palme investigation, he had expressed his definite opinion on the Palme case. It was Christer Pettersson who murdered Olof Palme, and what the prosecutor's office's work now "concerned in all essentials" was trying to construct a petition for a new trial that the Supreme Court could accept.

Banker Theo Tischler ended up in the investigation due to three different tips that were turned in from the group of private investigators in the Palme murder. According to these tips he was supposed to have had close contacts with police chief Hans Holmér, even after Holmér had been fired as investigation leader. According to the same informant, Tischler was supposed to have offered several million to Holmér so he could continue working on the so-called Kurd track. That was what every thinking private investigator right from the beginning understood to be a red herring, set out by Holmér and his associates to protect the real perpetrator.

Tischler had been interviewed for informational purposes about this in the summer of 2000, over fourteen years after the murder. He had not minced words. He had never met Holmér, much less given him any money. On the other hand he had been asked to do so by a mutual acquaintance a year or two after the murder. After having talked with his own contacts "within the social democratic movement and close to the administration" he decided not to give a krona to Holmér and his allies. In conclusion he then congratulated the two interview leaders for the swiftness with which they seemed to be running this case.

"If I did business the same way you gentlemen run police work, I would have been in the poor house thirty years ago."

The one interview leader regretted his attitude. Personally he and his colleagues were doing the best they could, and the mills of justice ground slowly as everyone knew.

"Sorry to hear that the bank manager has that attitude," said the interview leader.

"I'm a private banker," said Tischler "Not a fucking bank manager, for in that case I might just as well have applied for a job with the police."

The only one of the four that Mattei couldn't find on her computer was Claes Waltin, which made no great difference because Lewin found him anyway.

After that she returned to the police track. Mission: Find someone who knew Waltin. Find someone tall enough to tally with the witness statements. Find someone capable of shooting a prime minister in public, with scores of witnesses right in the vicinity. Find someone capable enough to escape unscathed.

However you find someone like that, thought Mattei, looking at the binders with all the police officers sitting in front of her on the desk. A total of a hundred police officers. Seventy of whom had been identified, questioned, investigated, ruled out. Another thirty whose identity was not certain, several of whom had probably never been policemen. Had only said they had been.

First she tried to sort them by height. That didn't go very well. Information about their height was missing in the majority of cases. Besides, almost all policemen in that generation would have been tall enough to shoot the prime minister.

With the help of their age, height, other information about physical features, and from those investigations that left no room for any remaining suspicions, she had nonetheless been able to cross out fifty or so of the seventy known colleagues who had been singled out. True, it had taken her almost the entire day, but she did it for lack of anything better to do, and she had to start somewhere.

Ordinary policemen had the peculiarity that they preferred to associate with other policemen, thought Mattei. Waltin on the other hand had not been an ordinary policeman. Which is why Lisa called her mother and asked whether she would have lunch with her. She was happy to. She had actually intended to call her daughter and ask the same thing. She would explain why when they met.

To save time they met in the police building restaurant, where they found a sufficiently isolated table. As soon as they sat down Linda Mattei revealed her intentions.

"Are you pregnant?" said Linda Mattei to her only daughter, Lisa.

"But mother. Of course I'm not."

"But you've met someone," she continued.

"The answer is yes," said Lisa Mattei. "What do you think about trading question for question?"

"Is he nice?"

"Yes again."

"Does he have a name?"

"Yes again. Johan."

"Johan?"

"Yes again. Johan Eriksson."

"So what does he do?"

"Studies at the university, in cinema studies, sublets a studio on Söder. Works on the side as a guard." I'm sure you've seen him, she thought.

"Lisa, Lisa," said her mother, shaking her head. Then she leaned over and stroked her across the cheek.

"Now it's my turn," said Lisa Mattei. "I have the right to six questions, and you'll get two free answers because I'm so nice and because you should calm down. Yes, you'll get to meet him. Yes, he's a little like Dad. Although twice as big. At least."

"I will get to meet him?" Linda Mattei repeated.

"The answer is yes. Seven questions. My turn."

"Okay. Ask away," said Linda Mattei, shaking her head and smiling.

"Claes Waltin," said Lisa Mattei. "Tell me what he was like as a person."

"Why are you asking about him?"

"Pull yourself together, Mom," said Lisa Mattei. "This is about work, and now I'm the one who's asking the questions."

"Okay, okay, okay," said Linda Mattei, making a deprecating hand gesture.

Then she told her daughter what she knew about Claes Waltin.

Already the first week after he had started at SePo he tried to make a pass at her.

"He made a pass at you. So what did you say?"

"I told him to go to hell," said Linda Mattei. "Then I basically didn't see a trace of him for the rest of his time with us. I was glad. Anything else you're wondering about?"

"What type was he?"

"Not my type anyway," said Linda Mattei, curling her upper lip. "According to what was whispered in the corridors he was a real creep. But I'm sure you've already heard that?"

"Ad nauseam," said Lisa. "What I'm wondering is whether he associated with other police officers. With regular colleagues."

"I have a really hard time imagining that," said Linda Mattei, shaking her head.

"Explain," said Lisa Mattei.

Waltin despised regular police officers. Waltin was very stuck-up. Regular policemen were much too simple for him. He never said that. He had shown it clearly enough without having to say it.

"So he didn't even have a humble confidant?"

"Humble confidant," said Linda Mattei, looking at her daughter with surprise. "Someone like me, you mean?"

"Some male colleague. One of those strong, silent types."

"I have a really hard time imagining that," said Linda Mattei. "Do you mean he's supposed to have been homosexual too?"

"Okay," said Lisa Mattei and sighed. "What do you think about actually eating lunch?"

Before she went home, for lack of anything better to do, she printed out a computer list on Berg and his associates on the riot squad, the dozen uniformed police who most often appeared in the Palme investigation's police track. Despite the fact that none of them seemed particularly credible as henchman for someone like Claes Waltin. Besides, half of them had alibis for the time when the prime minister was shot. Real alibis, not the kind they'd given each other or gotten from other officers.

63

The following day Mattei opened the binders that dealt with the thirty or so policemen who could not be identified with certainty. At the top of the first binder was a lead file where serious attempts at least had been made. At the top of the file, the anonymous letter that was the origin of the matter.

A handwritten letter, cheap lined paper, ballpoint pen. Surprisingly flowing handwriting. No misspellings. Basically correct punctuation. On the other hand no envelope, even though the envelope might often say more to people like her than the message that was inside. Especially if the sender pasted the stamp with the king upside down. Barely ten lines of text.

> Dear uncle blue. Saw on TV the other night that there were a lot of cops in the air when Olle called it quits. I myself saw an old acquaintance at the Chinese restaurant on Drottninggatan at the corner by Adolf Fredriks Kyrkogata. A real SOB who worked at the bureau out in Solna in the seventies. Then he became a fine fellow and got to go to SePo. Think what can happen when the hasp isn't closed. He was sitting there sucking on a glass of water when I came but I kept my cool and my mouth shut and that was probably luck because otherwise I'm sure my ass would have been kicked again. Mostly he looked at his watch and right before eleven he paid up and left. Maybe to guard Olle? Or else perhaps to come up with something else with Olle? Anonymous from personal experience.

. . .

If people could just give their names, Mattei was thinking as Holt entered the room.

"Everything okay, Lisa?" said Holt. "I saw on the voice mail that you were looking for me."

"Yes," said Mattei. "Berg and his associates," said Mattei, giving her the plastic sleeve with the information she'd produced.

"What do you want me to do with these?"

"Ask Berg if he or any of his associates knew Waltin," said Mattei. "Berg with the uniformed police that is. The one who's the nephew of the old SePo boss," she clarified.

"Do you think that's wise?" said Holt, weighing the papers. "Considering Johansson."

"You know Berg, don't you? You've talked with him at least. I think he trusts you. I'm pretty sure he likes you. The question is free. Pull a Johansson on him."

"A Johansson?"

"Yes, if you'd been Johansson and he'd been you. And was always getting himself worked up about something. What do you think he would have done?"

"I understand exactly," said Holt and nodded. "I'll pull a Johansson."

Nice to have colleagues who understand, thought Mattei, whereupon she returned to her binder.

The first letter had come in to the Palme investigation about a month after the murder. Nothing in particular seemed to have happened. A special file had been opened and entered under what was already—even in the building—being called the police track. But there was nothing else.

Not until the second letter was received, which arrived a month later. Only a few days after the TV news program *Rapport* had aired a major feature on what the TV journalists were also now calling the police track. The letter was postmarked Stockholm, May 7, 1986. This time the envelope had been saved. Even examined for fingerprints, on both the letter and the envelope.

> Dear uncle blue. I think uncle gets things a little slowly but I already knew that. Maybe ought to write direct to Rapport and tell about your dear colleague who was sitting in the bar and hoping for better times until he sneaked away and clinched the deal himself. If he really did it? What do you think yourselves? He is damned like the one who did it in any event but the witnesses must have seen wrong if it really is a cop they've seen. So of course it's cool for the sonofabitch who worked at the bureau in Solna before he became a fine fellow and ended up at SePo. Guess I'll have to call the complaint department on TV. Anonymous from personal experience.

After a week there was already a response from the tech squad. A number of fingerprints had been secured on the envelope. On the other hand none on the letter. Probably someone had wiped it off before it was put into the envelope. Of the prints that were found, one produced a result. A female drug addict with numerous convictions for narcotics crimes, theft, and fraud, Marja Ruotsalainen, born in 1959.

Maja Svensson, although in Finnish, thought Mattei. Sweet name, she thought.

Holt called Berg. Arranged a meeting at the same café as the first time. As soon as they sat down with their coffee cups, she pulled a Johansson.

"Claes Waltin," said Holt. "Former police chief superintendent with SePo. Drowned on Mallorca fifteen years ago. Is that anyone you knew?"

"Claes Waltin," said Berg, who had a hard time concealing his surprise. "Why are you asking?"

"You don't want to know and I can't say," said Holt. You knew him, she thought.

"Okay by me," said Berg, shrugging his shoulders. "Knew him is probably putting it too strongly. I met him twice. That was at the time when your boss was messing with me and my associates. Right after

New Year's, the same year Palme was shot. Sometime in January or February. We were back on duty, in any event."

This time things had happened, thought Mattei. The case seemed to have wound up with one of those officers who would be described by all other completely normal colleagues as "a zealous bastard." As soon as he found out that Marja Ruotsalainen's fingerprints were on the envelope things had happened. He realized she didn't work as a letter carrier as soon as he searched for her in the police registry.

In the summer of 1985 Ruotsalainen had been sentenced to two years and six months for felony narcotics crimes. A conviction that was never appealed and which she started serving at Hinseberg women's prison the week after the conviction. Ruotsalainen was tired of sitting in jail on Polhemsgatan and longed for the relative freedom at the country's only closed facility for women.

After six months she had been granted leave. She absconded and kept out of sight from the end of January until the middle of May, when she was arrested during a police raid on an illegal club in Hammarbyhamnen. She had been taken to the jail and had to go back to Hinseberg the following day. When the two anonymous letters had been placed in the mailbox she was on the run. Two days after the last one she was sitting in the jail on Kungsholmen.

Because the zealous colleague from SePo had the idea that it was a man who had written the two anonymous letters he searched for her male contacts in the police surveillance registries. Without success. Not because she lacked such contacts, but because none of those who were in the register could have sent the letter.

For lack of anything better he pulled out the papers from the police operation in Hammarbyhamnen during which she was arrested. Besides Ruotsalainen, who was wanted and immediately recognized by the Stockholm police detective squad who led the effort, another half a dozen individuals ended up in jail. One of them was a known criminal with twenty or more previous convictions for serious crimes, Jorma

Kalevi Orjala, born in 1947, and at that point in time he was strangely enough neither on the run nor suspected of anything else. About the same time that Ruotsalainen took a seat in the jail's blue Chevrolet to be transported to Hinseberg, Jorma Kalevi Orjala stepped out onto Kungsholmsgatan a free man.

The zealous colleague with SePo called the police inspector with the central detective squad who had led the raid against the club in Hammarbyhamnen. To save time and out of personal curiosity, because this was the first time he had crossed paths with one of the Stockholm police's great legends, Bo Jarnebring.

He had two questions. Why had Orjala ended up in jail? Was Orjala involved with Marja Ruotsalainen? On the other hand he never asked the third question. One that with reasonable probability might have led to his solving the murder of the country's prime minister barely four months after the event. The secrecy surrounding his work was so high that those ordinary questions, between fellow officers, were never asked.

Berg had met Waltin twice. The first time he had been alone. The second time four of his associates from the riot squad had been there.

A woman he knew had called him. She had been out with Waltin on one occasion. Then Waltin started pursuing her. Called her place of employment. The usual wordless panting. Sat in a car out on the street. Followed her. She called Berg to get help.

"I caught him in the act," said Berg. "He was sitting in one of SePo's service vehicles outside her workplace."

"I told him to lay off," he continued. "Unless he wanted a beating, of course."

"So what did he say?" asked Holt.

"He did as I said," said Berg, shrugging his broad shoulders. "Lucky for him, you know."

I can very well imagine that, thought Holt and nodded.

"The second time," she asked. "When you and your associates met him?"

. . .

The zealous colleague's conversation with Jarnebring had gone wrong right from the start. If not, it is very possible that the third question would have been answered anyway.

"I see then," said Jarnebring when he was asked the first one. "So which of my associates is it you're going to grill this time?"

"I can't go into that, as you understand," answered the zealous colleague.

"Imagine that," said Jarnebring. Then he replied to the two questions that were asked.

Orjala ended up in jail because Jarnebring always put people like Orjala in jail, as soon as he had the chance, and he got the chance because Orjala was in a place where there was both illegal serving of alcohol and illegal gambling. In addition Jarnebring had taken Orjala's keys from him, squeezed his address out of him, and had gone there while Orjala was resting up in a cell at Kronoberg.

"I didn't find anything in particular," said Jarnebring. "Other than Marja's bag and baggage. She was living with him while she was on the run. In principle I could have locked him up for protecting a criminal, but I guess I didn't have the energy to write up that kind of shit."

"Thanks for your help," said the zealous colleague. "I'll have to talk with Orjala."

"I'm afraid you're a little late," said Jarnebring. "The fire department fished him out of the Karlberg Canal yesterday morning. We thought about celebrating with cake on our next coffee break."

The second time was a few weeks later. Midmorning outside the police building on Kungsholmen. Waltin came walking up Kungsholmsgatan. They eased up alongside him. Waltin stopped them, got into the van, and told them to drive him down to Stureplan. If they didn't have anything better to do, of course.

"He was cocky, that stuck-up little prick. But sure. We were going in that direction anyway, so he got to ride along."

"Did anything in particular happen?" asked Holt.

"A sock in the jaw, you mean?" said Berg, smiling wryly. "No, nothing like that," he said, shaking his head. "But he did say two things that were strange to say the least."

"So what did he say?" said Holt.

"When we stopped for a red light up at Kungsgatan there was a very old lady with a walker crossing the street. The light happened to change but we stayed there so she could make her way across. Then Waltin leans over and says to the colleague who's driving that he should step on the gas and turn that cunt of hers into a garage. That the old lady was only pretending."

"Word for word."

"Yes, something like . . . the old lady is only pretending. Step on it and turn that cunt of hers into a garage. He said something like that."

"So what did you say?"

"I looked at him but didn't say anything. We were pretty surprised, actually. I mean, what do you say to something like that? I've never heard anything like it from another officer. Even though I've heard most everything. But this was just a nice little old lady."

"The other thing," said Holt. "What was the other thing he said?"

"That was even more peculiar," said Berg. "Although it took about six months before we understood it."

According to the forensic physician, Orjala had been run over by a car, fell into the water, and drowned. Blood alcohol concentration over .03. Hit-and-run accident, otherwise nothing to discuss, according to the forensic physician.

For lack of a better idea the zealous colleague took a service vehicle and drove to Hinseberg to talk with Marja Ruotsalainen.

The meeting at Hinseberg between the zealous colleague and Marja had hardly been constructive. She only said a single sentence. Repeated it until the interview was ended and he drove home again.

"Go to hell, fucking pig. Go to hell, fucking pig. Go to hell, fucking pig . . ."

Zealous as he was, he also wrote a memorandum on the matter and put it in the file.

Zealous as he was he had also visited the Chinese restaurant, brought along pictures of both Orjala and Ruotsalainen and showed them to the personnel. No one remembered either of them. Nothing special had happened otherwise during the evening when the prime minister was murdered, only a few hundred yards from the restaurant. There had been few customers the whole evening. Fewer than they usually had on a Friday evening after payday.

"We dropped him off at Stureplan," said Berg. "He was going to the bank, I seem to recall that he said."

"What else did he say?" Holt repeated.

"That was what was so strange," said Berg. "First he thanks us for the ride. Then he stuck his head in through the window on my side and said that I should take care of myself. Take care of yourself, Berg, he said. Watch out for all the eyes and ears that are on people like me, he said."

"How did you interpret that?"

"We talked about it. First we thought this was his way of flexing his muscles for us. It was about six months later that we found out that SePo had been investigating us for several years. That was when we started going in and out with those police track investigators in the Palme murder. Then it was in the newspapers too."

"He was trying to warn you?"

"Yes. I actually think so. A little strange, to say the least, considering who he was and considering his and my previous interactions."

The zealous colleague had not given up. Based on the anonymous letters and with the help of Orjala's personal file and his recorded contacts with the detective squad in Solna, he made a description of the unidentified officer that the anonymous letter-writer—probably Orjala—had pointed out. He sent the description to the secret police's personnel department and got an answer one month later. The one who matched the description best was a previous employee with the secret police who had service code 4711. His employment had ended in 1982. Since then he had resided abroad. The customary internal controls had been carried out. There was nothing that argued that he would have been involved in the murder of the prime minister or even in Stockholm at the relevant point in time.

So the zealous colleague had given up and his top boss, bureau head Berg, wrote off the matter.

Forty-seven eleven, thought Mattei. Where have I heard that? Wasn't that the awful perfume Dad used to give Mom when I was little? Kölnisch Wasser 4711, she thought. That's what it was called.

"There was another thing I wanted to ask you about, Holt," said Berg when they had finished their conversation and were standing by her car to say farewell.

"I'm listening," said Holt. Suddenly he's looking very strange, she thought.

"You are an exceptionally appetizing woman, Holt," said Berg. "So I was wondering if I could invite you out some evening?"

Goodness, thought Holt.

"That would have been nice," said Holt. "But the way it is now—"

"I understand," Berg interrupted. "Say hi and congratulations to him from me."

"Thanks," said Anna Holt and smiled. An exceptionally appetizing woman, she thought.

64

By exploiting her informal contacts with SePo Anna Holt found a woman who was alleged to have been involved with Claes Waltin at the time of the Palme murder. Jeanette Eriksson, born in 1958, assistant detective with SePo.

A co-worker of Waltin's thirteen years his junior who quit the police the year after the Palme murder to work as an investigator for an insurance company. She was still there, now head of the department, and she did not sound happy when Holt called her. The day after the meeting with Berg they met at Eriksson's office.

"I don't really want to talk about Claes Waltin," said Jeanette Eriksson.

"Not even a little girl talk?" said Holt. "No tape recorder, no papers, no report. Just you and me, in confidence."

"In that case then," said Jeanette Eriksson, smiling despite herself.

Claes Waltin had been her boss at the secret police. In the fall of 1985 they had started a relationship. In March of 1986 she ended the relationship.

"Though by then he was already tired of me, for otherwise he probably wouldn't have let me go. He already had another woman."

"I know what you mean," said Holt. "He seems to have been a full-fledged sadist according to people I've talked with."

"That's what was so strange," said Jeanette Eriksson. "Because I don't have that tendency at all. I've never been the least bit sadomasochistic. And yet I ended up with him. To start with I thought it was some kind of role-playing he was involved in, and when I understood how it really was it was too late to back out. He was horrible. Claes Waltin was a horrible person. If he was drinking he could be downright dangerous. There were several times I thought he was going to kill me. But I never had a single bruise that I could show to be believed."

"You were involved with him for six months?"

"Involved? I was his prisoner for five months and eleven days," said Jeanette Eriksson. "Before I could get myself free. I hated him. When I was finally rid of him I would sit outside his apartment and spy on him and wonder how I could get revenge on him."

"But you never did anything," said Holt.

"I did do one thing," said Jeanette Eriksson. "When I realized he'd acquired a new woman. When I saw her together with him the second time in a week. Then I found out who she was so I could warn her."

"You talked with her?" asked Holt.

"Yes, just the two of us. She worked at the post office. When she left work one evening I approached her. Told her who I was and asked if I could talk with her.

"It went fine. We sat at a café in the neighborhood and talked."

"So how did she take it?" said Holt.

"She didn't understand what I meant," said Jeanette Eriksson. "She seemed almost shocked when I told her what he'd done to me. Actually asked if I was still in love with Claes. Thought that that's what it was really about. After that not much was said. Not that we argued. We just went our separate ways. Since then I've never talked with her."

"Do you know what her name is?" asked Holt.

"Yes," said Jeanette Eriksson.

"So what's her name?" said Holt.

"Now it gets a little complicated," said Jeanette Eriksson. "I'm assuming it's not for her sake that you've come here?"

"No," said Holt. "I had no idea about this woman's existence until you mentioned her."

"May I ask a question myself?" said Jeanette Eriksson.

"Sure," said Holt.

"You work at the national bureau, you said. Isn't that where Lars Johansson is the boss? That big Norrlander who's always on TV?"

"Yes," said Holt.

"That's what makes this a little strange," said Jeanette Eriksson. "You see, he's married to the woman I talked with. Then her name was Pia Hedin. Today her name is evidently Pia Hedin Johansson."

"Are you sure of that?" said Holt.

"Quite sure," said Jeanette Eriksson. "I saw them together at a party at SEB a few years later, when I started working here at the insurance company. Then they were newlyweds. Must have been sometime in the early nineties."

"You're quite sure?" asked Holt.

"Quite sure," said Jeanette Eriksson. "She's a very beautiful woman. Pia Hedin is not someone you forget or confuse with someone else."

"I know," said Holt. "I've met her." What do I do now? she thought.

65

Despite his illness—after all he had suffered a serious stroke—Bäckström fought on and refused to let go of the case that had been his from the very start. Claes Waltin's involvement in the murder of Olof Palme.

Murders were about two things. Money and sex. Bäckström knew this from his own rich personal experience. What remained was to find out which of these motives had led to the victim's life being taken.

Right now there was much that argued that it was about sex. Both the perpetrator and the victim seemed to be literally bathing in money, which made it less likely that they were at each other's throats for that reason. Waltin had been as rich as a mountain troll. Everyone knew that. The victim had concealed tens of millions in various secret accounts in Switzerland and other tax paradises. Bäckström knew that, as did everyone else in the know, who had it from reliable sources. Besides, you could read about it on the Internet nowadays. How the Swedish arms industry paid out hundreds of millions in bribes to the murder victim and his shady companions from the third world.

There was also a witness to the murder who made a deep impression on an analytically oriented police officer like Bäckström. A witness who all his moronic colleagues only shook their heads at. A witness who waited until the third interview to admit that he had seen how the perpetrator talked with the victim and his wife before he started shooting at them. Presumably when they tried to get away, considering that the shots hit them from behind.

Murder victims and murderers almost always knew each other. Bäckström knew that too based on his long, solid police practice. The same dealings, vices, and desires, when it came down to it. When a man like Bäckström got the opportunity to let all the skeletons out of their closets. When the truth was finally revealed.

Waltin had undeniably been an extremely perverse type. Bäckström's meticulous survey left no room for doubt on that score. What remained was to link him with his victim, and there were already a number of circumstances that could hardly be owing to chance.

Both were multimillionaires, attorneys, had an upper-class background, had grown up in the same city. Surely socialized in the same circles. Ought to have, reasonably, considering all the rest. Besides the purely external likeness between them, that was almost striking. Short, delicate, skinny characters, with dark, dissolute eyes and moist lips.

I'll be damned if they weren't related to each other, thought Bäckström, experiencing a slight excitement.

It remained to verify this. To demonstrate beyond any reasonable human doubt. This would not be easy considering that his informant seemed to have abandoned him. First he had pursued GeGurra by phone and left a number of messages. His efforts were met by silence, and in that situation the only alternative was action. Bäckström watched for him outside his residence on Norr Mälarstrand. Saw when he arrived home. Rang at his door and of course covered the peephole while he did so.

At last the little coward cracked the door open carefully and asked what Bäckström wanted. Bäckström fixed his eyes on him and GeGurra unwillingly let him into the hall. Once inside he started by reminding GeGurra about an old common acquaintance, Juha Valentin Andersson Snygg, who despite his youth had a very extensive personal file in the police department's central archive. Nowadays it was missing, however that might have happened, and who could a known, respected individual like art dealer Gustaf G:son Henning really trust? If he only thought about it the least little bit? For it was hardly Anna Holt and her bosom buddies, who didn't even draw the line at secretly tapping other people's phones. If GeGurra chose that sort ahead of Bäckström he was lost.

· · ·

Of course he backed down. They all did when Bäckström started waltzing around them. Mostly to be nice and give GeGurra a chance to get his bearings, he also started off easy before things got serious.

"How did Waltin know Prime Minister Olof Palme?" said Bäckström, looking slyly at GeGurra.

"I had no idea he knew Olof Palme," replied GeGurra, looking at Bäckström with surprise. "Where did you get that from?"

"Listen," said Bäckström. "Just to save time. I'm asking the questions and you answer."

"Sure," said GeGurra, "but I'm really a bit surprised that—"

"Now I happen to know that Waltin talked a good deal about Palme," Bäckström interrupted, examining his victim.

"Didn't everyone?" said GeGurra. "Talk about Palme, I mean. At that time, at least."

"Exactly," said Bäckström. "Exactly, but now let's forget about what everyone else said. I want to know what Waltin said."

"I guess he said what all the others did. When they talked about Palme, I mean."

"So what did they say?"

"That Palme was an underhanded type," said GeGurra. "Yes, that he tried to socialize the country by stealth and let the government take over the companies with the help of those employee funds. At the same time as he personally took bribes from the defense industry so they could sell cannons to the Indians. It was the usual."

"That he was a Russian spy?"

"Yes, sure. I actually remember that I asked Waltin about that. Considering that he worked at SePo, I thought he was the right man to ask."

"So what did he say?"

"That he couldn't answer that, as I surely understood. But at the same time I obviously got a definite impression of what he wanted to say."

"What impression did you get?"

"That Palme was a spy for the Russians," said GeGurra, looking at Bäckström with surprise. "Didn't everyone know that? It was even hinted at more or less openly in the newspapers."

"Of a more personal nature then? What did Waltin have to say about Palme that was of a more personal nature?"

"That was probably personal enough," said GeGurra. "Saying that he took bribes from Bofors and was a spy for the Russians. I mean what do—"

"We're talking about sex," Bäckström interrupted.

"Sex," said GeGurra, looking at Bäckström, confused. "I really don't understand what you mean. Waltin talked a great deal about sex. About his own efforts in that area. But never in connection with Palme."

"But he must have known him," Bäckström persisted. "It's completely obvious that someone like Waltin must have known someone like Palme."

"Why?" said GeGurra. "If you ask me I think they never met each other. Why would someone like Palme associate with someone like Waltin?"

"How did you know Palme yourself?" said Bäckström.

"You're just going to have to give up, Bäckström," said GeGurra, putting up both hands to be on the safe side. "I never met Olof Palme."

"I think you should think about that," said Bäckström with an ambiguous smile. "On a completely different matter."

"Yes," said GeGurra, sighing. "I'm listening."

"Friends of Cunt. That perverse society Waltin was chairman of. Who were the other members?"

"Well, not Palme in any event," said GeGurra. "As far as the age difference is concerned he could have been their father, but I strongly doubt he could have had such children. Even if he had been a spy for the Russians."

"Names? Give me names," said Bäckström.

"Okay then, Bäckström," said GeGurra. "On one condition. That you leave me alone from here on."

"The names?"

"There were apparently four members in this illustrious little group of friends. All were studying law at the University of Stockholm. This was sometime in the mid-sixties. For one there was Claes Waltin. Then there was someone who became a well-known business attorney but he died rather young. I think his last name was Sjöberg, Sven Sjöberg. Died sometime in the mid-nineties."

"Waltin, Sjöberg . . ."

"Yes," sighed GeGurra. "Then there was Theo Tischler. He's a private banker and very—"

"I know who he is," Bäckström interrupted. "We know each other."

"I see," said GeGurra, who had a hard time concealing his surprise.

"The fourth man," said Bäckström. "Who was the fourth man?"

"Alf Thulin," said GeGurra, sighing again. "Nowadays a member of parliament for the Christian Democrats, although to start with he was a prosecutor."

Now this is starting to resemble something, thought Bäckström. A crazy SePo boss, a high-ranking prosecutor, a billionaire, and a so-called business attorney. Four pure sex lunatics. True, two were dead, but two were still alive and could be questioned. Now this is starting to resemble something, he thought again.

66

On Thursday the twentieth of September the coin dropped into the slot in Lisa Mattei's head. Some gray cell up there had been holding back for more than a day, and as soon as she stopped thinking about it, suddenly the answer came.

For many years SePo made use of four-digit codes to protect their co-workers' identities from the outside world. Their names would remain secret, and even when they testified in court they did so using their numerical code.

One of all the thousands of police officers who worked with the secret police during the past thirty years apparently had code 4711 until the early eighties. The person whom SePo's personnel department checked and removed from the investigation when their zealous colleague asked a question arising from an anonymous tip, employee 4711. Who had already quit in 1982, moved abroad, and for various unexplained reasons was not of interest in connection with the investigation's police track.

The coin dropped into the slot in Mattei's head and she suddenly recalled where she had most recently seen the same four-digit code. Not on the bottles of German eau de cologne her father bought as presents for her mother when Mattei was a little girl and long before a Swedish prime minister was shot in the street. Much later. Only a week ago. On a paper from the secret police tech squad, where an employee with an illegible signature and his four-digit service code, 4711, acknowledged receipt of the revolver that Detective Inspector Göran Wiijnbladh had given to Claes Waltin.

The same paper about which almost everything suggested that Claes Waltin had forged it. A chance coincidence, without the least relevance for their investigation? Or an unrestrained Claes Waltin, who could not resist the temptation to send a secret message that would never be discovered?

Johansson's third rule in a murder investigation, thought Mattei. Learn to hate the chance coincidence. Besides, it was time for another conversation with dear Mom, who had worked at SePo for over twenty years.

"Why do you want to know that?" asked Linda Mattei, giving her daughter a searching look. It was their second lunch together in a week and this time at a restaurant a good distance from the building. What is she up to? she thought, feeling slightly uneasy.

"I can't say," said Lisa, shaking her head.

"You've worked with us," said Linda Mattei. "For several years. You know what rules apply. What questions can be asked."

"Sure," said Lisa Mattei, shrugging her shoulders. "A simple rule. Someone like me may not ask any questions the moment I'm no longer working there, and someone like you may not answer questions because you're working there."

"Okay then. So why are you asking?"

"Because you're my mother," said Lisa Mattei. "What did you think?"

"If the person who had that identity code quit twenty-five years ago, I don't think it will be very easy to find out who he was," said Linda Mattei. "You have a code as long as you're working there. When you quit, the code becomes inactive for a number of years. Then someone else might get it. When sufficient time has passed so that no misunderstandings can arise. Just like when you change telephone numbers. And the only reason I'm saying this is because you already know it."

"Of course," said Lisa Mattei. "But I would like to know the name of the colleague who had that code up until 1982, when he quit. For reasons I can't go into, I cannot address a direct question to SePo."

"Your boss can," said Linda Mattei.

"Maybe he doesn't want to," said Lisa Mattei.

"Have you asked him?"

"No," said Lisa Mattei.

"Then do that," said Linda Mattei. "I can't answer. If it's any consolation, no one else can either. This is not information that we keep for twenty-five years."

If we're going to put any order into this a miracle will probably be required, thought Lisa Mattei when she returned to her binders after lunch. Only fifteen minutes later she experienced it. Or at least the hope of a miracle.

Feeling at loose ends, she did a search on Marja Ruotsalainen. Born in 1959 and almost fifty years old, if she was still alive. Heavy drug abuser since her teens. Criminal. Prostitute. Sentenced to several prison terms. Half of her life in foster homes, youth detention centers, institutions, and prisons, when at the age of twenty-seven she showed up in the papers of the Palme investigation. How great was the chance that she was alive today? Zero or one percent, thought Lisa Mattei while she entered Marja's social security number on her computer.

Marja Ruotsalainen. Forty-eight. Single. No children. Disability pension. No notations in the police registry in the past fifteen years. Living in Tyresö, a few miles southeast of Stockholm.

She's alive. A miracle, thought Lisa Mattei, shaking her head. Wonder if it would be possible to talk with her? she thought. The time before it hadn't gone so well, when the zealous colleague had visited her while she was incarcerated at Hinseberg.

67

Lewin read the two investigations into cause of death with regard to former chief superintendent Claes Waltin. One that the Spanish police had done at the scene on Mallorca in October 1992. One supplementary investigation that the Swedish police carried out as soon as his remains arrived back in Sweden in mid-November the same year.

Birds and fish had done a thorough job by the time he finally floated to land. The Spanish police identified him with the help of the report of a missing guest that the hotel had already turned in the day after the staff in reception saw him walking down to the beach. Identification was made using his swimming trunks and the room key in the pocket.

In the forensic facility in Solna they had been more thorough. First the corpse's teeth had been compared with Waltin's dental records. Despite the fact that the corpse was missing the lower jaw, the upper jaw spoke volumes. Former chief superintendent Claes Waltin.

Because he was who he was they had not been content with this, but also put the latest technology to use. Secured both bone marrow and tooth pulp. Took blood samples from his father and compared the two DNA samples that had been produced. The likelihood that the remains belonged to someone other than Claes Waltin were less than one in a million. Assuming that Robert Waltin did not have an unknown son, who had happened to drown in Mallorca while Claes Waltin was there on vacation and simply disappeared.

They had also been content with this. Claes Waltin was declared dead. His father buried him about the same time as he appealed the will. One year later his father and only surviving relative became his heir, after the district court invalidated his will.

Probable death by drowning, according to both the Spanish forensic physician and his Swedish colleague. Neither of them found any injuries to the bones or other parts of the body that would indicate he had been shot, stabbed, or beaten to death with the classic blunt instrument.

On the other hand there was nothing to rule out that he might have been drowned, strangled, suffocated, poisoned, or for example gassed. He could even have been shot, stabbed, or killed with a blunt instrument assuming that the bullet, knife, or object had not left any traces on those parts of the body that had been found.

I'm afraid we won't get any further than that, thought Jan Lewin and sighed.

To put at least some order into all these question marks he took out paper and pen and wrote a simple memorandum about the case that was casting a shadow over his life and preventing his two colleagues from engaging in more meaningful tasks. Unfortunately it was so bad that the most probable course of events was also the least desirable. The consequences were terrifying, which even someone like Lars Martin Johansson ought to understand.

Probability argued that Claes Waltin, sometime before the murder of Olof Palme, had come across a revolver from the tech squad. Sometime between the middle of April 1983, when the technical investigation of the murder-suicide in Spånga was finished, and the last day of February 1986, when the prime minister was shot.

Probably toward the end of that time period, thought Lewin. During the fall of 1985, maybe.

After that Waltin turned this weapon over to an unknown accomplice.

Probably in close or immediate connection with the murder, thought Lewin.

Probably Waltin also supplied bullets for the weapon. Special ammunition that could pierce through metal or, for example, a bulletproof vest. Not the target-shooting ammunition that the painter made use of when he took the life of his daughter, her boyfriend, and himself.

It was unclear where, when, and how Waltin acquired these special bullets. Sometime between the middle of April 1983 and the last day of February 1986. Probably right after he'd acquired the weapon, thought Lewin, and most likely he bought them in an ordinary gun shop. Showed his police ID, if they'd even asked. Paid in cash. Put the box of bullets in his pocket and left. A box of twenty, fifty, or a hundred bullets of the over six thousand similar ones that had been sold in Sweden in the years before the murder of the prime minister.

The perpetrator probably followed the prime minister from his residence in Old Town and just over two hours later seized the opportunity in flight at the corner of Sveavägen and Tunnelgatan.

After the murder he fled down Tunnelgatan, ran up the stairs to Malmskillnadsgatan, turned to the right, took the stairs down to Kungsgatan, walked Kungsgatan down to Stureplan, went down into the subway, and rode two stations up to Gärdet. The night of the murder he spent in one of SePo's secure apartments, which Waltin loaned out to him. The same Waltin who happened to park illegally the next morning when he came to clean up after the perpetrator, thought Lewin.

The day after the murder the perpetrator had disappeared. It was unclear when, how, and to where.

At some point after the murder Waltin smuggled the weapon back to the tech squad. To the most secure storage place of them all, assuming you were unrestrained enough to even think of it. And he was, thought Lewin.

Two and a half years later, in the fall of 1988, he secured the weapon by trickery from Wiijnbladh and got him to remove all traces of it. At the last minute, because he'd already been fired, thought Lewin. A man completely without boundaries. A man who thought he could succeed in virtually everything. Who actually had done that, and never had any intention of giving up the decisive evidence that he had done it.

What do I do now? thought Lewin when he was done writing his memo. First I'll talk with Anna and then she'll have to try to have a serious talk with Johansson. Personally he didn't even intend to try.

68

"Please sit down, Anna," said Johansson, gesturing toward the visitor's chair in front of his desk. "I've just read Lewin's memo that you e-mailed over. A model of brevity. One never ceases to be amazed. Dear Jan seems to have had a complete change of personality. Clear and precise, right to the point. Suddenly, just like that."

"So what do you think about what's in it?" asked Holt.

"Interesting. Unfortunately unsubstantiated. In the current situation, exciting speculations. An obvious lead file," said Johansson and nodded.

So it's along those lines hc intends to finish this, thought Anna Holt.

"If it's an obvious lead file, then I suppose it should be on the Palme group's desk," said Holt.

"In the present situation I think it's much too speculative for us to trouble them with this sort of thing," said Johansson. "Besides, they're fully occupied with other things, so I've understood from Flykt."

"So what is it you're missing?" asked Holt.

"If you give me a name of the bastard who did the shooting, then I promise that you'll see some changes around here," said Johansson. "Then I promise I'll call in the police's top five on the carpet, and it's perhaps not mainly our colleague Flykt and his friends that I have in mind."

"When you've got a name," said Holt. "And if you don't get one?"

"Then we'll have to think this through one more time," said Johansson. "At this stage we're embracing every situation."

Whatever that has to do with it, thought Holt.

"There's another thing we have to talk about," said Holt. "I'm afraid it's a troublesome story."

"You can talk about anything and everything with me," said Johansson.

"It's about Pia, your wife," said Holt.

"About my life, you mean," said Johansson, suddenly sounding serious. "What has she come up with this time?"

Holt recounted the conversation with Jeanette Eriksson, and that Johansson's wife apparently had a relationship, an affair, or in any event a personal involvement with Claes Waltin during the spring of 1986.

"I already knew that," said Johansson. "That too was a model of brevity," he said and smiled. "Besides, it was several years before she got involved with the right man in her life."

"How did you find out?" asked Holt.

"She told me about it," said Johansson. "That she'd seen Waltin a few times during the spring of 1986. The first time when Pia and a girlfriend of hers were out at a bar to meet guys. Although I had no idea that former colleague Eriksson supposedly warned her. Retroactive jealousy isn't something I engage in," said Johansson, shrugging his shoulders.

"So you've never been worried," said Holt. "Considering Waltin and what he might have got up to with your wife."

"About Pia?" said Johansson, shaking his head. "What would a fool like Waltin have been able to do to her? I'm sure you must understand, Anna? You've met Pia, haven't you?"

"Do you have anything against me talking with Pia? Considering where we're at, I'm afraid we probably have to."

"Sure," said Johansson. "Only I get to talk with her first. I can't imagine she would have anything against it. For informational purposes," he added, nodding toward Holt.

"Of course," said Holt. "She's not suspected of anything."

"Nice to hear," said Johansson. "Sometimes she can be a little adventurous for my taste. Not that strange, really. She's a lot younger than I am," he said and sighed.

69

In the evening Johansson talked with his wife, Pia. It was not something he was happy about doing. True, retroactive jealousy was not something that usually tormented him—he had put that behind him back when he was a teenager—but if he could have chosen he obviously would have preferred that the woman who was his wife had never met someone like Claes Waltin. Regardless of whether he seemed completely different to her from the person Johansson was convinced he had always been.

If it hadn't been for Waltin, it could have been a perfect evening. Pia got home before him, prepared a simple dinner that went well with mineral water, so that the evening could be devoted to talking and being together, perhaps with each of them reading a good book in their respective corners of the big couch with their legs intertwined. Instead he was forced to talk with her about the time, over twenty years ago, when she had been involved with Claes Waltin.

"What did you think of the curry?" said Pia, looking at him.

"Phenomenal," said Johansson. "Although there is something I have to talk with you about."

"Sounds serious," said Pia. "What have I done now?"

"Claes Waltin," said Johansson.

"I knew it," said Pia triumphantly. "I knew it."

"Knew what?"

"That he was the one who murdered Palme," said Pia. "Have you forgotten that? I said that to you at least ten years ago, but you refused to listen to me."

"I recall that you were harping on about it seven years ago," said

Johansson. "I also remember that we agreed at that time not to talk about it anymore."

"So why are you asking now?" said Pia with inexorable logic.

Sigh, thought Johansson.

So she told him about the time she met Claes Waltin. The first time she was at a bar with a girlfriend soon after the Palme assassination. She remembered it because that was more or less the only thing people were talking about at that time. She and her girlfriend, for example, who even considered canceling their long-planned trip to the bar. They decided not to and instead she met Claes Waltin.

Claes Waltin was good-looking, funny, charming, nice, single, and seemed completely normal in all other respects. All she desired that evening, because both she and her girlfriend had really gone out to meet a nice guy.

"He invited me to dinner," said Pia. "It was on Saturday, the same week. We went out and ate. Then we went to his place."

"I see," said Johansson. Why in the name of God didn't I let Anna take care of this? he thought.

"You're wondering whether I slept with him," said Pia, looking expectantly at Johansson.

"Did you?" said Johansson. Where does she get all this from? he thought.

"Actually not," said Pia. "I was even surprised that he didn't take the opportunity. He showed me all his paintings. He had a really amazing apartment. On Norr Mälarstrand, with a view of the water. I asked him how a policeman could have earned that much money, and he told me he'd inherited from his mother. She died in an accident."

I see, so that's how it was, thought Johansson.

"And then?" he asked.

"Next time I did sleep with him," said Pia. "At my place, actually. That time we had also been to the restaurant first. It was also just a few days before you showed up at my job and asked if I wanted to have dinner with you. I'm sure you remember that. When I explained that I was already occupied you looked like a little boy who'd sold the butter and lost all the money. At that moment I was on the verge of changing my mind."

Close doesn't shoot any hares, thought Johansson.

"And then?" he asked.

"If it's the sex you're wondering about then there was nothing special about it. Regular, normal first-time sex. Two times, if you're wondering. I realized it wasn't the first time he'd slept with a woman. It wasn't the first time for me either, and you know that too."

"That's not what I was asking," said Johansson. "I was wondering—"

"Although then a very strange thing happened," Pia interrupted. "I don't think I've told you this."

Jeanette Eriksson, thought Johansson.

"Do tell," he said.

A few days later a young woman had come up to her as she left work and asked to speak with her.

"Young, cute girl," said Pia. "Jeanette, Jeanette Eriksson I think her name was. Said that she was a police officer, and at first I didn't believe her because she looked like she was still in high school, but then she took out her ID and showed me. She wanted to talk about Claes. Said that it was important. We went and sat down at a café in the vicinity."

"So what did she want?"

"What she told me was awful. It was about what Claes supposedly subjected her to. That he was a sadist. That he almost killed her. I didn't believe her, actually. That wasn't the Claes Waltin I knew. I told her that too. Asked flat out whether she was jealous of me. The mood got very strange. Not much was said after that."

"So what did you do then?"

"Thought a good deal," said Pia. "At first I thought about asking Claes flat out. But that didn't happen. It felt strange, considering that we really didn't know each other very well. But I had a hard time letting go of it, so the next time we met, I think it was only a few days after I talked with that Jeanette, we also went back to my place. Don't know why. Maybe because I wanted to feel safer."

"So how was it," said Johansson. "Typical second-time sex?"

"Better," said Pia, looking at him seriously. "A lot freer, not as nervous. Although before he left he said something that I thought was a little strange."

"I'm listening," said Johansson.

"When he was about to go and was in the vestibule he put his hand on my neck, pretty heavy-handed, actually, and then he said that next time we got together we should go to his place. Fuck for real. Something like that, he said, and there was something in his manner that got me thinking about what Jeanette had told me."

"But you went home with him next time anyway," said Johansson.

"Yes," said Pia, smiling as she said it. "I did. And when I was in his bed and he went to the bathroom, I couldn't restrain myself. I peeked in his nightstand."

"Yes? And—"

"It was then that I found the pictures he'd taken of Jeanette," said Pia seriously. "They were not amusing pictures. They were horrible."

"What did you do then?"

"I went completely cold. Especially as he was suddenly standing in the doorway, just looking at me. He didn't say anything. He just stood there staring at me. Looked completely strange, actually."

"What did you do then?" repeated Johansson.

"I didn't get aroused, if that's what you're thinking," said Pia, looking acidly at him. "I was scared shitless, jumped out of bed, and started pulling on my clothes. Then he started wrestling with me."

"So how did it end?" said Johansson.

"Really amazing," said Pia. "It was only then that I understood the benefit of growing up with two older brothers who were constantly fighting with me," she said.

"Explain," said Johansson.

"I kneed him," said Pia. "A perfect knee right in his crotch. Just like my brothers had taught me. He fell down on the floor and just moaned. I grabbed my clothes, picked up my handbag, took the coat from out in the hall, and ran down the stairs and out on the street. It was then I discovered I'd forgotten my shoes. My new black high-heeled shoes. Expensive, super-nice-looking, Italian. Do you know who I got them from, by the way?"

"From Claes Waltin," said Johansson.

"Yes," said Pia. "The third time we met. I didn't have any idea he knew what my shoe size was. Fit perfectly. Really expensive."

"And then? What happened then?"

"Nothing," said Pia. "I never saw him again. No calls. Nothing. Although I miss my shoes," she said, shaking her head. "And I regret I didn't take those pictures with me, so I could have destroyed them. Someone like him shouldn't have pictures like that."

"I'm sure he had more," said Johansson. Wherever they've ended up, he thought.

When they went to bed he had a hard time falling asleep for once. He pulled her next to him. A little spoon against a big ladle, who didn't even need to pull in his belly anymore when he slept with his woman. Even though he put his arm around her he had a hard time falling asleep. What kind of arm could protect her if what he believed about Waltin was true? If it became obvious to everyone else? If the media found out about it? The story about the police chief who had a wife who had been involved with the man who was behind the murder of the prime minister. Even better, who had been involved with him at the point in time when he had just murdered the prime minister.

So that's an interview you can just forget, Holt, thought Lars Martin Johansson, and then he finally fell asleep.

70

"I have to talk with you, boss," said Mattei as she stood in the doorway to Johansson's office.

"It can't wait until Monday?" said Johansson. "I have a lot of things to do. Have to pick up my wife. We're going away this weekend."

"I'm afraid it's important," said Mattei.

"What's more important than my wife?" said Johansson.

"Nothing, I'm sure," said Mattei. "It's just that I think I've found the bastard who did it." The one the boss is harping about all the time, she thought.

"Close the door," said Johansson. "Sit down."

"4711," said Johansson five minutes later when Mattei was through talking. "Wasn't that some kind of mysterious German perfume?"

"That was why I happened to think of it," said Mattei. "That was when I remembered the service code on the so-called receipt that Waltin gave to Wiijnbladh."

"Although you don't know what his name is," said Johansson.

"Someone must have known. Someone at SePo must have known. Considering the answer from their personnel department that was in the file. I asked Linda, my mother that is, but she didn't want to talk about it. She thought it could be hard to produce. So long afterward, that is."

"Do you have any description of that mysterious perfume man?" said Johansson.

"The anonymous informant provided a description. The informant, who I think was Orjala, Jorma Kalevi Orjala. A known thug at that time who was run over in a hit-and-run accident involving an unknown perpetrator, and found drowned in the Karlberg Canal only a few months after the Palme murder. Doesn't seem as though Orjala liked our colleague from SePo, but maybe we shouldn't worry about that."

"What should we worry about then?" interrupted Johansson.

"He says that the person he saw at that Chinese restaurant on Drottninggatan the same evening that Palme was murdered had worked at the bureau in Solna, but that he had quit a number of years before and started at SePo instead. He is supposed to have left there in 1982 according to what SePo itself says in its response to the officer who had the question about the anonymous tip."

"Hell," said Johansson, sitting straight up in his chair. "Hell's bells. Why didn't I think of that? How could I have forgotten that bastard?"

"Excuse me," said Mattei.

"Hell," Johansson repeated. "It's Kjell Göran Hedberg you're talking about, of course."

North Mallorca, fall of 1992

First he intended to clean up after himself. As soon as he got rid of the body he intended to clean up after himself. Starting with his hotel room. Get his keys. Take the plane to Stockholm. Clean up his apartment on Norr Mälarstrand and his big house in the country. In the best case he could get back anything that rightfully belonged to him.

There was never time for any cleanup. As so often before when he planned things, the unexpected upset his calculations.

When he showed up at the hotel the next morning the police had already been there. A regular marked car was parked by the hotel entrance. Two uni-formed Spanish officers standing in reception, talking with the staff. The main key that was in his pocket, that he'd had to pay so dearly for, could no longer be used. He got rid of it. Threw it in the water when he turned in the boat he had rented. Traveling to Sweden was out of the question.

What remained was the hope that there wasn't anything to clean up. He laid low. Changed residence, waited, hid for months like a rabbit in its new hole. It was also then that he decided to have Esperanza built. As an extra insurance policy he could use to protect himself against the unexpected.

But nothing had happened. There hadn't been anything he needed to clean up. If there had been he would have noticed it. Then things would have hap-pened. All that had happened was that year was added to year, and soon it would be over for good, and worldly justice could no longer reach him. He had never had any reason to trouble himself about divine justice. On the contrary, it seemed to have been on his side all along, if you wanted to believe in such things.

Esperanza was no longer simply a boat, an insurance policy, and a reminder. It had also become a contribution to his livelihood, and it was Ignacio Ballester who had suggested it. Why not earn some extra money from all the charter tourists? Everyone who wanted to swim, fish, and dive. He knew the area, he knew the waters. He was an experienced sailor too, good diver, and capable fisherman. What would be simpler than putting out his card among all the others on the bulletin board down by the charter pier in Puerto Pollensa? Day tours, swimming, fishing, diving. Easy money and no tax authorities to torment anyone smart enough to give out only a cell phone number on the printed card.

Think of all the good-looking women he could meet, said Ignacio, winking at him. A man like him. In his prime and with a beautiful boat like Esperanza. All the beautiful women, practically naked, dressed for swimming and diving. And then the sun, the warm sea. Security, freedom, perhaps love too. Love. There was never anything wrong with a little love, was there?

71

Wednesday, September 26
and exactly two weeks left until October 10.
Headquarters of the National Bureau of Criminal
Investigation on Kungsholmen in Stockholm

Half an hour before the usual Wednesday meeting would begin, Lisa Mattei's mother stepped into Johansson's office. She closed the door behind her, sat down in the visitor's chair, and fixed her eyes on Lars Martin Johansson.

"No time for frills," said Johansson. "You're more beautiful than ever, Linda. Although that's probably not something any of your sallow colleagues have dared say to you."

"No time for bullshit either, Lars," said Linda Mattei. "Quick question. What are you up to with my daughter?"

"Nothing," said Johansson, shaking his head. "True, she's just as gorgeous as her mother, but as I'm sure you know, I've been a happily married man for many years."

"She's asking a lot of strange questions," said Linda Mattei. "I'm getting worried about her."

"I don't think you need to be," said Johansson. "If you ask me I'm convinced things will go very well for her. Things are already going well for her, and she can go as far as she wants. I'm sure she will too."

"Last week she wanted me to reveal the identity of one of my former colleagues. Is that something you've asked her to do?"

"Actually, no," said Johansson. "She came up with that all on her own, and I'm very grateful that she did."

"So it's not something that you're behind," said Linda Mattei.

"I helped her of course when she asked."

"You helped her?"

"Kjell Göran Hedberg," said Johansson. "How could I have ever forgotten someone like him?"

"So you knew," said Linda Mattei.

"It struck me suddenly when your gorgeous daughter was kind enough to describe him to me. The bureau in Solna in the seventies. Then bodyguard at SePo. Quit in 1982. Kjell Göran Hedberg. Same Hedberg who never should have become a policeman."

"Did you know he was called the Perfume Man? After that horrid German eau de cologne Kölnisch Wasser 4711 that my husband used to give me as a present," said Linda Mattei.

"Not a clue," said Johansson. "Must have been before my time. That wasn't what you were wearing those far too few times when I had the pleasure," said Johansson.

"Come, come now," said Linda Mattei. "You've never heard the story about the Perfume Man?"

"No," said Johansson. "Tell me."

Hedberg had started with SePo in the summer of 1976. He had been recruited from the detective division at the Solna police and was one of three who had been brought over from Solna and placed in SePo's bodyguard squad. First training, then service as a bodyguard. In addition, a service code to protect his identity from the outside world.

"He got the code 4711," said Linda Mattei. "There were no ulterior motives in that. At least not as far as I know. It was simply the code that was available, I guess. After a while he discovered that his colleagues were calling him the Perfume Man. After that German eau de cologne. He came to me and complained. I was office manager at the squad back then."

"I can barely contain myself," said Johansson.

"I told him not to be so damned childish," said Linda Mattei. "If any of his little classmates were being mean to him, he could always tattle on them to the teacher who would take them by the ear. Because he was evidently not man enough to rise above such childishness."

"So what did he say?" said Johansson.

"He slunk off," said Linda Mattei. "Didn't come back the whole time I was sitting at the counter, and that was at least a couple of years."

"He must have been occupied with other things," said Johansson. "First running off to rob the post office on Dalagatan and then killing two witnesses who happened to recognize him."

"I've heard that story before," said Linda Mattei. "Show me an indictment or even a preliminary investigation, then I promise to listen to you."

"Forget about that now," said Johansson. "Continue."

"My successor was evidently more sensitive than I was. It was Björn Söderström, whom you no doubt know. The one who later became head of the whole squad. In any event he liberated Perfume Man from his suffering. Gave him a new service code and saw to it that 4711 became inactive. For the same reasons you avoid having DIK on the license plate on your car."

"What would a real man do with a license plate like that?" said Johansson, shrugging his shoulders.

"No, maybe not you. But certainly one or two of your brethren," said Linda Mattei.

"That particular code I'm talking about, 4711 that is, has actually never been used since then. Not since the autumn of 1977 as far as I know. Although the story was well known, and that was certainly why our personnel department sent the reply they did."

"Although Hedberg was still there. Even after having robbed the post office and eliminated two witnesses," said Johansson.

"He was allowed to stay. Though he had left the bodyguards by 1978. For one thing, there was a lot of talk about what you just mentioned. For another, the boss at the time, it was Berg as I'm sure you remember, transferred him. Internal service for almost four years before he resigned."

"I've thought a good deal about that," said Johansson. "Why did Berg let him stay?"

"Well, it certainly wasn't out of consideration for Hedberg," said Linda Mattei.

"I understand exactly," said Johansson. "If it was concern for your daughter that got you to look me up, then you don't need to worry yourself in the slightest."

"Good," said Linda Mattei, getting up. "And if you were to get tired of your young wife you know who you can call."

All these women who love you, thought Lars Martin Johansson. In his conference room there were probably two more who were longing to meet him.

Not both however, as it appeared. When he showed up Anna Holt looked pointedly at the clock, even though he was only fifteen minutes late. Lisa on the other hand was energetic and happy as always, while Jan Lewin seemed almost absent. Although he was a guy of course. Not much of a guy, to be sure, thought Johansson, but who cared about such things?

"Read this," he said, giving them copies of the summary he had devoted the entire evening to while his wife sulked and finally disappeared to go to the movies with a girlfriend. Not with her husband, even though he had promised her.

"Kjell Göran Hedberg," said Holt. "Where have I heard that name?"

"Read," said Johansson.

72

Kjell Göran Hedberg was born on the fifteenth of August 1944, in Vaxholm parish due north of Stockholm. His father worked as a harbor
pilot. He was stationed in Sandhamn and lived in Vaxholm, when he
wasn't out piloting vessels through the Stockholm archipelago. He and
his family lived in a single-family house. Hedberg's mother was a housewife. Besides Kjell, the Hedbergs had a daughter three years younger
named Birgitta.

If Kjell Hedberg was still alive, and there was nothing to indicate that
he wasn't, he would have turned sixty-three just over a month ago. If
he was the one who shot the country's prime minister, he would have
been forty-one when he did it. Tall enough besides. When he applied to
the police academy almost forty years before he had been six foot one.
According to the information in his passport, now seven years old, these
days he was slightly shorter.

"Age takes its toll even on someone like that," Johansson observed.

After finishing nine years of comprehensive school, Hedberg worked for
a few years as a carpenter's apprentice at a small shipyard in Vaxholm
while he studied at evening school and earned a high school diploma.
When he turned eighteen he did his military service with the coast com-
mandos in Vaxholm. He trained as an attack diver and mustered out
with the highest grades in all subjects. As soon as he was a legal adult he
applied to the police academy and was admitted the following year. He
was then twenty years old and the year was 1965.

Once he was through with his year of police training, he ended up with the police in Stockholm as a trainee. He was promoted to assistant one year later, and after a total of ten years he applied for a position as a detective inspector with the police in Solna.

Hedberg got the position. Not only did he have good recommendations. He was also the kind of colleague everyone spoke well of. Someone who could be relied on when things suddenly heated up. Someone who always volunteered. Despite his youth, Hedberg was a real constable. The year was 1975 and he had just turned thirty-one.

After only a year at the bureau in Solna the secret police had been in touch. Spoke with Hedberg's boss. Spoke with Hedberg himself. Sent their usual recruiters there. Interviewed Hedberg, brought him to the mandatory test week at their training camp, somewhere in Sweden. Asked if he wanted to start with them. Got an affirmative reply. Took care of all the papers and got the go-ahead from his police chief and Hedberg himself.

Hedberg was placed with SePo's bodyguard squad. He was the Solna police department's best marksman. He was in perfect physical shape. Single, no children. There was nothing that would prevent him from living life as a policeman to the fullest. He looked good. Was careful about his appearance. Dressed well. Was courteous and well-mannered. Had everything required of someone who would be watching over the potentates of the realm, and in the worst case would take the bullet meant for the person he was protecting.

So far all was well known and well substantiated. What happened next was at best mere slander in the big police building on Kungsholmen. At worst it was true, even though Hedberg during his entire active time as a police officer had never been named as a suspect for the crimes he was supposed to have been guilty of.

Johansson's memo was about Hedberg's life up to the point when the wicked rumors had taken over. The boss pointed out that he had done it himself, that it was concise and a model of brevity, and that despite his advanced age he still managed to hit the right keys on his computer.

"So read and enjoy, because the rest I intend to do verbally," said Johansson. "You'll understand why immediately, and I don't need to even explain why this has to stay in this room. For the time being, at least. If it's as I think, there'll be some changes coming soon. We'll cross that bridge when we come to it," said Johansson.

"On Friday, May 13, 1977, Hedberg robbed the post office at Dalagatan 13," said Johansson. "His assignment was to guard the then minister of justice during the day. The minister of justice wanted to take the opportunity to visit his favorite hooker a few blocks from there. Hedberg got leave for a couple of hours and passed the time by robbing the post office. Got away with almost three hundred thousand in cash. A lot of money at that time, when a detective inspector like myself earned five thousand a month, before taxes and including all the overtime you accumulated."

"I'm sure I've heard that story a hundred times," said Holt. "Is it really true?"

"Yes," said Johansson. "How do I know? Well, I know. I was the one who found him, you see."

Then it got even worse. During the ensuing months Hedberg did away with two witnesses to the robbery by murdering them. The first was a young man whom he ran over with his car when the man was crossing the street outside the subway station at the Skogskyrkogården cemetery just south of Stockholm. That case had been written off as a tragic traffic accident—the victim had been high and more or less threw himself in front of Hedberg's car. The second was a completely ordinary murder. An elderly man and social outcast had his neck broken and was dumped in the same cemetery on December 24, 1977.

"On Christmas Eve," said Lisa Mattei, her eyes widening.

The suspicions against Hedberg could never be proved. What decided the whole thing was that the minister of justice gave him an alibi for the time when he was supposed to have robbed the post office on Dalagatan, and with that all the evidence collapsed like a house of cards.

"The whole thing ended with him being taken out of outside service," said Johansson. "He got to sit at SePo and shuffle papers. He sat there for four years before he resigned. Where he went then is unclear. According to the little there is, he's supposed to have moved to Spain a year later. That was in the fall of 1983. At the same time I have reason to believe he continued working for SePo during the following years. As a so-called external operator."

According to Johansson there was more to it than that. The only one who seemed to have made use of this particular external operator was then police chief superintendent Claes Waltin. It is probable that he had employed Hedberg in a mission that went wrong. A secret house search of a student apartment on Körsbärsvägen in Stockholm, Friday the twenty-second of November 1985.

"Waltin took care of the practical details. The target was an American journalist who was living there on a sublease. I had reason to believe that the operator he made use of was Kjell Göran Hedberg."

"Friday the twenty-second of November," said Mattei. "That's the day Kennedy was shot."

"Twenty-two years earlier," said Johansson. "This is probably one of those rare, chance coincidences."

"So what went wrong?" asked Holt.

"The journalist suddenly showed up. Surprised Hedberg. Hedberg killed him. Feigned a suicide by writing a farewell letter and throwing him out the window from the twentieth floor."

"This can't be true," said Mattei. "My first, real serial murderer. At least three murders on at least three different occasions. If he also shot Palme he's leading by a wide margin."

"Glad I can make you happy, Lisa," said Johansson. "But this particular bastard is not exactly fun to deal with."

"You must have met him," said Lewin. "How would you describe him?"

"I ran into him numerous times in service in the good old days. What's he like? Psychopath, ice-cold, shrewd, rational, dangerous. Everything you want. When I was operations head for the closed operation I entertained myself by reading his personal file. It was not fun reading. Someone like him should never have become a police officer. Nor is it so simple as being an ordinary sex murderer or a sadist. Hedberg has a distinctly practical nature. If a lightbulb burns out you put in a new one, and most of us can manage that. If a person threatens Hedberg's existence, he does away with him. In the same simple, obvious way as the rest of us change lightbulbs. So the part where he supposedly gets a kick out of killing someone I think you can forget. This is considerably worse than that."

"Is there any psychological evaluation of him?" asked Holt.

"All the usual stuff that everyone who started at SePo was subject to at that time. Where they obviously only have good things to say. To start with at least. Very good self-control, very high stress thresholds, constructive, rational, highly effective. After what happened in 1977, on the other hand, changes were made. The big boss at the time, Berg, had a very extensive psychiatric assessment done on Hedberg. Everyone sitting here surely knows what I think about such things, but for once I was inclined to agree with the doctor."

"What did he conclude?" said Mattei.

"That Hedberg was an evil psychopath with almost unlimited self-confidence. Someone who saw himself as an *Übermensch*. Totally incapable of deeper, emotional attachments to other people. With a very great, purely physical capacity besides."

"Everyone has their weak points. Even someone like that," said Holt.

"I think so too," said Johansson. "Hedberg had at least one, if you ask me."

"What was that?" said Holt.

"He was crazy for women," said Johansson. "That sort of thing costs. Sooner or later," he said.

"So this is the bastard we're looking for," said Anna Holt, when Johansson was finished half an hour later.

"I think so," said Johansson, while smiling and nodding at Lisa Mattei.

"What do you want us to do with him?" said Holt.

"Find him," said Johansson. "So I can boil him for glue." At long last, it was high time, and not an hour to lose, he thought.

"One more thing," said Holt.

"Yes?"

"Pictures of Hedberg. Do we have any good pictures of him?"

"Who do you take me for, Anna?" said Johansson. "I'm hoping that CIS e-mailed a whole photo album to you an hour ago. Thirty pictures of Hedberg, half a dozen of his parents, and about as many of his sister."

"Thanks," said Holt.

"You know what they say, Anna," said Johansson. "A picture says more than a thousand words."

There was a total of thirty-one pictures of Kjell Göran Hedberg, twenty-five of which had evidently been taken without his knowledge sometime in the late seventies or early eighties. They were typical police surveillance photos taken outdoors by means of a motor camera and telephoto lens. Hedberg going into a bar in the company of an unknown woman. Hedberg coming out of his residence. Hedberg getting into his car. Hedberg getting out of the same car in the police building garage. A 1977 Mercedes, Hedberg wearing a jacket with wide lapels, pants without cuffs but with flared legs, a white shirt with a long collar. A wide tie. A Hedberg of his time.

The photographer was naturally unidentified. Johansson and Jarnebring, in their futile pursuit of a colleague they suspected of a crime that would get him life imprisonment? Or a worried Erik Berg, who wanted to keep an eye on a conceivable security risk in his immediate vicinity?

Holt was captivated by one of them. An ordinary passport photo taken in the spring of 1982 when Hedberg was going to renew his police ID from the secret police, but instead decided to resign only a month later.

Kjell Göran Hedberg: somewhat thin face, regular features, straight nose, pronounced chin and jawline, short dark hair, dark and deeply inset eyes. Eyes that said nothing whatsoever either to the photographer or to a possible observer; eyes that appeared unaware of, or rather completely uninterested in the fact that they had just been photographed: unrevealing, sufficient unto themselves.

He looks good, thought Holt. You could clearly see that, and she would have thought that even if he'd tried to conceal his face by pretending to blow his nose. As on the evening of February 28, 1986, when he encountered Madeleine Nilsson on the stairs from Malmskillnadsgatan down to Kungsgatan.

73

After the meeting Lisa Mattei stayed behind while Holt and Lewin returned to what they were doing. There was not an hour to lose and everything essential remained to be done.

"You wanted to talk with me," said Johansson.

"The search," said Mattei, handing her boss a plastic sleeve containing ten pages.

"The search?"

"The search you asked me to do, boss. On that little society of law students," she clarified.

"Oh, that," said Johansson. "Well?"

"All of them were in the Palme registry. Sjöberg, Thulin, and Tischler. Although not Waltin, of course, but we found him ourselves."

"A leopard never changes its spots," Johansson observed for some reason as he weighed the plastic sleeve in his hand.

"Would you like a quick summary, boss?"

"Gladly," said Johansson. Anything that will save time, as long as it doesn't have to do with the case, he thought.

Sjöberg was interviewed for informational purposes because of the so-called Indian arms affair. He had nothing to add and was eliminated from the investigation early on. Besides, he had been dead for almost fifteen years.

"So we don't need that one," said Johansson and nodded.

"Thulin was there as one of the Good Guys. Substituted as prosecutor in the investigation on a couple of occasions. Served as an expert in one of the review commissions and as a political appointee on another."

"I know," said Johansson. "I've met him. I recall that he sat there the whole time harping on about Christer Pettersson. Real stuck-up little toad. Very stupid. It's a big, fucking mystery."

"What do you mean, boss?"

"How any woman would want to be involved with someone like that," Johansson clarified. "He seems to have won that fucking trophy they awarded to each other."

"That particular aspect doesn't appear in my papers," said Mattei. You too, my Johansson, she thought.

"Bragging, if you ask me," said Johansson. "We can forget Thulin. Next."

"Tischler," said Mattei. "At least three tips have come in about him, from the circle of so-called private investigators who allege he was involved in some way in a larger conspiracy to murder Olof Palme."

"How so? Involved?" That windbag, he thought. If it had only been that good.

"There are assertions that he supposedly offered the first investigation leader, Hans Holmér, a lot of money to follow up his Kurd track," Mattei explained. "Not because he believed in it, but rather to set up a little smoke screen to protect the real perpetrators."

"Forget it," said Johansson. "If Tischler had been part of a conspiracy, he and everyone else involved would have been in jail within twenty-four hours. You couldn't find a better guarantee for that than mister private banker's own mouth. Besides, did he ever give any money to Holmér?"

"No. According to what Tischler himself says, that came from information he received from individuals he knew. Within the social democratic movement. Besides, he's said to have spoken with individuals close to the government. All would have advised him against it. The Kurds had nothing to do with the murder."

"Did he mention any names?" said Johansson for some reason. "Of the people he talked to, I mean."

"No," said Mattei, shaking her head. "Individuals within the Social Democratic Party. Individuals close to the Social Democratic administration. Considering the time frame, it must have been during Ingvar Carlsson's stint as prime minister."

"But no names," said Johansson, nodding thoughtfully. "No names." Although personally I could think of at least one, he thought.

"Waltin," said Johansson. "He's the one this is about. Sjöberg, Thulin, and Tischler I think we can forget."

"I think like you do, boss," said Mattei and nodded. "It's a bit odd, at the same time, that all four would still be in the investigation."

"It's a small country," said Johansson. "Much too small," he repeated. Not least for someone like our murder victim, he thought.

"One more thing," said Johansson, just as Mattei was about to leave.

"Yes," she said and stopped.

"That thing with Hedberg," said Johansson. "You should get a big gold star for that. What bothers me is that I didn't think of him myself. I should have, you see, and that bothers me."

"Maybe you're starting to get old, boss," said Mattei.

"Yes," said Johansson. "Even I've gotten older." No matter how unbelievable that may seem, he thought.

74

The same evening Johansson met the special adviser at a seminar of the Turing Society. Though he had more important stuff he ought to take care of, because things had finally started to move after more than twenty years. Or more than thirty, perhaps, depending on how you calculated.

High time, thought Johansson. High time that a real police officer finally got to see the light at the end of the tunnel. In other respects the tunnel was completely different from the one the walking catastrophe who was in charge of the Palme investigation to start with had raved about. A completely different light too, he thought. A sharp white glare that struck him and people like him right in the eyes, without their being able to turn away or even blink.

The Turing Society was named for Alan Turing. Mathematician and code breaker during the Second World War. A great mathematician and the greatest of all code breakers.

Initially, it had mostly been an illustrious society where his Swedish colleagues, other mathematicians, statisticians, and linguists who had a past within the military intelligence organization were given occasion for both edifying conversation and a decent meal. They would meet quarterly to listen to lectures, hold seminars, or simply socialize. At the obligatory Christmas dinner, the first Sunday in December. At the exclusive gentlemen's club Stora Sällskapet in Stockholm, Christmas buffet, tails, academic vestments. Numerous shots and bottles of red wine. No one and nothing was lacking.

It was the special adviser who had invited Johansson. First when they had run into each other in Rosenbad. When they had bumped into each other at a reception at the American embassy a few days later, he had repeated his invitation.

The special adviser had been chairman of the Turing Society for many years, and during his tenure the society had taken in a new influx of members. Not only pure academics, but also the sort who mostly worked with military intelligence operations. Even an esteemed politician or two who took pleasure in talking about problems that ordinary people were not supposed to discuss.

"The subject of the evening really ought to entice someone like you," the special adviser tempted him. "We're going to talk about a particular aspect of the Palme assassination."

"The Kurd track or Christer Pettersson?" said Johansson.

"Not really," said the special adviser. "A purely academic discussion. The main speakers are going to start by presenting an analysis of the consequences of the various so-called tracks. If it turned out to be one way and not another. What political and economic consequences that would have, over and above the purely legal ones."

"Will there be many people there who were involved in the investigations?" asked Johansson, who had not the slightest desire to meet a certain female prosecutor in Stockholm.

"Are you joking, Johansson?" said the special adviser. "This is an educated society. That's why I'm so eager for you to come."

"I have quite a bit to do," said Johansson.

"For my sake, Johansson. For my sake."

"I'll come," said Johansson.

"Excellent," said the special adviser, beaming like the sun. "Then you'll also have the pleasure of meeting my successor. He's going to give the introductory address."

He was not particularly like the man he would apparently succeed. A tall, bony academic, half the age of the special adviser, with thick blond hair that stuck out in all directions and eyeglasses he constantly moved between the tip of his nose and his hairline.

He spoke slowly and clearly, chose his words with care, and took pains with both pauses and punctuation. Almost as if he were reading from a written text, while he also made a strangely absent impression.

Another one of the guys with a lot of letters in his poor head, thought Johansson in his judgmental way.

At the same time the speaker's message had been simple and clear. The advantage of the solitary madman who murdered a prime minister was that, in a social sense, he was primarily free of consequences. A man such as, for example, Christer Pettersson. What remained was the loss of a significant politician—controversial, to be sure—but otherwise nothing, and society would cope. As is known, even loss passes.

"Time heals all wounds," the evening's introductory speaker observed. He pushed his glasses onto his forehead and turned the page.

Despite the evening's purely academic orientation, the opening speaker had nonetheless granted himself a slight digression. Christer Pettersson also offered another essential advantage, not to be overlooked, because any critical thinker who was familiar with this case could not but conclude that he really was the one who murdered the prime minister.

"In a purely intellectual sense the Palme assassination is solved," he explained to his audience. "What remains to consider is thus not the collective trauma resulting from the unsolved murder, but rather the individual trauma that ensues from the fact that different recipients of this purely factual message have different bases for understanding how matters really stand."

What remains is to convince numbskulls like Holt, Lewin, Mattei, and me, thought Johansson.

The Kurd track and other similar descriptions of the event had limited consequences for Swedish politics and Swedish society. The geographic, cultural, and political distance between ordinary Swedes and types such as, for example, Kurdish terrorists made it possible to discuss the problem in terms of "us" and "them." Formulating a clear "dichotomy" where "we" were primarily all the ordinary, decent people while "they" in all essentials were only a kind of strange collective from a very distant part of the world. There would be certain limited effects on the general view of immigrants, refugee policy, and related issues. Increased resources to various agencies of social control, obviously. Calculated in budget terms, problems in the magnitude of several hundred million each. "In total at the most one billion per year, in the ongoing budget. Measures which in addition lend themselves to being handled within the already established bureaucratic structure."

Nice to hear that we don't need to come up with anything new, thought Johansson.

But then it quickly got worse. From an ordinary sneeze to a bout of influenza. What remained was more or less the choice between plague and cholera. Far-reaching political and social effects, social costs in the billions, collective mistrust of politicians and social institutions, loss of large portions of Sweden's credibility abroad. Suddenly a Sweden that had been reduced to an ordinary banana monarchy in the pile of African and Central American republics where heads of state, governments, and ministers were replaced without the least thought of political choices. And without triggering more than a yawn in the UN Security Council.

Whether the assassination did in fact concern a political conspiracy of the sort that befell Gustav III, or what was summarized in Swedish debate under the designation "the police track," was according to the speaker's considered opinion "a toss-up."

Because this comparison surely astonished many in the audience, he also wanted to take the opportunity to further clarify himself.

"In the society in which we live today, the police constitute a social foundation accorded the same respect as, for example, uncorrupted and democratically controlled political organs such as parliament and the government. The police today have a far greater significance than the military in Swedish society. We also live in a world in which security is discussed in police terms; although the means we use are still traditionally military. The point of view, the arguments underpinning it have their basis in a police mind-set, and focus has been moved from war to terrorism. The traditional military balance of terror between nations and blocs of nations is now history. Calculated in terms of damage, and compared with, for example, the so-called Kurd track, with the police track we are talking about social damages that are in the magnitude of a couple of powers of ten higher, and in which the majority of the loss comes from the outside world's depreciation of Sweden's democratic credibility," the introductory speaker concluded, adjusting his glasses down to the tip of his nose and inspecting his pensive audience.

A hundred times more worrisome. At least, thought Lars Martin Johansson, even though math had been far from his favorite subject in school. Even though we're only talking about two crazy policemen who never should have been policemen, he thought.

After the concluding debate they were invited to dinner at Rosenbad, where the government had made its own dining room available to them.

"So what did you think about my young successor?" asked the special adviser.

"Interesting person," said Johansson, who always tried to avoid quarrels when he accepted an invitation. "What does a young man like that occupy himself with?" When he's not talking shit in general terms, he thought.

"Military signals intelligence," said the special adviser. "But only because you're the one who's asking, Johansson," he added, holding his index finger up to his moist lips. "That's the young man responsible for the realm's connection with the American intelligence service. You know, all those eyes and ears high up there in the blue that see and hear everything we're up to."

"Yes, it's quite amazing," said Johansson. "Quite amazing," he repeated. To be putting something like that in the hands of someone like our crazy lecturer, he thought.

"Yes, it really is," the special adviser concurred, smiling happily. "And this they have the gall to call satellites."

After dinner was over the special adviser took Johansson aside once again to speak with him in private.

"By the way, what did you think about the wines?" he began. "For once really decent, even in this simple context, if you ask me."

"From your own cellar?" Johansson wondered.

"Not so, not so at all. A little haul that one of my co-workers made. Hidden away in a closet down at Harpsund. Someone forgot them, certainly. A regular little warehouse, actually, that we took the opportunity to walk off with."

"Is that really true?" said Johansson. "Or is it like with those deer in that park in Oxford?"

"Completely true," the special adviser assured him, nodding eagerly. "The previous owner seems to have left in some haste. By the way, have you thought about what truth is, Johansson? Really thought about it, I mean."

"Yes," said Johansson. My whole life, he thought.

"When an important truth is revealed to you," said the special adviser, who had now become so excited that he was tugging on the sleeve of Johansson's jacket, "when an important truth is revealed to you . . . you can be affected much more painfully than when you reveal a great lie. Truth touches you much, much more than a lie. When you truly see it before you, you fall freely, as if in a dream. As in one of those unpleasant dreams, you know. When you suddenly plummet, fall headlong straight down into a darkness that never ends, and it is so terrible that when you finally wake up it feels as if your chest could explode. When it can take several minutes before you are sure whether you're really alive or dead. Have you ever had a dream like that?"

"Never," said Johansson. "But once when I was a little boy they took out my tonsils and that was the first time I had anesthetic. With ether, actually, and the odor still sits in my nose. I remember that I fell like that. It wasn't particularly nice."

"But never in a dream," said the special adviser. "You've never done that in a dream? Completely exposed, lost and beyond all help?"

"Never in a dream," said Johansson.

"You are a fortunate man, Johansson," sighed the special adviser. "You're also happily married to a woman who is said to be beautiful, wise, and good."

Is he trying to tell me something? thought Johansson.

75

That same night Johansson had a hard time falling asleep. Not because he'd been dreaming, but because he'd suddenly been reminded of his childhood. Reminded of the time when he was eleven years old and had a cold the whole autumn. His worried father at last drove him all the way to the general hospital in Kramfors to have his tonsils removed.

A fresh memory, fifty years later. How he had to take off all his clothes and was handed over to them, in a white nightshirt from the county council. How they strapped him in an ordinary dental chair. How they bound his arms and legs with leather straps. How they bound his head tight. How they pried open his mouth. Two grown-ups with masks over their faces and holes for their eyes. Then they pressed the rag with ether over his nose and mouth. How he tried to tear himself loose before they suffocated him. The pungent odor of ether. Much more acrid than the gasoline, diesel, or even chlorine that he knew from life on the farm.

How everything turned black before his eyes, how his head roared, how everything around him started spinning, how he himself fell head-first straight down into the darkness, and how the last thing he thought about was his dad, Evert, who had not been allowed to come in with him, even though he had held him by the hand all the way up to the door.

76

Marja Ruotsalainen lived in a small apartment in Tyresö, a few miles southeast of central Stockholm. Considering the life she'd lived, she appeared to have managed well. A skinny little woman with a lot of henna-colored hair, who smoked constantly and only stopped when her hacking cough prevented her.

She did not seem particularly happy to see them. But she hadn't called them "fucking pigs," and she didn't tell them to go to hell. She even offered them a crooked smile when they sat down at her kitchen table.

"Girl cops," said Marja. "So what have you gals been up to the past twenty years?"

She did not offer them coffee. That sort of thing mostly happened in crime novels, but in reality people like her almost never offered police officers coffee. Nothing else either, for that matter. On the other hand she softened and started talking.

She and her boyfriend at the time had been at the Chinese restaurant on Drottninggatan that evening when the prime minister was murdered. She was living at his place. Hiding with him. She had been on the lam for several months. It was Friday evening and she was almost climbing the walls. Had to go out into town. Get out and move around so she could breathe, even though there were more suitable areas than downtown Stockholm where someone like her could go.

She was also the one who had recognized the plainclothes policeman who was already in the restaurant. Recognized him from ten years before, when she was only seventeen and she and another of her boyfriends twice her age had been arrested in a dope pad out in Tensta.

"A real fucking fascist. The type that twisted your arms up behind your back, called you a whore, and stayed standing in the doorway staring while the dyke jailers told you to take off all your clothes," Marja Ruotsalainen summarized.

Preserved as a bad memory. A year later she had seen him again, when she had yet another boyfriend twice her age. It was outside the Parliament Building, and the nameless policeman and one of the same sort got out of a big black Volvo and held open the door for a well-known politician they then escorted into the building.

"They just radiated SePo," said Ruotsalainen. "Might as well have had it printed on their foreheads. How clueless can you be?"

"That politician," said Holt. "You don't remember what his name was?"

"No," she said, shaking her head. "It must have been one of those conservatives. May have been in the summer of seventy-seven. When I got busted in Solna that time it was seventy-six. I remember that."

"Why do you remember that?" asked Mattei.

"Because it was my seventeenth birthday," said Marja. "Talk about a birthday present."

The nameless policeman from the restaurant she remembered. He had been sitting there when they came in. The time was about nine-thirty. He left after an hour or so. The rest she had figured out later when she read about the murder of Olof Palme.

"He pretty well matched that physical description. Dark, good condition, forty-ish. About six foot one. Dark jacket. I remember that, because he had it on in the restaurant. On the other hand I don't remember what kind of pants he had on. I guess I didn't think about it."

· · ·

Then they showed her pictures. Ten portrait photos of police officers taken twenty to thirty years earlier. The originals had been on their police IDs. One of them was of Kjell Göran Hedberg and was taken the same summer he was supposed to have accompanied an unknown politician into the Parliament Building.

"Not the foggiest," said Ruotsalainen. "They look like blueberries, the whole pile. How the hell do you tell one blueberry from another?"

"What do you think about this then?" asked Mattei, pushing a typewritten page over to her. A list of ten names of male police officers, the majority of which she gathered from the national bureau's personnel list, and one of them was named Kjell Göran Hedberg.

Pettersson, Salminen, Trost, Kovac, Östh, Johansson, Hedberg, Eriksson, Berg, Kronstedt. Ten names, and the surnames were not in alphabetical order.

"I recognize Östh," said Ruotsalainen. "That was another one of those Solna detectives. Also a fucking creep, but what his first name was I don't remember."

"Take all the time you need," said Holt. "We're in no hurry."

"Me neither," said Ruotsalainen. "These days I have all the time in the world. Before it was a lot of running around."

"No," she said, shaking her head. "Not the foggiest. They're all cops, I suppose, so I'm sure I've met them too."

"After the arrest out in Solna in 1976 you and your guy at the time were convicted of narcotics crimes. It happened in Solna district court in April of 1976. I have the conviction here," said Mattei, pushing a plastic sleeve over to Ruotsalainen. "What you said, that you were seventeen when you were arrested. That adds up; it says so in the conviction. Before you look at it I want you to think one more time about the name of that policeman who testified against you back then."

"Is this one of those psych things you learned at the police academy?" asked Ruotsalainen.

"Think now, Marja," said Mattei. "Think about that policeman who testified against you. Look at the list of names in front of you."

"Kjell Göran Hedberg," said Ruotsalainen suddenly. "That was his name. Damn, girlfriend. You're a fucking magician.

"That name," she continued. "I remember it. When that Nazi was sitting up there on the stand about to lie through his oath before he stepped on it for real. I, Kjell Göran Hedberg, do promise and assure . . . Guess whether I remember. How many people do you think there are who call me Marja Lovisa Ruotsalainen? Not even my mom."

Before they left they talked with her about her then boyfriend, Jorma Kalevi Orjala, who had been struck by a hit-and-run driver and drowned in the Karlberg Canal a few months after the murder of the prime minister.

"Cully," said Ruotsalainen and sighed. "He was a real fucking crazy, he was. Although I doubt that's why you came here."

"No," said Holt, who did not like lying, even to someone like Marja Ruotsalainen. "But we've read the investigation. According to the report, it was most likely a so-called hit-and-run accident. Someone hit him from behind with a car. He was thrown over the edge of the pier and down into the water where he happened to drown."

"Happened to," Ruotsalainen snorted. "Cully wasn't the sort that things 'happened to.' He was murdered. You must have realized that anyway?"

"In that case we've come for his sake too," said Holt, looking at her seriously. "So who do you think murdered him?"

"I wish I could say it was that fucking Hedberg," said Ruotsalainen. "But I don't really think so. There were a fucking lot of people who wanted to kill Cully. That evening, for example, he was at home with a girlfriend of mine, drinking and screwing her. He needed to I guess, and I was sitting in jail," she said, shrugging her shoulders.

"Do you have any names?" said Mattei. "For example, what was the name of your girlfriend that Cully visited? Maybe you have some idea who may have run him over?"

"Course I have," said Ruotsalainen. "The problem is that they're all dead. Cully's dead, my girlfriend is dead. Her guy at the time, who possibly ran over Cully after he came staggering out of his girl's pad, is dead too. You should have been here twenty years ago. Why weren't you, by the way?"

"Good question," said Anna Holt as they sat in the car on the way to the police building. "Why didn't we hold that interview twenty years ago?"

"I couldn't hold any interviews at that time," said Mattei. "I was only eleven when Palme died. It was Mom who did the interrogating at home with us. I used to sit on the edge of my bed in my room, and Mom squatted down in front of me and held my hand. Besides, that colleague of ours did make an attempt. To be fair," said Mattei, nodding emphatically.

"Although he wasn't as sharp as we are," said Holt. "So he can just go to hell. An ordinary fucking pig."

"Guys," said Mattei, shrugging her shoulders. "There's only one thing you need them for."

What has happened to little Lisa? thought Holt. Is she becoming a grown woman?

"But not Johan, exactly," said Holt.

"No, not him," said Mattei. "He's actually good for several things. You can talk with him, and he's really good at cleaning and cooking too."

"Can he see around corners too?" asked Holt for some reason.

"No," said Mattei and sighed. "Only Johansson can."

Not quite yet, perhaps, thought Holt.

77

The day after the meeting at the Turing Society Johansson decided to figure out who had dissuaded private banker Theo Tischler from investing his personal money in the pursuit of Olof Palme's murderer. It was just a sudden impulse, and as so often before he immediately gave in to it. Whatever this might be good for, really, he thought as he called the woman he wanted to talk with.

"I would like to speak with attorney Helena Stein," said Johansson as soon as her secretary answered.

"Who may I say is calling?" asked the secretary.

"My name is Lars Martin Johansson," said Johansson.

"What does this concern?" asked the secretary.

"We know each other," said Johansson. "Say hello to her and ask if I can meet her. Preferably immediately."

"One moment," said the secretary.

Know each other, thought Johansson. That's one way to put it. To be exact he'd spoken with her only once before. Just over seven years ago, when he was operations head of the secret police and responsible for carrying out a background check, because then undersecretary Helena Stein was going to be appointed minister of defense. At the time he discovered that she had a history that threatened to catch up with her after twenty-five years and would definitely put an end to her political career. He regretted having made this discovery and then congratulated himself for having rescued her from a fate that would have been considerably worse than that. In another time, when both she and he had been living another life.

"The attorney says it will be fine in half an hour, at her office," the secretary reported.

"Thanks," said Johansson, hanging up.

The office was on Sibyllegatan in Östermalm. A large, old-fashioned apartment with considerable space between the wall panels and the ceiling frieze. Painstakingly remodeled as a law office, which judging by the nameplate on the door she shared with three associates. A very stylish woman received him. She even managed to nod amiably and smile while being forced to mobilize all her strength to do so.

"Let me say one thing before we start," said Johansson as soon as he sat down in the chair in front of her desk. "My visit with you here today has nothing whatsoever to do with that story we talked about the last time we met. So you can put your mind at rest."

"So it shows that clearly," said Helena Stein. Then she smiled again and this time it was for real.

"I need your help," said Johansson.

"I'll be happy to help you if I can," said Helena Stein.

Then Johansson told her about his errand. Obviously without going into what it was really about. About why her cousin, the private banker Theo Tischler, decided not to give money to support Hans Holmér's private investigation of the Kurds' involvement in the murder of Olof Palme. Had Theo Tischler possibly consulted with her? A high-ranking member of the Social Democratic Party. A senior official with close ties to the government. It would be easy enough for someone like Stein to figure out what he was really looking for, thought Johansson as soon as he stopped talking.

"Holmér," said Stein, shaking her head with surprise. "When would this have been?"

"In the spring of 1987," said Johansson. A few months after he was fired, he thought.

"No," said Helena Stein. "If Theo says that, then he remembers wrong. It was much later that he came to me and wanted to talk about

it. Many years after Hans Holmér disappeared from the Palme investigation. In the spring of 1987 there was no reason to ask me for advice about
such things. I was an ordinary, newly hatched attorney who was working at a law firm. I've heard gossip about that in the family, that Holmér
wanted money from Theo, but that the whole thing ran into the sand
like so many of Theo's impulses and ideas."

"Do you remember when that was? When he asked you for advice?"

"Much later," said Stein. "Must have been in the late nineties. I was
undersecretary, that I remember. At a guess, 1999. Just a year or so before
you and I met, by the way."

"I've forgotten that time," said Johansson. "Tell me. What did your
cousin want? What advice did you give him?"

"He and one of his many friends, a very remarkable man by the
way and one of the richest in this country, much richer than Theo, had
apparently decided to let so-called market forces work to try to put some
order into the Palme investigation, given that our public judicial authorities had so sadly failed. Neither of them was a Social Democrat exactly,
to put it mildly, but that thing with the murder of Palme, and perhaps
even more the police fiasco, they both took very much to heart. So what
do you do in the world where Theo and his good friend live? You invest
a billion, buy up the best there is in individuals, equipment, knowledge,
and contacts and set about solving the problem. It's no more difficult
than that."

"This friend," said Johansson. "Theo's good friend. He doesn't have
a name?"

"Yes," said Helena Stein. "I'm sure you've already figured out who
I'm talking about. The problem is that he's been dead for several years.
Another problem is that I liked him very much. He was one of the most
remarkable men I've ever met and in a positive sense. So I don't know. I
get the feeling I've gossiped enough about him already."

"Jan Stenbeck," said Johansson. Sweden's answer to Howard Hughes,
he thought.

"Jan Hugo," said Helena Stein with a streak of melancholy in her
cool smile. "Who else, by the way, in the Sweden we're living in? But
it was actually not the case that it was my advice he and Theo wanted.

What could I have contributed where the murder of Olof Palme was concerned? In a purely factual sense, I mean."

"So what did he want from you?" said Johansson.

"They wanted to make contact with my lover at the time. Or boyfriend, as someone like that is called nowadays, regardless of age and emotional heat."

"So what did they want from him?" asked Johansson, who had already figured out his name.

"They wanted him to start working for them. Lead their private investigation. With basically unlimited resources, because he was the best they could possibly imagine."

"But personally he preferred to remain in the vicinity of the prime minister," said Johansson. So at least that got said, he thought.

"Yes, and because you know him I'm sure you can imagine how he formulated the matter."

"No. Tell me," said Johansson, sounding more amused than he intended.

"If I can be very brief, he wasn't particularly happy about Theo. I want to think he said that if he did have the power that all ignoramuses ascribed to him, then for starters he wouldn't have hesitated a minute to ensure that the authorities had my cousin Theo executed. With a dull, rusty broadax."

"I've heard tell of that broadax," said Johansson. "Just to see if I've understood this correctly. I already knew that Theo Tischler is your cousin. That you had a relationship with our own Richelieu was news to me. I didn't know you knew Jan Stenbeck either."

"People like us know one another. It's no more complicated than that," Helena Stein observed with a slight inclination of her slender neck.

"Though it never came to anything," she continued, shaking her head. "He talked with Jan and told him that he should hang on to his money. That this particular investment was a complete waste. He obviously refused to speak with Theo. He had no problem talking with Jan Stenbeck. They'd probably known each other forever and had numerous interests in common, which weren't limited to food and drink."

"He dissuaded Stenbeck," Johansson reminded her. "Why did he do that? Why was it a complete waste?"

"Because the murder of Olof Palme was already solved," said Helena Stein. "He already knew who the perpetrators were and why they had the prime minister assassinated. Out of concern for Sweden's interests it was best for all of us that we continue living in uncertainty."

"Did he say that to you?" said Johansson with surprise. Wonder just what he'd been stuffing himself with that time? he thought.

"Not to me," said Helena Stein, shaking her head. "He would never dream of doing that. On the other hand he said it to his good friend Jan. To my good friend too, for that matter. My very good friend, to be precise. He in turn told me only a month or so before he died. On the other hand what that would have been about in factual terms he didn't know. So when he in turn talked with Theo back then, he just said that he was tired of the whole idea. Not a word about why."

"No," said Johansson. We didn't have such luck, he thought.

"If it really is like that, what happened was probably best. That he didn't talk with Theo, because then all the rest of us would have read about it in *Expressen* the following day, I mean. Theo is not exactly discreet. Or do you think I'm attaching too much significance to my personal experience?"

"Not really," said Johansson with more emphasis than he intended, because his thoughts were already elsewhere. How do you go about holding an interview with a legendary Swedish multibillionaire who died five years ago? thought Lars Martin Johansson. Trying to question the special adviser was inconceivable. Regardless of whether he was alive or dead, and especially if there was anything to what Helena Stein had just said.

Though it can hardly have been out of concern for the completely inconsequential Christer Pettersson that he gave such advice to Jan Hugo Stenbeck, thought Johansson as he sat in the taxi on the way back to his office.

78

Hedberg's parents were dead. He had never been married. Had no children. None that were in the records, at any rate. What remained was his younger sister. Birgitta Hedberg, age sixty. Also single with no children. Lived in a condominium with three rooms and a kitchen on Andersvägen in Solna. The same apartment in which Hedberg had lived previously, before he reported that he had moved out of Sweden.

It'll have to do, thought Jan Lewin, for he had to start somewhere.

Hedberg's sister had worked as a secretary at a large construction firm until four years ago when she took early retirement after a car accident. As she drove her boss to a conference in Södermanland her car had been rear-ended; she suffered whiplash and became unable to work. The general pension system took over and gave her early retirement. Her employer and the insurance company added another couple million in damages for her suffering, and this was possibly the main reason that her assessed net worth came to over five million kronor in bank deposits, interest-bearing bonds, and fund shares.

Although perhaps not, thought Jan Lewin. Even before the insurance money was disbursed, she had reported assets of just under three million, and with the salary she had been drawing this seemed like quite a bit to Lewin.

A frugal life, good investments, a rich lover, or perhaps simply an older brother she helped by taking care of his money, thought Jan Lewin. The same brother who according to Johansson was supposed to have robbed the post office on Dalagatan in May of 1977 of 295,000 kronor. Five years' salary before tax for a detective inspector at that time. Lewin knew that as well as Johansson, because he had been working at the homicide squad when it happened and even remembered the case. Over thirty years later, this corresponded to almost two million, still five years' salary before tax for a detective inspector, thought Lewin, making a note of it.

If it's the case that she's acting as the bank for her brother, then they must have contact with each other, thought Lewin. Even if it isn't, she may be communicating with him anyway, he thought, even though sibling affection was unknown territory for someone like him.

Then he proceeded to fill out all the forms that were needed so he could make the usual checks on her in the registries that were at the disposal of the police, and he concluded that part by requesting a telephone check on her. So far everything had been routine, and there was still the more creative aspect to tackle before it was time to go home.

First he found a picture of her. Fortunately it was a current one, taken when she renewed her passport in February earlier that year. It showed a dark-haired woman in her sixties with her hair pulled back in a tight bun, regular facial features, straight nose, prominent jawline and chin, dark, vigilant eyes. Looks good, thought Jan Lewin. If it weren't for that austere, vigilant expression. Wrong, he thought. She looks mean.

Passport, foreign travels, credit cards, travel bureaus. Start with the credit cards, and if that doesn't produce anything, then check the travel bureaus in the area where she lives, wrote Jan Lewin.

Whiplash injury, disability pension, home help, complaints? Talk with home services, Lewin noted. If she's the way she seems in the picture, they'll probably remember her, he thought.

Then he wrote out his usual to-do list on his computer, for otherwise he wouldn't have been Jan Lewin. For the same reason he read it three times, added to it, deleted, changed and changed back again, before with a deep sigh he was finally ready to send it to Johansson. Then he shook his head meditatively once again. It was the fifteenth and final point that worried him, "Question Birgitta Hedberg?" It feels completely wrong, thought Jan Lewin.

First he deleted the question mark and then, after further pondering, the entire short sentence. Finally he replaced it with a new one. "Suggest that we wait as long as possible before questioning Hedberg's sister," wrote Lewin. Breathing deeply, he nodded and pushed the send button as the last official action of another day of all the days that made up his life.

Wise, thought Johansson ten minutes later when he was sitting in front of his computer reading what Lewin had written. Not only wise but necessary, he thought, if there was something in what Helena Stein had told him. Then he called in half a dozen of his most taciturn co-workers and gave them some quick instructions.

"Questions," said Johansson, letting his gaze sweep over the group.

They all shook their heads, three had already stood up, and colleague Rogersson had even managed to open the door on his way out.

"Good," said Johansson. "Get going."

Then he asked his secretary to immediately contact his counterpart with the Spanish national police, Guardia Civil, at their headquarters in Madrid. His Spanish colleague called back within fifteen minutes. Johansson told him in a suitably roundabout way about his errand and was promised all the help that matters of that nature required. Or more, if that were to prove necessary.

Never bad to have a few contacts, thought Johansson as he hung up and for some reason happened to think about the back room in that pleasant bar in Lyons. The bar where he and other really big owls some-times had the privilege of being nighthawks together.

All the strategic planning had taken him only a little more than an hour. Obviously without having said a word about it to Lewin, Mattei, and least of all to Holt, because he now found himself in a situation where the one hand shouldn't know what the other hand was up to. That was well and good, as long as he alone was guiding both.

Further information will be given on a need to know basis, thought Johansson contentedly. As he leaned back in his chair for some reason the one person he was thinking about was Anna Holt.

79

Lisa Mattei also looked at the pictures of Hedberg and his family that Johansson had distributed, and true to her systematic disposition she started with the ones who were already dead. Master pilot Einar Göran Hedberg, born in 1906, died in 1971 at the age of sixty-five. Then his wife, Ingrid Cecilia, born in 1924. She was eighteen years younger than the man she married the same year she gave birth to his son. Died in 1964, at the age of only forty.

He doesn't look nice, thought Mattei as she considered the Hedbergs' wedding picture. Einar Hedberg dressed in the ship pilot uniform, standing at an angle behind his wife, broad-shouldered, more than a head taller than she was. He would have looked good if it hadn't been for the vigilant expression, the absence of a smile, his military posture and body language.

His wife, Cecilia. That was apparently what she was called. Small, dainty, cute, anxiously smiling at the camera. Gaze directed a little to the right, and her husband's hand heavily protective as it rested on her shoulder.

Wonder what he did to her? thought Lisa Mattei.

Einar Hedberg seemed to have been a man accustomed to ruling over other people's lives, who not only piloted shipping vessels past shoals, reefs, and islets through narrow passages in the Stockholm archipelago. His obituary in *Norrtelje Tidning* mentioned his natural leadership qualities, his firmness of principle, and his considerable nautical and maritime knowledge. His "prematurely departed wife" had "stood faithfully by his side" in life, and if he was now mourned and missed in death, it did not appear so from his obituary notice. Einar Hedberg had "two surviving adult children," and there was nothing more than that.

Wonder what he did to them, thought Lisa Mattei.

Regardless of what the master pilot did to his two children, judging by Johansson's pictures things seemed to have turned out differently. If he had done anything, that is, thought the meticulous Lisa Mattei, aware as she was that pictures could be just as treacherous as words.

Among the ones she got from Johansson, four class photos from the comprehensive school in Vaxholm were included. Big brother Kjell Göran with teacher and schoolmates when he started first grade, and the same arrangement right before he left ninth grade and finished his studies. Corresponding pictures of his little sister, Birgitta, who went to the same school. There was a striking physical family resemblance between the siblings, especially if you knew what the parents looked like, but their similarities also ended there. It was their attitude to the outside world and the camera that set them apart.

The seven-year-old Kjell Göran Hedberg was a sturdy little thing who calmly observed the photographer. In contrast to the majority of his classmates, he did not smile. He observed what was happening, and what he saw did not seem to bother him in the least. His sister did not smile either, but because she seemed to have inherited their father's vigilant eyes, she looked almost suspicious.

The same slightly curly, dark hair, same brown eyes and harmonious facial features. Kjell Göran with his hair neatly parted on the side despite the curls. Sister Birgitta with a bow in her hair. The same neat clothes to which their mother, Cecilia, must have devoted considerable effort as she sat in front of the sewing basket in the parlor or in the laundry room down in the basement. But quite different expressions. Big brother ready to meet the world on his own terms, even though he was only seven years old and a handsbreadth tall. His little sister, always ready to defend herself against the same world, regardless of what it might be willing to offer her.

Nine years later little seemed to have changed. A sixteen-year-old

Kjell Göran in the center of the picture. As tall as the tallest of his male classmates, with broad shoulders, a narrow waist, and his arms crossed over his chest. With the help of a comb and Brylcreem, the slightly curly hair was replaced with a wavy black Elvis hairstyle, according to the custom of the time. The gaze was the same—calm, observant— but because he now permitted himself a slight smile he almost seemed amusedly indulgent about what was happening. Not so his sister. The long hair arranged in a ponytail, no bow anymore, but although in an objective sense she ought to have been the cutest of all the girls in her class, she could only offer the camera the same suspicious, dark eyes.

He must have treated them quite differently, thought Lisa Mattei.

80

School transcripts, thought Lisa Mattei as she closed the file of pictures of Kjell Göran Hedberg and his relatives. I have to see his transcript, she thought, and only five minutes later she was sitting with Police Superintendent Wiklander, head of the bureau's CIS squad, and in ordinary cases also her immediate superior.

"Transcripts? You want to see Hedberg's transcripts," Wiklander repeated, nodding at Mattei. "A strange coincidence," he observed, nodding again.

"What do you mean, coincidence?"

"A few days ago when our esteemed boss and I were discussing what data we should pull about Hedberg, for some reason he mentioned his transcripts."

"I see, he did."

"Yes. I remember that he said something along the lines of that perhaps it's best to pull his transcripts too. Not because he thought they seemed particularly interesting, in context, but mostly not to make you sad when you came and asked about them. And he probably did it because he really can see around corners."

"So that's what he said," said Mattei.

"Exactly that," said Wiklander. He sighed contentedly and handed over a thin plastic sleeve of papers. "Dear Hedberg doesn't seem to have been a typical intellectual. More like an ordinary, practical minded nobody, so perhaps you shouldn't expect a communion of souls."

"Thanks," said Mattei, getting up.

"No problem," said Wiklander, shrugging his shoulders. "Before you run off I have a message for you too. From Johansson."

"I'm listening," said Mattei.

"That you're not allowed to talk with Hedberg's teachers, old classmates, or anyone whatsoever who can even be suspected of having known him. Not under any condition."

"That's what he said?"

"Exactly that," said Wiklander. "So drop any thought of that. Otherwise you'll have the devil to pay. Direct quote from our top boss. His orders. To be on the safe side, mine too."

"I hear you," said Mattei, nodded curtly and left.

From an educational standpoint Kjell Göran Hedberg belonged to a long lost generation. During the nine years he went to school in Vaxholm, he got grades after every completed semester—nine years and eighteen semesters. Grades on a seven-degree scale, where a capital A summarized total success and a C complete failure, which to be on the safe side were supplemented by statistics that showed how everyone in the same class as Hedberg had done.

He was a typically mediocre student who was awarded B or Ba in almost all subjects. With the exception of history, metalworking/woodworking, and gymnastics including games and sports, the master pilot's son remained safely anchored within the class's median during his entire school career.

Already in his fourth year Hedberg got an AB in history, and along with two classmates shared the honorable first place. Two years later he had been raised to a small a, or "passed with distinction," which he then retained for the rest of his schooling. On the other hand, he lost first place. Statistics on the class's final grades showed that one of his classmates got a capital A, and that he was one of three who got a lowercase a.

I'll bet the others were girls, thought Lisa Mattei.

·   ·   ·

In metalworking and woodworking he was one of the better in the class and had an average of AB during his last three years in school. The same AB that gave him an honorable shared second place in woodshop and a shared ninth place overall. Of the first six places in the class, there were five needleworkers, divided into two capital and three small a's, but only one pitiful woodworker.

Wonder which ones they might have been, thought Mattei.

In gymnastics including games and sports Hedberg had been best in class throughout his time in school. With one strange exception that happened when he was in eighth grade. Already in fourth grade he had been the only one to earn a small a, and starting in grade five he had a capital A. With one exception. In the fall semester of eighth grade he dropped to a small a, which made him one of four. In the spring semester he got an AB and slipped down to a shared eighth place in a class with a total of twenty-four pupils. Then he found his way again. He received a capital A in the fall semester in ninth grade, and the only one with that grade when he finished the nine-year comprehensive school in Vaxholm in June of 1960.

Problems with puberty or something else, thought Lisa Mattei, and five minutes later she had already decided. She simply had to talk with Hedberg's old teacher. Regardless of Johansson, Wiklander, the devil, and all the other brethren who despite their worthless statistics tried to oppress her and her sisters.

Hedberg's teacher was named Ossian Grahn and he appeared in the class photo with Kjell Göran Hedberg and his classmates. A short man in his thirties with cheerful eyes and unruly blond hair. After fifteen minutes of the usual tapping on the computer, Lisa Mattei also knew most of what she needed to know about him.

Former secondary school teacher Ossian Grahn was born in 1930 and retired in 1995. He had been a widower for five years, with two grown children, lived in a single-family house on Båtmansvägen in Vaxholm, and was in the phone book with name, title, address, and number. A search on the Internet yielded a hundred hits besides and showed that Ossian seemed to be a very active retiree. Not only in the retirees' association in Vaxholm, where he had been on the board for many years, but also because of his intellectual interests. Interests that in the last five years alone had left traces in the form of three published writings. A book with the title *Boatmen and Peasants in Southern Roslagen*, where he was the sole author. An article in a larger work on Vaxholm's fortress. Another article, "Ancient Monuments in Roslagen," published as an offprint by the local historical society in collaboration with the municipality of Norrtälje.

He also answered the phone on the second ring.

In front of her Lisa Mattei saw a small, energetic retiree with cheerful eyes and unruly blond hair, which meant that playing with anything other than open cards was inconceivable.

"My name is Lisa Mattei," said Mattei. "I'm a police officer and work at the National Bureau of Criminal Investigation in Stockholm. I need to talk with you."

"Now I'm really curious," Grahn replied, sounding just as cheerful as his photo promised. "When did you have in mind?"

"Preferably right away," said Lisa Mattei.

"Shall we say in an hour?" said Grahn. "Because I'm assuming you drive a car and work in that ugly big brown building on Kungsholmen in Stockholm. The one you always see on TV as soon as some poor soul gets in trouble."

Lisa Mattei gathered up the papers she thought she would need with the class photo from 1960 at the top of the pile, borrowed a service vehicle, drove to Vaxholm, and met former secondary schoolteacher Ossian Grahn. He was seventy-seven, but judging by his eyes not a day older than in Mattei's almost fifty-year-old photo. The same Ossian Grahn who won her heart as soon as they sat down in his tidy living room and he served her the first cup of coffee.

"A question out of curiosity," said Grahn. "Is this Detective Inspector Lisa Mattei or Doctor of Philosophy Lisa Mattei who does me this honor? I looked you up on the Internet, in case you're wondering."

"Good question," said Mattei. "I actually think you're having a visit from both."

Then Mattei took out the class photo from 1960. The same photo that aroused Dr. Mattei's curiosity and made her want to ask certain questions. For reasons that inspector Mattei unfortunately was prevented from going into more closely, but which essentially concerned one of his pupils in the graduating class at Vaxholm school in 1960.

"I brought the class photo with me," said Lisa Mattei, giving it to him.

"There's one thing you should know, Lisa," said Ossian Grahn. "I was a teacher for over forty years. I have had thousands of pupils over the years. As far as this class is concerned I want to recall that I was their classroom teacher for three years, in grades seven, eight, and nine. I had them in Swedish and history, and one more reason I remember that is that the same autumn I started working at Norra Latin in Stockholm. It was there I got my first permanent position as an assistant principal."

"Do you remember any of the ones in the picture?" asked Mattei.

"Two," said Ossian Grahn. "And I sincerely hope it's not Gertrud who's the reason I've had a visit from Detective Inspector Lisa Mattei."

Gertrud stood in the back row to the left. Cute and well-dressed with long dark hair hanging over her shoulders. A shy smile toward the camera, fifteen years old but judging by her eyes considerably more mature than that. A father who owned the ICA grocery store in the middle of town and a mother who was a teacher and colleague of Ossian Grahn. She was one pupil among the thousands he had taught during a long life as a teacher.

"One of the best pupils I've ever had," Ossian Grahn observed. "If we're talking about such simple accomplishments as those that can be summarized in so-called grades," he added.

"More then," said Mattei.

"Gertrud is a very remarkable individual," said Grahn. "She's something as rare as a very charming person. She is educated, she is talented, and she is both kind and decent to others. She's good-looking too. Always has been, by the way. I've known her since she was a little girl."

"Do you still see her?"

"She's a doctor. Head of the district medical center here in Vaxholm," said Grahn. "Until a few years ago she worked at Karolinska in Stockholm, but then her new husband got sick and took early retirement and she moved back here. They actually live just a few blocks away. In her parents' old house, by the way. We usually say hi to each other a few times a week. Her name is now Rosenberg. Since she remarried. Her new husband also worked as a doctor. Although now he's on a disability pension, as I said."

"I didn't come here to talk about Gertrud," said Lisa Mattei. "Who was the other one who—"

"Let me guess," said Ossian Grahn. "You've come here to talk about Kjell? About Kjell Hedberg."

"Why do you think that? Why do you remember him?"

"Usually there are two kinds of pupils that someone like me remembers. On the one hand those like Gertrud, whom you always remember with joy, and there are not all that many of them, you should know. Yes, and then there are your problem children. And unfortunately there are usually quite a few more of them. Ordinary rowdy kids, although some of them can be really charming, and, unfortunately, there is the occasional little gangster. But the great majority of them were only the kind you really felt sorry for."

"Hedberg was a rowdy kid?" asked Mattei. Let's start there, she thought, because it was the last thing she could imagine.

"If it had only been that good," said Grahn, shaking his unruly light hair.

"It was worse than that?" said Mattei. Now this is starting to resemble something, she thought.

"I hope he was unique," said Grahn, squirming uneasily in his chair.

"What do you mean by that?"

"Kjell Hedberg is actually the only pupil, during my entire life as a teacher, that I was afraid of. Even though he never misbehaved. Not in my class in any event. Even though I was his homeroom teacher and even though I was twice his age. There was something about his eyes and his body language, his way of looking at you, that could be terrifying, to put it bluntly. As soon as something didn't suit him."

"Now I'm the one who's getting curious," said Mattei. "You have to explain."

"I don't think it's as simple as that he was an evil person. No fifteen-year-old is evil in that way. I think they only get that way later in life."

"So what was it?"

"I think he didn't understand the difference between good and bad," said Grahn. "The only thing that meant anything in Kjell's world was how he perceived you and whether he thought you were against him. It was probably my good luck that I instructed him in his favorite subject, history."

"He was interested in history?"

"Yes, in the way the very worst sorts are. He could rattle off lists of monarchs like running water even if you woke him up in the middle of the night. He knew the time and place of every battle, and his view of history was frankly deplorable. It was only about major personalities. Alexander the Great, Hannibal and Caesar, Gustavus Adolphus and Charles XII, Napoleon and Hitler. Great men who determined the fate of the world and in passing, so to speak, gave content and meaning to the lives of the rest of us ordinary mortals. I remember when we were reading about Gustav III. He came up to me after a lecture and told me that he was convinced that Gustav III was homosexual. He already knew that Gustav V had been. His father, the master pilot, told him that. About the old king who tried to rape his chauffeur, who drove into the ditch and nearly killed them both. Who had a curve in the road south of Stockholm named after him . . . I tried to reassure him by pointing out that they were not even related to each other."

"So how did he take that?"

"He had some long explanation about this being due to the inbreeding in our royal family. He knew they weren't related, naturally. It was about some kind of genetic depletion, and that one reason Gustav III had been shot was that it had been discovered that he was homosexual."

"But he still got a small a as a final grade."

"Yes, he did," Ossian Grahn observed and sighed. "It was mostly that he knew those lists of monarchs and all the dates, and then I guess I was cowardly, to put it simply."

"His grades in gymnastics," said Mattei. "Something happened there when he was in eighth grade. Is that something you remember?"

"Yes," sighed Ossian Grahn. "I was his homeroom teacher, so I got more than my allotted share of that story. From Kjell, his father the pilot, and his gymnastics teacher."

"So what happened?"

"When Kjell started eighth grade he got a new teacher, and already in the first class they were quarreling like two roosters in a henhouse that's too small."

"Why?"

"If you ask me I think it was because they were too much alike. Not that I know much about gymnastics and sports and such, but Kjell probably deserved the grades he always got. Considering his age he was unbelievably agile and strong. Best in school in soccer, handball, and ice hockey. Not to mention running and swimming and everything else."

"Was there anything in particular that happened?"

"I think the whole thing started when our school team was playing soccer against the team from Vallentuna. It was at the start of the fall semester. Kjell's new gymnastics teacher was the coach, and in some situation things must have heated up between them. One thing led to another, and in the first half his teacher told him to leave the field and sent in one of his teammates instead. Kjell seems to have gone straight to the dressing room, showered, changed, and hitchhiked home to Vaxholm. That's the way it was. Constant controversies."

"But the last year in school he was back on track again," Mattei observed. "I noticed he got his capital A back in the fall semester. Were they finally on good terms?"

"No," said Ossian Grahn, shaking his head. "He got a new teacher he got along with better."

"So what happened to the other one?"

"He was forced to quit," said Ossian Grahn.

"Quit? Why?"

"Only a few days before the fall semester was to begin he was in a serious car accident. He lived a few miles north of Vaxholm, out by Österåker, and one morning when he was driving to school to attend a meeting, where the teaching staff was getting ready for the start of the semester, he was in an accident. Drove into the ditch. It could have been really bad. Severe concussion and a number of broken bones. He was in the hospital for several months and he never came back to us."

"So what happened?"

"He seems to have lost a front wheel," said Ossian Grahn. "True, he drove like a maniac, but there was a lot of talk."

"About Kjell Hedberg?"

"Not as far as I recall," said Ossian Grahn, shaking his head. "He was only sixteen years old. It was the usual gossip about infidelity and jealousy, here and there. There was a lot of that out here in the country, you know. At the same time I have the definite impression that the police here wrote it off as an ordinary accident. That he is supposed to have been careless when he changed the tires on his car. Didn't tighten the lug nuts properly. You know what," said Ossian Grahn, looking seriously at Mattei, "perhaps you should talk with Gertrud, since you're here anyway. I'll give you her number."

"With Gertrud Rosenberg? About the car accident?"

"No," said Ossian Grahn, shaking his head. "If it were only that good."

81

The devil can stick it up his you-know-what, thought a contented Lisa Mattei as she drove onto the highway toward Stockholm three hours later. At the same moment her cell phone rang.

"My office in half an hour," said Johansson, sounding like he meant it.

"You have to give me at least an hour, boss," said Mattei. Goodness, she thought.

"For Christ's sake, it doesn't take an hour to drive from Vaxholm," said Johansson.

Goodness, goodness, thought Mattci.

"There's a lot of traffic, actually, and driving is not exactly my strong suit," Mattei lied.

"My office," said Johansson. "As soon as you set foot in the building go straight to my office," he repeated, whereupon he hung up without further ado.

We'll cross that bridge when we come to it, thought Mattei, giving it a little extra gas to manage what she intended to do before she met her top boss.

It's the first time I've ever seen him furious, she thought a little more than an hour later when she sat down in the visitor's chair in front of his large desk.

"How did you know I was out in Vaxholm, boss?" she asked.

"Our colleague Wiklander happened to see you down in the garage. Don't come in here and say you don't know we have GPS and tracking equipment nowadays in almost all our vehicles. I know to the last inch what you've been up to."

Didn't think of that, thought Mattei, shaking her head strenuously to stop the attack of the giggles she felt was on its way.

"You've been parked for over five hours outside Båtmansvägen 3 in Vaxholm, and I assume it's pure chance that Kjell Göran Hedberg's old homeroom teacher—that light-haired little bastard who looks like his pupils in that photo I was stupid enough to send you—has lived at the same address his whole life."

"I actually had no idea about that," said Lisa Mattei. That he'd lived there his whole life, that is.

"Forget about that now," said Johansson, glaring at her acidly. "Despite what both I and Wiklander said to you, you've been sitting chatting with him for hours. Despite the most obvious risk of a leak. What do you know about him and Hedberg? Maybe they've been involved since they met in junior high?"

"I don't think they've spoken to each other, actually. Not since Hedberg finished school."

"No," said Johansson. "And why do you think that?"

"I talked with one of Hedberg's classmates too. She was pretty convinced it was that way."

"You did what?" said Johansson, looking at her in amazement. She's sitting here fucking with me, he thought.

"I talked with one of his classmates," Mattei repeated. "She lived right in the vicinity, so I left my car and walked to her house. In case Wiklander wonders," she clarified.

"I hope," said Johansson. "I hope . . . that you have an extremely good explanation," he repeated, leaning heavily on his elbows.

"It's actually better than that," said Lisa Mattei.

"Lisa, Lisa," sighed Johansson half an hour later. "What am I going to do with you?"

"I was hoping for another gold star," said Lisa Mattei. "A giant one," she clarified.

82

The following morning the transcript of the interview with district physician Gertrud Rosenberg, born in 1945, was on Johansson's large desk.

The interview had been held in her home in Vaxholm. The interview leader was Detective Inspector Lisa Mattei. It was recorded on tape and already approved by the woman she had interviewed the day before. It took less than an hour to conduct, according to the times listed on the report. It was introduced with a brief summary by Mattei and concluded with her conveying to Gertrud Rosenberg a so-called disclosure prohibition.

Gertrud Rosenberg states by way of introduction and in summary in part the following.

She was a classmate of Kjell Göran Hedberg from the seventh to ninth grades in the comprehensive school in Vaxholm, from September 1957 until the beginning of June 1960. After completion of public school, Gertrud began at the high school in Djursholm. There she got her diploma in natural sciences with a biology major in May of 1963, after which she was admitted to the medical school at Karolinska Institute in September of the same year. In connection with this she also, about six months later, moved to a student apartment in Östermalm in Stockholm. Gertrud got her MD degree and was certified as a physician in June of 1970.

According to what she states, Kjell Göran Hedberg started as an apprentice at a small shipyard and boat builder in Vaxholm when he finished school in the summer of 1960. Because they were neighbors in Vaxholm, up to the middle of the sixties, they ran into each other regularly when they were in town, seeing mutual friends, etc. She has not had any closer association with Hedberg, however, neither during their time in school nor later. At the same time they have never been enemies and always talked with each other the few times they happened to meet.

During the following years they met more seldom. She knows however that he started at the police academy in the mid-sixties and became a policeman a few years later. It was her parents who told her that. Sometime in the early seventies, when she was working at the emergency room at Södersjukhuset, she saw Hedberg and an associate of his who were then working as patrol officers in Stockholm. On the occasion in question they brought in an intoxicated individual who had been knifed. On the same occasion they also had a cup of coffee together and exchanged phone numbers. The reason for the latter was that she and her husband at the time were thinking about buying a sailboat and she took the opportunity to ask Hedberg for advice because she knew he had worked at shipyards before and had some contacts in the boat business. No renewed contact on account of this was made, however.

Thereafter it was almost ten years before she encountered Kjell Göran Hedberg again. On a summer evening sometime in the late seventies when she and her husband at the time visited the hotel in Vaxholm to have dinner. Hedberg was there for the same reason, together with a woman she was surely introduced to but whose name she does not recall. On the other hand she remembers that he mentioned then that he was working at SePo.

The last time she met Kjell Göran Hedberg was about eleven o'clock in the evening, on Friday the twenty-eighth of February 1986, on Sveavägen in Stockholm.

LISA MATTEI: Tell me about the last time you saw Kjell Göran Hedberg. In as much detail as possible.
GERTRUD ROSENBERG: As I said to you earlier it was the same evening that Palme was shot. On that point I'm quite certain. I and the person I was with were walking on Sveavägen heading north. We'd had dinner at a restaurant by Kungsträdgården. We had booked a

room at a hotel by Tegnérlunden. There were a lot of people walking in the opposite direction. The movie theaters had just closed, which was probably why. Considering that we were actually both married to other people plus he was my boss, we chose to turn off to the left onto Adolf Fredriks Kyrkogata where there weren't so many people. So as not to run into anyone we knew. It was right then that I saw Kjell. At the intersection between Sveavägen and Adolf Fredriks Kyrkogata. Right by the hot dog stand that's there. On the same side of the street as the church and the cemetery. Just as we'd turned onto the cross street, he entered the crosswalk headed in the direction of Kungsgatan. So I saw him from the side at an angle at a distance of five or six yards, and as I already told you I have excellent vision in both eyes.

LISA MATTEI: And the time was . . .

GERTRUD ROSENBERG: Well past eleven. You see, we left the restaurant right after eleven, that I remember. Say it took perhaps fifteen minutes to walk to where we saw him. The weather was terrible so we were walking fast. We were in love, too, so I guess we were in a hurry to get back to our hotel room.

LISA MATTEI: A quarter past eleven?

GERTRUD ROSENBERG: Yes. A quarter past eleven. Not earlier.

LISA MATTEI: You're certain it was Kjell Hedberg you saw?

GERTRUD ROSENBERG: Spontaneously, yes. I was even about to say hi to him. At the same moment it struck me that perhaps that wasn't so suitable, considering that he had actually met my husband. Although you should know that I hesitated, went back and forth. Quite a while, then I decided that I'd only seen someone who looked like Kjell. Considering what happened, that is.

LISA MATTEI: Did he see you?

GERTRUD ROSENBERG: I really don't think so. He was walking fast. Seemed to have his attention directed at the other side of the street. Sveavägen that is.

LISA MATTEI: At the same time as he's walking straight ahead? In the opposite direction, toward Kungsgatan and at a brisk pace?

GERTRUD ROSENBERG: Yes. It was the way he walked too. Typical

Kjell. He was like that. Good condition, goal-oriented, always had his eyes open. The clothes were also Kjell, in some way. A practical, somewhat longer jacket. Dark winter model. Dark gray pants, not jeans, certainly proper shoes on his feet even though I didn't think about that. Nicely and practically dressed. That was Kjell to a T if I may say so . . .

"She's out getting a little on the side?" asked Johansson, looking up from the papers he had in his hand and at Mattei.

"Yes," said Mattei. "She and her boss. For a month by then. Married to other people. She was living on Kungsholmen with her husband and two children. He was living in Östermalm with his wife. Fifteen years older than her, so his kids had left the nest. Officially he was at a conference in Denmark. His wife was probably at home. Our witness, on the other hand, was a grass widow. Her husband had taken the children and gone to the mountains during sports week."

"So why didn't they go to her place?"

"I asked her that. She didn't want to. Thought there was a boundary there."

"Yes, I suppose there is," sighed Johansson. "So instead they go to Hotel Tegnér up by Tegnérlunden."

"Which I guess we should be happy about," Mattei observed.

"Why?" wondered Johansson.

"I haven't had time to tell you yet, but I found the hotel booking this morning. It was in one of those old boxes that Jan always sighs about. One of a couple of thousand hotel reservations that were never processed. Gertrud Lindberg, that's her maiden name, had reserved a double room for one night. Did it the day before, by phone. Gives her parents' address in Vaxholm."

"Who would have ever thought of her if they had rooted through those piles of papers?" sighed Johansson. "So why did she wait so long before she got in touch with us?" said Johansson. "Before she contacted our dear colleagues if I were to put it correctly."

"It's in the interview," said Lisa Mattei.

"I know," sighed Johansson. "Help an old man."

stop with the sighing already

499

"The reason she didn't make contact immediately was not that she'd been 'getting a little on the side.' That's not the decisive reason, and there I actually believe her," said Mattei.

"So what's the reason?"

"That she didn't think she had anything to add. At that point in time she didn't have the slightest thought that Kjell Hedberg could have been involved in the murder. She didn't see the Palmes. No Christer Petters-son character either. Or anything else that was shady or strange. She didn't hear any shots. It was a Friday evening after payday, lots of people out in town to amuse themselves. Apparently also an old schoolmate of hers. Perhaps on his way to a secret mistress?"

"Not a peep about the historical moment?"

"Yes, actually. In the summer of 1986 she met her old teacher Ossian at a barbeque at her parents' house in Vaxholm. They sat down and talked and like so many others they naturally got around to the Palme assassination. Then she told him what she had seen."

"That she'd been out getting a little on the side and missed the Palme murder by a couple of minutes?"

"Yes. She and Ossian seem to talk about most everything. By then she'd also left her husband."

"You've also checked that?"

"Yes. Ossian tells the same story."

"Then she would also have mentioned Kjell Göran Hedberg?"

"Yes, although mostly as an amusing story. That it almost seemed like a class reunion there on Sveavägen."

"But it was not until the spring of 1989 that she made contact with the police," said Johansson.

"Yes, it's a pretty amazing story," said Mattei. "I've checked it too, and everything she says agrees with our own records."

"I can hardly contain myself," said Johansson, leaning back in his chair and lacing his hands over his belly.

First there's the thirty-three-year-old who was arrested fourteen days after the murder, and in that situation it did not even occur to their witness that Kjell Göran Hedberg had anything to do with the murder of the prime minister. Then there was the summer and fall of 1986 when "everyone knows it's the Kurds who murdered Palme." Obviously not a thought about him then either.

Not until a year later did she start to think about it. The Kurds were ruled out by that time. Instead the police track had come onto the agenda in earnest. For various reasons she decided not to make contact. She was no longer so certain that it was her old classmate she had seen. Two years had already passed since the murder, and why hadn't she made contact previously, in that case? To get help and support she talked with her old boss, and lover, about it.

"He did the wave, of course," said Johansson.

"According to our witness he asked if she meant to kill him. Personally he did not have the slightest memory that they had run into one of her old classmates. How could he have? He was in Denmark at a conference when Palme was murdered."

"And now the bastard is dead," Johansson guessed.

"Died in 1997. Heart attack. Checked." Mattei nodded. Dead a long time like most of the others, she thought.

"But in March of 1989 she got in touch with the investigation," said Johansson.

"Yes. But not to give a tip about Hedberg, but to report that she had not seen Christer Pettersson when Palme was shot."

"That she hadn't seen Christer Pettersson. She calls the Palme investigation to say that she hasn't seen Christer Pettersson?" This is getting better and better, thought Johansson.

Christer Pettersson has been in jail for several months, suspected of the murder of Olof Palme. At that point "everyone who knows anything worth knowing" also knows that he's the actual perpetrator. To eliminate the slightest doubt about the matter, the Palme investigation nonetheless puts out an appeal to that great detective, the general public. They say they are interested in speaking with "everyone who was in the area in question at the time in question." Regardless of whether they'd seen anything or not. Even if they hadn't seen anything, it might be just as interesting to the police as an eyewitness to the murder itself.

Because Gertrud Rosenberg has seen neither the Palmes nor Christer Pettersson—or even anyone who is the least bit like Christer Pettersson—she decides to unburden her heart and talk. She calls the telephone number she saw in the newspaper. Talks for almost ten minutes with one of the investigators in the Palme group. Tells what she hasn't seen, without saying a word about her old classmate. Her information ends up immediately in one of the many binders full of so-called crazy tips.

"I have a copy if you want to see it, boss," said Mattei. "It's a regular surveillance tip. Handwritten."

"I'm listening," said Johansson, shaking his head dejectedly.

"Okay," said Lisa Mattei. "This is what our colleague wrote. I quote. Informant states that she has not observed Christer Pettersson. In addition she states that she has not observed the Palmes either or made any other observations of interest at the time in question. End quote."

"Wasn't that the kind of witness they were looking for? Sounds like an almost ideal witness," said Johansson.

"The colleague who received it doesn't seem as enthused as you, boss."

"So what does he think?"

"Quote. Bag lady. Says she's a doctor. End quote."

"So she ends up in the loony binder."

"Yes, although a more judicious colleague apparently entered her as a witness in one of the computerized registries. That's where I found her."

"And then?" asked Johansson.

"Then she never made contact again," said Lisa Mattei. "I understand her. She gives a very vivid description of that conversation."

"Conclusion," said Johansson, looking urgently at Mattei.

"She links Hedberg to the scene of the crime in immediate connection to the time. Probably right before he crosses Sveavägen and positions himself and waits for Olof and Lisbeth at the corner of Tunnelgatan and Sveavägen."

"I think so too," said Johansson. "Besides, she's a doctor, not some ordinary dope fiend who has reason to hate Hedberg."

"Yes," said Lisa Mattei. Not an ordinary drug addict, she thought.

"Do you know what one of the foremost signs of a bad boss is?" said Johansson suddenly.

"No," said Mattei. Now it's coming, she thought.

"That he has favorites," said Johansson.

"So there won't be any more gold stars," said Mattei.

"Between us I guess there will be," said Johansson. "If you promise not to tell anyone."

"I promise," said Mattei.

"And never do it again."

"I promise."

83

Despite his convalescence, Bäckström had not been idle. Now a crisis situation prevailed, and in a crisis situation "danger in delay" always applied. Every real constable knew that, and Bäckström knew it better than all the rest. Once he had been close to missing an open goal, just because he hesitated a little unnecessarily. True, it had worked out in the end. Obviously—what else was to be expected when Bäckström was at the rudder? He didn't intend to risk it this time, regardless of what the good doctor was harping on about. That he'd suffered a heart attack, minor stroke, or in the worst case both. What can you expect from someone who makes a living by dealing with a lot of malingerers? thought Bäckström.

First he talked with his relative at the police union. He was still sitting like a kind of spider in the police web, gathering in all the information that his members picked up as they were running around town. It was reasonable that someone like him ought to have a few things to say about Palme and his sex life. Even though he hadn't been one of their associates.

"Palme," said his relative. "How the hell would I know that? He wasn't a cop."

"Our colleagues, then. They must have talked a lot of shit about Palme, didn't they?"

"You're calling to ask if our colleagues talked a lot of shit about Palme. Are you joking with me? Are you sick or what? You're wondering about the guy's sex life? I guess he was just like everyone else."

"It seems to be considerably worse than that," said Bäckström.

"I suppose he took the opportunity," said his relative. "Who the hell hasn't? Must be a real shooting gallery if you were in his position."

"See what you can find," said Bäckström. You incompetent union bigwig bastard, he thought, slamming down the receiver.

Then he connected to the Internet. This bottomless source of knowledge and cause for rejoicing. Pretty soon he'd also found quite a bit that was both heavy and serious. First a lot of information about a famous female singer his murder victim was supposed to have been involved with. A lady who didn't appear to be one to play around with, if you believed what you read about her on the Internet.

Then he found a crazy artist hag who apparently supported herself by taking nude pictures of herself that she then dabbed paint on and sold for big money. She had written an entire book about her rich love life, and most of it was apparently about Palme. At least according to the newspaper articles about the book.

Surely just the tip of the iceberg, thought Bäckström. The guy must have been sex crazy. And on the very next search he hit gold. Pure gold. A vein as thick as his own index finger.

Two journalists had written a revealing exposé a few years earlier. It was about the Brothel Madam and the major brothel scandal that shook the establishment in Stockholm in the mid-seventies. One of her most frequent customers was apparently the prime minister at the time, who moreover had the nerve to flagrantly exploit two underage prostitutes. One who had just turned fifteen and one who was only thirteen.

The net is closing in, thought Bäckström, and at the same moment his phone rang.

"Bäckström," said Bäckström with a suitable damper on his voice because the Eagle of History had just flown past and touched its wing to his forehead.

It was his relative at the union. He had dug around a little and for practical reasons started in the break room at work. There an old colleague who had worked with the uniformed police in Stockholm in the seventies told him that Palme had evidently been involved back then with Lauren Bacall.

"You know, that dame who was married to Humphrey Bogart," the relative explained.

"So how certain is that?" asked Bäckström. "That old lady must be a hundred?" At least, he thought.

Quite certain, according to his relative. Bacall had visited Stockholm and stayed at the Grand Hotel. Late at night she had a visit from the prime minister.

"So how certain is that?" Bäckström persisted. A hundred years old, he thought. He jumped from teenagers to hundred-year-olds? Must have been crazy perverse, thought Bäckström.

Quite certain, according to the colleague his cousin had talked with. You see, he'd been responsible for security during the celebrity visit and had personally seen to smuggling the prime minister in through the hotel staff entrance, to be as discreet as possible.

Definitely crazy perverse, thought Bäckström.

After that Bäckström proceeded to external surveillance, which he initiated with a visit to private banker Theo Tischler. Bäckström had met Tischler in connection with an old case he'd been in charge of. True, that was almost twenty years ago, but their meeting at that time had ended in the best manner and Tischler still remembered him.

"Sit yourself down, Bäckström," said Tischler, pointing to the large rococo armchair where he usually placed his visitors. "What can I help you with?"

Danger in delay, thought Bäckström, and chose to get right to the point.

"Friends of Cunt," said Bäckström. "Tell me about it."

"No foreplay, just right to it," said Tischler, smiling. "What do you want to know?"

"Everything," said Bäckström. "Everything that may be of interest," he clarified.

"Sure," said Tischler. Then he told him. Just like he always did, and often without even having been asked.

"That little pathological liar Claes Waltin was expelled. He brought the society's name into disrepute, so I was forced to kick him out."

"So how did he do that?" asked Bäckström, even though he already knew. "Did he beat up the ladies he hit on?"

"No, hell no, it was worse than that. He had a prick the size of Jiminy Cricket's," said Tischler. "What the hell do you think the ladies thought about that? What the hell would they think about the rest of us in the society? So he was thrown out on his ears. Clearly I couldn't associate with someone like that. Do you know what my buddies called me, by the way? When I was in the Sea Scouts?"

"No," said Bäckström.

Then Tischler told him about the Donkey, and even though Bäckström had asked to know everything, he was forced to stop Tischler an hour later.

"I think I have a clear picture," said Bäckström.

"Impossible," said Tischler. "Then you must have seen it."

"This Thulin," said Bäckström by way of diversion. "Do you have anything interesting about him?"

"You mean the Apostle of Aquavit," said Tischler. "Back then he drank like a Russian, and when he was loaded he started raving about his strong faith in God. Though now he has become a fine fellow."

"I've understood that," said Bäckström. "There seems to have been a trophy too," he said, looking slyly at his interview victim.

"Trophy? What could that have been?"

"One of those prize trophies that you awarded to the one who hit on the most ladies. Cuntmaster of the Year I think you called it."

"No," said Tischler, shaking his head. "What would we do with something like that? I guess we didn't need a trophy. I was always the one who won. Why should I award an expensive trophy to myself? All the bar tabs I had to pay were enough."

He got no further than that, and as soon as he was outside on the street again he hailed a taxi. On the way home he made a detour to the usual greasy spoon because his empty stomach was echoing seriously.

High time to put a little something in my craw, thought Bäckström, ordering a sausage with red beets and fried eggs, double pilsner and an ample shot, for the sake of his digestion. Then one thing led to another, and when he finally got home to his cozy pad he lay down on the couch in front of the TV and started flipping between all the new and interesting channels he'd acquired.

Everything has its time, said Bäckström, like the philosopher he was, and the internal surveillance on the members of the Friends of Cunt Society could profitably be put off until the morrow.

84

Bäckström was used to having to toil like a dog. Strictly speaking he'd done it his whole life as a policeman, even though he seldom got any reward for his efforts. Mostly shit, actually, from all his envious, feeble-minded colleagues. During the last week it had been worse than that. He had been tossed between external and internal detective work. Forced to sneak around in the basement of the police building and then at the next moment sit for hours in front of his computer, hold discreet meetings out in town where he had to carry on whispered conversations and pick up the tab; he was even forced to visit the archive at Swedish Radio to get a copy of an old TV program in which one of his suspects was standing in a gravel pit in Sörmland shooting wildly in all directions with a Magnum revolver.

He had exploited all his contacts, convinced, persuaded, threatened, begged, and pleaded. Called in services and return favors and was even forced to bribe an unusually corrupt colleague with a bottle of his best malt whiskey.

On Wednesday evening it was finally done, and as he stood there with his Magnum Opus in hand—the bundle of papers still wafting their agreeable aroma from his computer printer—it was as if some force, even stronger than himself, touched his great heart.

"The murder of Olof Palme. Crime analysis, perpetrator profiles, and possible motives. Memorandum prepared on September 26 by Detective Chief Inspector Evert Bäckström," Bäckström read out loud.

Finally done, thought Bäckström. And if he'd only been able to take care of the whole thing from the very beginning, all of the nation's innocent citizens would not have needed to hover in uncertainty for more than twenty years.

A conspiracy with four members. He had been clear about this early on, as soon as he got on the trail of that secret society. True to his systematic disposition it was also there that he started. By mapping out the roles that the various perpetrators had played. That Claes Waltin was the brain behind the murder was apparent. A high-ranking policeman with SePo who had full knowledge of what the murder victim was involved in. Who had been able to more or less plan the deed in every detail.

Once that part was finished, the others had been allowed to do their bit. Prosecutor and member of parliament Alf Thulin, who had full insight into what the Palme investigators were doing the whole time, could even manage them for long periods and take necessary misleading or evasive maneuvers as needed. That was also where the wealthy Theo Tischler came into the picture, to put out smoke screens and also dole out a lot of money as needed to the first investigation leader so that he could continue chasing the life out of a lot of crazy Kurds. Then he too had been fired.

Which left the well-known business attorney Sven Erik Sjöberg. What had been his task when Palme was murdered?

According to reliable witness reports from the crime scene, which were also supported by various technical investigations, the perpetrator who shot Palme was definitely at least six foot one.

Claes Waltin was too short. Only five foot eight, apart from everything else that burdened a legal queen like him. Theo Tischler was even shorter, five foot seven, the same height as the victim. Squarely built and bald besides. It was even worse with Thulin, who according to the information in his passport could almost be described as a tall, stately dwarf at all of five foot five.

Sven Erik Sjöberg remained. A giant at five foot ten compared with the rest of the society, and both physically fit and powerful besides. Remarkably like the man that the witnesses described, and though he'd been dead for almost fifteen years, it was here that Bäckström made the first thrust. As always his intuition led him in the right direction.

Sjöberg had evidently been a diligent society brother and club joiner. Not just as a young law student in Friends of Cunt, for that was only a modest beginning. The introduction to a long career in social life that extended from the local Conservative association in Danderyd to the Employers Association in Uppland, the Friends of the Countryside Association, the Shareholders Association, the Taxpayers Association, the Association Against Employee Funds, the gentlemen's society Stora Sällskapet, Lilla Sällskapet, the New Society, Society for a Free Sweden, Rotary . . . And so on, and so on. All the way to the Swedish Hunters Union, the "Sneseglarna" sailing society, the Polar Bears winter swimming club, and the Magnum Boys shooting association.

The Magnum Boys, thought Bäckström, licking his lips, and by the next day he knew everything worth knowing about this illustrious confederation. Fifty-some men, marksmen, gun collectors, hunters who met regularly at a gravel pit in Huddinge, where they then passed the time by shooting at cardboard figures and empty gasoline cans with Magnum revolvers and automatic weapons.

When Bäckström read through their annual report for fiscal year 1990 he also found an item that reported that the vice chairman, Sven Sjöberg, had evidently made an appearance as the guest of honor in the noteworthy TV program *The Boys at Fagerhult* in October that fall. The very next day Bäckström acquired a copy of the program from the TV archive, and it was then that he ran across yet another vein of purest gold. Thick as his thumb this time.

After that there had been dinner, and it was then that the decisive piece fell into place. Sjöberg was invited to appear on the TV program not only in his capacity as a hunter, marksman, and society brother. In reality he was there to discuss the Bofors arms deal with India. In his capacity as member of the board of directors and the company's attorney for many years.

There was no doubt that you should buy your cannons from Bofors, if you asked Sjöberg, and if you had such a product to offer bribes were wholly unnecessary. Not much more had been said either; instead they proceeded to make a toast to the deal and discuss more essential things, such as how best to kill innocent animals.

In light of this new information Bäckström revised his previous analysis of motives. Not just sex, although there seemed to be strong bonds that united the perpetrators with their victim. Besides, he had found evidence for the second classic motive. Money. Lots of money, which Bofors paid out in bribes to both Indians and others. Not least to the murder victim, if you were to rely on the dozens of allegations in that direction that Bäckström had found on the Internet.

Sex and money. Perpetrators and victim who had a common past. A victim who had been murdered because he had a falling out with the others. With the brain Waltin, the mole Thulin, the financier Tischler, and the marksman Sjöberg.

The same Sjöberg who regrettably had died almost fifteen years ago and therefore could not be questioned. A completely natural death as it appeared. At the Santa's Elves Association annual Christmas dinner he rose to give the customary thank-you speech and started by opening his mouth, which he'd done his whole life. But instead of beginning to talk one more time he suddenly had a stroke, collapsed like an empty sack, taking a grilled pig's head with him in his fall, and died on the spot.

After a long period of illness. Jeez, Louise, thought Bäckström, who'd read his obituary in *Svenska Dagbladet* but was not as easily fooled as all the others.

85

It was time to move from words to action and confront the two perpetrators who were still alive, thought Bäckström as soon as he was done with his restorative Thursday breakfast of pancakes with fried ham, applesauce, toast with extra-salty butter, a big cup of strong coffee, and a gulp of Jägermeister to top it off. Then he ordered a taxi and rode down to the Parliament Building. Upon entering the reception area he handed a business card to the security guard and asked to see member of parliament Alf Thulin, on a matter that was both urgent and sensitive.

"Do you have an appointment, Inspector?" asked the security guard.

"Unfortunately there wasn't time for that," said Bäckström. "Win or lose, I took a chance and came here." Now suck on that, you little desk jockey, he thought.

It was a win, obviously. As always when he tugged hard on the reins. Five minutes later he was on the couch with the Apostle of Aquavit. Nowadays a fine, respected fellow, so it was crucial to be careful with the knife as you drew it against the whetstone. At least to start with, he thought.

"You wanted to see me, Inspector," said member of parliament Thulin, forming his short, thin fingers into a little church arch.

"I'll get right to the point," said Bäckström. "Even if my business is somewhat delicate."

"Be my guest. I'm listening," said the member of parliament, making an inviting gesture with his right hand.

"Friends of Cunt," said Bäckström, sticking out his round head toward the one being questioned to inspire added respect. "Isn't it high time you unburdened yourself on this point? Let's start there." Then we'll take the rest as we go along, thought Bäckström, who'd done more interrogations than most.

"Excuse me," said the member of parliament, looking at Bäckström with astonishment.

"I'm talking about the Friends of Cunt. A little society of comrades of which you were a member during your happy student days. I'm sure you remember it."

"I don't recall that we've dropped formalities," said the member of parliament, glancing at the closed door to his office for some reason.

Okay, thought Bäckström. If you're going to be that way. "Stop fooling around now, Thulin," said Bäckström, giving him the classic police stare. "I want you to tell me. Be my guest, Thulin. I'm listening. Or would you prefer that I call you the Apostle of Aquavit and take you with me to the confessional up at police headquarters?"

"Excuse me a moment, Inspector," said the member of parliament, smiling wanly. "I'm afraid I have to wash my hands. I'll be right back."

"Sure," said Bäckström. Before you wet your undies, he thought, and if he'd ever seen an interrogation victim who was soon going to be as docile as a sacrificial lamb, it was the Apostle of Aquavit.

Damn, he's taking a long time, thought Bäckström as he looked at the clock ten minutes later. Wonder if the bastard shit his pants? Best to check, he thought. He got up and reached for the door to see where he'd gone.

Locked. What the hell is going on? thought Bäckström, trying the door one more time to be on the safe side. Still locked.

What the hell is happening? thought Bäckström again fifteen minutes later. Dead silence on the other side of the door. From time to time he was able to perceive extremely faint sounds, even though he stood with his ear pressed against the door, and there had been a lot of running around in the corridor when he arrived. Stealthy footsteps, something heavy being dragged along the floor. Now there's some real shit going on, thought Bäckström, for suddenly it was so silent you could hear how silent it was. Damn it anyway, thought Bäckström. I should have brought little Sigge with me, he thought, feeling inside his jacket to be on the safe side. Empty. Who the hell would drag around a shoulder holster and a lot of scrap iron when you were only going to tongue-lash a dwarf? he thought.

That was also more or less the last thing he remembered when he finally awoke the following morning and gradually realized that he was still alive. Despite everything. Despite the Friends of Cunt, who evidently had tentacles that reached all the way to the top of police administration. Who evidently only needed to pick up the phone so the Lapp bastard up at the bureau could sic his own death patrol on Bäckström.

86

"How's it going?" said Johansson as soon as Lewin came into his office.

"It's rolling along slowly," said Lewin, nodding inquisitively at Johansson's visitor's chair before he sat down.

"Is he alive?" asked Johansson.

"I think so," Lewin replied. "I get that feeling, at least," he added with a cautious throat clearing. "In any event we don't have anything that indicates the opposite."

"His sister then? Runs out to the bar all the time and drinks champagne with all the interest on her accounts."

"She seems to live a very quiet life," said Lewin, shaking his head. "Judging by the records from her home phone she seems to socialize mostly with an old co-worker and a few neighbors in the area where she lives. Plus she's secretary of her condominium association. Not really any extensive socializing. She makes at most a few calls a day. I haven't located any cell phone. She doesn't have an account with any Swedish provider. But she does have a computer and an Internet account with Telia."

"She probably has one of those prepaid cell phones, like all the other crooks. A leopard never changes its spots," said Johansson as a police siren started sounding in the pocket of his jacket. "Excuse me," he said, fishing out his red cell phone.

"Yes," said Johansson as he always had the habit of doing when he answered the phone.

"You don't say," he continued. "Come here on the double so we can set out the shooting line.

"I see then," said Johansson, nodding. "Now you'll have to excuse me, Jan. I've got something else on the program, but I promise to be in touch."

Wonder what's happening? thought Lewin as he stepped out into the corridor from Johansson's office and was almost run over by the head of the national SWAT force and two of his bald-headed co-workers, on their way in at a fast march.

"What's happening?" said Johansson without nodding at his visitor's chair. Full battle regalia and grim faces. What the hell is happening? he thought.

"We seem to have a hostage situation down at the Parliament Building," said the SWAT chief. "At the office of the Christian Democrats. One perpetrator. Probably armed and dangerous."

"Do we know who he is?" said Johansson.

"The boys who are at the scene say it's Bäckström," said the SWAT chief. "Bäckström from lost-and-found. That fat little bastard. He seems to have taken one individual hostage and barricaded himself in his office. It's that Thulin. Do you know who I mean, Chief?"

"Bäckström, I know who that is," said Johansson. "Thulin? Are we talking about that sanctimonious bastard who's always on TV harping about all the wicked people he runs into all the time? Former prosecutor Alf Thulin?"

"Yes, boss. That Bäckström. Yes, boss. That Thulin. Yes, boss."

"Go down and tell the little fatso to behave properly," said Johansson and sighed.

87

She was a woman who seemed to live a quiet life. With one living relative. A brother who, according to what he reported to the Swedish authorities, had moved to Spain twenty-four years ago and was now living at a residential hotel in Sitges, south of Barcelona. He had kept that address for ten years or so, but when he last renewed his Swedish passport seven years ago he had apparently moved to 189 Calle Asunción, in Palma de Mallorca. Two Spanish addresses in twenty-four years. That was all.

I hope he's still living there, thought Lewin, who had spent all of his adult life in the same apartment at Gärdet.

Then he filled out all the papers needed for Europol to request that the Spanish police make a discreet address check on him, in addition to searching for Kjell Göran Hedberg in all the other registries to which they had access. Obviously he had also put a check mark in the box that dealt with individuals with a "suspected connection to terrorism."

That may put some urgency even into the Spanish colleagues, thought Jan Lewin, though he was normally not the least bit prejudiced. It's nice that you don't need to put things in envelopes and lick stamps anymore, he thought as he e-mailed his request to the officer at the national bureau who took care of the practical aspects and conveniently enough sat three doors down on the same corridor.

"Do you have a moment, boss?" asked Johansson's secretary as she knocked lightly on his open door.

"Sit down, damn it," Johansson hissed, waving toward the TV that was in one corner of the room.

SWAT team, Parliament Building, what's happening? she thought.

"What is going on?" she asked.

"Bäckström," said Johansson. "The little fathead has apparently gone completely crazy. Barricaded himself in the Christian Democrats' office and has taken that pharisee Alf Thulin hostage. I've sent the boys from the SWAT team to talk some sense into the bastard."

The SWAT team did as they had been taught to do when they were going to talk sense into someone like Bäckström. Someone who was suspected of being both armed and dangerous. In this case an extremely unusual police officer who unfortunately had access to the same service weapons as all his normal colleagues. The same Bäckström who regrettably—and literally—was standing in the way of the team's response itself.

First the door fell on him when they broke it down. Then the shock grenade that they threw in exploded only a foot or two from his head. Then four of them threw themselves over him and put both hand and foot restraints on him. All within the course of about ten seconds. The response leader had of course timed the operation.

When Bäckström was carried out on a stretcher and lifted into the ambulance, he was both unconscious and equipped with the necessary shackles. Ready for further transport to the psychiatric ER at Huddinge hospital and accompanied to be on the safe side by an escort from the same SWAT force that had nearly killed him.

During the following twenty-four hours a dozen of his bosses with the Stockholm police would devote the majority of their time to discussing how dangerous he really was. Because opinions diverged, finally they called his previous boss, Lars Martin Johansson, and asked for his assessment.

"A short, fat bastard who spouts nonsense all the time," Johansson summarized.

"Do you assess Bäckström as constituting a danger to the life and safety of others, boss?" asked the psychologist Johansson was talking with.

"Bäckström," Johansson snorted. "Are you kidding me?" Dr. Fridolin, he thought. What kind of fucking name is that?

But they got no farther than that.

88

On Friday morning Johansson called in Anna Holt and informed her that she and Lisa Mattei would be traveling to Mallorca on Monday morning. He had already organized a discreet link to the local police colleagues. All resources would be placed at their disposal. No stone would be left unturned.

Johansson even made sure the Spanish police would be responsible for the investigators' security during their stay. Not only the usual services provided to colleagues. Their contact person was a Spanish police superintendent about his age, who was acting head of the detective squad in Palma and an excellent fellow, according to one of his friends who was Spain's own Johansson. Among real Spanish constables he was called *El Pastor*, "the Pastor." Not because he was particularly God-fearing but mostly because he looked the part. A tall man with a stern, clerical exterior who could get even the most hardened offender to open up and cry his heart out on his bony shoulders.

"Mallorca," said Holt. An address seven years old that Hedberg himself had provided, she thought. The same Hedberg who probably had very strong reasons to keep away from the police.

"We have to start somewhere," said Johansson, shrugging his shoulders. "Besides, I'm pretty sure that's where he is."

"How can you be so sure?" asked Holt.

"A feeling," said Johansson, shrugging his shoulders.

"A feeling?"

"Yes," said Johansson. "You know, the sort of feeling you get sometimes, which means that some of us can see around corners.

"That's where the bastard is hiding out," he continued. "I feel it in my marrow. So now it's a matter of hiding in the bushes and not scaring him off."

"The prosecutor," said Holt. "I assume you've reached an understanding with the prosecutor?"

"Of course," said Johansson. "You're going to get all the papers within an hour. Signed and ready. Talk with the cashier if you need money. I get the idea the girls leave early on Fridays. If they've already left I can arrange it for you," he added generously and tapped the pocket with his wallet in it.

"You've talked with the prosecutor," said Holt. "With the prosecutor in the Palme investigation?"

"Are you crazy, Anna?" said Johansson. "I've talked with our own prosecutor. The one I always use. He's completely informed about my line of reasoning."

"So what is that?"

"That there are reasonable grounds to suspect that it was Hedberg who murdered Jorma Kalevi Orjala. That so-called hit-and-run accident, if you recall. In reality it was probably the case that Hedberg simply got a witness out of the way. One more witness. Just like he did that time when he robbed the post office on Dalagatan."

"Are you joking?" said Holt. "A case that was written off in May of 1986."

"There's nothing wrong with having a few papers with you," said Johansson. "As far as age goes it's fresher than Palme anyway. Besides, we have actually opened it up again. The colleagues at the group for cold cases took it over from Stockholm yesterday. High time they get something they can chew on."

"But, Lars—"

"Listen now, Anna," Johansson interrupted. "Sure. I understand exactly what you intend to say. Forget about Jorma Kalevi. I want Hedberg back here. I want him home in peace and quiet, and I don't give a damn how it happens, purely formally. Try to be a little practical, for once. Are we agreed?"

"No," said Anna Holt. "But I understand what you mean." Besides, you're the one who decides, she thought.

89

That same Friday morning Bäckström woke up in a bed in the psych ward at Huddinge hospital. A friendly minded fellow patient, who was only suffering from low-level compulsive thoughts at the moment and even had permission to visit the hospital store, sneaked the morning papers to him and asked for an autograph considering that Bäckström was on the front page of both *Metro* and *Svenskan*. Not by name, true, but still.

On the other hand *Dagens Nyheter* had been more restrained and even left an opening for alternative explanations. There it was said that a police officer on sick leave had contacted "a well-known member of parliament to make complaints against the National Bureau of Criminal Investigation's way of running the Palme investigation," but what happened beyond that was extremely unclear. According to the same newspaper's reliable sources, it had never been a question of a "hostage situation." The member of parliament in question had not submitted a police report and could not be reached for comment. The police response on the other hand was reported to both the Stockholm police department for internal investigations and to the ombudsman at the Ministry of Justice and the Office of the Chancellor of Justice.

By afternoon Bäckström had already been moved to the neurology department, where first his round head and bruised body had been stuffed into a torpedo tube of an X-ray machine. Then he got boiled cod with egg sauce, elderberry juice, and rhubarb pie. Before he fell asleep he had to stuff almost half a dozen tablets of various colors into himself, and when he woke up the following morning one of the Stockholm police department's human resources consultants was sitting beside his bed, observing him with a worried expression.

"How's it going, Bäckström?" asked the consultant, patting him on the arm.

"What's happening?" Bäckström wheezed. "Is there war?"

"It's over now, Bäckström," said the consultant, patting him a little more to be on the safe side.

"Now if you just take it easy and rest up, everything's going to work out fine."

"That's what you say," said Bäckström. What the hell is he saying? he thought.

"You're soon going to meet your very own support person," said the consultant. "The police chief himself has assigned Dr. Fridolin to that task. You know, the one you met at the gender sensitivity course where you had your stroke. Fridolf Fridolin, you know."

"Little Frippy," said Bäckström. What the hell is wrong with an ordinary shot to the back of the neck?

"It's going to work out, Bäckström," the consultant assured him. "Now just take it easy and—"

"I want to talk with the union," Bäckström interrupted. "Besides, I demand to be guarded so those fucking SWAT terrorists can't make another attempt to kill me. Just none of my colleagues. Bring over some reliable half-apes from Securitas."

On Monday he had been discharged and could go home. Fridolin, who had been at his side faithfully the whole weekend, drove him and even accompanied him up to his cozy pad.

"I'll see to it that someone from home services comes and cleans for you, Eve," said Fridolin with a faint smile as soon as he stepped inside the door and was confronted with the Bäckströmian home sweet home.

"Sit down, Little Frippy," said Bäckström, pointing to his couch. "We're going to have a serious talk, you and me."

Then Bäckström gave the good doctor his memorandum about the conspiracy behind the murder of Prime Minister Olof Palme. Complete with crime analysis, profiles of the four perpetrators, and possible motives. In addition, he produced a copy of the crime report against Waltin for his efforts with the candlestick on Walpurgis Eve, 1968.

"But this is terrible, Eve," said a shaken Fridolin when he finished reading half an hour later. "This is even worse than that movie by Oliver Stone about the assassination of Kennedy. We have to see to it immediately that you get security protection, so they don't—"

"Calm down, Little Frippy," said Bäckström, raising his hand like a traffic cop. "We shouldn't get ourselves excited unnecessarily and just rush off. Get me a beer from the fridge, then I'll explain how we should set the whole thing up. Get one for yourself too, if you want," he added, because he felt that he was starting to return to his old friendly, generous self.

Wednesday, October 10.
Outside Cap de Formentor in Canal de Menorca

"O blessedness to be young in morning light at sea," thinks the young count Malte Moritz von Putbus on his journey to the West Indies with the three-masted barque Speranza. We are traveling in a novel by Sven Delblanc, and the journey takes place the same year Gustav III was murdered at the Opera masquerade in Stockholm. The protagonist of the book is Malte Moritz, called Mignon by his friends. Young, idealistic, yearning for freedom, and still he has not discovered that Speranza carries a load of slaves. Much less has he given a thought to the fact that a hard fate can also put the freest man in fetters or completely destroy him. What the solitary man on board Esperanza thinks and feels more than two hundred years later we do not know. There is little to suggest that he is much like Malte Moritz as an individual, but seen from a distance, and in the morning light at sea, there is still much to suggest that he, at least at this moment, thinks and feels the same way. The calm breathing of the sea, the rustling of the waves against the stern, the sun smoke that encompasses him, the salt-drenched breeze that cools body and head. Then the rudder, controlled by his will and resting in his hands. At any time at all he can change course or completely redirect it. Security, freedom, "O blessedness . . ."

90

Ten days earlier, Monday, October 1.
Headquarters of the National Bureau of Criminal
Investigation on Kungsholmen in Stockholm

On Monday the first of October, Anna Holt and Lisa Mattei traveled to
Mallorca to try to find Kjell Göran Hedberg, and Lars Martin Johansson
showed a new side of himself. And did so in a wordy, roundabout way.

During the time Lars Martin Johansson had been a detective in the
field he had also—quite literally—put his mitts on numerous murderers
and violent criminals. The majority by sending letters or calling them
and asking them to appear at the police station for a little talk. A few
scattered times he and his associate Jarnebring had made home visits
without asking for permission first. Normally he and his best friend were
enough, and during his entire active duty neither of them ever needed
to reach for his service weapon. One time, "means one time," Johansson clarified, there was a "crazy Yugoslav" who had "behaved a little
stupidly" and started wrestling with Jarnebring, who in turn solved the
problem with the classic police chokehold, "you know the one that was
prohibited thirty years ago," while Johansson put the handcuffs on him.

"He was mostly sorry, the wretch," said Johansson. "Who wouldn't
be if you killed your best friend because you got everything turned
around?"

. . .

It had always been like that. It was still that way, in all essentials, and it would be in the future as well if Johansson had his way. Every drawn service weapon, every siren turned on, all harsh words, even every hasty, unplanned movement, was nothing other than an expression of police shortcomings that fortunately and almost never belonged to reality. Possibly with one exception. A former colleague whose name was Kjell Göran Hedberg.

"So be careful, ladies, and call home if anything happens," said Johansson.

"Above all," he said, raising an extra warning finger, "don't come up with any risky moves. Hedberg is a malignant bastard. If he shows up and starts making a fuss, shoot him."

"Are you saying we should take our service weapons along?" said Holt.

"You can always arrange that on-site," said Johansson, shrugging his shoulders. "You can't drag along that kind of shit on an airplane, especially these days when you can't even take a bottle of aftershave or a can of liverwurst. It's probably better if you fix that when you get there. I've already notified them about that, by the way."

Then he gave them a real bear hug. Put his arms around their shoulders and squeezed. The right one around Mattei and the left around Holt, and no particular ulterior motives were involved.

Lewin would stay in Stockholm to put order into all the papers. What Johansson would do was less clear. Look after his own business, presumably, and in other words everything was exactly as usual.

"He's actually kind of sweet," said Mattei as soon as their plane lifted off from Arlanda. "Johansson, that is."

"Oh well," said Holt. "Not only."

"He smells good too," said Mattei, who didn't seem to be listening.

"He smells like safety in some way. Clean clothes, aftershave—he smells like a real old-fashioned guy in fact."

"Lisa," said Holt, looking at her.

"Yes?"

"Give it up now," said Holt.

"Okay," said Mattei, taking out her pocket computer. If you're going to be that way, she thought.

91

Their Spanish guardian angel, *El Pastor*, was obviously a man who took his assignment with the greatest seriousness. As soon as their plane landed and taxied up to the gate, he was standing there, right outside the door to the plane, and when he caught sight of Holt and Mattei he nodded to them and took them aside to the little electric airport vehicle that was waiting.

A tall, skinny man in his sixties with jet-black hair, friendly, watchful eyes, and not the least like the Fernandel character who haunted Holt's fantasies. A few feet behind him stood his two assistants, half his age, who would apparently take care of the practicalities. They were several inches shorter, considerably broader, with narrow, expressionless eyes and hands crossed over their jeans-clad crotches.

Not like Hans and Fritz—the Katzenjammer Kids—more like Hans and Hans, and the only thing missing was the writing on their foreheads that clearly stated what they did, so you didn't confuse them with a couple of professional Mediterranean hit men.

Holt and Mattei did not see any trace of Spanish indifference either. Fifteen minutes later they were already in an unmarked police car en route from the airport to their hotel in central Palma.

"I assume that first you'll want to check in," said El Pastor, smiling courteously.

"Then I thought I would suggest a visit to my office where we can discuss your needs. After that, a simple dinner at a nearby restaurant that I often frequent myself, and where quite excellent seafood is served. Assuming you ladies don't have other wishes, of course?"

. . .

Holt immediately accepted the terms. Find Hedberg, she thought. Work on your tan along the way. That's how it will be.

The seafood and suntan were going better than the assignment. Escorted by Hans and Hans, they visited countless addresses in Palma and the surrounding smaller towns and villages, where they might possibly find Hedberg or perhaps someone who could give information about where he was.

The first address they visited was the one that Hedberg had provided to the Swedish authorities the last time he emitted a sign of life. Over seven years before, when he applied for a new passport. The address he provided proved to be a simple boarding establishment on Calle Asunción, in old Palma. The man in reception only shook his head when their Spanish assistants started asking him about Hedberg.

Bars, hotels, brothels, leasing firms, brokers and agents for all conceivable services. The usual squealers, informants, petty crooks, and the occasional ordinary person who might possibly have run into Hedberg. All simply shook their heads.

Only after five days, on Friday afternoon the fifth of October, did they finally get a tip that was worth the name.

92

As soon as Holt lifted off from Arlanda, Lewin suddenly had a lot of help from an unexpected direction. When he arrived on Monday morning he found a copy of his own list of fifteen points. It was lying on top of a considerable pile of papers. Plus a brief greeting from his colleague Rogersson: "From the Boss. Rogge." From the date he realized that the papers had been on his desk for over twenty-four hours, while in his usual solitude he had survived yet another empty weekend. I might just as well have been at work, he thought.

After another hour his colleague Falk knocked on his door and handed over a list of the transactions that had been made on Birgitta Hedberg's credit card during the past year. An ordinary Visa card that she used even more seldom than her home phone. One line was underlined in red. In early March, seven months earlier and a month after she had renewed her passport, she had booked a trip to Spain and paid with the card. A week with hotel and half-board. But not to Mallorca, to the Spanish Sun Coast. Either Hedberg has moved or else he simply chose to meet her there, thought Lewin.

The thought that she might have gone there on her own initiative did not even occur to him. Birgitta Hedberg is not the type to waste a week of her life swimming, sunbathing, or socializing with people she doesn't know. She wouldn't do it even just to relax, thought Jan Lewin. He realized that as soon as he saw the expression in her eyes on her passport photo.

"Thanks," said Jan Lewin.

"No problem," Falk replied, shrugging his shoulders. "There's more coming in a while."

"Before you go," said Lewin. "Just so we don't duplicate our efforts unnecessarily."

"I'm listening," said Falk, without sitting down.

"I'll make sure our colleagues down there get the information about her trip," said Lewin. "Ask that they check whether Hedberg possibly flew from Palma at the same time. What else might I do that you aren't already doing or have already arranged for me?" said Lewin, nodding amiably to soften what otherwise might be perceived as criticism.

"I think you can forget about that," said Falk. "We've already checked it, with the help of our colleagues at Europol. No Hedberg on the relevant plane from and to Palma, which doesn't necessarily mean a thing because we're talking about Spanish domestic flights and their procedures. What his sis was doing on vacation I also think you can forget about, simply because that will take too much time. Think about her cell phone instead," said Falk. "If you have any good ideas about how we can get the number."

"If she even has one," said Lewin, sounding as if he was thinking out loud. Although of course she does, he thought. He understood that from the expression in her eyes.

"She does," said Falk. "I've seen it myself. Most recently this morning."

"Do tell," said Lewin. Now we're moving, he thought.

"You probably have it in your e-mail," said Falk, looking at the clock for some reason. "Our colleague Wiklander is supposed to be sending you a memo."

Now things are really moving, thought Lewin.

Wiklander was the top boss of the National Bureau's intelligence department, the so-called CIS squad. For more than twenty years he had been Johansson's confidant, and most of all he was known for his discretion. Wiklander gathered information about the sort of things that were of interest to the police. About high and low, and the higher the better.

From everyone who had anything to offer, and if there was anyone who wanted something in return, it was crucial to show that you had very good reasons. Otherwise it was Wiklander and his staff of analysts who decided how the knowledge they were sitting on would benefit their colleagues, regardless of whether they had asked for it or not. Wiklander was a man according to Johansson's taste. A person he could sit and talk with quite openly about the most sensitive matters, because he always knew that the conversation had never taken place, if the wrong person were to ask.

Lewin had apparently passed through the eye of the needle. At least where finding out the number to Kjell Göran Hedberg's sister's cell phone was concerned. It's always something, thought Lewin, printing out the e-mail from Wiklander, because he preferred to read something he could hold in his hand and make notes on.

The external surveillance of Birgitta Hedberg had already started on Friday the week before, carried out by a group from the bureau's own detective squad under the command of Rogersson, even though he really worked in homicide. By Saturday morning they had already found a suitable "nest." It was a small apartment across the street from Birgitta Hedberg's residence and offered a full view into her bedroom, dining room, and kitchen. An ideal nest that was being sublet by an aspiring female police officer in her last semester at the police academy, who was completely unacquainted with Birgitta Hedberg, and obviously had no idea why they were interested in her unknown neighbor. She was burning with enthusiasm at the chance to help her future colleagues. At the National Bureau of Criminal Investigation, besides.

By Saturday afternoon she had signed the usual confidentiality agreements and for the time being was being lodged at a hotel in the vicinity and got a decent gratuity for the inconvenience. Then Rogersson fixed his eyes on her and told her sternly not only to keep her mouth shut but also to stay away. Not only from her apartment, but from the whole area.

· · ·

While Rogersson took care of the aspiring police officer and the judicial and social details, his detectives settled into her apartment and got their equipment in place.

"External surveillance from premises as per description above was initiated at 14:00 hours, Saturday September 29," Wiklander noted in the first point of his surveillance memo, and by Saturday evening things had already started happening.

They knew that not because

After having a simple dinner at six-thirty, Birgitta Hedberg disappeared into her living room to watch TV. Not because she could be seen—her living room was on the "wrong" side of the building—but rather because her TV could be heard by means of the microphone aimed at her kitchen window right across the street. However that might be, considering that parliament was still struggling with the issue of whether to approve the use of so-called concealed monitoring by the police.

Regardless of which, first she watched the news on TV4. Then she returned to the kitchen. Made coffee, took a bag of cookies from the pantry, and after ten minutes—when the coffee was ready—took both coffee and cookies with her and disappeared in the direction of her living room. Then surfed between various channels for over fifteen minutes before she finally started watching a Swedish movie on TV2 that started at eight o'clock.

When that was over she changed channels and watched the late news on TV4. Then she turned off the TV in the middle of the sign-off from the news program. At exactly thirty-seven minutes past ten she again became visible in her kitchen. Now in a white terry-cloth bathrobe, hair let down, without makeup, teeth brushed and ready for a night's rest. The sensitive microphone even captured the sound of tooth brushing and a medicine cabinet being closed, opened, and closed again. Of the water she ran in the sink, and three minutes later the flushing of the toilet.

On the other hand, the details of what she'd been doing on the toilet were unclear because any natural human sounds, the use of toilet paper and the like, were drowned out by the sound from the faucet in the sink that was still running. Then that too fell silent, and less than a minute later, thirty-seven minutes past ten that is, Birgitta Hedberg came back into the kitchen. With the coffee mug in her right hand and the bag of cookies in her left. After putting the cookies back in the pantry, she rinsed the coffee mug under running water, placed it in the dishwasher, sat at the kitchen table, and started working the crossword puzzle in that day's *Svenska Dagbladet*. After writing and erasing for over half an hour, she put down the pen, sighed with a bad-tempered expression, folded up the newspaper, got up, and disappeared in the direction of the hall.

"Excruciatingly exciting," observed Inspector Joakim Eriksson with the bureau's detective squad as he stood behind the camera under cover of darkness in their little nest.

"It hardly gets better than this," agreed his female colleague, Inspector Linda Martinez.

At the same moment Birgitta Hedberg came back into the kitchen with a red cell phone in her right hand.

"There it is," Eriksson observed as his motor camera with telephoto lens whirred into action and took the obligatory still pictures at a velocity of ten pictures per second.

Birgitta Hedberg then turned off the light in the kitchen, went straight to her bedroom, turned on the lamp on her nightstand beside the bed, placed the red phone by the bed lamp, turned off the ceiling light, went over to the window, and pulled down the shade. Ten minutes later she also turned off the bed lamp. The room behind the shade was in darkness. That didn't matter, because Martinez had already redirected the microphone toward her bedroom window.

From the audio recording it appeared that she had already fallen asleep within fifteen minutes. That she snored a few times during the night, audibly relieved the pressure in her bowels shortly after three o'clock, and woke up three hours later. When she pulled up the shade at six-fifteen in the morning she had already put on her bathrobe, and when she took the cell phone from the nightstand to put it in her pocket, officer Falk was already there and could see it with his own eyes.

During Sunday the same cell phone had been observed on another three occasions, and according to the memo that Lewin was reading, by Monday morning the team was already clear about her peculiar cell phone procedures. She did not seem to use it for her own calls. Nor did anyone call her. At the same time she made sure that it was always nearby. When she left her residence on Sunday to do a few errands on two occasions, she had it with her in her handbag. When she was at home it was in her pocket or near her. Apparently she made sure it was always charged. It was an ordinary, standard model Nokia supplied with a simple red plastic case. One of the most common cell phones in Sweden, but less common in Spain, and so far so good. What remained was to find out the cell phone number, so as to find her brother. If Jan Lewin was interested in tactical discussions in connection with this cell phone surveillance, he was welcome in Johansson's office at ten o'clock.

Two minutes ago, thought Jan Lewin. Getting up he straightened his tie, put on his jacket, and turned off his computer.

In Johansson's office the atmosphere was high-pitched. Johansson, Wiklander, Rogersson, Falk, Martinez, and Eriksson were there, and even before Lewin opened the door he was met by happy laughter from the other side.

"Sit yourself down, Jan," said Johansson before Lewin could apologize for his late arrival. "Have some coffee," he said, pointing to the tray on the table. "But be careful with the cookies. Linda just told us about the risks of eating too many cookies. Especially before going to bed. Increases audible intestinal activity in an unpleasant manner."

Linda Martinez, thought Lewin, nodding at her. Same age as Lisa Mattei, just as street smart as Lisa Mattei was wise. As an investigator in the field, there were few like her. Which perhaps was lucky, considering everything he'd heard about her escapades, thought Jan Lewin, sitting down.

"Okay," said Johansson. "The Hedberg woman has a cell phone. Almost everything suggests she has it for only one reason. To keep in contact with her dear brother. How do we get the number? Preferably immediately. Give me some bright-eyed suggestions."

"If we only want to get hold of her number, I can arrange that during the day," said Linda Martinez.

"How?" asked Johansson.

"By stealing it," said Martinez, shrugging her shoulders. "As soon as she goes out I can lift her cell, and in the worst case I'll have to grab her handbag too. But considering what I think you really want I would definitely advise against that. But, sure." Martinez threw out her hands in an expressive gesture to show her goodwill.

"There is a completely legal possibility too," Lewin objected with a cautious throat clearing.

"What's that?" said Johansson, who suddenly looked rather suspicious.

"That the prosecutor lets us bring her in and confiscate her cell phone." Like all normal police do, a hundred times out of a hundred, he thought.

"No way, José," said Johansson, shaking his head. "If we let Linda steal it straight up and down, and considering how she looks these days she could pass for an addict who just snatched one more bag, then the Hedberg woman is probably going to call her brother anyway and tell him she's lost her cell. By means of some other phone that we aren't aware of either.

"It's the same thing with your solution, Lewin," he continued. "As soon as she gets the chance she's going to warn him. Then we're definitely cooked, considering that we've brought her in. Besides, we can't rule out that they have some established security procedure we don't know about. That she calls at regular intervals to confirm that everything is calm."

Although of course there are no differences otherwise. Purely legally and such, and never in Johansson's world, thought Jan Lewin.

· · ·

The latter—some kind of security procedure—Wiklander had already thought about. For that reason at that very moment his co-workers were installing a special mobile monitoring device aimed at her residence. If her cell phone emitted a sign of life the monitoring device was ready. Likewise if Hedberg made contact with her. At the same time the problem was apparent. They were short on time. Assume they only communicated once a week. Or even worse. Once a month. Or never, if there was no particular reason to do so.

They could also forget about pinging cell phone towers. Because they didn't have her number, that was practically hopeless. Monitoring calls from cell phones in the vicinity of her residence made to recipients on Mallorca—if that was even where Hedberg was—wasn't a meaningful way to search for the number either. The apartment on Andersvägen was wall-to-wall with the north approach to Stockholm, and denser cell phone traffic than in that area could hardly be found in the whole country.

"I hear what you're saying," Johansson interrupted. "What do we do?"

"If we can just call from her cell phone to one of our special cell surveillance numbers, we can get her number directly. Then we can start searching for what numbers she has called. Our computers are going to have a hard time of it, considering the extent of traffic. If we can get a certain day or a certain time too that would be a great help."

"So you say," said Johansson.

"In that case I propose the fifteenth of August of this year," said Lewin.

"Why then?" asked Falk.

"It's his birthday," said Lewin. "I think she's the type who's meticulous about calling her older brother and only relative on his birthday. Even if he might prefer that she didn't."

"I think so too," Johansson agreed. Every thinking colleague must understand that, he thought, glaring at Falk.

"If we ping from the relevant cell towers for the fifteenth of August this year we'll be sitting with tens of thousands of calls," said Wiklander.

"Considering all calls made from cars en route to and from Arlanda, thousands of them are going to be calls abroad. It's going to take months to follow them up. We've got to have her number. Otherwise it won't work. If we just have the number, we'll manage it in a few hours tops. Assuming she's called, of course."

Birgitta Hedberg was a disability pension recipient and as such she had the right to home services. And she'd had run-ins with those same home services since the first day. The current controversy was over a promised major cleaning that had not yet happened. The primary reason was that the majority of those who worked with home services would have rather quit than set foot in Birgitta Hedberg's apartment.

Wiklander tugged on a few of the usual threads. Almost immediately he found a colleague at the Solna police who had a wife who worked as a supervisor with the municipal home services. Discretion a matter of honor. Already by Tuesday afternoon the colleague's wife had called Ms. Hedberg and reported that they could initiate the promised major cleaning as soon as the following morning.

High time, according to Birgitta Hedberg, and she could receive the long-promised help herself as early as eight o'clock the following morning. Then she hung up without a word of thanks.

Hope the old bag gets life, thought the Solna colleague's wife, because her dear husband's involvement in this particular home services matter gave her some hope on that score.

"Well, well then," said Birgitta Hedberg for some reason when on Wednesday morning she opened the door to her apartment and scrutinized Linda Martinez. The same Martinez who nonetheless did her best to play the role of submissive immigrant in the service of Swedish Cleanliness.

For the next two days Linda Martinez scurried around like a white tornado in Birgitta Hedberg's three-room apartment. Swept and scrubbed so that even Cinderella in the classic Disney film looked like a real shirker in comparison. On the third day she was then granted all the favor that someone like Birgitta Hedberg could offer someone like her. First she was allowed to go along with her to do the shopping and carry all the bags. Then she stood outside the bank and waited while her new matron did errands that didn't concern someone like her. Finally they went to a nearby bakery where Birgitta Hedberg bought two Napoleon pastries. Once back in the apartment Martinez first had to help with lunch. Then set out the coffee. Two cups this time, and a pastry for each.

When the coffee was finished Martinez was given additional instructions for the rest of the day. Then Birgitta Hedberg went to the bathroom and left her handbag behind on the kitchen counter.

As soon as she shut the door, Martinez fished the red cell phone out of the bag. She entered the number Wiklander had given her, and then ended the call the moment after she'd made contact with the recipient. Deleted the call from the phone's memory. Put it back in the handbag and proceeded to clean away the traces of their little *kaffeklatsch*.

Hope the old bag gets life, thought Linda Martinez, even though she had no idea why Birgitta's cell phone number seemed to have almost decisive importance for her top boss.

Fifteen minutes before Jan Lewin meant to go home for the day, Wiklander stepped into his office and his contented smile was answer enough to the question Lewin had had in mind for the past week.

"The fifteenth of August at zero eight zero two hours Birgitta Hedberg made a call outside the country from her prepaid cell phone to a Spanish prepaid cell phone. The same time there as here," Wiklander clarified. "The last cell tower that forwarded the call is on north Mallorca. A little over a mile from a little town called Puerto Pollensa. The call went on for seventeen minutes. You have both numbers and all the rest of it in your e-mail."

"I'll call Holt immediately," said Lewin.

"Do that," said Wiklander.

93

On Friday morning the fifth of October, Holt, Mattei, and their Spanish colleagues finally detected a sign of life from Kjell Göran Hedberg. True, it was seven months old, but compared with what they'd had before this was fresh produce. It was irritating that the tip had been there all along. Not at the detective squad in Palma, but instead with the so-called terrorist squad at Guardia Civil's headquarters in Madrid.

In early March Hedberg had rented a car at the Hertz office at the airport in Málaga. It was the day after his sister had arrived there on vacation and checked into a hotel in the vicinity. Three days later he called Hertz and reported that the car had been stolen. They asked him to come to their main office in central Málaga. There a theft report had been filled out. A photocopy of Hedberg's passport had been made and he told the little he knew.

In the evening he had left the vehicle at the parking spot outside the hotel where he was staying. When he came out in the morning it was gone. That was all, and if they wanted to discuss it further they could reach him at his residence at 189 Calle Asunción in Palma de Mallorca.

In the tourist country of Spain thousands of rental cars were stolen every year, and for many years such crimes had been routine matters in the pile. Something that the car rental company, the police, and the insurance company handled without involving the person who rented the car. In later years this had changed. Domestic and international terrorism was the cataylst. The Basque separatists in ETA, the Islamist terrorist bombing at the railroad in Madrid where two hundred Spaniards had lost their lives.

Rental cars that were stolen, and especially those that were rented by foreign nationals, suddenly became interesting as a so-called pre-incident crime, one of several stages in the preparations for a terrorist attack. The registry that had been built up to sort out both stolen rental cars and those who had rented them already included tens of thousands of vehicles and individuals.

One week earlier, Friday the twenty-eighth of September, the terrorist squad in Madrid had received an inquiry from their counterparts with the intelligence department at the Swedish National Bureau of Criminal Investigation. A fast-track inquiry because their own top boss had already been in contact and given orders that everything that came from that Swedish agency should be handled with the highest priority. For the time being at least.

The basis for their questions was also nicely detailed. They were interested in the female Swedish citizen Birgitta Hedberg, age sixty, and her brother, Kjell Göran Hedberg, three years older. Birgitta Hedberg was said to have been in south Spain between the third and the tenth of March, where she stayed at the Aragon Hotel outside Marbella. On the other hand, where her brother was to be found was unknown, but at the same time his whereabouts were extremely interesting.

They found Birgitta Hedberg immediately. Inquiries at the scene indicated that she had stayed at "the hotel in question during the week in question." The computers in Madrid had already found her brother the following day in the registry of stolen rental cars. On the other hand he had not stayed at the Aragon Hotel in Marbella, as he had stated in his theft report to Hertz. There was no registration in his name in any event, and if he had shared a room with his sister, this must have happened in secret and in an ordinary twin bed. Considering that the car was picked up at the airport in Málaga, it was also strange to say the least that the man who rented it could not be found in the lists of flight passengers. Neither from Palma nor from any other destination on the day in question.

His home address in Palma did not seem to tally either. On Thursday the case had therefore been sent on to the colleagues in Palma with a request for help. Considering the sender, it crossed El Pastor's desk right before he was to go home to prepare for the evening's dinner with his delightful Swedish colleagues. Suddenly there he was, the man he had been looking for in vain for more than a week, and not because he'd asked the ones whose help he had requested but because they were asking him. As sometimes happens when the one hand isn't clear about what the other hand is up to.

First El Pastor had given free rein to his Spanish temperament. Called his counterpart in Madrid and told him what he thought. Then he unleashed the remainder of his frustration on his incompetent co-workers.

As soon as he'd regained his balance he had Holt and Mattei picked up from their hotel, conveyed them to yet another seafood restaurant by the blue sea, and did not say a word about what had happened the whole evening. Why ruin an otherwise pleasant evening with that kind of thing? thought El Pastor, looking deep into Anna Holt's eyes as he raised his glass. What an amazing woman, he thought. As beautiful as a young gypsy from Seville, in Bizet's opera.

The following morning Hans and Hans drove back to the boarding house on Calle Asunción. Took the man in reception aside and in Holt's and Mattei's absence had a serious talk with him. It hadn't helped. He still shook his head and refused to acknowledge any Kjell Göran Hedberg.

"*Nada,*" said Hans and Hans with a joint shrug of the shoulders when they returned to the office in the afternoon to give a report to the dark Swede.

"*Nada,*" Holt repeated with a faint smile just as her cell phone rang.

"Hi, Anna," said Lewin. "How's the weather?"

"Excellent," Holt replied. "Are you thinking about packing your bathing trunks and coming down for the weekend?" You might be challenged to a duel by El Pastor, she thought.

"If it were only that good," said Lewin and sighed. "We've found her number now. She has made only one call, as it appears. The fifteenth of August this year. Hedberg's birthday, as I'm sure you recall, and you have all the information in your e-mail. The call went via a tower that's a few miles from a town called Puerto Pollensa on north Mallorca, but I don't know exactly where that town is located. Probably simplest if you ask one of our Spanish colleagues."

"Can you wait a second, Jan?" said Holt, setting down her cell phone on her desk and turning around in the office where she was sitting. I knew it, she thought. I knew it. He's been here the whole time.

"Puerto Pollensa," said Holt. "Is that anywhere near here?"

"It's sixty-five miles north. Takes about an hour, depending on the traffic," answered Pedro Rovira, who spoke considerably better English than the other colleague, Pablo Ballester.

94

Bäckström had almost immediately seen about instilling some manners and style into his so-called support person Little Frippy. He was even getting sort of fond of the bastard, though he looked like a painful animal experiment and sounded like a bad book.

Reminds me a little of Egon, after all, thought Bäckström. Though not as taciturn, of course.

Egon was his dear goldfish, which an unusually malevolent colleague unfortunately had taken the opportunity to put to death when Bäckström was out in the countryside on a murder investigation. Then the colleague got rid of the body by flushing it down Bäckström's toilet. Although that fate probably won't befall Little Frippy, I hope, thought Bäckström. Because he—as stated—was starting to get attached to him.

After only a few days Little Frippy had asked Bäckström to stop calling him Little Frippy.

"Okay then," said Bäckström. "If you'll stop calling me Eve, I promise that your name will be Fridolin in the future."

"I thought you were called Eve," said Little Frippy with surprise. "Don't all your buddies call you Eve?"

"I lied. I've never had any buddies," said Bäckström. He shook his head and knocked back a little good malt.

"That's sad," said Fridolin, sipping his beer and sounding like he meant what he said.

"Do you want some good advice, Fridolin? From a wise man."

Fridolin nodded.

"Whatever you do, don't ever get yourself any buddies. You see, in this fucking world you can't rely on a single fucking person."

With that the ice had been broken, and together with his now faithful squire Bäckström discussed how they would get his message out to the general public, whom all the shady powers that be had kept in the dark for more than twenty years.

Fridolin got straight to the point and suggested that he should speak with the provincial police chief in Stockholm. He "had her ear" and was pretty sure he could arrange a meeting in which Bäckström could make a presentation about the truth behind the Palme murder.

Nice to hear it's not a more vital body part, thought Bäckström.

"What's the point of that?" he asked.

According to Fridolin it was well worth trying. There were three good reasons. People like Waltin and his companions were at the top of Ms. Police Chief's own political agenda. Fridolin had—as stated—her ear, and besides it was an open secret that she was being considered as the next national police commissioner.

"Okay then," said Bäckström. If it's war, then so be it, he thought.

95

Puerto Pollensa on north Mallorca. They already knew this on Friday afternoon, and the fact that the cell tower that had finally conveyed the birthday call to Kjell Göran Hedberg was only a few miles from the place where former chief superintendent Claes Waltin had been found drowned fifteen years earlier had not surprised Anna Holt and Lisa Mattei in the least.

Nor El Pastor, as it appeared.

"I remember that a high-ranking colleague of yours from the Swedish secret police drowned up there many years ago," he said for some reason when he, Holt, and Mattei were having lunch on Saturday.

"Yes," said Holt. "Yes," she repeated, with a broader than usual smile.

"I understand," El Pastor replied, bowing his head slightly. "It's very important to move ahead carefully," he said. "I have a feeling he's still there. Right in the vicinity, and soon we'll arrest him."

Though not on Sunday. Not on Monday and not on Tuesday. Even though the activity around them increased by a hundred percent and even though neither Holt nor Mattei understood a word of anything their Spanish colleagues said to one another.

"Patience." El Pastor consoled them when he had them driven home that Tuesday evening. "Patience, my ladies."

· · ·

At six o'clock the next morning he called Holt at her hotel, and because she had long been prepared she was already wide awake when she answered on the second ring.

"We've found him," said El Pastor. "Right now he's at home asleep in his residence. If you want to be present at the arrest I can pick you up in fifteen minutes."

"We'll see you in reception," said Holt, rushing to the shower.

Mattei was already waiting when Holt came down. At about the same time the police car braked outside the hotel entrance.

"Have you thought about one thing, Anna?" said Mattei, looking at her watch.

"What's that?" said Holt, heading for the entrance.

"Today is Wednesday the tenth of October. Only eight weeks since we were rolling our eyes at Johansson and all his strange ideas."

"No," said Holt. "I hadn't thought about that. Right now we have other things to think about."

96

Driving to Puerto Pollensa was out of the question. Not even with flashing lights and a siren and even though at this time of the morning the trip took less than an hour.

Only half a mile north of the hotel their car drove right out onto the beach, where a helicopter was waiting.

El Pastor had of course helped them into the cabin, made sure their seats were okay and that they were properly secured in them. They were joined by El Pastor, Rovira, Ballester, and another three colleagues from the detective squad in Palma. Filled with the seriousness of the moment and equipped to meet it. Protective vests, automatic weapons, silent, closed faces.

El Pastor helped Anna put on her vest, offered her a holster with a pistol, which she fastened to her belt with a metal clip. Lisa Mattei had to help herself and in addition declined the weapon that their colleague Rovira tried to slip her.

"Okay, Lisa," said Rovira. "As long as you keep behind me. Promise?" he asked with a broad smile.

"Promise," said Mattei, smiling back. God, how exciting, she thought. Just like everything Johansson had warned them about. Besides the fact that they were with the Spanish colleagues who were known to keep their hands closer to the trigger than did all her co-workers at home.

Two minutes later they had company in the darkness above. The lights from another helicopter that positioned itself right alongside them. Also from the Guardia Civil and the largest model.

"Our SWAT force," El Pastor explained. "Two groups of six men. We'll have him soon," he said, patting Holt on the hand. "We'll land in fifteen minutes, and we plan to make a forced entry into his house in no more than forty minutes, quarter past seven at the latest," he clarified, indicating with his watch.

"Is he still there?" asked Holt, who felt a certain unease. Not least considering what Johansson had said when he said goodbye to them.

"To be sure," said El Pastor, nodding.

Then he told them. Late yesterday evening they got the decisive tip from one of their local informants. Only a few hours ago they had found the house where he lived. Hedberg lived in a small gatekeeper's cottage on a large estate, apparently owned by a wealthy English couple who were seldom there. The estate was well isolated from the rest of the settlement up in the mountains, six miles southwest of Puerto Pollensa. Hedberg could live there for free in exchange for keeping an eye on the property, and apparently he had been living there for the past two years. What he was occupied with otherwise was still unclear.

"Enjoying the good life, perhaps," said El Pastor, smiling and shrugging his shoulders.

"I talked with my colleagues up there only half an hour ago," he continued. "Just after they located his house. The light above the outside door is on. The shades in the bedroom are pulled down. His car is parked in the yard outside. He has no watchdog to warn him. He's sleeping, and there's not a chance in the world he can escape."

In the end it still turned out just as Johansson had feared, thought Anna Holt half an hour later. She was squatting behind some bushes only fifty yards from the little gatekeeper's yellow-pink limestone cottage where it was hoped that Kjell Göran Hedberg was getting his beauty sleep. Everything indicated that. Silent and peaceful. The light on above the outside door. The car in the yard. The shades pulled down. Just like El Pastor said.

The twelve colleagues from the Spanish SWAT team silently approached from all directions. Shadows of black, impossible to make out in the darkness that surrounded them. Black overalls, boots that went up to their thighs, helmets, bulletproof vests, automatic weapons. Then suddenly completely quiet.

"Now," whispered El Pastor where he squatted by Holt's side, and at the same moment all hell broke loose.

The whole thing was over in ten seconds. The sound of the outside door being knocked down as all three windows were smashed. The four shock grenades that were thrown in. The blasts, the flashes of light and the roars from those who came after. Then silence again, and for some reason Holt happened to think of Bäckström.

After half a minute the response leader came out the door, now sagging to one side. Taking off his helmet, he rubbed his hand over his stubby hair and shrugged his shoulders regretfully.

"*Nada*," he said to El Pastor and shook his head.

97

Late on Tuesday evening the ninth of October Johansson got an unexpected call at home in his residence on Söder. It was Persson, and this was the first time he had ever called Johansson at home.

"Persson," said Johansson. "Nice to hear from you. All's well, I hope." He's hard to hear, he thought. Poor reception. Must be all the cell phone traffic out in Solna that Wiklander keeps on harping about.

"Feeling great," Persson confirmed. "I'm not even calling to borrow money. There's something I want to talk to you about."

"When were you thinking?" said Johansson. Sounds serious, he thought.

"Tomorrow evening if you have time. I have a few things to arrange beforehand. Thought about inviting you to a little dinner out in the country. I've got a little cottage down in Sörmland. It's less than an hour south of town. Down by Gnesta."

"I thought you'd bought a house in Spain," said Johansson.

"Did that too," said Persson. "Sold it after a couple years. The only thing you can do down there is drink and play golf. I don't play golf and I prefer to drink at home."

"Wise," said Johansson. "What time were you thinking?"

"Come around seven," said Persson. "Then we'll have time to take a sauna before we eat. Actually thought about serving fresh perch. If you eat fish? Otherwise we can have something else."

"Perch is good," said Johansson. Almost as good as whitefish, he thought.

"You don't even need to bring any aquavit along," said Persson. "For once I've got some at home. There's only one thing you need."

"What's that?" said Johansson.

"Directions," said Persson. "Do you have the work GPS with you?"

"Always," said Johansson. Anything else would be dereliction of duty, he thought.

"Give me the number, then I'll send over the coordinates," said Persson.

"You can text them straight to my cell," said Johansson.

These are different times now, thought Johansson as he hung up. Wonder what he wants? he thought.

Red cottage with white corner posts, one large and one small outbuilding, a lake fifty yards south of the house. Dock with a sauna down by the lake. Persson met him in blue pants and sweater and a becoming suntan.

"Welcome, Lars. I see you have your henchman with you," he said, nodding at Johansson's service vehicle and his driver who was in the front seat talking on his cell phone.

"Considering the aquavit with the perch," said Johansson. "He's probably sitting there telling his wife how I've ruined his evening."

"Wise," said Persson. "We may need a few hours given that we're going to sauna, talk, and eat."

"I'll send him home," said Johansson. "There must be taxis even out here in the wilderness."

"Wise," Persson repeated. "You see, I need to talk to you face-to-face."

Wonder what he wants? thought Johansson.

A well-fired sauna. A lake that you could cool off in. Just jump right out from the dock down into the water that was still forty-eight degrees, even though it was well into October. A string bag with beer placed to cool in the lake.

"You didn't get that suntan here at home," said Johansson once they were sitting on the sauna platform, each with a beer in hand. Not at this season, even if the summers are getting more and more tropical.

"I took a week," said Persson, wiping the beer foam from his lip.

"Greece, Spain, Turkey?" Johansson suggested.

"Mallorca," said Persson. "There was something I was forced to do."

"Mallorca," said Johansson. How was it he hadn't already sensed it as he got out of the car?

"Fine this time of year," said Persson. "The best time, actually. Warm without being hot. Cool at night so you can sleep."

"Curious coincidence," said Johansson. "I actually sent a couple of my co-workers down to Palma as recently as Monday of last week."

"I know," said Persson. "Holt and Mattei, who are supposed to try to find Hedberg."

"So you know that," said Johansson. Although I guess I sensed that too, he thought.

"You can bring them home," said Persson. "It's already been arranged."

"Tell me," said Johansson. What's happening? he thought.

In Canal de Menorca outside Cap de Formentor,
early in the morning the same day

So the boat was called Esperanza. That means "hope" in Spanish. Hope for a successful future or in any case a future over which you yourself have control. Esperanza was given her name fourteen years earlier. It was the boat's owner, skipper, and only crew member who had christened her, and considering what was about to happen to him and his craft, he could not have chosen a worse name.

98

There wasn't that much to tell, according to Persson. Twelve hours earlier, at eight o'clock local time on north Mallorca, which by the way was the same time as here at home, he had solved the problem of Kjell Göran Hedberg by blowing him and his boat into the air.

"Approximately fifteen nautical miles outside the harbor in Puerto Pollensa, if you know where that is."

"I know where that is," said Johansson. "That's about where Claes Waltin happened to drown." Is he joking? he thought.

"Oh well," said Persson. "It was Hedberg who drowned him. Although it was a good ways farther into the bay."

"How long have you known where he was?" said Johansson.

"Since I did the house search at Waltin's home and realized who he'd been involved with. For quite a few years after Hedberg had to quit us, Waltin used him as an external operator."

"I've realized that," said Johansson. "I also think I've realized why Hedberg was forced to kill him."

"Waltin was going downhill," said Persson and nodded. "He was drinking too much, talking too much, associating with the wrong people. Waltin was a security risk, and Hedberg did not intend to serve a life sentence because of him."

"I hear what you're saying," said Johansson. "So how long has Hedberg been on north Mallorca?"

Basically the last twenty years, according to Persson. Most recently he'd been living in a little house up in the mountains north of Pollensa. A gatekeeper's cottage he got to live in for free, in exchange for guarding a house for a wealthy English couple who had a large estate in the vicinity and were almost never there. He also had a car that he leased. A small fishing boat that he owned and had built in the spring of 1993. A boat that he took tourists out in. To swim, sunbathe, fish, and dive.

"So how did you find him?"

No great art, according to Persson. Not considering all the traces of Hedberg he'd found in the house search at Waltin's. When he went down to Mallorca ten days ago he already knew everything he needed to know. About his boat, for example.

"As soon as I found out he had a butane tank on the boat, I decided what I would do. The bastard had installed one of those stainless steel gas grills up on deck, and those crazy Spaniards placed the butane tank under the deck and ran a fucking lot of cables back and forth. Couldn't be better."

"Explain it in layman's terms," said Johansson. He had never unscrewed the detonator from a rusty four-hundred-pound mine, he thought. He didn't even know if you dared lick the snot from your upper lip while you were doing it.

He had arranged the practical details late in the evening before the morning when it happened. Right before he called Johansson at home and invited him to dinner, by the way. He made sure that Hedberg was at a safe distance. Used ordinary dynamite from Nitro Nobel. Three pitiful small charges, and he needed to use only a couple of ounces of this classic Swedish product. One hollow charge under the deck to split the butane tank open. Two on the gas lines that were run inside the cabin bulkhead. He was done in half an hour. He even had time to relieve pressure on the lines from the tank.

"Butane is odorless, as you know," said Persson, indicating a toast with his beer can.

"So when he started the engine up it exploded," said Johansson.

"Who the hell do you take me for, Johansson?" said Persson. "I'm not a fucking mass murderer. First I made sure he was out in open water so there were no innocent people in the vicinity. I followed him in my own boat."

To ensure this humanitarian aspect, Persson made use of a regular cell phone as the trigger mechanism. It was a prepaid cell he had bought on Mallorca. Paid cash and it couldn't be traced. With a pre-set delay besides.

"As I'm sure you understand I was fucking tired of that bastard considering all the grief he's caused in the past thirty years. You know that better than anyone, by the way. So I decided to send a final greeting to mess with him."

Once Hedberg was out in open water Persson first called him on his own cell phone. As soon as Hedberg picked it up and answered, he called the cell phone that triggered the explosives a few seconds later.

"How did you get the number to his cell phone?" said Johansson.

"Already had it," said Persson. "It was the cell phone he used for running his boat charters. An ordinary Nokia. With the same old signal they all have, which means you start reaching in your pocket as soon as anyone in the area gets a call."

"So did he answer?" asked Johansson.

"Sure," said Persson. "I was in my boat a short distance away looking at him through the binoculars. Although he didn't answer by name."

"So what did he say?"

"*Sí*," said Persson and chuckled.

"And you," said Johansson. "What did you say?"

At first he thought about sending him one last greeting from his colleagues, but after closer thought he refrained.

"Who the hell wants to be a colleague of someone like that? So instead I asked him to say hello to the audience. 'Say hello to the audience, Hedberg,' I said. You should have seen how fucking surprised he was. Especially when another phone started ringing with the same ringtone as soon as I started talking to him. I even had time to wave at the bastard.

"Yes, and so then the boat blew up. First three short cracks when the charges went, and then a big fucking ball of fire when the butane burned off. I saw the bastard as he flew away. At least thirty feet up in the air. Saw one of his legs fly off in a different direction. If you ask me, I think it was the stainless steel cover on the grill that took off and sawed off his stump. His boat went straight down. It was fifteen hundred feet deep in the channel."

"I see, I see," said Johansson. "So what did you do then? Flew home to Sweden to have grilled perch with an old colleague?"

"No, the hell I did," said Persson. "It's not over yet. More is coming. Do you want another beer, by the way?"

"Thanks, this is fine," said Johansson. "I have some left," he explained, showing the can so as not to be impolite.

"So what happened then?" he repeated.

Persson had maneuvered closer to the wreckage to be able to see better. Stayed there a few minutes to check the situation while it finished burning.

"As I'm lying there looking, the bastard suddenly pops up right by the side of my boat. Sooty and burned, and gasping like a fish. Bleeding like hell. But he was alive. Strangely enough."

"'Help me, help me,' he said, extending his hand toward me. 'Sure,' I said and handed him my fist. Then I took a piece of pipe I had in my tackle box, to kill off the rougher morsels you can get down there, in case you're wondering, and then I banged him on the head a few times. I guess that was all. He sank like a stone, and I sent the piece of pipe along as a reminder."

"And then," said Johansson.

"Then I took the boat back to the hotel. I was staying in a little pension across from the charter pier where he had his boat. Checked out. Got in the car to go to his house up in the mountains and do a little discreet house search."

"So did you find anything?" said Johansson.

"No," said Persson. "There wasn't time. The area was already crawling with Spanish officers, so I continued straight to the airport in Palma and took the flight home. Landed at Skavsta just a few hours ago. But if you ask me I think he basically just had a bed to sleep in. Hedberg was not as careless as Waltin, so I don't think we need to worry about that detail."

"So you were down there at the same time as Holt and Mattei," said Johansson.

"I was actually there first, if you want to quibble. A fucking piece of luck it was, by the way. If I hadn't been there he would have gotten away from us. If we'd missed him now, we never would have seen a trace of him again."

"What makes you think that?" said Johansson. What the hell is he sitting there saying? he thought.

"He was warned by one of your so-called colleagues," said Persson, shrugging his shoulders. "What do you say to a piece of perch, by the way?"

In the deep channel outside Cap de Formentor on north Mallorca in the morning the day before

Finally it had happened anyway. What he thought would never happen. Instead of sheering ninety degrees port and setting course toward the woman in the big house down by the beach in Cala Sant Vicente, he continued right out into the deep channel. Entered a new course on his GPS navigator at the same time as he congratulated himself that Esperanza always had her fuel tanks filled. Enough diesel to take him three hundred nautical miles to Corsica, where there were many like him and at least one he trusted unconditionally. Who could give him a refuge for the remainder of his life.

Not like the woman, who said she was from the U.S. and was renting the large house on the beach in Cala Sant Vicente. Who talked about her wealthy husband whom she never saw. Who was twenty years younger than him, with her long dark hair, her white teeth, her large, pendulous breasts and the prom-ise in her eyes. The one who had approached him only a week ago when he was scrubbing the deck on Esperanza to make her fine before autumn, when the vacation season was now finally over. The one who asked him if he spoke English, if he knew any good places where she could dive. If perhaps he, or someone else, could help her?

The woman who could actually dive as well as he could and who had shown that the very first time she went with him out to sea. The woman he was sup-posed to have picked up at the large house in less than an hour. The woman who must have betrayed him, despite the promise in her eyes. Because there was no other explanation. Because Ignacio Ballester had come to see him early in the morning. Told him what his nephew had said and chose to warn him instead of betraying him.

He only had time to take with him the essentials and the small bag that was always packed. Completely sufficient, because there was nothing in that cottage that could say anything about him or the life he had lived since that Friday evening at the intersection of Tunnelgatan and Sveavägen more than twenty years ago. He had left his car because it was safest that way, and what would he do with it now? Ignacio drove him down to the harbor and Esperanza. Shook his hand and wished him luck at sea. There was no alternative, and that was why Esperanza was berthed there. A beautiful little boat, but also an insurance policy and a constant reminder.

Security, freedom, and at a low price. Simply yet another day and night at sea.

99

Grilled perch, butter and lemon, boiled potatoes, beer and a cold shot of aquavit. It couldn't have been better in all its simplicity, but despite that Johansson had problems with his appetite.

"Which one of my people was it who warned him?" asked Johansson as soon as he'd taken the first bite.

"You must have asked the Spanish colleagues to assign some local talent to protect the little ladies you sent down. One of them happened to be the nephew of the man who owned the shipyard where Hedberg built his boat. He suddenly realized that your co-workers were searching for one of his uncle's old customers. Called his uncle and let his mouth run. Then his uncle went to Hedberg and warned him. It's not the first time this sort of thing has happened, but I guess I don't need to tell you that."

"No," said Johansson. "You don't need to."

"You're eating poorly, Lars," said Persson. "Why aren't you eating? Here I've been standing at the stove and exerting myself."

"What the hell do you want?" said Johansson. "It never occurred to you that I'll take you up to Stockholm and put you in jail?"

"No, never," said Persson with a smile. "For what, if I may ask?"

"For what you just told me," said Johansson.

"No," said Persson, shaking his head. "That thought has never occurred to me. And if you do that anyway, I will have no idea what you're talking about. That's one of the advantages of sitting in a sauna when you're going to talk about such things. Not a lot of clothes where people can hide microphones and other garbage. Cheers, by the way."

. . .

"Cheers," said Johansson, emptying his full shot glass.

"Although I have every sympathy that you're a little moved," said Persson. "Who wouldn't be after such a cock-and-bull story. But as soon as you get a little perspective on it you're going to thank me."

"Thank you," said Johansson. "For what? Because you killed Hedberg?"

"Because I solved a problem for us. For you and me and everyone else like you and me. For my only friend, Erik, not least. If it hadn't been for his sake I might even have let the bastard live."

"You must have had help," said Johansson. Because you're already sitting here you can hardly have flown commercial, considering what you were up to this morning, he thought.

"I would never dream of talking about such things," said Persson. "A good fellow takes care of himself. How the hell would it look if people like you and me didn't dare stand up for one another?"

When Johansson was in the taxi on the way home a few hours later his red cell phone rang. The cell to which only his closest associates had the number.

"Yes," said Johansson, who never answered with his name when the red phone rang. Holt, he thought.

"Where have you been? I've been looking for you for hours." Holt did not sound happy.

"Had a few things to take care of," said Johansson. "So I turned off the cell."

"We've found Kjell Göran Hedberg," said Holt. "We think so, at least. We're pretty sure it's him."

"What the hell are you saying?" said Johansson. "Tell me. I'm listening."

"He's dead," said Holt.

"Dead," said Johansson. "What the hell are you saying?"

100

The Spanish police had acted with uncharacteristic swiftness. Their investigation of the boat accident outside Cap de Formentor arrived by courier from the national bureau's liaison in Spain only a few weeks later.

In purely technical terms they didn't have much to go on. Scattered pieces of the boat had been found. The only part of Kjell Göran Hedberg that was found was the lower left leg. Shark-infested waters so it was completely natural. There were even white sharks in the area. Known not to leave much behind when they were finished. That it was Hedberg's leg was however established beyond any reasonable doubt. Comparisons with the DNA material that had been secured in the house search ruled out that the appendage had been attached to anyone other than him.

The investigators had to rely on eyewitness reports instead. Three individuals, who were standing at the lookout point out on the promontory when it happened, told the police what they had seen. Everything indicated an accident involving gas, caused by leakage from the tank to the grill that was on board. Probably when Hedberg lit it to make his breakfast.

Johansson's Spanish ally El Pastor made contact via a letter addressed directly to Johansson. He had no reason to suspect foul play. On the contrary, he shared the understanding that his colleagues in the tech squad with the police in Palma had arrived at. It was the kind of unhappy occurrence that unfortunately could obliterate the most well-planned police efforts.

Johansson had the head of his international unit write a brief, friendly thank-you letter. Obviously without saying a word about El Pastor's loose-lipped associate. How could he say anything about him without getting into problems? Besides, it wasn't his responsibility.

The right thing in the right place, thought Johansson as he placed the investigation into an interoffice envelope for forwarding to the colleagues at the National Bureau of Criminal Investigation who took care of the identification of Swedish citizens who perished in accidents abroad. In reality they should have been investigating the murder of the Swedish prime minister, but the lack of meaningful assignments in that case meant that for several years now they had mostly been engaged in other things.

101

Three weeks after Kjell Göran Hedberg's demise, Johansson devoted three days to cleaning up after him. First he gathered all the papers that were the result of his and his three associates' efforts. Most of them he ran through the shredder and the rest he put in a binder. In the evening, when all his co-workers had already gone home, he personally went down to the Palme room and distributed the contents of his binder among the thousand that were already there. Just as in ancient Rome, he was going to let justice rely on chance when all else had betrayed it.

Then he turned off the light and left. Inwardly he also wished future archival researchers good luck.

The following day he had a long lunch with the female chief prosecutor in Stockholm, who was also the head of the Palme investigation. He turned over to her the memo he had asked Lisa Mattei to write about the future registration of the Palme investigation's material. How this gigantic pile of papers could best be stored for the future, while he and his associates took back the office space they so desperately needed for the things they were actually working on.

"If we could be content with ordinary diskettes and computer memory," said Johansson. "If we could just transfer all the material to computers and store it according to the latest technology, there is nothing to prevent you from carrying it around with you on a simple cord around your neck," he said. "Within the foreseeable future in any event," he clarified.

. . .

In order to underscore that he was serious, he fished his computer memory out of his pocket. This one already held ten gigabytes, attached to his key ring, taking up less space than his keys, even though the device could hold a whole wall of binders.

"Although I want an amethyst on mine," the chief prosecutor replied, smiling at him.

"Of course," said Johansson. "I'll treat you to that. If you take care of the confidentiality issues and tell us how you want it implemented in practical terms."

"Of course," she said. "Who else would do it? And then I'll be obligated to inform the government too, naturally."

"No problem," said Johansson. Down in the cellar with all the papers, he thought. Twenty-five to forty years of secrecy, regardless of which it no longer concerned him. Hardly anyone else either. Possibly a historian or two with a lot of letters in their little heads.

What remained was the most important thing. That he talk with his co-workers. First Lisa, because that would be easiest. Then Lewin, because that was actually not interesting. Finally Anna Holt, because that could certainly get tricky.

"What do you want to do now, Lisa?" Johansson asked as he personally served her coffee in order to really underscore his goodwill.

"I was thinking about going back to my old job at CIS," Mattei replied.

"Is that what you really most want to do?" said Johansson.

"Yes," said Mattei.

"Okay then," said Johansson. "That's what we'll do."

Nothing more than that was said.

Jan Lewin was not sure he wanted to return to his old job at the bureau's homicide squad. He had even considered resigning from the police after more than thirty years in service.

"What good would that be?" said Johansson, looking at him with surprise. "Once a policeman, always a policeman. You know that, don't you, Jan?"

If it really was that way, unfortunately it didn't apply to him. The profession had taken its toll on him. Besides, maybe he wasn't suited for it to begin with. In later years he had gotten more and more depressed.

Johansson tried to cheer him up by talking about a dissertation in police research he had just read. According to the author, the slightly depressed investigators were the very best ones. Completely superior to all the thoughtless, excitable colleagues.

"Apparently you shouldn't be so fucking cheerful and high-spirited," said Johansson. "Then you would start to lose in precision and reflection."

"So you say," said Lewin. "The problem I guess is that it wears you down. It eats you up from inside, if you understand what I mean."

"I hear what you're saying," said Johansson. "Do you know what I think?"

"No," said Lewin.

"You need a woman," said Johansson.

Johansson quickly elaborated on his thoughts on Lewin's actual needs. Every man needed a woman. Good guys needed good ladies. It was no more complicated than that, but to be on the safe side he repeated the message twice.

"Do you have anyone in particular you intended to suggest?" said Lewin.

"Holt," said Johansson. "Anna Holt. She likes you, for one thing. Besides, you're the same age. You should be careful about running after younger talents. They have a fucking capacity to grow away from you."

"In a collegial sense, possibly," said Lewin, squirming. "Besides, I'm actually twelve years older than her."

"Yeah, who the hell can believe that," said Johansson. "You don't look a day over forty-five, and Anna is forty-seven if I remember right, so I'm sure that will work out."

"So you say," said Lewin, smiling hesitantly.

"Because you know she's twelve years younger than you, you've presumably already thought about it," Johansson observed.

"Why do you think that?"

"Any real policeman could see that," said Johansson. "If you know something like that, you've already checked out the lady in question."

The conversation with Anna Holt went better than he had thought. Considerably better than he had feared.

Holt also wanted to return to her regular work. Not only that, she assumed that she would do so.

"Sure," said Johansson. "You'll get everything as you wish, Anna. I'm sure you already know that."

"Thanks," said Anna Holt. "What I already have is good enough."

"Then that's what we'll do," said Johansson.

"I have just one last question," said Holt, getting up.

"I sensed that," said Johansson.

"What happened to Hedberg was a strange coincidence, wasn't it?"

"Yes," said Johansson. "It was probably one of the strangest things I've encountered in my whole life."

"And," said Anna Holt.

"I was just as fucking shocked as you were when you told me what had happened," said Johansson, looking seriously at her with his honest, gray eyes.

"I believe you," said Anna Holt. She nodded and left.

The following day Lewin went into Holt's office and after the usual hemming and hawing squeezed out his real errand.

"I was wondering if you'd like to have dinner with me?"

. . .

Holt thought it sounded like an excellent idea. She suggested they could do it that same evening and preferably at her place. True, there was nothing really wrong with the restaurant he'd invited her to, but in the long run she thought it was a little tedious to go out. Unnecessarily expensive too.

"Gladly," said Lewin without clearing his throat. "Is there anything you want me to bring?"

"It's enough if you bring yourself," said Holt. If I ask you to bring along a toothbrush, I'm sure you'll call to cancel right beforehand, and if need be you can always borrow mine, she thought.

The provincial police chief in Stockholm was a busy woman. Not until the same day that Johansson and the chief prosecutor in Stockholm decided to carry the Palme investigation down to the basement of the police building in the greatest possible secrecy did she have time for Bäckström's presentation on the same case.

To begin with it had looked fairly promising. The police chief's own conference room. A small, highly qualified group. She herself, the attorney for the Stockholm police, the presenter Bäckström, and his faithful squire Fridolin.

"The Friends of Cunt," said the police chief with an incredulous expression. That was how the whole thing started, and then it only got worse.

An hour later it was over. Ms. Police Chief nodded curtly at Bäckström and requested a private conversation with Fridolin.

"I'm disappointed in you, Fridolf," she said as she closed the door on the two of them.

The following day her attorney called Bäckström's home number to clarify certain legal and employment-related matters.

As a private individual Evert Bäckström had great freedom to have his own opinions about this and that, such as for example about the murder of Olof Palme, and to the degree that he violated laws and regulations it was his own responsibility. Concerning Inspector Evert Bäckström it was also very simple. Memoranda of the type he had submitted to him and to his superior the day before should not be signed with his official title, because the contents did not have the slightest thing to do with Bäckström's position with the police. If he nonetheless did so, it was as stated a matter of his own criminal liability. In order to avoid any misunderstanding on this point, the attorney had also written an explanatory letter that was already in Bäckström's mailbox.

"What do we do now?" said Bäckström, giving Fridolin the evil eye. You little dickhead, I should flush you down the john, he thought.

According to Bäckström's squire it was too early to throw in the towel. On the other hand perhaps an alternative plan of action ought to be chosen.

"What do you think about TV, Bäckström?" said Fridolin, leaning forward. "I have quite a few contacts in the media, too."

"Journalist bastards," Bäckström snorted, already missing Egon so much it hurt.

"These are no ordinary journalists," Fridolin assured him. "I know a guy at TV4. A heavy dude, really heavy. He works at *Cold Facts*," Fridolin stated, sounding more and more like his new mentor.

"So he does," said Bäckström, nodding and taking a meditative sip of the good malt in order to think even more clearly. "So he does," he repeated. Wasn't it the case that in war all means are permitted? he thought.

102

On Thursday the second of November the special adviser departed the era in which he had lived and worked for over sixty years. Not because he had consumed enormous quantities of pea soup and warm *punsch*, but rather from completely natural causes. His bad heart, his high blood pressure, a lifelong excess of food and alcoholic beverages that his doctor had advised him against. Constant negligence with his medications, even though the same doctor emphasized how important it was that he follow his prescriptions to the letter. Completely natural causes in other words, and the great mystery was really how he had lasted a day beyond the age of thirty considering the life he had lived.

Just like his mentor, old professor Forselius, he died as a result of a massive brain hemorrhage. According to the autopsy report there were a number of good reasons, but because the pathologist would be asked anyway he wanted to point out one of them in particular. That his blood had been thin as water, due to a severe overdosage of the blood thinner warfarin, which he was forced to take due to his bad heart. It was a classic rat poison that had also been beneficial in the art of medicine, even though in combination with large quantities of alcohol it was much worse than rat poison. His high blood pressure had taken care of the rest, producing a logical conclusion. The great mystery was, as stated, how he had lived as long as he had.

In the investigation of the death there were also two interviews. One with his housekeeper, who found him dead in the morning. The second with the last person who saw him alive and had dinner with him the same evening he died, former detective inspector Åke Persson. Persson had worked the majority of his active career with the secret police, and according to him that was also how he and his host had gotten to know each other.

A simple three-course dinner. Swedish home cooking. First some herring with a couple of shots and a beer for each, then sailor's beef casserole with which they shared a bottle of red wine, for dessert home-made apple pie made by the host's housekeeper. A little cognac with coffee, and possibly a thing or two he'd forgotten, but absolutely no extravagance.

They finished the evening with a game of billiards and a little evening toddy. Then Persson went home. His host had as always been in the best of spirits and even sang to him as he got into the taxi. On the other hand he had no memory of what it was he sang. Whatever that had to do with it, by the way.

The special adviser had thus died of natural causes, and as far as the witness Persson was concerned he could have gone on living as long as he wanted.

He was mourned and missed by those near and dear, friends and co-workers. A man with a good memory besides, who only a few weeks before his death made a codicil to his will in which he bequeathed an old book about Magdalen College, Oxford, to the head of the National Bureau of Criminal Investigation, Lars Martin Johansson.

To my dear friend Lars Martin Johansson. In memory of all the deer in the park at Magdalen, in memory of all the stimulating conversations we have had, and because I personally have now finally had my say.

103

Johansson was present both at the funeral and at the cemetery, Norra Kyrkogården, as well as at the ensuing luncheon at Grand's French restaurant. Persson had been there too, and when they were through eating and said goodbye to the closest mourners, they went home to Johansson's to have a memorial highball to the dead man and talk in peace and quiet.

"What does your wife have to say?" asked Persson as they were in the taxi on their way to Johansson's both pleasant and spacious apartment on Söder.

"Not a smidgen," said Johansson. "She's at a conference. Won't be home until this evening."

Johansson did not waste any time on small talk. Led his guest into the office, mixed two ample highballs for them, offered him the larger armchair and sat down on the couch himself.

"I got a little worried when I read the investigation into the cause of death," said Johansson. "Are things so bad that your sense of orderliness has started running amok?"

"Forget it," said Persson, shaking his head. "Neither you nor your associates have anything to worry about. Our mutual friend ate himself to death. Burned his candle at both ends. To be on the safe side he lit a fire in the middle too, and it's no more complicated than that."

"Nice to hear," said Johansson. "So what do you think about Bäckström? I heard from Jarnebring, when we talked last week, that he's more or less climbing the walls when he's not hovering like a blimp due to all the conspiracy theories he's full of. There was some journalist at TV4 who called Bo to ask whether he knew anything about the mysterious sex track in the Palme murder that Bäckström has been raving about."

"Couldn't be better," Persson grunted. "If Bäckström is saying it, then even those lunatics on TV should understand that there's no truth to it. Besides, isn't he on sick leave? And at a guess, the little fatso is going to stay that way for a good long while."

"So you say," said Johansson. "On a completely different matter. So when did you figure out how things stood?"

"The fall of 1992. When we got word from the Spanish colleagues that Waltin drowned in Mallorca. Then Berg decided we should do a home search at Waltin's. If he hadn't done it, I would have done it anyway," said Persson, nodding.

"I ran it myself," Persson continued. "Neat and tidy. No carelessness. His apartment in town, his estate down in Sörmland, three different safety deposit boxes, an extra apartment at the top of the building on Norr Mälarstrand where he lived. Registered to some company that he owned."

"So did you find anything interesting?" said Johansson, without sounding the least bit curious.

"No," said Persson, shaking his head. "Just a bag of old clothes, shoes and winter clothes, a knit cap. I burned it the same day. Nothing to trace. The clothes weren't even washed. Some other trash of no interest that mostly concerned little Waltin's special orientation went into the same fire."

"Nothing else?"

"Nothing you want to hear about," said Persson. "That particular part I took care of when I and the woman I'm involved with took the boat over to Finland. Somewhere on a level with Landsort where it's supposed to be three hundred feet deep. She's Finnish, by the way, so we were going to see her elderly parents. Old as the hills, frisky as squirrels. Must be the sauna."

"Berg," said Johansson. "Did you tell him?"

"No," said Persson. "Why would I do that? He had enough troubles of his own."

"So why did you wait fifteen years with Hedberg? Couldn't you just as well have left it at that?"

"Your fault, Lars," said Persson. "When you showed up at my place a few months ago and started asking about Waltin, I realized the hour had come. You're the man who can see around corners," said Persson and grinned.

"So it was really my fault," said Johansson.

"Depends on what you mean by fault," said Persson, shrugging his shoulders. "True, you did say to me that you wanted to boil the bastard for glue, but I really did it for Erik's sake."

"For Erik Berg's sake?"

"Who else?" said Persson. "What do you think would have happened to his reputation if you'd dragged Hedberg into Stockholm District Court? What do you think would have happened to the organization? To you too for that matter. You were operations head with us for six years. If Erik had still been alive, he would surely have ended up in jail too. I did it to be on the safe side, if nothing else. I think you would have been able to keep from laughing when the media vultures started feasting on you. Because you don't really think they would have been content with Waltin and Hedberg?"

"I understand what you mean," said Johansson, and as he said that he thought of his wife.

"So who helped you?" said Johansson. It's over now, he thought.

"Last question," said Persson. "Are we agreed on that?"

"Yes," said Johansson. "After this we draw a line through this."

"Cheers to the deceased," said Persson, raising his glass. "That man was more than just a mouth."

"Cheers to him," said Johansson. You already knew that, didn't you? he thought.

"I have a present for you, by the way," said Johansson. He stuck his hand in his pants pocket and handed over the copper-sheathed lead bullet he had brought with him from work when he went to the funeral.

"The renowned seventy-five-percenter," said Persson, holding it up between his thumb and index finger in his improbably large hand.

"So you know that," said Johansson.

"Our deceased friend told me," said Persson. "He had pretty good ears, you know."

"I've understood that," said Johansson.

"I have three brothers and three sisters," said Persson. "Combined they've collected a dozen kids. Have I told you that?"

"No," said Johansson. "I actually have three brothers and three sisters too." Combined we have even more children than you all, he thought.

"I know that too," said Persson, studying the bullet he was holding in his hand. "My nephews and nieces are grown now, although when they were little I used to do magic tricks for them. Whenever they had a party, Uncle Åke would do magic for them. I got pretty good, actually. Probably could even have supported myself doing that. It's in your fingers, and once you learn it, it never goes away."

"I believe you," said Johansson.

"Good," said Persson. "How would it be otherwise? If people like you and me couldn't trust each other."

"Not so good. Really bad, maybe. I believe that," Johansson agreed, sipping his highball.

"So what do you think about this?" said Persson. He pulled down the sleeve on his right arm, showed the bullet he was holding in his fingers, raised his hand, clenched it, turned his giant fist before he opened it again and showed his empty hand.

"Abracadabra," said Persson.

104

The same evening, when his wife came home and they'd gone to bed, he dreamed. The only nightmare he could remember having as an adult. No ether-induced stupor this time; he hadn't had very much to drink, and he was definitely not eleven years old anymore. Even so he had fallen freely.

Fallen freely, as if in a dream. Simply whirled down and down, fell headfirst into a black hole that never ended. He sat upright in bed without knowing whether he was alive or dead. He must have done something more, because Pia was holding his arm so hard that it hurt. Even though his muscles were tensed like rope.

"What's going on, Lars? God, I was frightened."

"I'm alive," he said. Am I? he thought.

"Of course you're alive," said Pia, stroking his cheek. "It was only a dream. A nightmare. I guess you're not used to them. Don't forget you've promised me to live to be a hundred."

"I haven't forgotten. I promise," said Johansson, shaking his head. I'm alive, he thought.

"Nothing else has happened? Is there anything you want to say? Nothing you've forgotten to tell me?"

"I'm going to quit my job," said Johansson. "I've already talked with them. I'm through with this now. I really thought I never would be, but now I am."

"And nothing else has happened? Something I ought to know?"

"Nothing," said Johansson. "Nothing has happened." Finally, he thought. Finally it's over.

Truth, myth, or just a simple tall tale? Regardless of which, early on Friday morning the first of December a single shot echoed in the park behind Mary Magdalene's College in Oxford. The previous night had been cold. The ground was white with frost, shrouded in fog that rolled in from the river Cherwell, when the largest of the park's deer had to sacrifice his life. Still the largest of them all but declining the past few years. Now he mostly created disorder in the herd, bothered the hinds and held back the younger, more energetic stags. For that reason someone decided he should be removed.

The man who held the shotgun was a thirty-year-old professional hunter from one of the nearby estates. Among many other things his employer was also a senior fellow of Magdalen, and his own hunter took care of the wildlife at the College as a part-time job. But no proctor in a Spanish cloak and tall black hat, because that belonged to a time long past. Instead a young, very professional game warden in a green cap and oilskin jacket who made certain there was a proper backstop behind the prey before he shot, who had loaded the bullet the evening before so as not to unnecessarily disturb the peace in the halls of learning, who made the suffering brief and put the bullet in the deer's neck.

The deer that collapses on the spot, on head and horns, with curled-up front legs and a few final kicks with the back hooves. The red blood that colors the white frost, the final snorting exhalation. Red blood that shows up especially well against white frost, time that stops for a moment. But no more than that, and for the others in the herd life will immediately go on.

Truth, myth, or just a simple tall tale? Regardless of which, on the first Sunday in Advent, Sunday the third of December, there was a dinner at Magdalen College in memory of a recently deceased honorary fellow. Not a remarkable dinner, simply a typical English gentlemen's dinner, with venison steak, brown gravy, and overcooked vegetables, but the wine they served was excellent. A Romanée-Conti from the great year of 1985, a large quantity of which the special adviser had purchased long before at three-hundred-year-old Berry Bros. & Rudd on St. James Street in London, and also took the opportunity to send a couple of cases to the wine cellar at Magdalen.

The English upper classes have the good custom of almost never giving speeches during dinner. Dinner is eaten every day, dinner speeches are given only on special occasions, and this particular day one of the dinner guests did give a speech. A memorial speech to the deceased.

The speaker was himself both an honorary fellow and a member of the governing body of another college. It had been founded more than five hundred years later and in a completely different era than when the buildings were erected to honor the memory of the foremost of Jesus's female disciples. It was called St. Antony's College, which was an honorable enough name compared with all the other colleges at Oxford, but insiders simply called it "The Spy College." Founded after the most recent world conflagration by donors who almost always wanted to be anonymous and all of whom seemed to have unlimited amounts of money. As an academic institution the logical answer to the Western powers' demand for better, more educated, and more reliable brains in the Western security agencies. Perhaps the historical inheritance of the five traitors from Cambridge, if you preferred to think along such lines.

The dinner speaker was named Michael Liska, born in Hungary during the Second World War, fled as a teenager to the U.S. after the revolt against the Russians in 1956. He had no notable academic credentials, especially not in the company in which he found himself. He had worked his entire adult life for the CIA, a successful career, and when he had retired a few years ago he had been deputy director of the organization. Even substituted as its director on a few occasions when circumstances compelled the president of the United States to make rapid, radical changes.

A big, burly fellow who was always called "The Bear," even though "Liska" means "fox" in Hungarian. Michael "The Bear" Liska, who was now a healthy retiree of sixty-seven. Even though as a teenager he climbed up on a Russian T54 in the streets of Budapest, threw a Molotov cocktail through the open turret door, and sent a volley of bullets through the body of the driver when he tried to crawl out of his burning tank.

About this and other things of the same sort he had of course not said a word. Instead, for his learned listeners he talked about his Swedish friend and comrade-in-arms of almost forty years.

He began his memorial oration by recounting his friend's scientific achievements. The decisive contributions he had made to harmonic analysis in mathematics, about their significance for coding and encryption in an intelligence operation.

Liska also placed him in a historical perspective. The last, and youngest, of the three great Swedish mathematicians who used the gift that only the Lord God Almighty could have given them, to protect freedom and law.

Arne Beurling, who had been the first of them. Professor of mathematics at the University of Uppsala, who in 1940 reluctantly reported for service as a sergeant with the Defense staff's intelligence division. Then in fourteen days he broke the Germans' secret telecommunications codes with the help of paper, pen, harmonic analysis, and a highly unusual mind.

His contemporary colleague Johan Forselius, professor of mathematics at the Royal Technical Academy, who with the computers of the new era and his own contributions to prime number theory made sure that the messages the democracies of the Western world chose to conceal would also remain concealed in practice. In the spirit of the time that was then required.

Then the youngest of the three, for whom they were now gathered to grant a final farewell. Forselius's disciple, professor of mathematics at the University of Stockholm at the age of twenty-nine. His dissertation on stochastic variables and harmonic divisions for many years considerably facilitated the uncovering of every dictator's evil projects and secret traps.

Liska concluded his talk by quoting the final words in a letter he had received from his old friend only a month or so before he died.

"*Regardless of whether truth is absolute or relative, and quite apart from the fact that many of us constantly seek it, in the end it is nonetheless hidden from almost all of us. As a rule out of necessity, and if for no other reason than out of concern for those who would not understand anyway.*"

ABOUT THE AUTHOR

Leif GW Persson has chronicled the political and social development of modern Swedish society in his award-winning novels for more than three decades. Born in Stockholm, Persson has served as an adviser to the Swedish Ministry of Justice and is Sweden's most renowned psychological profiler. He is a professor at Sweden's National Police Board and is considered the country's foremost expert on crime.

A NOTE ON THE TYPE

This book was set in Monotype Dante, a typeface designed by Giovanni Mardersteig (1892–1977). Dante was originally cut by Charles Malin between 1946 and 1952. Its first use was in an edition of Boccaccio's *Trattatello in laude di Dante* that appeared in 1954. The Monotype Corporation's version of Dante followed in 1957. Although modeled on the Aldine type used for Pietro Cardinal Bembo's treatise *De Aetna* in 1495, Dante is a thoroughly modern interpretation of the venerable face.

Typeset by Scribe, Philadelphia, Pennsylvania
Printed and bound by Berryville Graphics, Berryville, Virginia